L.A. LOVE

Liam's Story

CARLOS DUVAL

authorHOUSE®

AuthorHouse™ UK Ltd.
1663 Liberty Drive
Bloomington, IN 47403 USA
www.authorhouse.co.uk
Phone: 0800.197.4150

Published by AuthorHouse   05/05/2014

ISBN: 978-1-4969-7978-0 (sc)
ISBN: 978-1-4969-7979-7 (hc)
ISBN: 978-1-4969-7980-3 (e)

FOREWORD

Liam Parry, a 'Student of Life', takes you on a roller coaster journey through several decades of life's pleasures and trials. This journey, starts in the 60s era in Liverpool. Liam will take the reader through many experiences they can identify with happiness, sadness, love and desire, an amazing soup of life's twists and turns. Enjoy the ride.

CHAPTER 1

I discovered a Readers Digest writing competition. I thought I'd enter and began thinking of what children might like to read. I decided to write about my early teen's experiences. After some deliberation I centred my piece on the first time I fell in love. The story was about one special day in my life, which I wanted to relive. I called it '1963 The Day Of The Goddess.' The story did well in the competition; but there is a part two. Part two started many years later, re-discovering a love once thought to be lost. Let me first of all tell you about the day that started everything off. It was one day which stood out above the rest. One of those life changing days which is always remembered?

1963. THE DAY OF THE GODESS.

Monday, 8.30am first-day back to school after the Summer Holiday. It was a crisp, autumn, morning, the type which maps out the course of your breath from the mouth. I leave the house, a new Council House on the outskirts of Liverpool. I attended one of the few schools of the day at which a school uniform was worn. We were semi—posh Scoucers.

On the 15-minute walk to school I passed the time with a favourite game. I listened to the sound of vehicles and tried to identify them. Many vehicles of the day had very distinctive voices, and some required a keen ear for pitch and tone to get them right. I was very skilled at this game.

I arrived at the school playground. The peace of the morning was shattered by the sound of hundreds of children. I weaved my way between groups of girls whispering giggly secrets to one another, and boys, who tended to be much noisier, shouting over each other like stags at the rut. Then, having found my group of friends, I barely had time to join them when the whistle blew, mowing down each pocket of sound like a machine gun.

The Deputy Head stood in a commanding position on a raised area at the school end of the yard. Everybody quickly lined up in front of him, like iron filings to a magnet. The process of entering the school was speeded up this morning by a light shower. We entered the hall, which doubled up as a dining hall and gymnasium. We waited while the Teachers took up their seats on the stage and the Head Master Mr. Stanway, complete with cap and gown, arrived at his post behind the lectern. He stared us down to silent compliance before churning through the formalities of morning assembly. Throughout Assembly sheepish late comers were directed to the front of the hall. They stood, facing their fellows, waiting a caning at the end. After witnessing the pseudo executions we filtered into the main building, staircases and corridors like a disease entering the body.

I arrived at 6A; washed into the classroom by a wave of fellow pupils. I landed at my desk. Small groups formed and bits of paper and insults flew around the room. James Cook allowed a loud 'rasping fart' to escape. This caused a ripple of laughter amongst the boys and condemnation from the girls, who moved quickly to less affected parts of the room. Due to some genetic defect girls never farted, only boys had the skill to turn this bodily function into an art form or competition.

The registration bell rang out as Mr. Stanway entered the room, followed by a young lady. Immediate silence descended and the lady was introduced as Miss Hughes, a new teacher. The Head introduced us as 6A; and demanded the very best behaviour for Miss Hughes. As Mr. Stanway left my eyes locked on to the heavenly body that was MISS HUGHES. She wasn't like any teacher I had ever seen before. She was a Goddess. Not tall, but beautifully formed. The tightly curled brown hair topped a beautiful face. Bright happy eyes and perfectly formed lips confirming her relative youth compared with other staff. Perhaps she was newly qualified or a student. She introduced herself. I heard nothing. I was at that moment in the business of falling in love with Miss Hughes. Every movement, every shape she made every gesture and smile just hit me like a hammer. I was smitten, bowled over, hooked. I, Liam Parry, was truly in love for the first time.

The first order of business was registration. As Miss Hughes took her seat behind the desk, she emptied a fat briefcase onto the desktop. I recognised the folders as our homework entries. She began calling names in alphabetical order. As the names progressed towards the letter "P" I became more anxious. Each pupil confirmed their presence; then it came to—Parry? I hesitated. She looked up and smiled a little, searching the room for my raised hand and verbal confirmation of my existence. My face exploded and I could hardly speak. She must have thought I was an idiot.

Another bell, first lesson, History. Miss Hughes was to stay for this session, observed by Mr Sternway. She must have been a Student Teacher. I could drink in the magnificence of her beauty for another 40 minutes. The first matter was that of feedback from our History homework. The fabulous Miss Hughes was to give her opinion on our efforts to be Historians. I so wanted to impress her. The subject was, the voyages of Captain Cook, I had decided to write my work from the point of view of a 14-year-old lad joining the Royal Navy as a cabin boy. I tried to imagine what it would have been like in those days. The sights, the sounds and smells, the social standing, the hardships and pleasures of the day, the anxious feelings before the first voyage in a man's world. I had tried to enjoy the experience of writing my first story. Then, after some reviews of other people's work, it was my turn.

I recognised the cover of my folder. My heart rate increased.

'Now then; Liam Parry.'

Face explosion time again. I wish I could control that.

'This is an excellent piece of work, I'm very impressed. Do you know, when I read this I felt I was really there? I enjoyed it very much, well done.'

She spoke to ME!!! Again my face exploded, my heart rate increased, but I felt wonderful at the same time.

'Now for the remainder of the lesson the subject is "The influence of the Monarchy on the Expansion of Empire.'

I loved History. At any other time I would have taken it all in and enjoyed living through the unfolding events in my mind. Not today; today was Miss Hughes's day. I watched her every move and gesture like a hawk. When she first entered the room she wore a grey business suit, jacket and skirt, with a white blouse. Now she removed the jacket to hang it over the back of her chair. She had a lovely curvy figure. The 'V' neck blouse was tucked into the tight fitting skirt which hugged her thighs down to just above the knee, where it gave way to the best legs on the planet. The best thing about the blouse was that when she bent over the desk to check something, the eyes feasted upon just a hint of cleavage. My boyish eyes developed a telescopic zoom on such occasions. I took in nothing of what was said during the lesson. I didn't write anything or answer any questions. I just sat there, hot, with mouth open. She was the honey pot I was the Bee.

The lesson endeth; Time to leave my new-found love. As we filed out of the room I searched my mind desperately for something to say to her. Others gathered around her to ask questions or collect folders. I held back in order to get the chance to say those killer chat up lines to make her laugh or get any reaction. Now I was there, at the desk. She was sitting now and about to hand me my folder. Again my systems broke down. I wanted to thank her for a very interesting lesson. I thought that was better than "How are you fixed for tonight miss?" Just as I was about to force some words from my lips, "The cleavage syndrome" again stunned me. At this point the Head returned to the classroom and diverted her attention. I quickly took my folder and left. I desperately wanted to pee now.

The remainder of the school day does not feature in my long-term memory. I know that although I had experienced a life changing moment, I couldn't discuss it with my mates. I would have been the subject of scorn forever more. The finer attributes of the gorgeous Miss Hughes had not gone unnoticed by my mates of course, and I was obliged to join in with the banter, but I didn't like the way they spoke about her. I didn't like the comments bathed in teenage lust. For me it was love.

4pm, the final bell of the day. The virus, which had infected the building this morning now, dispersed to infect the Newsagents and Chippy across the road. As I was about to leave, the Goddess once more crossed my path. She was chatting with Mr. Penlove, the Art Teacher.

'Good bye Angela' he said 'see you tomorrow.' ANGELA. I now know her name. Angela Hughes. As she passed by she smiled. My eyes remained glued to her as she made her way to the car park. She got into a red soft top Triumph Vitesse. It had one of those easily recognisable engine sounds. I watched until she disappeared from view.

As for today though, this morning I was a school kid, this evening, I was a man.

So that was my contribution to the writing competition. It was in the top 100 in the Country. An achievement, of which, I was quite proud. This would not be the last I would hear about Angela Hughes, but it would be a long time before our paths would cross again.

Of course there were other important events this year even though Angela was perhaps the most important to me. President John Kennedy was assassinated. It was the worse winter weather for perhaps 100 years.

Casius Clay was knocked to the floor of the boxing ring for the first time in his career. Dr. Beeching destroyed the Railway Network. The Profumo affair rocked the Political world. Martin Luther King gave his 'I have a dream' speech. The series Dr. Who started. Quite a year, for everyone.

CHAPTER 2

After leaving school I had other concerns. Getting a job and learning to cope with the next phase of my life. Of course you know everything, don't you? You've done all the learning you need to do; and everything you need just falls into your lap. Well that's the theory anyway. So on we go, into the big wide world, to experience the ups and downs that life has to offer.

In the early sixties, it was reasonably easy to find work. I started in the retail trade working for a shop chain called Berties, the forerunner of the modern Supermarkets. I enjoyed the work and quickly proved myself worthy of promotion to management in just six months. However, I was about to learn my first workplace lesson. I was given all this extra responsibility due not entirely to my talent, but because I was cheap.

Having discovered this fact, I found the job I loved most in my life. Everything that came after this was never quite up to the pure enjoyment and satisfaction I got out of my next job. I became a student Psychiatric Nurse at Rainhill Hospital, near St. Helens. This job armed me with the life experience which would shape my future. It is in this location that I continue the story of the first major phase of my life. I regard this period as my awakening.

. This was the place which gave me a firm grounding for the future. It gave me more understanding of the "Human Condition" the tragic and the lighter side of life. Rainhill provided my 'Life Apprenticeship' and I missed it so much when it came to an end. The Hospital was an 800 strong Family of Staff caring for some 2000 Psychiatric Patients. It was one of the largest hospitals in Europe at the time. It provided my first romantic experiences and a very rich diversity of life experiences, which made it a wonderful place to be.

I don't know what prompted me to apply for this job. I had brief glimpses of the place whilst passing on the bus from time to time, but the high walls veiled the full extent and character of the place. One day, whilst contemplating my future I decided to write an enquiry letter. Ten days later I received a reply with an application form. Soon after I found myself standing at the gate, about to enter a New World; one which would completely change my life and many of my attitudes to it.

The call for interview included directions to the main offices. The Hospital was split into two sites. The main area was known as "Avon Division" and the other 'The Annexe'. I walked through the gate to the main site. It was late autumn 1967. It was 09.45hrs on a pleasant sunny morning. I didn't know what to expect. I found a rather pleasant looking area along the main drive. There were flowerbeds, a playing field and a bowling green with a range of buildings from the Victorian era to more recent additions from around the 40s. There were a number of uniformed nurses and white coated doctors, which I later discovered were male nurses. There were also many people I judged to be patients walking around. At the end of the drive there was a roundabout flanked by parked cars. An imposing Victorian building which, on enquiry was found to be the main offices, backed this area.

Apprehensively, I entered. The large hallway was imposing, very high ceiling with elaborate chandelier, oak panelling and beautifully carved highly polished oak furniture. There were also wall lights, which reminded me of one or two old Pubs I'd been in. I selected a large, winged green leather armchair and sat down. The place smelled mainly of polish blended with the smell of food. It was a few minutes to ten. My appointment was for ten. At the appointed hour a lady seemingly in her fifties, appeared from behind a large oak panelled door and asked if I was Mr. Parry. As I stood and confirmed my name, she shook my hand and asked me to follow her. She wore a dark green uniform with white collar and a matching belt with a large fancy silver buckle. I later learned that this was the uniform of a Sister Tutor.

She introduced herself as Sister Morgan, Senior Nursing Tutor. She sat behind an oak office desk with green leather inlaid top. I was invited to sit as she opened a folder on the desk. I was nervous, but soon put at ease. There followed a surpassingly friendly interview, which culminated in my being offered a place in the Nursing School as a Student Nurse for the next intake in January. I was very pleased, even more so when I was informed that I could start as soon as I liked and serve an induction period whilst waiting the first School session. I was then given an overview of the terms and conditions of service. The shifts were long but days off quite generous.

Students were not classed as staff on the wards, but would do all the jobs everyone else did as part of the Training Programme. The wage was lower than I had been getting, but I couldn't wait to start. As soon as I could, I gave my week's notice to Berties and counted down the hours. I couldn't wait. I was so excited.

My Family and friends thought I was mad. I used to reply that if I was, then I was going to the right place.

Soon I found myself at the start of a 3-year Nursing Course to qualify as a Psychiatric Nurse. 08.45 am, the first day. Just 2 weeks after my interview, here I was again, walking through the main gate towards the offices. I entered the main hallway, which looked just as it did before except there was a different background food smell; breakfast.

This time a Staff Nurse Tutor, Gregory Mason, greeted me. I was taken into an office and asked to fill in some forms. It turned out that Gregory lived not far from me. I lived in Page Moss; he lived in Knotty Ash. Mr. Mason, possibly in his mid 20s, seemed different from the average person the moment I met him. He was one of those people who can be instantly regarded as 'professorial' and eccentric. Agitated by being required to do something menial like paperwork, he seemed absent, not here with me. He had the demeanour of a much older person. Deciding to end the torture of administration he lifted the telephone and called in what he described as "a spare 3rd. Year" to complete this task and show me to the next phase the proceedings.

Enter Student Nurse Wilkinson, a pretty blonde girl. Typical image of a nurse, complete with uniform. We were introduced and Mr. Morgan quickly made his exit, passing on the admin to Patricia. Paperwork complete, I was escorted to the tailors shop on the Annexe side of the Hospital via a tunnel under the main road. Having reached level ground after the steep tunnel gradient, I saw for the first time exactly what lay behind the mysterious high walls. Heavily wooded areas giving way to low grassy banks flanked the main drive. There was lots of rhododendron, bushes. The trees were very mature, oak, ash, birch and a few willows. There were flowerbeds, recently bared ready for new plants. Leaves were starting to fall and the colours change. The sun was shining, creating variety to the images along the way. To my left stood rows of large 2 storey ward blocks between clumps of trees. We chatted as we walked. Pat gave me an introduction to the Hospital and a little of the history. She came from Doncaster and lived in the female nurse's home, within the grounds.

She asked if I was to live in also. She pointed out the location of the male nurses' home as we passed by. I hadn't thought about it, and I asked if living only 6 miles away would preclude me as a resident. She wasn't sure but suggested I ask, as there were many benefits to living in. It was very cheap and food was subsidised, plus she felt it was a better atmosphere to study. It was worth considering. We entered the main corridor part way along. It seemed to go on forever. Pat informed me that it was the longest hospital corridor, certainly in Europe, and possibly in the world.

My guide took me to the tailor. On the way the staff canteen was pointed out and I was asked to meet Pat there when I was finished. I was introduced to "Jack the Tailor" and asked to wait a while. Pat left for the canteen. Then I was ushered to an area behind the counter and all my measurements were taken. At the back of this area was a room where ladies did repairs and staff laundry. I was told that my uniform suit would be ready in a few days but I would be given my Whites straight away.

'What colour tabs?' Jack asked. I didn't know what he meant. 'What are you being employed as?'

'Oh, I've come as a Student' I replied.

Armed with this information he called out student tabs to one of the ladies who set about sewing red tabs to the collars of several full length white coats. After a short delay I was handed a pack of white coats and sent on my way.

I made my way to the canteen and sat down to a cup of coffee and a chat with my escort. She had spoken to 'The Chief' about accommodation and it seemed there were a few rooms available if I was interested. They would be basic but functional I was told. They were low cost and there would be an automatic deduction from pay. I was asked would I like to see a room on my way to the ward where I would start work. I agreed and was taken to the male nurse's block, which was above the Annexe admin offices. The room was quite large with typical high ceiling and large sash window. The heating was by radiator under the window. There was a single bed, an armchair and an office type desk and chair. There was a large full-length mirror and a framed print of an old pub. The toilet was communal along the landing. I liked it. I liked the idea of becoming independent and doing my own thing, and home wasn't far away if I needed anything. I decided I would arrange this as soon as possible.

CHAPTER 3

Now back into that amazing corridor. I discovered that the Annexe was divided between male and female sides, the dividing area being the offices at the central point. We were on our way to ward 13. On the way I was told that this ward had 120 beds. The Patients were, on the whole, able to look after themselves and that I wouldn't experience any major problems starting there. Pat thought it was a good initiation ward, and the Charge Nurse, Paddy O'Hare was a great bloke to work with. It was 11.45 already as I entered the ward. There was an entrance corridor with doors to the right and left and I could see a very large room at the far end. A short distance in we turned into the Charge Nurses office. Greetings and introductions followed and Pat wished me luck and left. Paddy informed me that due to a cold virus, claiming several staff, there was a shortage on the ward today. He would have normally shown me around and introduced me to everyone. He was so sorry, but today I'd have to be thrown in at the deep end. I said I was ok with that, but I'd never worked in a Hospital before.

'It's OK son, by 7 o'clock you'll either love it or hate it.' He called out for Julie, who promptly appeared at the door. 'This is Liam, a new Student. Take him under your wing today darling, and be gentle with him.' And so it was that Julie, a State Enrolled Nurse, in possibly her 50s, was given the job of breaking me in

Looking a little concerned, she reminded Paddy that she was dealing with little Kenny and was that OK? Or should she do something else as I'd only just started. I didn't know what the problem was but Paddy said, 'Well he'll have to deal with it sooner or later, may as well be sooner.'

Julie then took me across the corridor to a side ward containing 12 beds. They were all empty except for the first one on the left, which was screened off. Julie stopped me a moment.

'Now listen love, I'm sorry to put this on you straight away, but little Kenny has died, and we are going to get him ready for the morgue. It'll mean cleaning him up, making him look as good as we can for his relatives to see him. Have you ever dealt with a dead person before?'

I said that as a member of the St. John Ambulance I had dealt with only one death after an accident. Other than that I'd viewed a few bodies before funerals, but that was it. I'd do my best.

I was then asked to get a white coat from my pack and wear it. I was now on duty. I popped back to the office to retrieve one of the coats from the pack I had been given. I was quite excited about opening up the crisp starched coat and putting it on. I felt properly installed now. Returning to the care of Julie she noted my red collar tabs.

'I didn't realise you're a Student.'

'Oh I'm not quite yet, I just started early ready for the new intake in January. They thought it would benefit me to gain some experience until then.'

Julie took a trolley from a corner of the ward.

'Well here is your first lesson. I'll promote myself to Tutor' she said with a smile. Julie then took me through all the requirements of a 'laying out trolley', together with all the reasoning behind it. Then, asking if I was ready, she opened the curtains and pushed the trolley in beside the bed.

'Little Kenny' was covered with a pristine white sheet, only his face was visible. He was bald. His skin was very white with blue vein, rather like a roadmap, on his face. It was so quiet, that's what I felt most. There was just nothing from him. Still, what else should I have expected? After all he was dead. Julie asked me to take hold of the top of the sheet and follow her method of folding down the sheet until Kenny was fully exposed. He was so thin. The skin had settled on his bones, which made him look starved. I was told that the Duty Doctor had signed the certificate and we were free to continue. Under instruction, I helped wash the body. Julie was so caring and she spoke to him as if he could hear. She told him everything we were about to do and even apologised if a procedure would have been uncomfortable. I was then given the job of plugging all the orifices. Using tweezers or tongues I had to block off the nose, mouth, ears and anus. The most difficult thing I was required to do was tie off the penis with a bandage. Even though I knew he couldn't feel it, I felt it for him. The final jobs were to tie the label to his left toe with his details, put on his shroud and finish off his nails and hair. Julie said her farewell.

'There you are Kenny darling; you look like a million dollars now.'

Then we placed Kenny onto a large trolley with aluminium cover. He was put to one side while we remade the bed after disinfecting it. Then we took Kenny to the mortuary, which was a separate building removed from the main wards and surrounded by trees. Once we arrived there a porter who I assisted to place Kenny into the fridge met us. On the walk back to the ward, Julie complemented me on doing a good job. I certainly didn't expect that to be my first job, but I was quite proud of how I coped with it. I never admitted it, but the visions of 'little Kenny' stayed with me for some time afterwards.

Back on the ward and it was now dinnertime. I was now passed into the care of Barry Hartley the Staff Nurse. I wasn't sure at this stage where a Staff Nurse stood in order of ranking, but he was certainly senior to me. Barry took me to the staff canteen midway down the main corridor. Barry was a fun guy. Always there with the humorous quips. He had an endless catalogue of jokes and some very strong views on various aspects of life. All this I found out during the break. He was quite amused about the fact that I was required to deal with a death so early in my career. It was obvious from our time in the canteen that Barry was a very popular bloke, especially with the ladies. From the time we left the ward to the time we returned I was constantly entertained, but later in the evening I couldn't remember much of it at all in order to pass it on. The most enduring memory of Barry would be his famous (within the Hospital) statement when he agreed with something you said.

'This is indeed a statement of extreme fact and truth, against which neither argument or logic can prevail in fact.' That was Barry. In spite of his light hearted and frivolous nature, I was to develop the greatest of respect for him. As far as the job was concerned, he knew his stuff and he was always willing to listen and help if it was needed.

On returning to the ward I was passed on again to Emily. Emily was an Assistant Nurse, in her own words, 'the bottom of the pile'. Emily took me around the ward so I knew where everything was. As we toured the ward I was introduced to many of the characters that made up the Patients compliment. Some were quite friendly and seemingly 'with it'. Others were either less friendly or absent from the world altogether. I was told that many of the Patients on this ward were Epileptic and that I would soon learn how to deal with various types of fit.

It was tea time. Everyone filtered in to the dining room like cattle going to be milked. A few needed reminding or actually escorted to their table. Everyone had his or her place. Our job was to get the meals out as quickly as possible, making sure that the correct diets were served to the appropriate patients. The food was very good and prepared in each ward kitchen; not like a conventional hospital were meals were delivered from a main kitchen to all the wards. The 3-course meal was over within 90 minutes. Everything cleared away and tables re set within 2 hours. Then the staff took breaks in 2 sessions. I was on the 2nd, at which point more of the staff were properly introduced. The last hour was taken up with settling everyone down. A few went to bed early but most sat in the day room or games room. It was a more relaxed time during which I witnessed what was called a Grand Mall fit being dealt with. At 7pm it was time to leave. The day left me with a lot to talk about, should anyone wish to listen.

CHAPTER 4

That evening I decided to visit my mate James. Although the evening was wearing on quite late, I made the effort to make the trip to his house. I was keen to bring him up to date with the day's events.

He was keen to get a full report about the Lunatic Asylum as he so in appropriately put it. He expected to hear about crazy people intent on rape and murder, foaming at the mouth and screaming. I had to disappoint him, but he was impressed by 'the body' story. That night I slept well, but I wasn't keen on getting up at 5am, in order to be in by 7am, using buses. I had own a motor cycle, but I was short of money so I couldn't use it until I got my next pay packet. Fortunately, the pay was weekly, so not too long to wait.

Soon my friends and family got used to the idea of my working at Rainhill. I was getting to know more about the place every day. It was vast. I stayed on ward 13 for the whole of my induction period and luckily the old bike, which I bought from the Police Auction for £15 kept faithful to me and got me there each day regardless of the weather. I wished I could afford a car though; I didn't have appropriate motor cycle kit for winter temperatures. Christmas seemed to pounce upon us suddenly. There seemed to be no shortage of money to celebrate it to the full at the Hospital. Decorations and lights arrived early in December. A large conifer already existed in front of each main office and these were festooned with lights. Maintenance staff decorated all the communal areas. And nursing Staff decorated each ward. The whole place was transformed from an imposing Victorian Hospital into a fantastic winter wonderland. It was just wonderful. I was acutely aware of many of the poor souls for whom the world they lived in was constantly fraught with troubles, misunderstandings and delusions; denying them the pleasures of life. We all did everything we could to give them as much of the joy of the season as possible.

The week leading up to Christmas was party time. A staff drinks trolley was to be found in the ward staff room. Only off duty staff was allowed to sample the delights of this trolley. During this period many off duty staff and their families would visit the wards and help entertain the Patients, perhaps share a drink with them or play games, or even just sit and talk. Many of the patients loved seeing the children. The People, who were permanent residents, never got out into the community. However, we were in a period of change and this would give rise to a few funny incidents, which I will tell you about later.

I was given Christmas off, but like many others I visited each day to socialise and partake of the hospitality. We were like a large family. Christmas Eve we had a significant snowfall. I couldn't get home on the bike and the buses stopped at 6pm. I went with a group of Staff to The Brown Edge a nearby Old World pub. It was packed and I could hardly see to the end of the lounge because of the density of cigarette smoke. It was a great night and Barry played a major role in providing the entertainment. All except two of us lived in the Hospital Houses or in the Nurses Homes. We all left in a group at 11pm. And made our way back to wherever we wished to go. We spread out all over the road and had snowball fights and challenged the odd sliding motorist to miss us.

Now wet and cold, Gerry Finlay and I, continued to pelt a couple of the girls with snowballs until they reached the female nurses home. They managed to get inside and lock us out. Gerry was having none of this. He was convinced that one of the girls fancied him and he was determined to have his way with her. He hammered on the door, but to no avail. Then it opened, and his face lit up. His delight was short lived when he was confronted with the Matron who whacked him with an umbrella and gave him a matronly scolding. We started to leave the scene when Gerry had another idea.

'Just hang on a minute Liam' he urged, Helen's in room 8 on the first floor. I know which one it is. Come on lets go round there!"

I followed him in the pursuit of his Dream Girl. Gerry pointed out room 8. The light was on and there was a narrow gap in the curtains.

'You don't expect her to climb down here do you, daft bugger'. Gerry surveyed the scene and weighed up the options. As far as I could see there were no options except to leave. Gerry decided to emulate 'The Beatles' and began to sing a love song. The 'love song' turned out to be Penny Lane. I didn't quite grasp the logic of that, but he was happy and possibly even in love. After throwing some snowballs at the window, the curtain opened, the sash window was lifted and Helen appeared telling us to go away or she'd be in trouble with Matron.

'We're not frightened of that old bat' Gerry announced bravely.

'Aren't you, indeed!' Matron announced from behind us. 'Now if you don't want the spike of this brolly up your anal passage, I suggest you go back to the hole you emerged from, NOW!'

We turned in horror to see the little but mighty Matron standing there, cloaked in a woolly night-gown, but still wearing her Matrons cap. We left.

Gerry lived in Litherland. Neither of us fancied walking home. After roaming the Annexe corridor for a while, the night staff on ward 7 found us a bed each in padded rooms. Perhaps we were safer there. The next morning I awoke at 8.45. After my brain kick started itself again I realised that I was in the padded room and remembered being allowed to reside there by the night staff. I got out of the bed, feeling slightly groggy; I walked to the door. It was shut and no internal handle. I looked through the observation glass, which had a limited view of the corridor. Now and again a figure would flash by but of course I couldn't be heard. It occurred to me that as the room would be thought empty; no one would be likely to check it. When a patient was known to be in one of these rooms, a staff member would be allocated to constantly keep a check on the Patient, and a note would be made in the report book and an identity label would by fixed to the door. The Night Staff would have gone off duty at 7am and Gerry and I wouldn't be in the log; we weren't supposed to be there. That was a bit worrying.

After waiting for a while I heard the outer handle being turned and the Charge Nurse asked how I was. The Night Staff hadn't forgotten us, after all. Having been released from the 'padded cell', I made my way to my ward where I collected my topcoat helmet and gloves, and decided to try and get home on my trusty steed. The main roads were ok now, so I made it home by 10 O'clock. My Parents and younger Sister Annette were a little shocked when I told them I'd spent the night in a cell, until I explained. Annette thought it was hilarious.

There then followed the traditional Family Christmas Dinner with Mum, Dad and Annette. It was nice to be home, but my heart was still at work. Each Christmas after this, most of my time would be at the hospital. Mum was concerned about my move to live at the hospital, just like a Mum would be. Dad was fine with it and Annette said I was a nuttier anyway and that's where I belonged. We settled down with full stomachs for the Queens speech and then a John Wayne film, during which I nodded off. I did awaken later to see Bonanza, which I liked. Other viewing included 'No Hiding Place', 'Alfred Hitchcock Mysteries' and 'Emergency Ward 10', which was nothing at all like Rainhill. Boxing Day was spent mainly with my mate James in the City centre. Both penniless, we just walked around and window-shopped.

CHAPTER 5

The rest of that week was quiet and routine. New Year provided another period of fun and frolics but I was working over this period, so I didn't end up in any more padded rooms. On New Year's Eve I went to the staff party in the Social Club. That was a great night. My first romantic interlude happened that night. Her name was Kathy, a Staff Nurse from what we called 'the sick ward.' This was a ward where patients, who fell ill with medical conditions, were nursed. Someone she didn't want to be bothered with was annoying Kathy. I sat at the same table with a group from ward 1, most of the evening and we had chatted, from time to time, with some difficulty over the disco music volume. However, a Male Nurse from Prestwich Hospital had taken a fancy to Kathy and became a bit of a pest. Kathy asked me if I wouldn't mind pretending to be her husband for a while, just to get rid of him. I agreed. The next time he invited her to dance; she pointed me out and told him it was her husband's dance now. He politely bowed out and I danced with her to complete the deception. This turned out to be the last six dances, then Midnight. Someone announced the count down. We stayed in a sort of loose hug until the midnight 'Happy New Year' and the kiss, which continued for some time. Then more dancing, and without saying anything we continued to dance together until 1am. I was on duty at 7am. I did mention this fact but we couldn't part. Kathy was about 5' 4" tall, slim but not thin. She had long black hair, lovely complexion and blue eyes. She wore a black full length dress which had a sort of inlaid glitter and black shoes which I stood on many times. I wasn't a good dancer. I gathered that she lived in St Helens very near the town centre in a terraced house. She lived with her parents and one older brother. I guessed she was around my own age.

It felt so good holding her. The silky dress seemed to accentuate her form. For some reason I was constantly fascinated by the feel of her bra strap and the slight fold around her middle. She would have been mortified had I mentioned it, but I found it rather sexy. Her thighs rubbed mine frequently and her breasts pressed against me just below my own. Kathy wore little make up. Many of the other women were overdone. Her lipstick was pale pink and her eyes were accentuated by shadow. The ear rings sparkled under the disco lights. I occasionally had to apologise for stepping on toes. There were some dances which were more vigorous and meant dancing apart. We flowed like courting birds and I loved the way she moved. When close I detected beautiful perfume. Her hair was soft to my face. Occasionally we spoke to each other in short sentences, mostly nonsense, but it helped with the bonding process. Kathy spoke with a Lancashire, distinctly St. Helens accent, with local colloquialisms like "ye mornt" for you must not. Her voice was soft and feminine. She was very intelligent and later conversations covered a wide variety of topical subjects she admitted to prefer listening to my ramblings.

We left the dance floor at 2am and attempted to get a taxi. Of course nothing was available. We decided to stay near the door and ask people if there was space in their taxi to share. The kissing and cuddling continued throughout this process until at 3.15am a space was found. I remembered to ask to see her again, and she agreed. I kissed her into the taxi and watched the car disappear into the dense cold mist. I was very happy. I forgot to suggest a date and time, but I knew where she worked and I could get in touch again. I made my way to ward 13 and lay down on the sofa in the staff room. 3.45am about 2 hours of sleep before being on duty again. At least I wouldn't be late; I was already there.

It was 3 days before I encountered Kathy on duty again. I was concerned that perhaps it was a one-night stand. Much to my relief she was delighted to see me again, and she had the same reservations. We arranged the date. Our days off overlapped so we were able to meet without complications. The other good thing was that she had access to her mum's car, a Ford Anglia. Great.

The day of the date arrives. I'm nervous. I've always been rather shy of girls and didn't regard myself as anything special. I was so happy that this lovely girl wanted to go out with me. I could hardly believe it. We were to meet at 5pm. Mum wanted to meet me. That made me even more nervous. I arrived a little early and mum greeted me. Much to my surprise I discovered that mum also worked at the Hospital. Her name was May and she was a Sister on one of the female wards. The connection was useful. We got on well chatting until Kathy came in looking great. The shiny long black hair flowed over shoulders onto a white knitted jumper. She wore a checked mini skirt and white calf length boots. Her smile lit up the room.

'Do you drive?' May enquired, offering me the keys.

'Well yes' I confirmed, rather surprised at the offer.

The car was outside in the street. It was dark and the car was already starting to mist over with the cold air. After fiddling about for a while trying to find everything and wiping the windows and mirrors, we were on our way. It was great to be in a car for a change. I was used to buses and a motor bike. I had passed my test in my mate James's' car. His family was quite well off. He had an Austin Westminster, which I had driven quite a lot.

Having checked out the venue, I took Kathy to the Mersey View club at the top of Helsby Hill. There was live music tonight and the 'Chicken and Chips' was a good price. On the drive out we just chatted about work mainly. We both felt relaxed and at ease with each other. Kathy had never been over the Widnes Bridge before. At night it was a great sight. She stopped talking for the whole length of the bridge in order to take in the views. We were counting Christmas Trees on the way and before we set off I suggested we guess the final total. My guess was 1020; Kathy's 500. As we entered the car park at Mersey View the total was 720. Kathy wins. It was a frosty night. Kathy took a long warm coat from the boot before we treaded with care across the icy car park to the entrance. The club was warm and welcoming. The group hadn't started yet so we went downstairs to the dining room for the bargain 'Chicken and Chips'.

During our conversations it transpired that Kathy had serious ambitions. She had looked into the possibility of nursing in America. It seemed there was a shortage in some areas and Qualified Nurses from Europe were in demand. She had done a lot of research, and I got the impression she was very keen on the idea. Her parents had reservations, but they seemed to centre mainly on her being so far away. I asked when she thought she might go. No firm decision had yet been made, but that glint in her eye at every mention of it told me it was 'a definite possibility'. What I didn't realise was that Kathy had already completed her SRN (State Registered Nurse) qualifications at Whiston. She was now doing the 18 months to do what we called double qualification. I was impressed. At the back of my mind I did a quick calculation. It would seem she was a couple of years older than me. I didn't enquire at this stage. In conversation over our meal, she told me she was a bit disappointed with nursing at the General Hospital. She liked to get more involved with the people and General Nursing tended to be more detached, more concerned with paperwork and ticking boxes. She enjoyed Rainhill much better. I asked if it wouldn't be the same in the states. She thought the Americans would be more down to earth and less formal. She had researched the experiences of other nurses who had made the change and was satisfied it would meet expectations.

The evening went very well. We had a lot of fun and I managed to remember some of Barry's' jokes. The time at the club flew by and seemingly in an instant it was time to leave. Outside I encouraged Kathy to walk to the outer wall to look at the view of which the club was aptly named. This view never failed to amaze me. I had been here many times, but each visit was better than the last, plus this time I had a pretty girl on my arm, or actually, wrapped within one arm. It was bitterly cold, especially at the cliff edge. The wind swept across the Mersey directly into our faces. She loved the view and I pointed out all the places of interest. The Airport was located by following the flight path of a plane landing. The two large oil refineries were obvious due to the thousands of safety lights on the gantries and of course the ever burning flame at Stanlow. Frodsham below looked like a toy village and further out we could pick out the City lights, The Wirral Peninsula and the Welsh hills. Wonderful though it was we didn't stay long. I offered to return with her in the summer. Her agreement told me that this date was not a one off.

We returned to the car and started the engine to warm up the car, and commenced to kiss and cuddle to warm us up. I kept it just nice. I didn't want to go too far and put her off. But I kept questioning the wisdom of this reasoning. My experience was very limited here. It seemed to be the right thing to do. The car now being defrosted, we set off back to St. Helens. I asked if she preferred to return via the Bridge or the Tunnel. She had never been through the Mersey tunnel either, but elected to go over the Bridge again. Kathy suggested we stop off at the Hospital so I could get into the home without getting buses again. I told her I was still at home at Page Moss. My residence was to start in a few weeks. So it was that we went to my home first; stopping for a while near Huyton Teachers College for a last cuddles session. She assured me she didn't mind taking herself home from my house. We moved on and stopped outside my house. We kissed again, the sort of kiss, which says, don't go. Kathy thanked me for a lovely evening, and with a knowing smile asked if she had impressed me enough to do it again. With some embarrassment I gave out an apologetic laugh and assured her that I would love to do it again.

'I'm new at this darling' I said, 'I wasn't sure about the procedure.' I smiled back.

'Well, so, when Romeo?' We both giggled.

'Let me get starting at the School out of the way, get some dosh together and I'll take you somewhere magnificent next weekend.'

'Sounds perfect to me. You know where I live, where I work. If anything changes let me know. We can always go Dutch. I don't mind.'

We managed to reluctantly Part Company. I watched the car disappear. For the first time, I was in love with someone who was willing to return it. I was over joyed.

CHAPTER 6

The time to commence my Training School induction was upon me I was given the Sunday to move in to my room My Family came with me I felt like a child going to boarding school for the first time. Mum wasn't at all impressed with the place and Annette joked that I belonged in a Mental Hospital. Dad thought it was very good, he wouldn't mind staying in it. After brief goodbyes; you would think I was going to South Africa not just six miles away; I began unpacking my belongings. I had very little to unpack. The wardrobe and desk looked distinctly light on goods. Still, I now had 3 years in which to fill the empty spaces. Everything in its place, I stood at the large sash window, placed my hands on the radiator and peered out into the car park. It was raining. The trees across the drive looked drab. I suddenly felt alone.

There was a knock at the door. I opened it to see a beaming smile. It was Kathy. 'We are not really allowed here, but I got permission to come to your room just to wish you good luck. I'm happy for you.' She edged her way in. 'I'm sorry, I can't stay. Just know that if there's anything you want, any help or anything; Well, I'm around.'

I thanked her. We kissed briefly and with a smile she left.

'See you at the weekend then?' She said as she left.

'Yes, see you at the weekend. I'll meet you in the canteen to arrange times, OK?' 'OK' came the reply, together with a smiley glance back.

Tomorrow I am about to embark upon two new phases really. I officially become a Student Nurse. By now I have some idea of the immensity of what I have got to study. And of course, I have a wonderful girl friend who evidently loves me so much; she's willing to go Dutch. WOW! I decided to have a look at the Communal Lounge. There were a few lads, milling around there. Some were here for the first time and about to start in the same school as me. There were also a couple of old hands sizing up the competition for the females. We all sat down on the instruction of one of the older students. We were all asked to introduce ourselves to everyone in the group, together with where we came from. Students arriving today came from Scotland, Wales and places in England such as London, Cambridge, Lancaster, Doncaster, York and 'Page Moss'. There was one Student from Cape Town South Africa and one from Gibraltar.

That evening all the new students gathered in the female nurse's home lounge; this was the suggestion of one of the Tutors. The gathering was a social affair for the purpose of getting to know one another and to meet any Tutors or Senior Staff who could attend. The formal introductions would be dealt with on the first school morning next day. I was able to play a significant role because I was already reasonably familiar with the hospital. It gave me a lot of pleasure to help and perhaps settle some nerves. I didn't mention what my first ward task was.

The first school week was an induction. We were shown around the departments and wards and given the information we needed to function. Everyone was kitted out with uniform within days. By the weekend it was obvious that some couples had already found romance. But I could only look forward to my own date with Kathy.

The periods in the school allowed for weekends off. Kathy was also off this weekend so we met at 11am on Saturday morning. A bitterly cold January day, we spent it in Chester. The shopping areas were more sheltered. Not that we did any shopping, we just looked around, walking and talking hand in hand. We had dinner there then walked around the City walls. I was able to show off a bit because history was a favourite subject of mine, so I was able to bring many of the Roman areas to life. It began to rain and the walk became a run back to the car. We left Chester. I was put in charge of the driving. I thought Kathy would like to visit Port Sunlight on the Wirral, so it was there that I headed next. Again I became a sort of tour guide and told her why Lord Leverhulme built the village. I pointed out the individual character of each house and it turned out that this visit was the right thing to do. She loved it. The Lady Lever Gallery was closed when we arrived, so no posh cup of tea in the café. I stopped in a secluded area and we kissed and cuddled awhile. She was so beautiful. I wanted to tell her then that I loved her, but held back. She told me I was a lovely man, and perhaps she was holding back too. Anyway, I was enjoying the day and it seemed she was too. We decided to go to Kathy's house for tea and spend the evening there. After tea her dad suggested we all go to the Labour Club for the evening, and so we did. It was a very enjoyable evening. This occasion was a bonding time with the family. Kath's dad,

Ron was a Bus Driver and her elder brother Jake worked at Bold Colliery at the coal face. Ron and Jake were proper "Lancashire Lads". Worked hard, played hard and enjoyed good booze up. This get together confirmed to me that Kathy was not a one off date. That was fine with me. On return to the house we were diplomatically left alone in the front room to get on with our courting, another sign of acceptance and trust from the family.

January was dominated by the new Nursing School and of course Kathy. Kathy and I were soon serious lovers and made concentrating on study very difficult. We wanted to see more and more of each other and now almost every meeting concluded by making love in the back of the car. Not such an easy task in the restricted back seat of a Ford Anglia, but as they say, true love will find a way. It was during this period that I had to learn the delicate art of applying condoms at just the right moment. This I always found much fumbled and even at times off putting but that skill was nothing compared with the need to obtain these items. Despite being very mature in so many ways, I could not bring myself to buy condoms in a Chemist shop. It would almost always be a woman serving and I would be acutely embarrassed to ask for them. I had to resort to buying mail order. Fortunately I could arrange deliveries to my room at the hospital. Doing it this way gave rise to all sorts of unwanted mailings prompting everything from domination accessories to prostitution services. These I had to dispose of at once in case cleaners found them or someone who might regard them as unsuitable for a person in a Nursing roll to have. I did have a sneaky look first though before throwing the stuff out.

CHAPTER 7

Valentine's Day. I agonised for ages to find the right idea for Kathy's present. My mate 'farty' James and I had once had a meal at a place called 'The River Room' restaurant at the Pier Head. It was a first floor restaurant right at the riverfront. It was classy, not too expensive and the food was good. I booked it, making sure I saved enough for the special day. I could only get lunchtime booking as they called it, dinnertime to normal people. We were both supposed to be working, but as luck would have it we were able to arrange the day off together. I was overjoyed to see her reaction to the venue. We had a lovely-uncrushed meal and a sit in the lounge looking at the river. It was a bright sunny day. A bit 'crisp', but we still walked around the Pier Head taking in everything that was going on. It was always very busy. A Royal Navy Ship must have been in because there were sailors everywhere. We walked through the bus station, passed the 'greasy spoon café' where the ordinary people ate. They also had an external hatch where you could buy food on the go. I liked the hustle and bustle of the bus station. There must have been about 50 stands with queues at each one. The buses moving in and out like ants around their nest.

After walking for a while, Kathy suggested we return to her house. She had a surprise for me. Try, as I might on the return journey, I couldn't prize out of her the secret surprise. Back at the house, Kathy let herself in and I followed. She took off her coat and stoked the coal fire.

'Do you want a drink?' she asked as she walked into the kitchen.

I confirmed my desire for a cup of tea. I sat on the sofa having taken off my coat and raised my hands to warm them from the increasing heat from the revitalised fire. Kathy re-entered the lounge.

'Kettle's on, I'm just going to the bathroom.'

She went upstairs and I picked up a copy of 'The Echo' and flipped through it. After a while I was aware of Kathy returning to the room. Her silence made me lower the paper to reveal Kathy standing at the door in a black negligee. It was layered so I couldn't see everything, but enough to realise that we were not about to drive off anywhere else today. I stood and walked to her, put my arms around her and kissed her forehead.

'You're beautiful' I whispered as I held her too me. The heat of her body quickly filtered through my own clothes. I was instantly aroused. We kissed passionately for a few moments, and then after being assured that we had plenty of time alone I was guided, if guidance was needed, to her bedroom. My clothes seemed to float away and as we sank onto the bed, the negligee also disappeared. This was the first time I had been in bed with a woman since I was born, even better, a gorgeous naked woman who also wanted to be there.

Now I felt all the beautiful skin, the shapes, and the warmth. I could feel her entire body next to mine. Her lips felt sexier than before, her breathing faster. I was able not only to feel her, but see her in all her beauty.

'I don't have any condoms,' I admitted nervously.

'I'm ok at this time of the month, don't worry.'

Reassured I increased my seduction technique as much as I was able with limited experience. Perhaps it was me who was being seduced. I didn't care. Now, without restriction I was able to feel and play with her fanny, to fondle her breasts and kiss her ever more inviting lips to the fullest of joy. Later I would realise that on this occasion I was carried away with my needs rather than Kathy's, but future experiences would resolve that issue. For now everything was heavenly. This was the most wonderful experience of my life so far. Soon, perhaps too soon in the excitement, I was fully inside her. The heat, the motion, the feeling was so intense that I come very soon. When I was spent I realised that Kathy was yet to orgasm. I placed my knee between her legs and massaged her till she climaxed several times. We collapsed together and held each other tenderly. We had made love before in the back of a car, fully or partly clothed and often in a rush. This was altogether different, like it should be. It was so wonderful. Neither of us wanted it to end. All too soon it was time to return to reality. Valentine's Day would never be the same again.

Kathy and I became ever closer for the next few months. Then on a Saturday evening date at the end of March I detected a change of mood in Kathy. She seemed on edge and quiet on the drive to our destination in Liverpool City Centre. I parked near the station. It was a mild evening. The Sun was warming the evening air after a day of showers. I took Kathy into the Adelphi Hotel and we climbed the entrance staircase to the large lounge area. Kathy settled on one of the sofas while I went for the drinks a Pony and a Coke. When I returned I 'took the Bull by the horns' and asked what the problem was. I had inkling already. My worst fears were confirmed when she told me her offer had come through from the American Hospital and all the paperwork had been approved. She would be departing in a Month.

Though devastated inside, I put on a brave face and began the discussion about how we would keep in touch and make every effort to see each other whenever we could. I still had a way to go before qualification but committed myself to join Kathy at that point to start a new life in the USA. I liked the idea. I was enthusiastic and I could visualise the new life. Kathy was tearful, but I reassured her that I was fine with it; I was expecting it and she had my full support. She produced some leaflets and documents and began talking me through the practicalities of her new adventure. She kept asking me if I was sure it was OK. As the evening progressed we began to dream of the life ahead of us, together. Neither of us had even the slightest doubt about the future. The evening ended with a simple kiss and cuddle, our emotions were mixed. We needed some time to take it all in properly.

CHAPTER 8

We met as frequently as possible over the following Month. It just flew over and as the time drew nearer we became more emotional and reluctant to part at all, then came the dreaded day for Kathy's family and me. The departure lounge at Manchester Airport, lots of nervous waiting because of the checking in times hours before boarding. Then the tearful hugs and kisses before Kathy was taken by the flow of passengers out of sight. We made our way to the observation area to see the plane leave. It was raining and as the aircraft roared along the runway smothered in its own spray, I found myself willing it to rise from the ground. We lost sight of it for a moment over a hill. I held my breath. Then the plane appeared again and rose like a Swan into the low cloud base and was soon gone. This flight was a short hop to London where there would be a changeover to the New York flight.

The mood was of sadness as we made our way to the car park, the correct one of which we couldn't find for ages. We left the airport having paid the equivalent of a second mortgage for parking and drove back mostly in silence to St Helens. I was dropped off at the Hospital.

Back in my room I felt so alone. Kathy had become so much part of my life. I wanted to compose a letter to her but I couldn't motivate myself to do anything. I left my room again and out into the hospital grounds. I walked out through the back way, a narrow lane flanked by the hospital farm. I walked with only my sad thoughts for company all the way home. It was early evening when I arrived at the house. I spent the rest of the day with my parents and Annette . . . I told them how the day went. They knew I was feeling low and I was given tea and sympathy. Annette took me to the pub for an hour, and then I caught the bus to the hospital. I was on duty next morning.

All I could think of now was when would the first letter arrive? It wasn't long before the first airmail letter just confirming that all was well, lots of love, miss you. Not a lot could be fitted on that one blue sheet. It was 10 days before the first proper letter. What was the next few years going to be like?

'My darling, Liam. I miss you like mad. Keep thinking you'll appear at my door any minute. I am now reasonably settled at Jefferson Memorial in Queens. The area around the Hospital is quite run down but the People seem fine. The Hospital itself is nowhere near as big as Rainhill and you'd find it a bit clinical, but the Staff are great and they want to know all about England. It's a private company who owns the place but they do take Patients whose circumstances would preclude them from normal hospital care. One of the Surgeons always walks around with a cigar in his mouth; yes really!

There isn't a nurse's home. I'm living with a family in the suburbs, Martha and Jake Rubinstien and their 8yr old son Alex. In return for some Nannying, I live almost free. Jake is a Cop (Policeman to you) and he works long hours on shifts, so Martha and I spend a lot of time together. The House is what we would call a large bungalow with a 2-car garage, complete with 2 cars. My licence is of limited use here, so Jake will help me through the process of getting a permanent licence. The houses have open plan front lawns and small rear gardens and patios. It's a nice quiet area. Don't like the kids around here much, they tend to be a bit rude and cheeky? They've got everything and seem to want even more. What I do like is the pay and the lifestyle. Can't wait for you to share it with me, I'm coming home for Christmas and New Year. I know its months off, but if we keep busy it'll soon pass my darling. I love you so much. Go and see Mum soon, I've sent her photos and some other stuff for you all to see. Keep your handsome head in those books and off the female nurses.— Kath. XXXXX'

For just a few minutes I felt closer. I immediately wrote my reply.

Thank you, so much for the lovely letter. My love is also with you my darling, and I miss you so much too. I'm glad you've found a nice family to live with and a Cop eh? Wow! I'm impressed. The area sounds lovely too, I'm so happy for you. Everything here is much the same as you left it.

You remember we had started to try out ways of getting some patients more used to living in the community? Harry Barlow and I were given the task of taking 6 Patients out for the afternoon for a bus ride and perhaps some shopping. We travelled only a short distance on the bus because Billy Williams started playing with the hair of a lady he was sitting behind, so before she became too uneasy we made a diplomatic exit with apologies to the lady. Harry decided it might be a good idea to let the lads experience a Laundrette, as when they were discharged, they would no doubt have to use one. So in we went. All seemed to be going well. We showed them how to fill the machines, how to get the detergent and use the slots and coins and how to get assistance from the attendant if needed. We borrowed some of their excess clothing to demonstrate the process, sat on the benches and awaited the results. After a few minute we could smell burning. On investigation we discovered that one of the patients had put his plastic mac into one of the dryers and thick black smoke had started to fill the place. 15 minutes later the Fire Chief was as unamused as the attendant. Exercise curtailed.

On the positive side, the Patients had experienced some excitement in their hum drum lives and they'd seen the Fire Brigade in action.

Hurry to me the day when I can be at your side for always. I cannot imagine any life without you. I wish I could do this in person, but I can't wait till Christmas. Will you please consider marrying me? I know I'm only a Student, and you are a Super Yankeedoodle Mega Nurse, but I'm crazy about you. When I post this I'll be a nervous wreck until I hear from you. How much is an overseas telephone call? I do love you so very much, you and only you. I knew it from the day we met.

All my love is with you. No matter how far. Liam. XXXXXXXX'

CHAPTER 9

Now it was the waiting game again. I expected to see May soon at work and arrange to go to view the photos etc.: For now it was time to try and get back into the books and the classes and discover ever more fantastic facts about the human mind and associated problems. This period was also a good time to reacquaint myself with my old school pal James whom I had neglected recently due to falling in love.

It was a Saturday, a day off. I met James in Huyton Village outside the Post Office. As we walked to his car he explained that he had arranged to look after his two nieces for the day. We were to collect them from his house and go first to Alder Hey Hospital to visit his Nephew who had been given skin grafts after being scalded

'So it's a busman's holiday then?' I enquired. James apologised, but I didn't mind at all.

James lived in a large detached house near Pex Hill, Cronton. His Father was a Royal Navy Officer and away for months at a time. His Mother was clothing wholesaler with a warehouse in Salford. They were what we called 'well to do', nice people though. James worked in the warehouse learning the trade. He wanted to join the Navy, but mum wasn't keen to have both her men away all the time. She always worried about John, the Dad; he was a Submariner and spent much of his time tracking Russian Subs and Spy Ships, could be dangerous.

The house was lovely and made me envious. Jane, his mum was home with the nieces and a friend of hers, Mirriame. They were anxious to go shopping in Wrexham and couldn't wait to palm the kids off onto us. Once we took charge of the two little girls the ladies were off in the 2.8ltr. Jag, all glammed up and ready to spend spend spend. We helped ourselves to a snack and James gave me the keys to his Austin Westminster. I loved it. A none-standard midnight blue with leather seats, walnut dash and lots of chrome. She glided along with ease and grace. The girls sat in the back and argued with each other while we tried to listen to Radio Luxembourg.

It was a lovely sunny day. We decided to take the girls for a trip after the hospital visit.

Half an hour later we parked at Alder Hey and made our way to the ward. We were a little early for visiting hours so we looked around the place. I spoke to several Nurses and was intrigued by the fact that they all had Welsh accents. It was as if as if a Slave Trader had gathered them up from the Mountains and Valleys herded them to ships at Llandudno and transported them to Liverpool to work here. Bells rang, and people filtered into the wards. On the way to the Hospital we had stopped at St. Johns corner Huyton to call in at a corner shop. This shop was well known in the area and had the unique characteristic of a Jacobean style front and a witch's hat shaped tower. We had to decide what to take for our 6-year-old patient. As I was the National Health Representative in the party I was asked for advice. I concluded that everyone seemed to take Lucozade and grapes to visit patients. Oh, and flowers. James questioned the wisdom of taking flowers to a 6-year-old lad, so he bought an Airfix kit of H.M.S. Ark Royal. 'Sorted.'

We walked down the ward and sat around the bed the kid was asleep, so we just sat. The Girls were getting fidgety and began to crawl around under the bed and punch each other. We placed the Lucozade and Ark Royal on the bedside cabinet and began to eat the grapes.

'Why don't you wake him up?' James asked, looking at me.

'Why me?" was my reply.

'Well you're the Nurse.' was his logical conclusion.

'You don't have to be qualified to wake someone up' I said. 'He's your Nephew, you wake him up.'

One of the girls took the notes folder from the bottom of the bed.

'Don't play with them, put them back'" I shouted, but in a whisper. At this point a man and woman appeared at the foot of the bed. The woman looked lovingly at the sleeping boy.

'Ah, just look, he must be tired. Are you boys Bill's Kid?'

James stood to greet the new comers.

'Who's Bill?' asked James, rather puzzled.

'Billy Armstrong, his Dad' the lady answered, equally puzzled. The penny dropped. This wasn't James's Nephew. With some embarrassment we departed and went to find the right patient. We accidentally left the Lucozade and Ark Royal with Bills kid. We Found Ben, the real Nephew, sat with him and ate his grapes. James assured him that we would bring him something next time and what would he like? Turned out he wanted comics anyway. I wonder what Bills dad thought about the Ark Royal and who drank the Lucozade?

It was so boring we left after only 20 minutes. Now, how do we entertain two little girls? I know how to entertain big ones. James was equally stumped. Again it was down to the Health Service Rep. to think of something. James was now driving. I directed him to 'The Diddymens' Houses" nearby, the creation of Ken Dodd. The girls seemed fairly interested. Lizzy, the youngest but most inquisitive, asked about the 'Jam Butty mines' and did they exist? Well I didn't want to destroy the girl's imagination, so I offered to show them the 'Jam Butty Mines.' Helen, the slightly older, but all knowing girl told me not to be stupid, there wasn't such a thing as a 'Jam Butty mine.'

We stopped just after the Diddy Houses. There was a low stone wall backed by some wasteland, which had possibly been an old railway cutting. I led the intrepid explorers down the embankment to the mouth of the tunnel under the road, now blocked off mid-way, through it served as a conduit for some large water pipes. I described it to the girls as the entrance to the 'Jam Butty mines.' Helen was of course still not convinced. Then, as if by some miracle, on the ground at the foot of the tunnel entrance was — a real Jam Butty. Probably thrown away by someone passing over the bridge, but there it was indisputable evidence of the existence of the mine. I could hardly believe my luck. Helen was gobsmacked; Lizzy simply accepted it and even James had to think again. James laughed out, 'To coin a phrase, you Jammy Bugger!'

That was the only miracle that day. We took the girls to a Burger Bar in Old Swan for tea, then back to Cronton to the Super House to watch T.V. and eat until the ladies returned heavily laden with shopping bags two of food and nine of clothes. Uncle Harry collected his reasonably good children at 7pm. The girls excitedly recounted their exploration of the Jam Butty Mine and un—noticed by me, Millie had brought back the now curled up and hard Jam Butty to have for supper. Good luck with that I thought.

Now we spent a boozy wine evening with the ladies. Mirriame got a bit randy by 11pm; but was bungled off into a taxi before she went too far. What a shame. She had begun to insist on playing strip poker, but protective mum was having none of it. James and I offered to drive

Mirriame home, but Jane joked that she'd eat us both alive and reminded us that we were also unfit to drive.

I stayed the night in the guestroom, which was originally intended for Mirriame. Lovely, soft double bed. I wished Kathy was also in it. I thought about her and our time together. I thought about what it would be like to start a new life in the USA. As I did so I drifted off to sleep. I had slept over here many times before. It was as quiet as a graveyard here at night, not much noisier during the day either.

Next morning, after freshening up in the en suite bathroom, I followed the wonderful smell of Breakfast to the dining kitchen area. There was also a dining room proper. Jane was as bright as a button considering how much wine had been consumed the previous evening. James came down half an hour later. After breakfast, Jane carried what looked like two tons of Sunday's papers and magazines into the conservatory and settled down to a good read. James and I washed the three cars, his Austin, Mum's Jag and Dad's Vintage Austin Mayflower. Then we played pool in the games room, which had an array of Royal Navy pictures, posters and models. Late afternoon I was dropped off at home where I wrote my next letter to Kathy, leaving it incomplete so I could use it as a reply to her next letter.

CHAPTER 10

Communication quickly became more orderly. A couple of letters written each way every week and on Sundays I would join Kathy's family for a communal telephone call either too or from New York. Kathy was due home for Christmas, and we made it known that we intended to get formerly engaged at that time. Everyone was looking forward to it and my sister Annette was already thinking about her Bridesmaid's dress even thought she hadn't yet been invited to be one.

I threw myself into my work, hoping time would pass quickly, and then weeks did indeed fly by. Kathy also worked hard, lots of extra shifts to put money away for the big visit home at Christmas. Jake Rubinstien, the Cop, got an award for talking down a potential suicide victim from the top of a 60-storey building. In the same week he was wounded by a knife wheedling drug addict, but recovered quickly. Kathy was now working in the Emergency Trauma Unit, which we were told in New York was as busy as a Superstore checkout, by which she seemed to mean the till area of a large Department Store.

The letters described the changing mood of the USA at the time. Hippies were appearing with flowered clothing, love beads and free love. In one letter Kathy asked me if I was into free love. I told her I wasn't planning on charging her. There were also a number of labour disputes going on and Vietnam War Veterans were upset about their treatment which led to marches and demonstrations in New York and elsewhere. Jake was involved in tackling these events which worried them quite a lot. My news was not as exciting as I mainly gave news of what was happening at work or special local events. We were just peddling towards the big day really. I was now having tea every Sunday at Kathy's house and was soon regarded as part of the family.

July 1969, a Friday, a day which I would never forget. I was working on Ward 1A. The Sick Ward, where patients who had physical illnesses would be treated or patients who had been to theatre would recuperate. It started out to be a routine day. There were only a dozen patients in at this time so it wasn't very busy. Sister Morgan was in charge today. She was a bit picky most of the time so you had to be on your toes for her, but she could be relied upon to stand by you if you needed anything or had a problem. Staff Nurse Colin Graye was instructing me on the administration observation and management of drips. We were in the process of changing a saline drip for a postoperative patient. Sister Morgan came from the office directly to me. She had a purposeful look in her eyes. I thought I was about to be told off for something. She placed a hand on my shoulder.

'Liam, come to the office with me. Colin, can you manage?'

Without really listening to Colin's positive reply, she ushered me into the office. There, sat with her head in her hands and obviously very upset was May, Kathy's Mum. I moved quickly to her, put my arm around her and asked nervously what was up? Briefly recovering some composure she looked up at me with wet red eyes, the indentations of her fingers still on her cheeks. I kneeled, so as, to at the same level. Between sobs and sharp intakes of breath, I was given the news. 'She's dead. She's dead, passed away. Our Kathy's dead'. Her head returned to its burial in her hands and the sobbing increased. I was stunned. I said nothing at first, I just held May tightly, her body shaking out of control. She was red hot. The extreme shock was oozing from every pore. I managed some words.

'Oh my God. Oh my God. What happened?' Sister hugged us both. May couldn't get the words out to tell me more.

May was assisted out of the ward by some relatives. I fainted. Next I remember being on a bed in the ward. Sister Morgan and a man I didn't recognise looked down at me. I felt a cool sponge being pressed against my forehead and eyes. Sister excused herself and left. The man introduced himself as Phil, Kathy's Uncle.

'I'm so sorry to meet you under these horrible circumstances Liam. How do you feel? Stupid question! Do you want me to tell you more now, or would you like to rest more first?'

'Please tell me what happened now. I'm as ready as I'll ever be'.

I still couldn't take it in properly. Was this a terrible dream? I knew it wasn't a dream and steeled myself for the details. Phil sat down and holding back his own tears began to tell me about it.

'She had gone to a shop; the Police called it a Drug Store, near the Hospital after work. A drug addict had apparently raided the store for drug money. The Shop owner had resisted and the thief shot him. The Cameras showed Kathy entering moments later and being unaware of what had happened found the owner lying wounded on the floor. She called the Ambulance and tried to help the wounded man. Unfortunately the thief was hiding behind the counter. As his escape was blocked and on hearing the approaching Police, he panicked and shot Kathy too. It seems she died instantly at the scene. They got the Bastard though; they got the Shit bag. He tried to shoot his way out and they killed him. Best thing that could have happened to the Bastard. Jail would have been too easy.'

Phil broke down and I raised myself up to comfort him. Someone helped him away. Sister Morgan returned to me. The Family had gone now and the Deputy Chief had come to take me home.

I was taken home and dreaded breaking the news to my family. Sister had phoned ahead so I was greeted with full support and sympathy. I spent the next 12 hours in bed. The Chief had told my parents that I was to come back in my own time. Nobody would bother me unless I asked for anything. That's what the Rainhill Family was all about. For the next few days I kept in touch with Kathy's Family. And, when I was fit, I visited them and stayed one night. May had taken it hardest. I suppose a Mother would. I hated the fact that Kathy would have to undergo what the Yanks called 'an autopsy'. I cried for her going through that. She was perfect and shouldn't have been treated like that. But I knew it had to be.

Eventually, her body was flown home. The funeral was to be held at the family's local Parish Church with cremation at St. Helens Crematorium near Windle Island. The dreaded day arrived. My friend James drove me to Kathy's house, and stayed with me for the whole funeral except when I was asked to travel in the limousine for the cortege. The New York Hospital and the New York Police Department sent huge bouquets. Remarkably, Martha and Alex Rubinstien also came from the States to attend, which I thought was so lovely of them. May asked me would I please say a few words at the Crematorium. I agreed but I was so anxious about it.

Since that day I have always tried to avoid the roads between the Church and Crematorium. The memories are so painful. On the ride in the limousine I looked out of the window and hated everyone for just carrying on. Some impatient drivers overtook the cortege which in my opinion is a 'no, no' out of respect. I wanted to jump out and punch them. Then the Crematorium came into view. Kathy would be destroyed there. I broke down and sobbed until I was helped from the car. I took a deep breath. May came and kissed me and put her arm around me.

'Are you sure you can do this? I understand if you can't' I kissed her back.

'This is the last thing I can do for her. I hope I can make her proud.'

The coffin was shouldered and slowly we followed on. The Funeral Director showed us to our seats and we settled down whilst some classical background music played. Kathy's close family members hugged each other and cried. James eased in next to me, put his arm around my shoulder and asked if I was ok. I couldn't answer.

The music stopped. A clergyman appeared and stood at the lectern. He opened a book and looked out at everyone. He gave his oration, many things I actually didn't know about Kathy's life. Then he said a few prayers whilst standing with one hand on the coffin. Then he announces me. I stood and walked in silence to the lectern. I looked at the gathering. I recognised the close family and a few of her friends from Rainhill and the Rubinstiens. There were so many people they stretched beyond the doors. I stood for a moment, which seemed like a Month, the words stuck in my throat. I hadn't prepared anything. I decided to speak from the heart.

'None of us expected to be here today to say our last farewell to beautiful Kathy. We expected to share a wonderful future with her in our lives, making our lives ever better for her being here. My love, my understanding, my empathy goes out to you, her Family and Friends. She would be amazed to see how much love people shared with her. The Vicar has very ably taken us on a brief journey through her life. My time with Kathy was so brief, like the blinking of an eye; but I recognised all the wonderful loveable qualities Kathy had. It would have been my great privilege and honour to share that life with her in a new country with a new beginning. In just one moment, that was taken away by an armed thief. Kathy died doing what we would all have expected her to do. She was helping a wounded man. That was the Kathy we all know and love, selfless, brave and compassionate. Even though her stay in New York was brief, the impact she had on the people there is demonstrated by the magnificent tributes they sent back with her and we are so pleased to welcome the Rubinstien Family to share our grief on this day. To, Kathy, my darling I will always love you. Whatever twists and turns my life may take you will always be with me in my heart and mind. Goodbye beautiful'

Holding back my tears I returned to my seat. May looked over to me and mouthed a thank you.

The music started again. After a brief pause the coffin sank slowly below the plinth. The curtains closed and the Funeral Director beckoned us towards the exit. Everyone gathered outside for a while. It was a warm day. I was asked if I was returning with the family for a buffet. I declined, after asking May if she didn't mind. She said, 'You go ahead lad. I wish I could just be alone right now'. We kissed and hugged. 'Doesn't be a strange" she said, drumming up a smile.

James had followed in his car. We left together. We drove to Ottespool and went for a long walk along the path at the edge of the River. We stopped for a drink in the Pub in the park. I drank Whiskey, several glasses. We left and lay down on a grassy bank in the park. The warmth of the sun sent me off into a sleep. I awoke to a cold feeling. It was dark. James had allowed me to sleep for nearly four hours. He understood my need to rest. I was taken home to the comfort and reassurance of my family. I lay on the sofa with my head on Annette's lap. She massaged my forehead and I told her about the good times.

CHAPTER 11

I spent a few days just travelling around on my bike. Just to keep my mind occupied. Then after four days moping around I decided that I would be better off back at work with my other Family. I contacted May to find out what she was doing. She was already, back at work. That's where she got most of her support from and she was kept busy. I was asked to call round when I could. There was a parcel for me of some things May thought I might like from Kathy's belongings which had arrived from the Rubinstiens. She didn't know what was in it. The Inner parcel was addressed to me and unopened. I said I would collect it soon.

Next day I went to the Hospital and spoke to the Chief Nursing Officer about returning. He told me he thought I was doing the best thing. He reassigned me to a unit called 'the Villa', a Tuberculosis ward which was small and quiet with only 24 beds. At this time though it only had 8 patients in.

'Just see how you go,' he said.

He called Joe Williams the Charge Nurse and explained the situation. I was to start next day at 9am for my induction. It was a specialist unit so you couldn't just walk in and start like the main wards. I returned to my room in the home. Alone again, I looked through the letters again. Strangely they perked me up a bit. Before tea I rode over to see May. She was at work but her sister was in and gave me the parcel. I resisted the urge to inspect it immediately and took it back to my room. Still resisting, I had tea in the canteen before finally getting up the courage to open it up.

I removed the parcel from the plastic bag. The brown shoebox belonged to the NYPD Evidence unit. I hoped I hadn't accidentally been sent a gun or a body part. I peeled back the tape and opened the lid. The contents were wrapped in tissue paper and there was an envelope on top. It wasn't sealed. I took out the folded paper.

'Dear Liam,

We are so sorry for your loss. We were deeply shocked the day this happened. Jake was actually on the call to this incident and took part in the shootout which followed with this crazy drugs idiot. When it was all over and Jake found out who the victim was, he was truly devastated. We all loved Kath and she became a true friend of mine. She was always talking about you; we feel we know you very well.

I was so moved by your talk at the funeral. We miss her very much too. When we were deciding what to send back to the family, there were some things, which would obviously have been intended for you, so we decided to pack them separately. We hope you find some comfort in these things. There is a last letter. It was addressed and ready to go. We left it as it was and didn't read it. If you find yourself in a position where you can visit New York, then please come and see us. You will be more than welcome. Likewise, should we be able to visit England again, we would like to look you up if that's ok.

If you would like to stay in touch, then that's fine.

Lots of love and best wishes.

Jake, Martha and Alex. XXXX.'

Carefully unfolding the tissue paper I looked inside. There I found a few photos of us. Each location brought back vivid memories. The Hospital Social Club, one of many evenings spent there. This one was a 40s night. I wore a Royal Air Force mock up and Kathy wore an ARP uniform complete with helmet, which belonged to her Granddad.

The River Room Restaurant at the Pier Head. It was taken by a professional, for sale at the venue.

The Post Office Tower Restaurant, taken on Kath's 21st. Birthday. Didn't know it would be her last Birthday.

Me, outside the Adelphi, standing by an Aston Martin DB6. Pretending it was mine.

The 1967 New Year's Eve staff party, both of us awaiting the taxi. Don't know who took it. The night we first met, made me very sad.

Kathy, in her Uniform, outside Jefferson Memorial.

Kathy, with friends, outside Macey's Store, New York.

Kathy, with the Rubinstiens, and the Dodge Station Wagon outside the house.

Jake Rubinstien in his Police Uniform, didn't realise he was a sergeant, standing next to a Black n White.

My letters to her and her last letter to me.

"My lovely Man.
Your letters are the highlight of every week. I can't wait to read you beautiful words. I can tell that you worry about my possibly meeting someone else here, that I'll need the love of someone else. Well I have met another love of my life. He's much taller than I am. Brown skinned, strong, brave and very handsome. He snuggles up to me when we meet and I just love to feel his gorgeous muscles. He'd do absolutely anything for me and we meet every Saturday without fail. His Name is Sammy. He has gorgeous dark blue sad eyes and he is probably my best American friend. I absolutely adore him. He's in the Police Force and he's even got a medal. I'm with him now as a matter of fact. I'm waiting for him to get his new shoes. —From the Blacksmith. Sammy is my favourite Police Horse. Jake introduced us and it was love at first sight. You definitely have competition my darling.
I can't wait to be with you again and you can put a saddle on me. I have to walk back to the stables now with Sammy. I'll finish off later and get to the post.'

Even now it raised a laugh. She was full of fun. I'm so glad she was happy there. There was a Horseshoe, maybe from Sammy, I don't know, a leaflet showing engagement rings, a notebook with lists of patient's medication and diets, some postcards, of New York scenes and a $10 dollar bill. That was it, the last gifts from Kathy. I looked through once more then put them away in my locker.
Thinking about Kathy, I fell asleep. My dreams were filled with anger and rage. After some hours I awoke shouting and wet with sweat. This

was to be the way of it for several weeks. Eventually I settled down with support from family, friends at work and my long suffering mate James.

I was now working on a newly formed rehabilitation unit. A former Victorian Gate House on the South Gateway. This was a quiet spot. This gate was not used by anyone to access the Hospital. The future of this type of hospital was now in doubt as more progressive ideas on the treatment and management of Mental Illness came to the fore. The house had been refurbished to enable staff to help with the rehabilitation of long term patients with a view to relocating them to semi-independent accommodation in the community. Our task was to teach basic skills such as cooking, cleaning and day to day self-help in various domestic situations. This would be backed up by providing all the Hospital and Community Support Services as and when needed with nursing staff on site at all times to provide support at what was determined to be a half-way house. The ultimate aim was to enable the residents to achieve full independence if possible. This was purely an experimental project at this time. We didn't expect to discharge anyone for the time being.

This was a very enjoyable and often rewarding assignment. We were to be as informal as possible; no uniforms. We were to teach rather than do everything for our patients. We had 12 patients and 12 Staff working in a 'Day Hospital' situation. The patients stayed in the house with 2 supervisors at night. I was tasked with thinking up and managing a skill task which could possibly encourage patients to take up a pass time or hobby; something which was outside the routine of Hospital Life. Institutionalisation was the major obstacle to becoming independent. Although it was the middle of summer, I decided to get a small team of 4 patients together with the project of building a sledge for the winter snow. Something they could build to an achievable deadline and something they could enjoy the use of, albeit for a short period. So, the project provided opportunities to take part in the design process, using tools, safety, varnish and paint and perhaps some artwork, with the pleasure of using the product of their labour for fun on completion.

I put the idea to Len, the Charge Nurse with my report on the benefits and outcomes, and he approved it. I was then allocated a workspace in the large loft area. A budget was approved for materials, the patients were selected and we had the go ahead from the Chief. The project was commenced in September and was to be completed by Christmas in anticipation of the snow. Of course I had lots of other work to do.

This only took up a few hours each week and I had a School Block in between. However, this was the best thing that could have happened. I had a comprehensive list of responsibilities in this new unit which kept me busy.

CHAPTER 12

Now the time had arrived for the intermediate examinations, the halfway-point to determine how everyone was progressing. The examination was a mock-up of what we could expect in the finals. There was a theory section lasting two hours and then on the following day, a practical section; setting up trolleys and drips and the like. We all passed, now onward and upward.

I didn't spend much time in the Hospital Social Scene this year. I saw a lot more of family and my mate James. His life was also changing. He got himself a girlfriend called Gail. I wasn't very impressed with Gail. She was pretty, yes; but too perfect. Always painting and polishing various bits of her. I would have been frightened to kiss her in case I spoiled her lipstick. Poor James was hooked though, and he was her personal cash machine. James wasn't short of a few bob, but I suspected he soon would be. Gail was very slim. She wore bright colours and never enough clothes, she was always cold. Gail was a 'pretend blonde', for now anyway, and very much into the pop music scene, demanding to be treated to the most high profile gigs. She was also a fashion icon and had to be dressed accordingly, mostly at James's expense. She worked in Boots Chemist shop where 'the look' seemed to be more important than the actual job. Though having a job didn't seem to mean spending anything. The biggest crime she committed in my view was persuading James to sell his beloved Austin Westminster in favour of a Mini Cooper S. The Westminster was too square for her taste, she could better flash her skinny legs with the mini skirt when exiting the mini and of course her super ultra-white knickers.

Still, James was in love and she could do no wrong, so I said nothing to upset the Apple cart. Frustrated by the fact that I could no longer see James alone, I devised a cunning plan to visit James in his new love nest in Widnes with my Sister Annette. Annette was tasked with keeping Gail occupied while I had some quality time with my Hen pecked mate. They were now living in a flat in the darkest depths of Widnes near the Town centre. It was November before I could swing into action with my plan. Anne and I mounted my sturdy stead without proper winter motorcycle gear, and we were off to Widnes. Twenty minutes later we arrived outside the flat feeling like two ice lollies. We painfully manoeuvred our way off the saddle and moved like Robots towards the ground floor door. I rang the Westminster Chimes and a hazy white figure approached seen through the frosted glass. The door opened to reveal the heavily painted skimpily dressed and densely aromered Gail. A forced smile greeted us as Annette pounced like a Tiger onto her prey with a big unwelcome kiss and a loud Liverpudlian HI Ya !I passed the pair of embracing Females; one warming up, the other rapidly cooling and found James in the lounge trying to untangle Christmas Lights. The flat was nicely done. Painted tastefully rather than papered. Leather suite, latest T.V., low glass coffee table, polished wooden floor and rugs rather than carpet. 8 track sound system, a couple of picture prints of seascapes and a mirror. There was a long low cabinet with central drawers and end cupboards for nik naks. On top of which were family photos and a bowl of real fruit.

Annette did her job well and quickly contained Gail in the living room while I chatted to James in the kitchen. I helped him untangle the Christmas Lights while we caught up with events. It became obvious to me that he was regretting taking the steps he had in order to gain his independence. Living apart from mum wasn't all it was cracked up to be. Fortunately James's Dad, being a Naval Officer, ensured that James was equipped with all the life skills he needed, which was just as well, as the fabulous Gail couldn't even fry an egg, so the cooking, as well as just about everything else was down to James. Confidentially I was informed that Gail's days were probably numbered. 'All that glitters isn't Gold' came to mind. I felt sorry for him and so did Annette. Having untangled the lights, James and I returned to the living room where Annette was being dolled up courtesy of the few skills Gail had to offer. I helped James start with the decorations and erecting the tree. After a while we all settled down for a chat and some 8-track music. Everybody but me had several glasses of Australian Wine, which lubricated the evening. At 11 pm., Annette and I wrapped ourselves up, donned our helmets and said our goodbyes. I kissed Gail's lipstick; it was so thick I couldn't get near the actual Gail. The door was opened to reveal a heavily frosted ground and a white crystal motorcycle which was as inviting as a nude dip in the sea on New Year's Day.

Carefully, we supported each other as we walked to the Bike. Slipping, sliding laughing. James offered to drive us home, but I needed the Bike for work. I removed the frost from vital areas of the machine before mounting it. Annette slotted in behind, putting her arms around my waist. I waved; pulled down my visor and moved off. The main road had been gritted but the journey home was hazardous due to mad drivers treating the roads like it was a normal day. We made it. The warmth of the house was wonderful. The experience renewed my enthusiasm for car travel.

Staff Nurse Barry Hartley came up with a bright idea to help patients experience more of the outside world. Actually, I think it was a way of getting a day out for us. He proposed that we hire a coach and take the more articulate members of the ward to a Pantomime one afternoon, with a Pub stop on the way back, the emphasis being on the Pub stop. The idea started out as a joke, but Barry soon realised the positive side of the project. He submitted the idea to the Charge Nurse at a morning break. The idea was adopted and the big day was arranged.

The Pantomime was Cinderella and the performance was at Blackpool. 40 Patients were selected and luckily I was one of 12 Staff pressed into service on this first ever Patients Coach Trip. Barry thought it would be quite amusing if we wore our white coats to see what the public reaction would be, however this did not happen.

So off we went. The Coach Driver looked a little on edge when closely inspected by curious mad men, but we reassured him that he would not be murdered or eaten as long as he didn't upset anyone. Some did indeed need some calming for the first half-hour of the journey, but sweets, tablet s and plenty of fags made everyone happy. Even the Patients settled down eventually.

Our arrival at Blackpool excited many of our charges and some just continued to rock back and forth uttering nonsense as usual. Some had never seen the sea before. The illuminations had finished but we agreed that if trips like this one proved useful, then perhaps a lights trip next year. There were still plenty of brightly lit shops and amusement arcades to see though.

The Winter Gardens came into view but we couldn't stop outside. Our first test of organisation and security was passed when we managed to herd our 40 Patients 100 yards from the Coach to the Theatre, through the lobby and up flights of stairs to our pre booked rear seats. We didn't want to be in front of anyone and we may need an escape route in case of problems. Each nurse was allocated 3 or 4 patients to look after and after some initial confusion we settled down. Pantomime, being a rather noisy audience participation event masked some of the antics of our more vocal Patients. Everything was going well for half an hour or so, then some disruption. One of the female nurses was trying, between bouts of laughter, to dissuade one of her group to stop doing something. It transpired that having found one or more of the leggy dancers irresistible he was masturbating and reaching orgasm before any control could be exerted upon him. Not that she could have done much about it anyway. We could safely say that he enjoyed the show very much.

We emerged from the Theatre without anyone getting arrested and retained all 40 Patients for the next part of the trip. It was a problem finding a Pub, which allowed Coaches, but we stopped at an unsuspecting venue near Preston. It was quite busy but we found a perimeter area to seat everyone. Drinks and fags kept the patients happy and calm. Barry pointed out a funny event-taking place without any customers noticing what was going on. A little skinny Patient called Billy was observed sitting and rocking as he normally did. But his eyes surveyed the bar area for prey. When someone would turn away from his or her drink to talk, Billy would dart over like a Greyhound and steal his or her drink. Returning as quickly to his seat he would consume the stolen drink in one then sit quietly rocking again. The customer would turn again to continue with their drink but it had disappeared. This went on for a while. He was never caught.

After about 2 hours we returned to our Coach and back to the Hospital. Despite the wanking and thieving the day went well. Nobody was lost or arrested and everyone was happy.

CHAPTER 13

Soon it would be my third Christmas at Rainhill. This one should have been my engagement to Kathy. Her Family would find it hardest to bear. I resolved to spend some time with them. I was brought up a Catholic and I was still practising my faith. However my faith was diminishing, which was in no small part due to the events of the year. Not only Kathy, but events around the world made me step back and think again.

I made arrangements to see my local Parish Priest about the issue but first he urged me to await the arrival of two Jesuit Priests to the Parish who were to conduct a special mission to encourage and strengthen faith in our Parish. They were a sort of SAS Priestly task force sent to cure the ills of the community. They were due this weekend and would stay for two weeks leading up to Christmas. There would be special Masses and Confessions conducted by them and the opportunity to have one to one guidance on any issues.

This seemed to be an opportunity not to be missed. I may gain strength and better understanding to help me cope with my loss and deal more effectively with other issues on my mind.

So they came, the SAS Priests. I attended the extra Masses as often as I could.

The extra confessionals were also useful to lighten the load of my guilt. Then, one evening I plucked up the courage to ask for a personal talk after confessions were over. My request was granted and although quite nervous about it, I comforted myself in the fact that this Priest didn't know me so I could let all my feelings out and get an independent view on the subject.

I sat with the Priest in a side chapel and he listened to all I had to say. Then he said he had to meet his companion in the Catholic Club at that time. I was offered a few leaflets and a couple of book suggestions and off he went. I felt like I had been left in the middle of a lake in a rowing boat without oars. Rather deflated, I left. My next plan was to arrange to talk to my own Parish Priest to see if he could help, at the same time offer my opinion of the value of the SAS Priests mission.

I got my meeting with the Parish Priest a few days later. This was even more difficult because he knew my family well. I had taken a very active part in the life of the Church. Nervously I met the Priest privately to discuss my concerns. Again, the listening part was ok, but all I got was

'I can't help you from outside, you have to be inside.'

I have no idea what that meant. What I do know is that my Catholicism ended at that point Thereafter I regarded myself as an Atheist.

At work my sledge project was nearing completion. It had changed over the months from being a one-man sledge to a two-man sleigh. The idea was that it should be pulled along by a porter's mini tractor, either inside or outside. Fully decorated it would carry Santa around the internal roads and main corridors carrying gifts or raising funds. Great! The final job was to fit a set of four large pram wheels with axles and the tow bar fitting. One week before Christmas, and the project completed on time, I got my team together for a congratulatory gathering. The Charge Nurse and a few other staff attended the occasion. I said a few words. The Charge said a few words. We arranged for the porters to give the vehicle a test run. The team gathered around the sleigh to move it out to the driveway. The problem was; the sleigh was wider than the doorway.

A few days after this embarrassing event, the sleigh was partly dismantled to get it out of the building, and the show did get on the road. Throughout the Christmas period a small group of volunteers manned a small tractor complete with reindeer antlers, to pull the sleigh around the Hospital grounds to distribute gifts and good cheer. Maintenance staff rigged up strings of lights around the tractor and sleigh and some genius set up a sound system to play festive music on each of its tours.

Local businesses donated gifts for the sleigh and staff also pitched in to make the idea a success. I would have liked to extend to local estates to raise funds for extras such as outings or other treats for patients, but there was a problem with insurance. Those of us who took part in the project enjoyed it very much. The group who constructed the vehicle were very proud of themselves.

CHAPTER 14

My project completed at the gatehouse, I was now allocated to 15A on the Annex. This was a ward for the long term patients with a variety of mental illnesses. It was a ward full of characters that saw the world in a completely different way to everyone else. Their world was one of routine and everything done for them. Fully institutionalised they were content with their plight and very easy to manage. It was a happy place though. We kept the patients busy and entertained. Some, by necessity were heavily medicated to maintain their mood. The most exciting event would be the occasional Epileptic Fit or brief conflict arising between patients born of some disagreement or misunderstanding.

Whilst doing the bed round one morning, my eyes were momentarily diverted by a lovely pair of long, long legs. A new assistant Nurse had joined us from somewhere, maybe heaven. Later I had the pleasure of working with her. We worked together on an exciting project. Checking and trimming finger and toe nails. She, Angela, held the limbs, I did the trimming. Angela was quite tall, the same height as me, 5"10". She had brown curly hair, flawless complexion, and bright brown eyes with long lashes. She had a face I would describe as Irish, with just the right amount of red lipstick. The slight dimple on her chin was cute. The moderate Irish accent added to her charm. Angela was slim, shapely and extremely attractive. We got on well together and our association did not end with toe nails. We had lunch together. She had worked for 6 months on the Female side but didn't like it much there. She told me women could be bitchy and women in authority could be swine's. This was her first day on the male side, and so far she liked it very much. I hoped that meant me. Having established that she was single, I plucked up the courage to ask her out. Much to my surprise and delight, she agreed.

Saturday, my day off, and a date in the evening. I'm almost skint. I borrow some money from Annette. I recently bought a lovely grey suit from the Trafford Catalogue, I've polished my shoes to death and I'm ready to go. I partake of a light snack in the canteen so I can enjoy the meal later. Back in my room I have a second shave, apply the smellies and dress to kill. I am to meet Angela at 5pm at her house in Thatto Heath, not far from the Hospital.

I dismissed the idea of the bike, Angela didn't seem keen. Proudly I walk along the drive to get the bus. I'm nervous and a bit hyped up. It's a crisp but sunny evening. I decided not to wear a top coat as I wanted to show off the suit. Half way to the gate I look down to check the shine on my shoes. Then my head explodes and a sudden rush of blood floods from my nose. My shirt, tie and lovely suit change colour instantly. Inside my mind the words "fuck me!" resonate as I turn to go back to my room. I look like the victim of a frenzied knife attack. Passers-by give me a wide berth as I run breathlessly back to my room.

The blood stained clothes are thrown onto the bed and I change quickly into an older Pierre Cardin suit I'd had for a couple of years. I must have put on weight because the waistband clip was a nightmare to fasten. I found some cotton wool and plugged my nose. Now I'm late. I run to Thatto Heath, stopping at the end of her street to slow down my panting. Walking to the house I feel sweaty again. My hair is now windswept and I left my comb inside my blood stained suit. I wanted to die. What on earth would she think of me? I'm late and I look like a tramp.

The door opens. Mrs McFerrin, Angela's' mum peers out at me. You must be Liam she says in a broad Irish accent. I'm warmly invited in and sat down opposite Mr. McFerrin for inspection. 'Is it whendy?' He asks.

I explained my problems with the nose bleed and the fact that I'd left my comb behind. I was immediately presented with a comb. It was stainless steel and had some hairs tangled into it. I accepted it gratefully and combed my hair. My offer to return it was refused. I was now the proud owner of a hairy metal comb.

Angela appeared. She wore a cream pinafore dress, quite short, and a military style mac in matching colour. It was left open with the belt hanging down. She had calf length patent leather boots and glossy black shoulder bag. Having established that I was ready we quickly left to avoid further scrutiny by the parents. I told Angela that the Rolls had a technical problem and that we would have to use buses. She was fine with that. As we walked she linked my arm and we talked and laughed constantly.

On the two bus journeys to Liverpool we sat close and held hands. I pointed out places of interest as we passed them; she seemed to know remarkably little about the areas we passed through. I was pleased to enlighten her about such places as my own home which we passed, Knotty Ash and the diddy men's houses, my old Berties shop at Old Swan, the Ice rink and finally the vista from the top of London road of the whole City centre, Paddy's' wigwam, the Anglican Cathedral, the Post Office Tower and the Liver Buildings.

We got off the bus in Lime Street in front of the Empire theatre. It was dark and not as cold as I expected, though I already regretted failing to wear a top coat. We walked hand in hand, crossing Lime street and past St. Georges Hall then past the Everyman and onward to Church street for a spot of window shopping. As we left the shelter of the city buildings we walked across the plateau in front of the three graces. The cold wind from the river made us rush to the restaurant. I was pleased to arrive in the warm entrance hall to the River Room, the venue for my romantic evening meal, which posh people called dinner for some reason.

Of course I was acquainted with the layout, having been here a number of times before. I directed Angela ahead of me so I could admire those beautiful legs. As we got to the top of the stairs we (or rather Angela) were greeted by a plump Italian waiter in crisp black and white uniform, looking like a Penguin.

'Table for two Sir?' he enquired, without even looking at me.

He cupped Angela's elbow and whisked her to a table at the window. The chair was pulled and re set as Angela sat down. The napkin was shaken out and presented to her like a prize. While this was going on I sat myself down like a spare part, shook out my own napkin and presented it to myself. Magically, our waiter produced a wine list out of nowhere. I opened it and looked knowingly at the three columns of wines. It might as well have been a French Railway timetable for all I knew.

He stood waiting for my deliberations. I asked Angela what she would like, in the hope that she might know what she was doing. Alas, she didn't.

'Do you have any Australian white?' I asked.

The wine lists were retrieved quickly and snapped shut.

'Of course sir' he replied, looking at me like I'd committed some atrocity

'Would that be two?' Angela nodded agreement.

We didn't see him again. Perhaps he went to commit suicide. A girl came with the wine. We gazed across the river. The clear sky, the stars and full moon made it a lovely romantic scene. The tide was in so a couple of small cargo ships and a tanked passed slowly by. Two ferries hurried back and forth between Seacombe and Birkenhead. The cotton wool plugs were getting itchy and I fiddled with them from time to time. "Would you like to get them out?" she asked. "Well perhaps later if you like, but I must get rid of these cotton wool plugs first". We both started to laugh. Each of us thought back to that quip for the rest of the evening. When either of us started giggling, we both knew what it was about.

The meal went well. We frequently held hands across the table and the conversation flowed with the help of an Australian Vineyard. I was offered a share of the bill but declined, even though I could have done with the help. The food, in three courses, was delivered by three different waiters who made it abundantly clear that Angela was considered the main dish in that place tonight. When she asked for directions to the bathroom, the waiter and the manager escorted her almost to the toilet seat itself. Then it was time to leave. Again, it took two waiters to help Angela on with her coat. In my head I asked' do you want to shag her for me too'? But of course I knew the answer to that. We giggled our way down the stairs. She sopped me in the entrance hall, pulled me towards her and kissed me with a softly spoken

'Thank you' We left, arms around each other, to be greeted by a cold breeze. It didn't matter. We walked along the river front, stopping from time to time to kiss. The kisses became longer and more meaningful. I sat on a bench. Though the lattes were wooden, it was still freezing to the bum and legs. Possibly more sensibly, Angela sat on my lap which was undoubtedly softer and considerably warmer. We hugged and kissed some more. The cold no longer mattered. The cuddling was wonderful. I was aroused, and she knew it and obviously fine with it. Sadly time ebbed away so quickly. Buses took ages to get anywhere. A wonderful night ended in a wonderful feeling. At her door we kissed good night and made arrangements for out next date. I was over the moon. On the 20 minute walk back to the hospital I didn't feel the cold at all. I was in heaven. In the background though were thought of Kathy. I couldn't help feeling that I was cheating in some way; then another part of me said don't be silly, you have to move on at some point.

This would be a Christmas of mixed feelings. No Kathy, no engagement. My Sorrow would be felt more so for May and the family. I imagined how much more unbearable this would be if I was alone. At least I had the support of my family at home and the Rainhill Family at work and of course my friend James. Money was also an issue. I wanted to buy so much for so many. For most I hoped a nice card and a social visit would suffice.

I spent a lot of time walking and thinking in Parks or Town Centres. Positive reflection was good for me. I planned to socialise more and concentrate better on my studies, which had drifted recently. James telephoned to tell me that the fabulous Gail was no longer on the scene and that she had moved back home. I went to see him a few days before Christmas.

The bike, which was a shaft driven had worn out a bearing and was off the road. I couldn't afford the repair. So after lunch at home on a Saturday, I walked to Cronton to what I called Cookes Mansion. Many houses were now decorated with window lights and trees. A few had been adventurous and decorated garden trees as well.

After an hour and a half I arrived at the mansion. The Mayflower was standing proudly on the drive suggesting that Commander Cooke was home on leave. The Cooke family had gone to town on the lighting. All the eaves and porch were edged in lights. A weeping willow in the garden was no longer weeping but full of lights. The two large front sixteen pane windows were edged in lights and large Christmas trees filled them.

I rang the bell, which had been switched from Big Ben to the Popeye theme.

James' Dad, John, opened the door. For some reason I was surprised to see him out of uniform. A gush of warm air enveloped me carrying the smell of mulled wine and mince pies. John shook my hand firmly as he announced my arrival to whoever was inside. He took my coat, patted me on the shoulder and ushered me towards the lounge. The whole house was decorated from ceiling to floor. Above the fireplace was a banner 'welcome home.' Sat around in the lounge were Mirriame, Jane, James, and a man who was introduced as Tony, a fellow Officer friend of Johns. After being told off for walking to the House, I settled down to an evening of good conversation, lots of Navy tales a game of Chess with Tony; which I lost quite quickly, and then Monopoly which was given a time limit of 90 minutes, followed by a count up of assets to determine the winner. Then it was a lovely meal, lashings of alcohol and daft party games. It was a great evening. During the evening it transpired that John was to be promoted in the coming months. He was to take Command of a Training School in Scotland. John and Jane would be moving there. James however was to stay. He too was to be promoted to General Manager of the Salford

Warehouse. He would look after the business here while Jane hoped to expand into Scotland. Cooke Mansion was to be sold and James would live somewhere else after overseeing the sale, which could take months. Everybody except Mirriame seemed happy with all this upheaval. I was happy that James was to stay around. Mirriame was to stay the night. I was sent home in a taxi in a happily intoxicated state. Times like this were exactly what I needed. I began to think that I could get through this period and move on.

Christmas Eve. It was a working day. 7am to 7pm. It was a hectic day trying to make it special for everyone else. All the patients were well stuffed and watered by the end of the day. A Salvation Army Band had been around the wards which added to the atmosphere and an Irish Dance group also entertained the patients after tea. At 5pm. I had to accompany one patient to the General Hospital by Ambulance. He was suspected of having eaten some tree decorations, some of which were sharp when broken. I was with him at Whiston until 8pm. It was of course one of the busiest nights at casualty. It turned out that he hadn't actually swallowed anything after all, but we had to be sure. I got off duty at 9pm. After a quick wash and change in my room I made my way to the Staff Club for the Party.

Part of my mind told me I should not socialise, that I should be alone in mourning. Another voice asked me what I would advise anyone else to do under the same circumstances? The answer was to carry on with life as normal. Keep treasured memories and ask yourself what your loved one would want you to do? If the situation were reversed I would want Kathy to remember me fondly but live life to the full. You never know how much of it you've got left.

CHAPTER 15

The cold night air gave way to a blast of heat and the glare of flashing lights as I entered the club. I was immediately enveloped and heavily kissed by a large lady who gleefully pointed up to mistletoe hanging above the door. As I began to remove my coat I was treated to two more kisses, this time from fellow students—female fellow students. This was a good start. At the bar I found many of the people I knew, some of them already at the stage of talking nonsense and going on for ages about it. The music was loud, the conversation incoherent and the women dressed to impress. As I got merrier I was persuaded to join in with the dancing. After a while I found myself in the tender clutches of a girl called Helen. She was an assistant nurse on the female wards. We liked each other and soon began to kiss and cuddle in a quiet corner. Then the conscience cut in. I felt guilty and somehow unfaithful. I had to explain to Helen what was going on, assuring her that it wasn't anything she had done or said, but I had to go. I think she understood. She said that should I feel any different at any time I was to contact her. I left the party. It was late. I was so confused and upset. I couldn't decide what was right or wrong. I walked for over an hour in the grounds trying to sort my thoughts out but failed. I retired to my room by 3am. I was on duty again at 7am. It could be a tough day ahead.

Christmas day was very busy. After the patient's breakfast everyone was dressed in their best clothing ready for the special day ahead. At 11am a Choir arrived from a local senior school. They sang carols for half an hour with some unwelcome accompaniment from a few of our less tuneful patients. The choir was treated to lunch with the patients and a good party atmosphere prevailed. The afternoon was enjoyable with visits from a few relatives and off duty staff who all played a part in making the day a happy one all around. I was able to take my mind off my darker thoughts. After another party at teatime we were able to relax. Most patients were worn out with all the activity and I, together with the rest of the duty staff just sat and played games with those with enough energy to join in.

In the evening after leaving the ward, my mind turned once again to Kathy. I looked once more through the parcel of memories then went walking in the grounds. It was freezing. No one was about. I could be truly alone with my thoughts and just walk. The peace and absolute quiet helped me to remain calm. I cried a little from time to time. At one point I passed near a Hillman Husky owned by Dave Prentice, a fellow student. There was some movement of the body and the windows were steamed up. Made me smile as I imagined what he was doing with Emily Williams of the same class. I was tempted to frighten them with a knock on the window, but decided against it. Then thought of Angela lifted my spirits. Perhaps she would be the one to help me turn the corner at last.

The period between Christmas and New Year's Eve, flashed by. During this time I saw quite a lot of James and Family and I also visited Kathy's Family twice. Everyone seemed frightened of saying or doing the wrong thing, including me, so it made it an awkward time.

New Year's Eve. I went to Liverpool Pier Head with James and his parents. A Royal Navy Frigate was in port and we had VIP Invitations to the on board celebrations. John was in his Uniform and Jane wore a long black formal dress, I must say I rather fancied her. James and I wore suits and ties on Johns orders. Lots of Navy families were on board. A sort of marquee was set up aft of the main superstructure. A generator hummed in the background to provide extra power. A Royal Marine Band played popular music, including some Beatles hits, which sounded much better than I imagined it could do from a Military band. We were first escorted to the Officer's wardroom for drinks and buffet. Some of the fancy food I didn't recognise so I didn't eat it. I stayed with the safety on sausage rolls, sandwiches and cakes. I was offered rum to drink. I accepted it like an old salt and knocked it back in one. First there was the heat in my throat, then seconds later the world exploded. I had never had rum before. John observed my expression and laughed. I was informed that this was the best rum and that I should take it easy if I was to stay on it. I changed to Guinness.

I was introduced to a number of people during the evening, mainly Officers and their Wives. I found the Officers very jovial and friendly, but some of the wives were very snobbish. I quite enjoyed being addressed as Sir by the white coated Stewards serving drinks and by the Petty Officer assigned to show James and me around the ship. I asked James why his Dad called his vessel a boat and this was referred to as a Ship. He informed me that in the Navy a surface vessel was a Ship and a Submarine was a Boat.

The tour of the Ship was very interesting. There was a lot more crammed inside than I imagined. After half an hour of climbing and descending ladders, squeezing through hatches and banging my head more times than I could count; we arrived at the marquee. The area was now crowded with guests and the snobby women were more amiable. The magic hour approached. The Band stopped playing and the countdown began. 10-9-8-7-6-5-4-3-2-1. — The Liver Clock rang out its' first chime. The whole River Front erupted into the sounds of Ship and vehicle horns and screams of "Happy New Year". Every female was embraced by someone and kissed then passed on to another and another. I received more kisses in a few minutes that in all my previous life. The Marine Band played Auld Lang Syne and everyone joined hands to dance in a large circle around the deck. One section of the circle collapsed into a heap of officers, ratings and women. Lots of legs and knickers appeared between stripes and white caps. Snooty women were no longer evident just laughter and more kissing. The Band returned to normal service as the Liver clock rang out its' twelfth chime. The noise of horns, bells and fireworks continued for almost twenty minutes before a normal party atmosphere returned.

CHAPTER 16

1970 had arrived in some style. It was a memorable night. James had disappeared with a girl. I stood at the outer rail looking across the River towards Birkenhead.

'Are you ok Sir?' a Steward enquired.

I assured him I was fine. I was a bit dizzy due to the alcohol but steady enough to gaze for a while. Then I suddenly became aware of the rocking motion of the Ship. It must have been slight as we were tied up on a calm river, but it was enough to make me sick over the side. I wasn't the only one. Others were at it too. I went for a drink of water. When I returned the Band was packing up their gear and some guests were leaving the Ship. It was 2am. By 3am. I was reunited with the Cook Family. We were escorted off the Ship to a waiting Mini bus. John's car was left behind as we left the dock for home. John and Jane seemed quite with it; but James and I were a bit worse for wear. James informed me that there was a new love in his life called Sandra. I wondered what course my future would take in the love stakes. Then I fell asleep again. I remember being helped into the spare bedroom at James's house then nothing until 1pm, New Year's Day.

I had dinner with James John and Jane. Then I was taken home. On the journey James and I decided to have a holiday together in the spring. We discussed a number of places and settled on London. I had been once on a school trip but it was only a day trip by train with only a short time to cram in as much as possible. I didn't remember much about it. So I was now looking forward to a proper holiday in the capitol.

The next day I saw Angela again. This time is was just a quiet drink in a Pub in Prescot. She seemed a little on edge on this occasion. There was a greeting kiss when we met; we remained attached to each other as much as possible. There was lots of conversation and humour and in the pub we were very close. There was, a but though. I knew Angela had something on her mind. Eventually she plucked up the courage to tell me the earth shattering news. Angela had been divorced for a few months. She also had a daughter, two years old called Christine. She apologised for not telling me when we first went out, but she thought it might spoil a lovely evening. I squeezed her hand tighter and told her not to worry. Yes it was a surprise but. I was honest in saying I didn't know quite how to deal with the situation at this moment, but let's see if we can work it out together.

I put a brave face on it, but I was deeply shocked inside. This news did change the atmosphere a bit. Angela was obviously upset and worried, I was unsure what to do or say. I asked her to tell me about Christine. She took some pictures from her bag and began to describe the scenes to me. She was obviously very proud of her daughter and I think it made her feel easier that I showed interest. Thereafter I was asked from time to time whether I still wanted to continue with the relationship. She would understand if I wanted to call it a day. I asked for time to digest this new situation. We agreed to meet again soon. Our parting that night was sensual but cautious I would say. We indicated a mutual desire to continue, but I felt it was a 'watch this space' scenario. Tonight I wasn't as overjoyed as last time. I had a lot of serious thinking to do. I had limited experience of women, and no experience of children.

After a couple of days at home I returned to work for a session in the School. The theory work was now getting more detailed and I had to work hard to keep up. Just like the school days as a child, there were the' know all's' who seemed to find everything so easy, and then there were the plodders like me who had to work at everything. I enjoyed the school blocks though. We were all good friends and a few courting couples. We enjoyed each other's company and we bonded as a group.

During this school session we were required to observe a post mortem. Most of the lads, including me, put on a brave face and cracked jokes about it. This was a nerves settling exercise. The day arrived. We filed across to the mortuary like "Lambs to the slaughter". Many of us had visited the morgue before, but simply to deliver bodies. Each would be I.D. Checked before being places into the fridge. That was normally the end of it for us. Now we were entering a new zone, the post mortem.

On entering the examination room the atmosphere was different from that of previous visits. The odours were a mixture of cleaning and embalming fluids, and perhaps what people describe as 'the smell of death'. On the examination table lay a corpse covered by a white sheet. A mortuary attendant indicated the positions in which we were to stand so that he and the examiner had room to work easily.

We stood silently. A couple of the girls linked arms in support of one another. The blokes tried to look macho and unconcerned. A door clattered and in walked a large bearded man in full theatre dress. He was still tying on his cap as he marched purposefully to a position behind the table facing us.

He introduced himself as Doctor Bruce (he looked like a Bruce) Bentham. The first thing he told us was the locations of the toilets and the exit. He tried to make us feel better by announcing that anyone who needed to leave should do so and not feel bad about it. He then gave an overview of the procedure and the reasons why thing were done the way they were.

Then, with the aid of the attendant the sheet was rolled down and removed to reveal the body of an 86 year old Woman. The post mortem would not normally be required in her case but permission had been granted by next of kin for the purpose of research. My mind turned to Kathy. I was so sad that her body; her beautiful body would have been subjected to what I was about to witness.

The laying out work done on the ward was immediately undone. Dr. Bentham dictated and the attendant made notes as the procedure commenced. The skin was parted from the neck to the groin. The twenty observers were immediately reduced to eighteen. Embarrassingly, it was blokes not girls who were the first casualties. We wouldn't hear the last of this later. Two further cuts were made at the top, outwards towards the shoulders to facilitate the folding back of the skin to reveal the ribs and abdominal organs. A few more disappeared. As the rib cage was sawn open and the removal of internal organs commenced, our group was reduced further still. The organs were examined, samples taken and weighed. Then the top of the skull was removed. The brain was taken out and kept for research purposes. It was very interesting if not messy. The smell almost beat me rather than the views, but I managed to stay the course. By the time the body was sewn up and washed off, only six observers were left. It was interesting and educational, but I wasn't in a rush to see any more.

The relationship with Angela was decided for me by fate. The next date I failed to attend the date because my Dad was taken to Hospital with an Angina attack on the day we were supposed to meet. That was accepted. The details of the rearranged date were leaked to a couple of the older female nurse with whom I worked. Having decided that Angela was too old for me, and taking into account that she had a kid, and possibly that her dress was too short and seemingly in my best interests; one of them told me that Angela was unable to see me that evening. The result was that I let her down again. The next day Angela told me that she now had my answer to her question as to whether or not we should continue. She said she understood and that she hoped we could remain friends. I tried to explain what happened but she didn't want to accept it.

February arrived. I was allocated to 'The Benedict Clinic'. This was a specialist unit, within the hospital grounds but separate from the main buildings. The senior staffs here were Psychologists rather than Psychiatrists. The patients were being treated for such things as gambling and drug addictions and a variety of behavioural problems. The unit also contained the Hospital Operating Theatre used by visiting Consultants.

I was to spend two months in the main unit and one month in the theatre and recovery wards. This would take me to April, so I booked my holidays for the end of my attachment here. I checked with James that he was in agreement with the dates. Now I had London to look forward to.

The main unit had unique challenges. Those with drug and alcohol problems made it their business to find ways of beating the system. The twice-daily searches revealed stashes in the most ingenious places. Alcohol could be found in gutters and drainpipes. Lucozade bottles were a favourite. Drugs may be found in hollowed out books and furniture legs or buried in flowerbeds or sewn into clothing. The drugs were the hardest to find. They could be secreted anywhere there was a gap or recess. In radios, T.Vs. curtain seams, pens; the list of possibilities was endless, but it made the job that much more interesting. Treatment here was based modifying behaviour rather than using drugs to help patients. It was hard work and often very frustrating. The deception rate was very high, so you were never quite sure how successful you had been in any particular case. The re admission rate was high

I was quite proud of the fact that I brought about weekly Staff/Patient meetings at which Patients could express any feeling they had or complaint or give praise or make any suggestions to improve things. Due to the fact that it was my idea, I was democratically made Chairman of these meetings. This created a problem for me near the end of my period of duty here. At what was to be my last meeting as Chair, the patients had organised a whip round to buy me a few gifts. My acceptance of these didn't go down well with a couple of the staff. They were of the opinion that we all contributed to the work of the unit and I should have declined the gifts. I must say, this upset me. I thought I might offend people if I declined. In the event I offended people anyway. Sometimes you just can't win.

One amusing thing that I recall from this unit was an incident at one of the Weekly Dances. A fellow Student called Harry Duker was found cornered in the kitchen by a voluptuous lady called Ruth who was, amongst other things, a Nymphomaniac. She got poor Harry in a corner and stripped naked; inviting him to have his way with her. He was terrified. Fortunately he was rescued from this fate before it went too far. I had danced with her from time to time on these occasions and she was quite determined in her quest for seduction. I'm sure many of the male patients benefited from her generosity.

It was during my time at the Clinic that I found myself infatuated with a S.E.N. called June. She was perhaps 10 years older than me, maybe even more; but she just bowled me over. She was very attractive, light brown curly hair, slim and shapely with a lively and friendly personality. She was good company. I wasn't sure about her marital status. I didn't see a ring, but many Nurses didn't wear rings if they had sharp stones in case they injured a Patient. I established that she wasn't married or courting. She still lived at home. I didn't ask her age. My colleagues guessed she was anything between 28 and 35, which didn't help. Anyway, I thought she was great. However, I didn't make any attempt to ask her out at this point. The brakes were still on. I was troubled though because she was constantly on my mind. Perhaps later in the Year.

In April I was allocated to the operating theatre block. The staffing was, a Staff Nurse, John Maytree, the Charge Nurse, Vince Nutall and I. Within myself I was a bit nervous about working in the Theatre. I imagined having to deal with scenes of blood and guts and handling parts of people which had been removed. In the event it wasn't anything like as nauseating as I thought. The first two weeks was my induction period. I didn't go into the operating theatre at all. My job was based in the small ward of 8 beds, which was the preparation and recovery area. I kept the beds ready for admissions, looked after patients when they arrived and tried to reassure them about their treatment. I washed shaved and painted with Iodine the areas required for operations, dressed patients in caps and gowns ready for theatre; then having capped and gowned myself I would wheel them in and help get them into position on the table. Then I would leave to prepare the ward for the recovery. Remake and disinfect the bed.

Make the bedding up for the patient's return. Make up the appropriate dressings trolley and ensure that any special equipment was in place, and then have a cuppa or lunch. Usually the Staff nurse or Charge, in company with the Anaesthetist would return the patient to me in various states of consciousness and I would keep an eye on them until the recovered. If special equipment was used I would be instructed how to deal with it and the Staff Nurse would ensure that I handled the situation correctly until the patient was discharged from the care of the Theatre staff, fully recovered. Depending on the operation, they would stay with me for anything from a few hours to several days before being returned to their own wards.

I soon got used to this and became very proficient at it. I rather enjoyed the status of walking around the unit in my theatre garb from time to time. I felt important. In week three I was joined by Student Nurse Emily Williams who took my place in the recovery ward in between bouts of sex with Dave Prentice. She was a 'dizzy blonde' and needed careful supervision. I was moved to do more theatre work and my nervousness returned for a while. Now I was introduced to the work of a Theatre Technician. Now I would really earn my theatre garb. This work was a lot more involved and detailed my contribution to the proceedings more important. John, the Staff Nurse was careful to ensure that I fully understood everything before I was let loose. I had to learn about the gas cylinders and their various uses, the instruments, the dressings the technical language and the regulations. It was now my job to get the theatre ready for the operations. Make sure everything was spotlessly clean and vital areas sterile. I got all the instruments ready and dressings laid out. The Anaesthetists equipment in place, the lighting and sockets tested. Then I tested all equipment that was going to be used. Patient's notes were available and any special requirements that the Medical Staff requested was on site. During the operations I was to count every item in and out so that nothing was left inside the Patient. Every swab had to be accounted for and this was the most common cause of delays at the end of procedures. This work was so demanding that I hardly ever noticed the previously feared blood and guts. At the end of each session I cleaned up and accounted for everything. Sterilised the instruments and disposed of waste including and tissues removed. Then I rechecked theatre stocks and re ordered what I needed. Checked that notes had gone to where they were needed next and reported to the Charge Nurse to have my work checked and signed off. My next job was to check on the patient's condition whilst in the care of Emily. Job done.

In days gone by little emphasis was placed on dental care, so there were a lot of total dental extractions. Many Patients came in with yellow toothed smiles and left with sunken cheeks and gummy. The most intriguing procedure was an abortion. The foetus was required for the lab so it wasn't destroyed. It was Male and could easily fit into the palm of my hand. Several Staff showed interest in seeing it. I was amazed at how perfect it was. Every feature right down to the soft finger nails and peacefully closed eyes. I felt sorry for the little soul as I placed him in a jar of formaldehyde for preservation.

On occasions the Consultants would agree to do minor surgery for Staff. On one occasion during my watch, Sister Anderson, the Wife of one of the Chiefs was admitted to have piles removed. I felt uneasy about the prospect of closely observing the bum of a Chief's Wife. I consulted John about it but he told me to just treat it like all the other jobs and not think about it. In the event I need not have worried. Only a tiny area was visible and it could have been anyone. She recovered in a private ward attended to by Female Staff.

Other than those two things, which stood out in my mind, the rest was routine. I enjoyed my time there and learned a lot. Now it was holiday time with my best mate James. I had been looking forward to it for ages. The Theatre assignment had taken a lot out of me and I was now ready to let my hair down.

CHAPTER 17

I hadn't seen much of James of late due to his courting Sandra. She was a travel consultant and as luck would have it she was working on an assignment in Disneyland, Florida for the whole of April, so no conflict of interests thank goodness. Cook mansion had not yet been sold so James often had his guest stay over; lucky swine.

Friday evening was my time to pack for the adventure. That meant just about everything I had in my flat was to go with me. James came to the hospital to visit. He had a surprise for me. I followed him out of the building, he was obviously excited. He offered to take me home for a while to check that I had everything I needed. The reason for the excitement became clear when he took the car keys from his pocket and inserted the largest of them into the door of a Rover P3.

'WOW!' I said as I admired the executive lines. 'I knew the Cooper wasn't you'. I was invited to sit inside. I melted into the firm leather seat, my eyes taking in the classic dashboard. The 3ltr. Engine was brought to life and purred. Then we floated as if on air along the drive and out into the traffic. The ivory bodywork enhance with chrome fittings and grille found many admiring eyes on the journey to Huyton. At home I looked around for anything I might need over the next two weeks. I said my farewells to the Family and was given the delightful privilege of driving back to the Hospital. What a beautiful car to drive with bags of power waiting to unleashed at the right moment.

Having packed my meagre belongings into the massive boot, we set off for a final visit to Cooke's mansion as James had forgotten an envelope which Jane had left for me. She had decided that I was poor and left me a subsidy to help with holiday expenses. I felt a little embarrassed about it but I was relieved that I wouldn't have to worry as much about spending. James had been left in charge of booking accommodation for our trip but had told me nothing so far. I asked him had he sorted a place to stay.

'Oh my God, I knew there was something else I had to do!' was the rather surprising response.

'You're not seriously telling me you haven't booked anything?' I looked across for a reaction.

'Well no, I haven't booked anything,' then the grin. 'But Dad has' The grin turns to a smile. 'We are staying at the House of one of his Navy buddies, Sir Malcolm Carstairs; he works in the Ministry of Defence in London.' I looked at him again.

'Yeah, yeah'. Now where are we really staying?" James smiled again.

'No honestly, when I told Dad the plan he offered to contact Malcolm and see if he could put us up for two weeks. No hesitation, no problem. That's the way they are, all for one and one for all people. I've never met this bloke but Dad says he's a great friend. I've got the address and directions. I'm told he won't be home 'till 8 this evening but there will be someone to meet us if we are earlier.'

I wasn't 100% convinced about this story, James was a bit of a practical joker at times, but he seemed sincere now. I would reserve judgement and awaited our arrival at Butlins or a guesthouse somewhere. After a snack and a short detour to drop off the house keys to a neighbour; we commenced the adventure at 1215; estimating our arrival in the London area by about 6pm. James drove the first leg, which turned out to be an arm and a leg. We stopped at Watford Gap on the M1 at ten past five. I had slept part of the way; it had been a journey dogged by hold-ups. We took trays from the leading end of a long counter displaying a variety of hot foods. It was busy and I didn't notice the astronomical prices until we arrived at the till. Fortunately we would only be doing this on the journey out and back. By the time we got to a vacant grubby table with the previous occupants left overs my steak pie and chips had cooled under the congealed gravy and crusty peas. I suggested we find a café off the Motorway on the return trip. The main meal finished I turned my attention to a cup of muddy tea which had also cooled as if to accentuate the terrible flavour. As we digested the offering I remembered the envelope from Jane. James was reading a Telegraph whilst I opened the envelope. Inside I was amazed to find £30 and a note.

'Dear Liam. I hope you don't mind my doing this, but I am aware of how little you are paid in your work. John and I often talk about you, in the nicest way of course. I would like you to think about working for me in 'The rag trade.' James is now running the Salford Warehouse and I'm sure he would love you to help. You would easily earn more than the Health Service pays you and we know you well enough to recognise your skills. No pressure. Do think about it. Talk it over with James if you wish. He has the authority to hire you without further reference to me. Hope you enjoy your well-earned holiday. Love, Jane and John.'

'Did you know about this?' I displayed the contents of the envelope.

'I didn't know about the cash, but the job offer is something I have discussed with Mum. What do you think?'

'Well I wasn't expecting this. Let me think about it.'

James took a last gulp of cold mud. 'That's fine. No rush. Whatever you decide is fine. I know you love the Asylum.'

'Psychiatric Hospital' I declared as a correction.

'Yeah, OK; the Nuthouse.' The cold mud made him cough as he laughed.

We left to continue our journey amongst high volumes of traffic which after about five miles ground to a halt. Several emergency vehicles passed us on the hard shoulder; conclusion, an accident. James began his promotional talk designed to entice me into the business. He talked about emerging markets, new trends and possible expansion. I found it interesting, but I wasn't composing my notice just yet. It passed the time anyway until we were able to file passed the mangled wrecks, which had been moved over to get the traffic moving again. It was 8pm before we arrived at the gates of a large and very real Mansion near Royal Tunbridge Wells in East Sussex. I still couldn't quite believe that this would be our home for two weeks until the electronic gates opened as if by magic, allowing us to continue up the circular drive to the front door. It reminded me of a TV comedy 'The Beverley Hillbillies'. As we approached I started singing the theme tune and James quickly joined in.

The only sound was the crunching gravel, which eased off as the car gently stopped. As we emerged from the car the large front door opened and a lady appeared, dressed in a grey trouser suit and black court shoes. She was nicely tanned and has black tightly curled hair. Descending the six wide steps she held out her hand in greeting.

'Good evening Gentlemen, I'm Maria Genero the Housekeeper. Sir Malcolm and Lady Carstairs will be here soon. Please follow me; we will attend to your luggage shortly. This is Gordon the chauffeur, if you let him have your keys Gordon will look after your car for you.' We were taken through a large hallway to what was described as the reception room. On route we were asked how our journey was but I suspect it wasn't a serious enquiry. Maria took our jackets and indicated the position of the chairs in which we were to sit

'Would you like a drink? Dinner will be served as soon as your hosts return.'

We requested tea. Maria left the room and background music drifted around the room from somewhere. After several minutes admiring and commenting on the surroundings, Maria reappeared with a large silver tray on which the teapot and cups were laid out around the milk and sugar jugs. Having checked how we would like our tea, it was promptly served. We were then left alone.

'I thought you were joking about this,' I said.

James admitted also being a little overwhelmed by the status of our hosts. He knew that his Dad and this Malcolm had a long naval association but he knew nothing about Malcolm's status. The gravel crackling was again apparent. James stood to look out of the window. I was informed that they had arrived by Taxi. A bit puzzling as they had a chauffeur. Minutes later we stood to be introduced to Sir Malcolm and Lady Louise Carstairs. Sir Malcolm, who later insisted on first names only, immediately greeted James with a firm handshake.

"You've got to be James, you are the image of the ugly buggar; oh, not that you're ugly, you're a lot better looking than he is!' Louise interjected.

'Oh you terrible man, don't take any notice James, it's lovely to meet you, and who's this?' Louise looked at me.

'Oh sorry, this is my friend Liam, since our school days'

Both shook my hand and I was made welcome. The Carstairs went to 'change for dinner'. Maria ushered us into the dining room and again indicated the seats we were to occupy.

The oblong highly polished dining table was set for four. It seemed that dinner was later than usual and cook was concerned about it. Darkness had descended and it was so quiet outside. The smell of good food wafted around the room. The sound of muffled voices could be heard from the kitchen and plates clattering. The Carstairs returned. They had changed but to informal wear. They sat opposite us and asked about our journey, but they actually wanted to know about it. Malcolm asked how John liked his training camp posting in Scotland. He was of the opinion that John would want to be back at sea before long or at least under it.

A plump lady came in with the first course.

'This is Marjorie, our fantastic cook' was Louise's introduction.

Marjorie said 'good evening' as she served the food.

Malcolm placed his hand on her arm. 'So sorry we are late Marjorie, we were held up in traffic.'

The creamy potato and leek soup was gorgeous. Then came the rib of beef with help yourself vegetables, then a fruit pie and custard or cream, I had cream; then the cheese board and tea or coffee. Then Malcolm opened a large box of Players cigarettes and he had a cigar. We were offered cigars but declined.

After dinner, about 1030 by now, we retired to the lounge and talked until 1.30am. Maria had gone to bed soon after dinner. She lived in. Cook had finished by 1130 and was driven home by the chauffeur. Louise showed us to our rooms. My room was, as I would imagine a posh hotel room would be. Quite large, oak panelled nice paintings. The furniture was oak and smelled of fresh polish. All the fittings were brass. The room was en suite with beautiful bathroom and a separate shower. The large bed stood on a richly decorated carpet and the window looked out onto pitch-blackness and a star studded sky. It must have been fields on my side of the house. I undressed, sank into the bed and fell asleep almost immediately. It had been quite a day.

9. 15 Am. Sunday morning. I stood at the bedroom window looking out across fields and woodland. For a moment I could not believe my own eyes as three deer walked calmly between clumps of trees to take a drink from a small pond. A kingfisher sat on a fence pole above a stream not far from the house and two rabbits rushed between hedgerows in the large garden. To be greeted by such a lovely scene on the first day of my first proper holiday away from home was just wonderful.

I heard voices downstairs. Reluctantly I left the window scene and made myself presentable in the pristine bathroom. I made my way to the dining room to be greeted by Louise.

'Good morning young man, did you sleep well?'

'Oh yes thank you. What a lovely House you have. I just saw some deer out of my window. I was told to expect a lot of wildlife around here.

The Staff didn't work on Sundays so I was invited to help myself to breakfast. The kitchen, which I didn't see yesterday, contained a small dining table. I selected Cornflakes and sat down to eat. Louise was in the process of cooking bacon and sausages. I was invited to help myself when ready.

James joined us soon and at this point I felt more at ease. After some exploration of the cupboards he found everything we could want and a good relaxed breakfast was washed down with lashings of tea. Malcolm arrived on the scene. He informed us that should we wish at any time to accompany him into the City, he left either by 7am or 10am to avoid the worst of the traffic. When working, he used the Chauffeur. 10am departures would often be in company with Louise who would lunch with friends. However, should we wish to drive into the City, he would lend us his parking permit. Then of course we could drive part way and use the tube. Today though was relax day for the Carstairs. Louise suggested we may like to explore nearby Tunbridge which was a lovely little Town Centre.

So began an upper crust sponsored holiday I would never forget. We used each of the travel methods suggested to get into London. Being chauffeured in the Austin Princess Limousine was perhaps the best experience. Driving in ourselves tended to be a getting lost experience followed by several near misses with cars driven by Arabs, then failing to find the house easily on the return journey. Many of the evenings at the Mansion were spent in the company of VIPs, a High Court Judge, a Cabinet Minister, retired Vice Admiral and the permanent secretary to the MOD. They were without exception very nice people, but in some respects made me fear for the future of the Country.

I fell in Love with London. I've loved it ever since; just to visit though, I don't think I could live in the City. We managed to see most of the most important places. I was amazed at how small Horse Guards Parade was. The televised trooping of the colour made it look massive. I loved the parks and the Tower and Madame Tussaudes. I could spend a long time just people watching in places like Piccadilly. Plus I developed a fondness for the iconic Routemaster Buses. All too soon though the two weeks disappeared into history and we were headed home, avoiding the rip off poor quality Services. What a wonderful luxurious holiday it had been. Now back to reality.

CHAPTER 18

My first allocation on returning to work was a period in School another mock exam was due and this was a revision period with mock tests and lots of practice on setting trollies and making specialist beds and questions questions questions. This was quite a stressful period because there seemed to be a shortfall between the questions and corresponding answers but we were reassured that we were at the level expected at this stage. Then we were released again onto the poor unsuspecting patients.

My next allocation was a period of secondments to outside agencies, Liverpool City Centre Social Services. There I experienced working with people who had experienced the most horrendous social problems. Homelessness, I had no idea there were so many people living on the street, sleeping on and under benches archways and Railway Tunnels. They utilised any shelter they could to eat and sleep. It was summer now. How they managed in winter was unimaginable. Each day in company with a Social Worker, we visited a Salvation Army Hostel. I didn't like this place. People seemed to be treated like scum. There were many of course who were untrustworthy; who would bully and even harm others in order to achieve some sort of higher archy status amongst the dregs of Society. Still, I felt there should be a better way of helping these poor souls. I also encountered the problems of drugs and domestic violence, exploitation and prostitution. This was the world of nightmares. In just two weeks with this unit we found 3 People dead. One had fallen into a coal fire and the head and shoulders were cooked. One had committed suicide under a train and the third was a drugs overdose. We had organised 4 section 28 Psychiatric hospital admissions. (Compulsory orders) 3 due to violence and 1 was an old confused woman who had filled her house with rubbish to the extent that only one room was accessible. Plus she was sharing the house with 33 Cats. This assignment put me off Community Social work. It was Hell on Earth.

Next it was a small specialist Children's Unit. These children had the most horrendous behavioural problems. The problem was that it was small. From 8am till 5pm the screaming and banging, the assaults and the uncontrolled bowel and urine explosions were in your face all day without respite. The 30 minute lunch was pure heaven. I had the greatest respect and admiration for the Staff there. Again, not for me, in the future.

Then, the Crème De La Crème, Ashworth, the Hospital for the Criminally Insane. Here, you dare not go anywhere alone. An Experienced Officer escorted me everywhere. Now I was training to deal with Psychopathic Murderers, Rapists and People who were ready to take you into their confidence to get anything they wanted. Even the Patients were quite bad. Seriously though, this was a high risk, high security establishment were your life was very much on the line if you became complacent. Here I could work. It was potentially dangerous but very interesting too. Deep down there is a fascination with danger in all of us. I enjoyed it here. The Staff were just a great solid team and that made it a satisfying place to be.

September 1970. My external adventures over, I was able to scare the living daylights out of the Female Students who had yet to partake of these activities . . . Now it was 3 Months nights. 7pm. 'till 7am, four on and three off. I had never worked nights in my life. I was apprehensive. My worries were not eased by the fact that I was to do my nights on ward 7, The Refractory ward, our own mini version of Ashworth. On the Friday before a weekend off, I went to visit the Charge Nurse for ward 7, Mr Kevin Williams. He took me around the ward and talked me through the system. I was introduced to Staff and Patients. The most likely trouble makers were pointed out. I was told that most of the patients were in their rooms before the night staff took over. These were individual lockable rooms. There were 20 room plus two padded rooms for those who required a period of calming down after a violent episode. I recalled my night in one of them.

For this weekend I was, at the invitation of Commander Cooke, to spend 2 days at the Submarine Training School in Scotland. James and Sandra were also invited. Another Guest was James friend Mirriame. Mirriame's husband Jerry had a Range Rover and we were invited to travel in that this weekend. Jerry was Financial Consultant. He was a very busy man and sent his regrets but he had to work in London this weekend. As he used the train, we were given the use of the Car.

CHAPTER 19

Our Destination was 'The Clyde Submarine base, Helensburgh, Dumbartonshire. The shared driving commenced with James accompanied by Sandra in the front. We were all excited about the trip. Mirriame was looking forward to seeing her best friend again. They had known each other since school and it was hard on them to be parted because of John's job. The party set off at 4pm on the Friday, intending to arrive at the pre booked Hotel at Helensburgh before midnight. I sat with Mirriame at the back. I was tired and soon nodded off. We were past Carlisle before I woke up again. It was time to change over. I was next to drive. We all swapped around so the 'couples stayed together . . . We got to know a lot about each other. I had previously thought of Mirriame as a bit self-cantered and full of herself, but now I was warming to her. She was actually a lot of fun to be with and didn't have the selfish traits I had attributed to her at all. One thing which became obvious was that Jerry was away a lot and Mirriame was a bored Housewife. She made it quite obvious that for her at least, this weekend had nothing whatsoever to do with Submarines.

The third and final driver change was passed to James again. Mirriame had no interest in driving. As we sat at the back she asked if I'd ever had my palm read. As the light began to fade across the fields this new game began. She had obviously studied the meanings of all these lines and bumps and I was intrigued at her pronouncements as she looked at my palm for clues to my future. It seemed that I was to enjoy a long life with several partnerships and two Children. My financial status would improve but only in the latter part of my life. I would have a significant health problem perhaps in my middle years, but it would have a positive outcome. Finally, I would move away from my home town to find my true destiny.

After thanking her for that very interesting reading, my hand was not released. She said it was a pleasure, leaned over and kissed me on the cheek. My hand remained captured within both of hers for some time. We made eye contact and smiled at each other. I now looked at her in a fresh light.

I was turned on, and she knew it. As darkness came we became bolder. Our touching secretive as we didn't want to advertise the newly discovered attraction to James and Sandra. Now with arms around each other we felt skin and explored a little. We arrived at the Hotel at 1140pm. Jane was in reception to meet us and hugs and kissed were shared. James and Sandra had one room and Mirriame and I separate rooms, but not all night.

John arrived before midnight and bought a round of Aberdeen Angus Burgers. They were enormous and together with some salad and a glass of whiskey went down very well. We chatted until 12.30am and then dispersed to our rooms. Mirriame made sure I knew where her room was so that I could make good on her invitation. I sorted out my bits and pieces in my cosy room. Showered, shaved and made my way to Mirriame by 1.15am. Now nervous I knocked on the door. I entered to find Mirriame in a full length night dress, cotton with a Japanese Lion pattern. The moment the door closed we were locked together in a firm passionate kiss. As the kiss lingered on for a while I furled up the back of the nightie until I could feel the firm smooth and hot buttocks. As I massaged that area the kissing became more like a meal. I was gently led to the bed without releasing any of the grips we were now locked into. At the edge of the bed the nightie drifted away in company with my own clothing.

We sank onto the soft mattress and pulled over the Duvet. Her naked body was very hot and very sexy. Every area was perfectly shaped and firm. I'm not sure what I expected, but perfection in a woman nearly twice my age was not at the forefront of my imagination. I spent some time confirming what I couldn't quite believe, but she was indeed flawless. I couldn't understand why any man would neglect her and leave her open to other relationships. Still, at this point I wasn't complaining. I tried to hold out with the foreplay as long as I could but she was just too much. In any case she seemed as keen as I was to get on with the intercourse bit. This was to be a conventional session with Mirriame lying back to think of England and me bringing the Jumbo Jet in to land on runway one. She was hot and wet and sexy and I soon offloaded what felt like 200 gallons of sperm into her. She nearly crushed me between those well exercised legs. It was over too soon and we collapsed into kissing mode again. After about half an hour of post coytal stroking and words of love, I was urged to leave as it probably wouldn't look good it we left the room together in the morning. Reluctantly I agreed. She was so gorgeous; this was the last thing I wanted to do.

Our pre-arranged group meeting for breakfast took place at 9am. John joined us and set out our options for the day. He suggested the girls may like a shopping trip and the men a visit to the Base. It was during this meeting that I discovered two new things. The first was that Porridge could be eaten with added salt rather than sugar and the second was how difficult it was to pretend that nothing had happened between Mirriame and me. On the journey up here I thought mainly about the Navy and Submarines. Now I just thought about sex.

10 Am. The Girls went on a shopping tour of the Highlands in James's Jag. We departed in a Royal Navy Land Rover for the base. Soon we arrived at the Base, greeted by four armed Pickets (Navy Police), in belts and gaiters. The senior of the group, a Petty Officer, approached our vehicle in company with an Able Seaman carrying a metal pole. The P.O. saluted John and asked for passes. We had been given special passes. As the passes were scrutinised, the second man checked under the vehicle with a mirror on the end of his pole. The Petty Officer opened the back to check inside. Having satisfied themselves that all was well we were saluted through the gates. James questioned the need to be so thorough with the Commanding Officer. John explained that everyone was checked like that. In any case he commanded the training school not the Base. He had obtained permission to show us round from the Base Commander. We had an interesting tour of the less sensitive areas of the base and then lunch in the wardroom with the actual base commander and a few officers. After lunch we were allowed to clamber in and around a submarine. This boat was John's previous command. A hunter killer type, it was armed with torpedoes for an attacking roll. It was smaller than the large Nuclear Subs and therefore more cramped. In fact the biggest space was the central corridor between compartments. When on patrol it would carry about120 crew. The kitchen was very small and I asked how they carried enough food for such a large crew. It seems they left port stuffed full and could manage for a 90 days minimum. The crew were very highly trained and knew their jobs to the highest possible standard. Lives depended on it, even on routine patrols. I quote from the Petty Officer in response to my question about living and working in such confined spaces.

"We can find room for anything, except mistakes".

After our tour we were driven off to the separate training school. Once again we went through all the security procedures before John proudly showed us around his empire. We left at about 5pm and we were treated to a scenic drive before returning to the Hotel for dinner, (Tea Time to us). The Girls arrived back laden with shopping bags. We had dinner at the House, about a mile out of town. It was a stone semi detached house belonging to the Navy. During the meal John indicated that they would be returning to 'The Cronton Mansion' later this year. He wasn't keen on running the Training School and if not offered another sea job he may retire early. Mirriame was over the moon at the prospect of rekindling her friendship with Jane, and now there appeared to be a new member of the gang in the form of Sandra. This was deemed to be a serious relationship when they announced their engagement. This created a fantastic party atmosphere which could only be held in the local pub. The evening of drunkenness and merriment was made all the better by the fact that the amourous clutches displayed by Mirriame and myself were evidently regarded as harmless fun by everyone, so we took full advantage of it.

It was at this party that I was introduced to and permanently went off Haggis. It made me very sick for a while but didn't put me off another wild sex session with Mirriame in the Hotel later. This event was more of drunken shag than a love making. It was furious and mind blowing sex. This time we did leave together in the morning, largely due to being incapable of leaving anyway. All she was worried about in the morning was looking a mess. I was ordered to stay under the duvet until she had got fully dressed and had 'put her face on.' I complied. Nobody saw us anyway

CHAPTER 20

Sunday was launch day. John had purchased a 45' Catamaran for his probable retirement. We were going along on 'her' sea trials at 1pm. Mirriame was nervous about it and to be honest, I was too. It was longer than a Bus and possibly just as likely to sink. I had once done a weekend sailing course at Hollingworth Lake. That was the full extent of my experience. James had done quite a lot with his Dad. The rest of us had no idea what to expect. James tried to re assure us that this Motor Launch was well equipped and stable with the double hull. It had both sail and motor power and was very comfortable.

'Your Dad does realise that he's supposed to stay on the surface with this, does he?' I quipped.

Several nervous laughs supported my question.

'It'll be great fun, you'll love it' was James reply as he observed the arrival of the Navy Land Rover. John assisted us all into the back of the Land Rover with re assuring smiles and pats on the back. Then we were on our way to the Harbour; part of which was reserved for small private craft. We stopped at a payment kiosk for the car park. John fiddled for change. A broad Scottish voice resonated from within the kiosk.

'Auk am Nort Charrgin yeu Sar.' We were waved through.

'Ex Submariner' explained John with a smile. 'He shouldn't be sitting in that hole taking car park money. It's a disgrace.'

We piled out of the vehicle. James issued us with life jackets and made sure they were tied off correctly. Then we were told about the lights and whistles, attached to the jackets, not very re—assuring. Now down the steps, along the footway between lots of craft, some very posh indeed. Then we came across 'Pride of Perth,' the Silver Catamaran. Cabin sited centrally with Pilot deck on top. It also had a very tall mast with furled sail and two massive motors, one at the aft of each hull. She; I was told it was a She, was quite large compared with most of the craft there, but certainly the smallest in which I'd ever been to sea. John had prepared and checked everything, as you would outside. John rechecked our life jackets then told us what we could and could not safely do when under way. He asked us to note the dingy stowed behind the cabin. This was for use in emergencies. Then John took his place on the little bridge whilst James was sent to various parts to confirm safety checks. Then it was "'Cast off forward. Cast off aft,' and we edged away from our mooring into the walled dock. Both James and I accompanied John on the bridge. Perhaps it was called cockpit being so small, I didn't ask. Anyway, it was the helm, but there was another steering unit below in case of bad weather. It was a nice day. Very calm and I thought "this is ok; should be fine. We entered a lock with an observation tower. We were observed by a man from the tower as he closed the gate behind us and opened the gate ahead of us.

We powered up and moved slowly out into the channel. The behaviour of the craft immediately changed. It was lovely and calm within the dock, but now we were already rising and dipping noticeably and we hadn't reached the sea yet. John applied more power which had the effect of raising the hull a little and smoothing out the ride. The channel was marked by buoys which ended about a mile out, and then it was just sea ahead. I looked back to gain a reassuring glimpse of the land. Now we were at sea proper and waves lashed over the bow splashing stinging spray into our faces. More power was applied and we began to bounce a little. Excitable screams emanated from the cabin. 'She's great isn't she?' James called out over the noise.

Both John and I replied 'yes she is'. I retreated down the ladder and entered the cabin. Mirriame was sat quite rigidly holding on to the dining table. Sandra was more relaxed, she was stood holding a brass rail looking out of the window. There was a lot more noise inside and not much could be seen. Jane was doing something in the small galley but I'm not sure anyone was ready to eat yet. I asked Mirriame if she wanted to go up top. She thought she may feel better if she could see more. I assisted her out of the cabin to the ladder. We went up the ladder in tandem to make her feel safer. It did the trick. Now she began to enjoy it more. The throttle eased and we headed into a Sheltered Bay. Once there we stopped, anchored and had a snack. John went round checking everything again. He was delighted with his purchase. When they moved back to Cronton, John intended to sail to Fleetwood or Widnes to a permanent mooring. He said the craft was big enough to do channel crossings and possibly Spain for holidays. Jane didn't seem as confident.

John announced the imminent arrival of a poor weather front from the North East. We had to return to port. We powered up and left the bay, encountering heavier weather on the return journey. We were knocked about quite a bit as the winds and higher waves closed in fast. We were pleased to see that observation tower on the dock gate again. As we slowly edged up to our mooring again the rain caught up with us. We were just in time to avoid the worst of the weather. John was at pains to point out that' Pride of Perth could easily handle bad weather so we need not have worried. Back at the Hotel we got ourselves back to normal and had a meal together. John had firmly made up his mind about his options and resolved to talk to the brass about it during the coming week. We were all pleased to hear it. Again we chatted well into the early hours and drank plenty. Tonight I held back. Mirriame was still on heat and I wasn't going to let her down. However Mirriame retired to her room with the Girls for a 'Girly night.' Rather deflated I returned to my room and settled down for a good sleep. My night duty period was due to begin at 7pm tomorrow so I needed as much rest as possible.

It was about 3am when I was disturbed by a knock on the door. I opened the door and a rather tipsy Mirriame announced herself as 'Room Service'. She eased passed me and weaved her way to the bed, giggling all the way. The room floor reminded me of one of those movie bedroom scenes. I tripped over the shoes then followed the trail to the bed. Dress, bra, combined knickers and tights and oddly, one glove. The Duvet was pulled over Mirriame who fell asleep almost immediately. I joined her but did not disturb her. I took the opportunity to have a short exploration but then drifted off myself. It felt lovely.

I was awoken by the 8am by News on the clock radio. I turned towards the clock to be met by the bright brown eyes of the beautiful Mirriame who admitted to turning on the radio. We kissed and I ran my hand down her back to her thighs. She raised her leg to cross my body. I pulled her over till she was looking down at me, raised on her arms. I fondled her breasts as she lowered herself onto my ridged penis. My hands moved to the cheeks of her bottom and the motion began. She sat straight and bounce on me, her breasts, now shaking up and down. Her panting became a series of moans and I was gritting my teeth as the orgasms shook our bodies. She collapses onto me which took my breath away for a moment. She dug her teeth into my shoulder then sucked the air from my mouth. It was over. James banged on the door.

'Are you ready for breakfast you two?'

My brain panicked as the words 'You two' were digested. Oh shit!

Mirriame just said 'Whoops' and smiled at me. 'Don't worry Chicken, no one will say anything.' We showered together, dressed and made our way down for breakfast.

It was a serve yourself breakfast. I found myself in company with James as we picked our way through the delights on offer. He nudged me.

'You dirty Bastard; well lucky dirty Bastard. Don't worry; your secret is safe with me; and everybody else.'

'What?' I was panic stricken for some reason. James laughed. 'I'm only joking mate. But actually I don't think anyone would care. We all know Mirriame is not happy. Don't worry. I think she only wants the sex, she doesn't want to tie you down, oh, unless it's for sex, smile again.

'To be honest I fancied her myself before Sandra. Mum knew it and always made sure I was never left alone with her. Enjoy it whilst it's hot.

Breakfast went without incident, but everyone seemed to be scrutinising me, perhaps my, guilty, imagination. John and Jane arrived to bid us farewell and safe journey, and off we went. When not on driving duty, each of us slept during most of our free time. I relived my Mirriame moments and worried about how I would cope with night duty, especially the first night. I peeled myself away from Mirriame outside the Nurses home at 4.15pm. Thanked everyone for a great weekend and went once more to bed for a few hours.

I didn't unpack. I just flopped onto the bed, set the alarm for six and nodded off. In what seemed to be ten seconds the alarm rang out. After a quick wash and shave I visited the canteen for tea before reporting to ward seven at a few minutes before seven.

CHAPTER 21

It felt very strange going to work at this time of day. My first partner on duty was a 3rd. Year Student, Antonio Paroni. Fortunately he was good company, essential when spending 12 hours together each night. We had 2 hour breaks at night at times arranged between ourselves. For the first month I was introduced to great Italian food cooked in the ward by Antonio. However many night time breaks were spent in the company of Mirriame which didn't help with the energy levels for the rest of the night after wild sex sessions. In the middle of the night it was easy to smuggle her into my room. This went on two or three times each week for about a Month before she seemed to have found a fresh conquest; I'm not sure exactly why but it fizzled out. We remained friends though and there was never any awkwardness at future meetings and social gatherings. My sexual endeavours with Mirriame were enhanced with several expensive gifts, gold watch and cufflinks, new clothes and shoes and study materials. It was a period of exciting diversion for both of us and it remained a secret, even from Jane.

I didn't stay on ward 7 beyond the first month. The duties were mainly security there, the patients potentially violent. Several times Antonio and I found ourselves being thrown around by one of our charges and having to press the alarm bell to summon help. One night we received a call to collect a patient from the Main Office, who had been brought in on a section 28 (compulsory admission) by the Police. Being the junior I was sent to collect this man and return with him to the ward. I walked across from the Annex to the main building. There I found a Police van and 2 cars. At reception I was greeted by 8 Policemen, a Doctor and a Social Worker. My admission was handcuffed and guarded by two burly Constables. He was quite calm and even polite. The situation was explained to me by a Police Sergeant and I signed a couple of documents before the 20 stone Patient was released to my care. I was informed that this man had attacked his family with an axe; injuring but not killing two of them. He had a history of Psychiatric Problems including violence. Armed with this knowledge, the full complement of escorts left and I was then left with the prospect of escorting this Person on my own to the other side of the Hospital, and keeping him calm at the prospect of being taken to a secure ward and a locked room.

I addressed him by his first name, Michael, and asked him to call me Liam. I offered him a drink or food before leaving reception. He declined. I then asked him to walk with me to the ward where he could get some sleep. He had been medicated to calm him down. I avoided talking about the problem which got him arrested. I asked had he been to Hospital before. He told me about several previous admissions; one to Rainhill and two to Prestwich. He was fine with it and knew what to expect. Fortunately he was not at all upset about his situation and believed it was best for him. I kept the conversation going for the 15 minute walk. He settled in well and I was very relieved

Month two was in ward 5, a much more tranquil ward with 80 beds. By now I was quite used to night duty and the rest from sexual exploits meant that I could devote more energy to the task. This time my partner was Daniel Hartwell SEN. Dan was mid 20s and had worked at Rainhill for eight years. He was well suited to the job, always jovial and good to be with. On a number of occasions we talked about the old tales of the Hospital. The Hunch backed Monk who was said to roam the grounds at night, strange goings on around the mortuary and church and the Ghost of Rainhill who was said to walk the full length of the Annex Corridor each midnight.

On occasions Antonio and a few others on breaks would visit and Antonio would cook for us. For fun we decided to conspire to promote the Rainhill Ghost story to frighten the Female Nurses. For a week or so we planted the idea in the minds of others that strange sounds were recently heard in the Annex corridor which couldn't be explained. When the stage was set, a couple of us would gain access to the maintenance corridor beneath the main corridor. Then, with the aid of chains or knocking on water pipes, we would walk the maintenance corridor from end to end moaning and pulling chains and banging. The Female Nurses and probably others not in on the prank would rarely venture out of their wards at night. To the best of my knowledge, the secret of the Rainhill Ghost was never revealed and was often a topic of conversation in the canteens.

Antonio became so well known for his nigh time Italian feasts we would often have a dozen of more guests in ward 5; some off duty, to sample the wonderful dishes. Some years later when the future of the Hospital was doubtful, Antonio opened a successful Italian Restaurant in Liverpool.

Month three was spent in ward 13, the sick ward. Not so restful here. Patients required constant monitoring or intensive care. This was a busy ward all night every night. My first job of laying out on my first day at the Hospital became almost a weekly event here. The ward offices were all equipped with quality VHF radios. One of the favourite pass times was to listen to the Police band. It was often dull routine stuff but occasionally a chase could be monitored or serious crime dealt with. One nigh whilst sitting with a lad called Jim Knox, we heard an officer calling in about his inspection of an abandoned car which he suspected had probably been stolen and dumped. When the registration was given poor old jimmy realised that it was his car. We couldn't call the Police to confirm this because we were not supposed to know about it. The Police gave him the news next morning at home. The down side was that he was later fined for failing to tax the vehicle. The thief was never found.

At the end of my period of night duty, I had another week's holiday. James persuaded me to have a go at working in the warehouse part time to see if I would consider entering the business. I reluctantly agreed and during the weekend prior to this trial we spoke about the prospect at length. I was to be paid for my trial period which was very nice. Just four or five hours a day, I was to be shown how each department operated and do some hands on work. James thought me capable of management and wanted to train me to do so over a twelve month period. Instead of £8 to £12 per week I would be on £20 to £25 per week increasing after training. The money sounded great, but I was apprehensive about it and didn't want to seem ungrateful by possibly letting him down. Anyway I agreed to try it out.

So now I changed tack. Like a fish out of water I began part time temporary work in a wholesale clothing warehouse. My first job was loading and unloading vans, some the company vans and some customers vans. Most customers came in cars; shopkeepers buying in small quantities. They looked after themselves. At times I helped check the goods as they left. This was heavy work at times, especially the large rolls of material. I did 3 days of that and it was more than enough, even just a few hours a day

Then I did 2 full days in the office working alongside James as he lorded over his empire. Whilst at the Hospital I discovered that I had a talent for administration. I was good at keeping records accurately and I could see ways of improving systems if they were inefficient or ineffectual. Using diplomacy and acting as a background voice I was actually able to make a difference in the short time I was there.

First; there was too much duplication of effort. James was one of those Managers who had to be involved in every detail. This made some staff feel undervalued and certainly underutilised. I was able to persuade him to take a step back and consider giving more responsibility to people who had more experience. Then James could concentrate on running the business overall. Telephone orders were often dispatched within an hour of the call. This meant the vehicle delivering was hap hazard, perhaps visiting a particular area several times a day. I asked did customers ask for immediate delivery and I was told no. So I suggested planning the delivery routes to serve allocated areas on selected days of the week, thus cutting costs significantly. The clothing, shoes accessories and bulk materials departments sent out information to customers separately; so many customers would get three leaflets from the same company in separate envelopes on the same day. I suggested amalgamating the information so that only one posting would be required. I also found out by carefully scrutinising electricity bills that 'Style Ettoes Exclusive Fashion' was paying for the warehouse and some of the street lighting. Several months later they got a significant refund for that error.

I made such an impression that the whole family took me out for a meal a few week later in order to try and persuade me to change careers. I didn't. Anyway, for my one week part time effort I was paid a fantastic £50. That was like winning the pools to me.

It was now the first week in December 1970. The Cookes had decided to retire at the end of the year, or at least John had decided. Jane was not yet entirely comfortable with the idea for herself. John was taking his accumulated leave at home and Jane had stayed in Scotland until Christmas to sort things out with the Scottish Business she had started. James was now a fully-fledged manager at the Salford Warehouse.

CHAPTER 22

For December I was allocated to ward 9A. The Patients here were all over 60yrs. Old, commonly known as Geriatrics. All of them had been here almost all their lives and were deeply institutionalised. The Charge Nurse was Ted Murray almost a Geriatric himself. He was just as Institutionalised as the Patients. This was a ward run in what was becoming an outdated fashion. Ted was peddling towards retirement and wasn't in the right mind-set for any change. The patients got up from 7am. Good basic care was the order of the day. Everyone was expected to be washed, shaved and decently dressed before breakfast. Assistance was given were needed. Everyone had the same place for breakfast. Then it was medicine round and move to the day room where everyone had their place around the edge of the large room. The wooden floor remained polished and un—used in the middle. Everyone just stared or rocked away. A T.V. entertained itself in one corner and some of the more articulate patients would play board games or cards with each other or staff when available.

There was a games room containing a billiard table, used mainly by staff. On two mornings a week a Doctor or Psychiatrist would visit and some patients would be seen in the consulting room. For many, this was the highlight of the week. Ted was a nice chap. He always made sure his patients were well looked after in terms of general welfare, it was simply that he was not in the market for new ideas. No rocking the boat. The Staff also had set responsibilities only the Staff Nurses did medicine rounds, so we never got the chance to discuss medications or administer them. Only the Charge and Deputy did ward administration, so we never had case studies. The Assistant Nurses always did bedding and clothing. SENs did personal care and special diets. The Students, well, we just talked to people and kept them entertained. We were allowed to do TPRs (Temperatures Pulse and Respiration Charts) and take bloods, urine and stool samples for the lab. The trouble was there wasn't much call for that sort of work

However, we worked on him and gradually got permission to take small parties out into the grounds for gardening and tidying the grounds, picking litter and such. It was winter now so we did the litter picking and during a brief period of snow, some snow shifting. The Gardeners were persuaded to let us help keep the empty flower beds tidy. Whatever we could think of to serve as occupational therapy we took part in.

One day whilst tending to a flower bed border, I was knelt down using a trowel when I was hit on the back of my head with a spade, luckily, the flat part. Had it been side on, I wouldn't be telling this tale. It seems that one member of my group had decided for some reason to see what happened if he bashed a Nurse with his spade. My assailant, Gordon, was a quiet man, hardly ever spoke. So it was quite a surprise to be assaulted by him. I took my group back to the ward and reported the incident. Mr Murray was most concerned and insisted that I go to Whiston Casualty to be checked. Our own Hospital Ambulance was summoned. It was a 1950s long nosed Bedford, used mostly for internal work. Today it was having an outing. Sister Morgan accompanied me to casualty. Discovering that it was quite busy, she returned to Rainhill suggesting that I telephone when ready.

I registered and was asked to sit in the waiting area. Sister Morgan had established that I had not been cut. It was hurting for about 15 minutes, now I just had a feint neck ache. After about 2 hours, bored stiff and now without any pain, I told reception I was fine and got the bus back to Rainhill. I informed Sister Morgan and Mr Murray, filled in a report and was relieved of duty early.

I took the opportunity to visit James. We had now agreed to disagree about the benefits of my joining the rag trade. He was quite shocked at the story of the attack by 'The Mad Man'. We went to The Black Horse at Cronton. It was a nice pub but the clientele were a bit snooty. The Manager knew the Cooke family so the 3 or 4 deep queues weren't much of a problem. Sandra was due back the following weekend. He hoped she'd be in season

The Hospital was now decked out for Christmas. As always I walked around the grounds to marvel at the wonderful atmosphere created by this metamorphosis. The children of the few visitors and the Staff would be transported into a giant grotto for their delight. Ted Murray was a bit of a 'bah humbug' about Christmas, it upset his routine. Fortunately this year he was off duty and the Deputy Len Murray, not related, was more amiable to having a good time. During the week I was on holiday the staff and anyone else who could help had been clearing out ward 9 on the ground floor. It was due for a face lift. As a result we had our bed allocation increased from 80 to 100. All the other wards took their share of ward 9 patients. Ted had booked Christmas and New Year off so he didn't have to cope with the disruption. We took this opportunity to make some changes in the hope that we could persuade Ted to keep them on when he returned. We intended to use the excuse of extra patients to deal with to make our adjustments. The changes were largely student driven and Len just went along with it.

Using some of the furniture from the cleared ward we sectioned off parts of the large dormitory into units of 8 or 10 beds, doing away with the regimented rows. We managed to get lockers for many of the beds so patients could have some personal items with them. The 6 side rooms which had been used to store junk were cleared and made into nice bedrooms with locker and wardrobe in each. The day room was fully utilised with tables and comfy chairs laid out in a random order, covering all of Ted's, prize, polished wooden floor. This would be a major problem when he returned. We took the 24" T.V from ward 9 and replaced our 14". Putting it into the games room where it could be actually watched. We were a bit cluttered with extra furniture on a temporary basis which didn't please the ward maid, and the dining room had more tables which made meal times a bit harder, but on the whole we managed and knuckled down to making Christmas and New Year a very happy one for our Patients.

Christmas shopping was a stressful experience with limited income. I always tried to get presents which were out of the ordinary. No socks or gloves or hats. For my Dad who was a pools and racehorse enthusiast, I got a form book. For my Mother who was a housewife who enjoyed cooking, I go a' days gone by' cookery book. For Annette, who was into Cliff Richard, I got a book about the background work to putting on his shows and making records. James, my best mate, qualified for a Dictaphone. He frequently had ideas he wanted to follow up when we were together but never had a pen or notebook.

During my time at the Benedict Clinic, I became infatuated with a SEN (State Enrolled Nurse), June, who whilst being a lot older than me, I was very fond of her and deep within me I knew I fancied her too. I bought her a quality necklace which I hoped would impress her. I wanted to ask her out. This was my courting strategy.

Early one afternoon, having established that June was on duty, I made way to the Clinic to present her with this fantastic necklace. It was only whilst on the walk to the Clinic that I began to ask myself some important questions. I knew she was divorced some time ago so she was free, but did she wear jewellery? I thought I had seen a necklace around her neck before but I wasn't sure. Even so, would she like this necklace? And whilst it was expensive to me, it might be cheap rubbish to her. I began to wish I had gone for the safe Chocolates. But then would she be on a diet? Oh my God! I don't actually know what I'm doing here. My nervousness increased as I approached the building.

I entered the lobby. Took out the box and examined the necklace again. I liked it. I would soon find out if June liked it. Deep breath and in we go. Nell Gleeson, a fellow student classmate approached. She was a big Girl. 16 stone of enthusiastic woman pounced on me shouting Merry Christmas Liam! She planted a big sloppy kiss directly onto my lips. When I was released from the crushing embrace, I enquired as to the whereabouts of June. I was directed to the day room.

I opened the entrance door. A significant group of people were gathered. All of them appeared to have drinks and I was offered a glass of wine as I moved further into the room. Beyond the main body of people and facing everyone stood a smart looking gentleman who I didn't recognise, the Unit Sister Mary Lunt, the Deputy Charge Harry Oldman and June. It was obvious that something was going to be said by one of the group, perhaps some sort of award ceremony. I excused myself to the front, quickly presented my gift, hurriedly said Merry Christmas. June thanked me with a smile and a look of surprise as I retired to blend in with the spectators again. The man I didn't know started speaking to the group

"Well thank you everyone for coming to this celebration. For those of you who don't know me, I am Dr. Morgan from Whiston Hospital. It's a pleasure to be here and meet all of you. June thought it would be nice to have this little gathering, to be amongst her friends and colleagues on this very special occasion. I know how much the work here means to June and how important you all are to her. Likewise I've invited many of my friends and colleagues from Whiston to join us here to celebrate our Engagement. June is a wonderful Lady and the love of my life —"

My heart sunk. My Mouth went dry. And I was deeply embarrassed. June had not yet opened the gift box but had set it down on a table next to her with other gifts which I had only just noticed. I couldn't bear to stay any longer. I walked briskly out of the building avoiding another attack by the massive Miss Gleeson. To make things worse, I'd put a note inside the gift box.

"June. I hope you don't mind but I wished to give you something special this Christmas. During my time at the Clinic you were very kind and supportive and I truly appreciated it. Working with you and getting to know you was a lovely experience. You have a lovely personality and I became very fond of you. Have a wonderful Christmas. If you're agreeable, I would very much like to treat you to a meal or even just a social evening. I really love your company. Lots of love. Liam. XXXX."

Oh my God. What on earth will she think of me? Giving her a date proposal at her engagement party! I didn't bloody know! She didn't ever mention a boyfriend. All the conversations we had. Not once did she mention a boyfriend. She told me about her divorce, her car, her holidays, and tastes in food, clothes and all about her family. Every bloody thing except a boyfriend! And what about the necklace? Half a week's wage. Will she give it back to me? It's probably gone now. Perhaps she will be too embarrassed to talk to me about it; or too angry

All the way back to my room I was so angry with myself. How could I have been so stupid1 I never heard from June again. I never got the necklace back. Soon after this fiasco, June left to live with her Doctor. They got married in April.

Meanwhile back at the ward, another woman entered the arena. Vera, the ward maid. She may have been in her late 30s or early 40s, not easy to tell. Vera was a bit of a tease. She did a lot of flirting and liked male attention. Despite her apparent age she was reasonably well formed. She had died bronze hair which was thinner than it should have been. Perhaps the colouring was intended to disguise this fact. Her face couldn't be described as pretty, but her bubbly personality made you like her. She had a nice body though. The Ward Maid uniform tended to enhance her shape. It was a pale blue, one piece overall, zipped full length down the front. Our Vera didn't wear a bra because the actual shape of her breasts and nipples were abundantly obvious. Her waste curved in and then fanned out to enhance, by means of the tight fit, the very shapely bottom and thighs. Interestingly, there was never any sign of a "knickers line", a fatal flaw of many tightly fitted garments. She didn't ware tights. Her lower legs were muscly, but the thighs appeared firm and smooth. She was required to ware flat shoes, but I suspected that heels would have accentuated her legs more. Not that I noticed of course.

At break times Vera would conduct her usual flirting techniques with the men around the table; patting and stroking heads, perhaps the odd hug. She would often make suggestive remarks or wiggle enticingly. The Women hated her. On one occasion she went a little further with me, though what I did to encourage her I'll never know. She sat on my lap, turned in the same direction as me so that her legs were over the top of mine. She joked with the others about my being aroused. I laughed it off, but I was actually being aroused. She wiggled her bottom and it felt good. I placed my hands on her thighs and stroked them. It was lovely. Nobody was taking any notice. This was just Vera messing around. I took advantage of this and pressed myself hard against her so she was in no doubt that I fancied her. She changed her motion from a wiggle to up and down. I almost come. She stood up laughing and left. It took a few minute for me to settle back to normal status.

Somewhat shell shocked I returned to ward duties. I thought that was it. A bit of sex play then on with the job. I couldn't have been more wrong. I had just finished the bed making round with one of the girls. Walking past one of the side rooms with the linen trolley I was swept in. Vera clutched me like a prize and kissed me seductively. In a flash she had pulled me onto the bed on top of her. Again I was aroused and the passionate kissing lasted a minute or so before I pulled away. I suggested we were taking a big risk of discovery here. I asked her to meet me in the empty ward when she finished at 1pm. She eagerly agreed and I asked for my dinner break at that time. All systems go. I just couldn't get her off my mind now and the flirtatious smiles and touches continued throughout the morning.

At 1pm. I made my way downstairs to the empty ward. Fortunately the heating was still on. I stood by one of the large sash windows and looked out into the grounds. I heard the door open followed by quick female steps. Trying not of appear too eager I continued to stare through the window. Her arms wrapped around my waste and squeezed tight. I felt her breasts pressing into my back. The vice like grip was released accompanied by a sexy groan. I turned and engaged her lips softly. I had hoped to slow her down with the gentle approach, but she was on a mission, and I was it . . . The padded rooms still contained beds. They had been forgotten in the clearance. It was to one of these that we quickly migrated. I was invited to unzip the overall dress. I began to ease it down. She held me at arm's length so I could take in the unfolding view. Then for what seemed like an eternity, disaster struck. The zip jammed at the half way point. As I struggled to rectify the problem we both burst into laughter. That eased the tension. The zip freed and we were back in business. The reason for the absence of a knickers line became clear. She didn't wear any. Beneath the snugly fitted overall our Vera was naked.

Rolling back onto the bed she pulled me with her. Skilfully she helped me out of my clothes until we were both as nature intended. This encounter was frantic. No foreplay was required. Increasingly sensual kissing gave way to almost violent screaming intercourse culminating in explosive orgasms for both of us. Trying to be a bit romantically calm afterwards didn't seem to matter so much. Vera was happily satisfied and ready to go. It was like I imagined being with a prostitute might be like. To be honest though, I wasn't objecting. I knew instinctively that no relationship was on offer, just sex. I hoped there would be more. There was no indication one way or the other that this would be the case. We parted with a simple kiss and a final feel of her bum. I returned to duty after a quick snack and tried to focus on the work at hand, but it was impossible.

CHAPTER 23

Christmas and New Year celebrations went well on the wards. Vera was on holiday she did visit the ward a few times to tease us, remarkably even with her husband in tow. I felt embarrassed for him. He just put up with it, even looking disinterested.

One evening about eight O'clock I was relaxing in my room listening to Gustav Holst Planet suite. There was a knock at the door. I opened it to see Vera, smiling brightly and holding a feather duster in her hand. She wiggled her duster in the region of my groin.

Hello Liam. Is there anything you want dusting off that hasn't been used for a while?'

Her free hand pushed my chest and I eased back into the room. The door closed and I was firmly kissed and hooked like a fish onto the Vera sex line. I pulled her to me and explored her bum. This time I detected knickers so it would take a few seconds longer to get down to business. I unzipped the back of her one piece dress and assisted its' fall' to the floor. The trip to the bed was swift and the black bra and knickers were soon removed along with my own clothes. I kissed her hard and continued to kiss my way down to her fanny. She had shaved the area so the vaginal lips stood proud and inviting to the touch. I thought about licking her out but decided to use fingers instead. My lips returned to her nipples as I inserted two fingers into her hot wet fanny and began to manipulate the internal muscular waves. As she got more excited I returned to kissing her lips and tongues became involved too. We rolled over and Vera was on top. We were both ready. She eagerly mounted me like a horse and literally bounces up and down and began screaming. The Music by chance became punchier as I too began shouting in orgasmic spasms. The description of 'Earth moving' seemed appropriate at this time as we took every single ounce of energy from each other. The eruption over, Vera bit my chin and ear quite hard. Her final romantic words were.

"I want to shag you to death then fucking eat you, you big sexy bastard!" I wasn't sure what the correct response was to that, so I said, "Would you like a cup of tea instead"?

We both collapsed in a heap and laughed our way into a more relaxed state. The Planet Suite would never seem quite the same again

Mr. Murray returned in the New Year and as predicted was not impressed by all the changes to his ward and the routines. We managed to retain the day room set up because of the amount of furniture we had. The dormitory though was returned to military style

Again, the lockers and partitions were taken to storage. He didn't seem to notice the new T.V. arrangements, so that stayed in place.

As Vera returned to work, I went on leave. I spent this time at home. I thought I'd better reacquaint myself with the family, having been obsessed with the job for some considerable time. Apart from my time at Rainnhill being a significant effect of my life, my upbringing was also an important element of who I am. I was born in Huyton. Living in Page Moss all of my life, my experiences and personality were moulded by 50s and 60s Liverpool. I loved the City and knew it very well. I was a bit of an odd ball in that I had no interest in sport. All the other lads I knew were either Liverpool or Everton football supporters. I found it all rather boring. My main objection I suppose was that few if any of the team members belonged to the City. Some were even foreigners, which I thought made a mockery of the game. The Clubs I saw simply as big rip off businesses draining all the money they could out of the swearing, spitting supporters. As a member of the St. John Ambulance I was obliged to attend some football matches. I must admit to enjoying many of the games. The fans could be a bit of a handful at times but on the whole I enjoyed it. I preferred cinema or garden fete duties. My roll was mainly in training and I enjoyed helping with recruiting events. I regarded my membership more as a hobby. There were many dedicated members who devoted all their spare time to the cause and I had a great deal of respect for them.

The family home was in a terrace of white Council Houses on Liverpool Road, near Page Moss shops. It was a nice comfortable house with front and rear gardens, coal fires and 50s furniture. We wanted for not much at all seemingly, but as a boy I was aware of the use of Freemans Catalogues and a weekly visit from Mr. Connor who collected loan repayments. There was also a Trafford Catalogue in use and it was this that I also used from time to time.

There was the weekly visit from the Parish Priest, Fr. Walsh. Money was also given to him, which he probably spent later in the Catholic club on whiskey. We had relatives in various parts of the City, but visits between members of the family were rare so I didn't get to know any of them very well.

My upbringing and that of my Sister was strict. Any transgressions on my part were punished with my Fathers belt. In later years that may have been frowned upon, but I think it was thought of as good practice by Irish descendant families. Anyway, I didn't grow up with any lasting effects, as far as I know. I don't think my Sister was treated in the same way. She tended to be 'kept in' for a number of days depending on what was done.

My Father, Ben Parry was a paint blender and worked in a factory in Kirkby. At this time he was 48yrs old. Also born in Liverpool, he served in the Merchant Navy in the War on Atlantic Convoys. He never talked about it, but I know he once spent several days in a lifeboat after being torpedoed and almost died. He and Mum had never gone on holiday anywhere. Dad had health problems due to working with chemicals. His chest was a mess and he also smoked.

Mum; Maureen, was born in Ireland in a place called Balbriggan, not far from Dublin. I understand that the residents there were not fond of the British. Mum was a dedicated Housewife and Mother. Her world was the house and family and Huyton Village for the shops. She had no desire to explore any further. She was 4'11" slightly plump and had an inbuilt dynamo. She always wore a pinney. I never saw her without one.

My Sister, Annette was 22 at this time. Annette was slim and very energetic. She was attractive and went through boyfriends like a combined harvester through wheat. She had a bubbly personality and could remember all the jokes I couldn't. We got on well and liked to spend time together whenever possible. Annette was a hairdresser and worked in Prescot shopping centre

On the first Monday of my week at home Annette and I decided to do to 'The Pool' to see what was on for the sales. Annette didn't work Sunday or Monday. It was raining so the bike was not a consideration. We decided to go on the train, a rare treat. We set off at 11 o'clock and walked via Twig Lane up to Roby Station. On the way we passed the park and St Aloysius Church which I had now fallen out with. I liked this area with the different styles of housing. Crossing Western Avenue we climbed the moderate hill up past St. Barts Church and the bigger Victorian Houses, the garage complex and into the station subway to the Ticket Office. On the way we shared Annette's little umbrella and the constant playing about with it, pulling from one to the other, including doing our own rendition of "Singing in the rain" along one of the gutters, meant we may as well have left it at home. On arrival at the station the rain had stopped. We sat like two wet cabbages on the platform seat, steaming a little as the sun came out until the drab looking train clattered into the station.

The doors opened on the front carriage and Annette boarded with several other passengers. I quickly ran to the second carriage and boarded, then watched through the connecting door as the train set off and Annette anxiously looked around for her brother. When she seemed to resign herself to the fact that I had not got on the train, I sneaked up to the seat behind her and whispered into her ear. I received a smack for that. The sun was shining now and the carriage was warm so we were able to dry out and get more comfortable. As we left Edge Hill and began to descend between the high cuttings, towards Lime St. I couldn't help being in awe at the enormous fete of those labourers excavating these massive cuttings by hand all those years ago.

We arrived at Lime St. Station. I liked this building. It had lots of character. It was always full of interesting people and lots of things going on all the time. I was always jealous of those boarding the London Trains from platform one. The mixed smells of coffee, doughnuts, bacon, perfumes and diesel entertained the senses. The noise of engines, horns and whistles, punctuated by the sound of tiny wheels on suit cases and peoples voices bombarded the ears. The eyes feasted upon the contrasts of ironwork, window displays and advertising boards, clothing and hair styles. Shafts of sunlight pierced the scene from the high arched glass roof and provided momentary warm patches to bath in. This was the world under one roof.

We left the station to Skelhorne St. At the bottom of the hill was a greasy spoon café, 'the punch and Judy'. The food was average and the prices low, but the main reason for going there was the legs. Not legs of Lamb, but legs of ladies. You see much of the seating was below street level and afforded a wonderful view of the ever flowing parade of mini skirted girls passing by. Annette was of course fully aware of this, and as she was facing uphill, I was given advanced warning of any potentially good ones about to come into view. However, even that distraction didn't quite make up for the poor quality catering tea they served.

After dinner it was Paddy's Market where we purchased only once, from the fantastic nuts stall. I liked Cashews, Anne, salted peanuts. Next stop Lewis's department store, entering below the statue of what Annette described as 'Donkey Dick'. Here she bought a pair of shoes in the sale to add to the other forty pairs she had strewn all over her bedroom. On route around the ground floor she tried lots of different perfumes which soon became overpowering and indistinguishable one from another, but she was happy. I bought a Parker pen which would make me that much more intelligent. After a quick exploration of the other floors we left for Church Street and Marks and Spencer's. I liked M&S because the assistants tended to be the best looking of all in the City shops. There was one I fancied in particular and I hung around her section for a while. This must have seemed a little strange to Annette because it was the lingerie section.

Then we got a cab to the Philharmonic Pub, one of Liverpool's classic establishments. Fine ironwork with gold plate, beautiful chandeliers solid oak pub furniture in richly decorated Victorian style rooms. One of the most well-known features being the Men's toilets which have very distinctive urinals. Annette of course had to go in, as many female visitors do to see what all the fuss is about. You can sit in any public room on quality leather seats and drink fine wine at rip off prices and maybe see someone famous from the classical music set. The Philharmonic hall is just across the road. Annette let it be known that I was Vaughn Halger, a world renowned conductor. Where she got the name from I don't know, but it was intended to get us some free drinks I think. In the event it got some Japanese visitors quite excited and I signed some autographs and featured in a photographic frenzy. I overheard a Liverpudlian lady nearby telling a friend she had heard of me.

It was time to return from our adventures. At Lime St. we looked at the departure times. Our train from platform 14 was leaving in a matter of minutes. Hurrying through the checkpoint we dashed for the nearest door, boarded and flopped down into our seats. The whistle blew. The train left exactly on time. The front half, our carriage, remained it was only at this point that we noticed that no one else was in our carriage. With some embarrassment we alighted again and asked the man with the whistle when the next train was. Fortunately it was only 20 minutes and only the front two carriages would be leaving the platform. Right got it.

CHAPTER 24

Final Examinations month. This was an anxious time, not least because it had been delayed because of some administrative problem. The Tutors tried to put a positive spin on it, saying we had more time to prepare. The fact was we just wanted to get on with it. Normally we would have sat our exams at our own school, but it was decided to amalgamate the exams for a number of Hospitals and everyone was to sit the exams at Prestwich Hospital. This was an extra worry. At our own school we knew where everything was, we were 'at home' and comfortable with the surroundings. Now it was to be a visit to a strange hospital and outside our comfort zone.

The sorely anticipated day arrived, a Tuesday morning in February 1971. There had been an overnight flurry of snow and the coach was late. The exam was due to commence at 10am. The coach was due to pick us up at 8am. It arrived at 8.45. The journey would normally take 30 minutes, but it was poor weather with slow traffic and hold up's. We arrived at 9.45 and hurriedly shuffled through the snowy car park to the school entrance. Once inside we were met by a Prestwich Tutor who announced that everyone was delayed and the examination was put back to 1pm. We were to be provided with lunch.

Several students, myself included, found this very stressful. Toilet visits increased and very little conversation took place. It was like waiting for a dental appointment. We were given free lunch vouchers for the staff canteen. I didn't feel much like eating until I got to the counter. The display of choices and the wonderful smells enticed my troubled brain to give priority to food for now. I sat with a petite, pretty student nurse called Millie. She was from Grange Hall in Southport and very nervous. She started reciting lists of things from her memory like facial nerves and types of medication. I gently stopped her; reassuring her that she had done 3 years study and surely must be ready by now. I asked her to tell me about Grange Hall and how she had chosen this career. This took her mind off lists. As we left the dining room for the school, I kissed her on the cheek together with a gentle hug and wished her good luck. She half cried, half smiled and thanked me, squeezing my hand.

The exam went well, although I think I may have waffled a bit on a few answers. Fortunately for the practical section we worked in twos I had the good fortune to have a partner from my own class, Luke Granger. Luke was a big lad, about 15stone. He was always in trouble for being sloppily dressed. He hated ties and often wore trainers. His shirts were often pink instead of white and he coloured his hair in quite loud colours. He also wore various colours of glasses. He had a fat, jolly, face, a good sense of humour and he got on very well with the ladies. He is Homosexual. He knew his stuff and he was great with the patients, especially the more vulnerable of them. My camp friend prevented me from making some fundamental nervous mistakes. He wasn't nervous at all. He had a 'what will be, will be' attitude.

Exams over, we made our way to the coach. I caught a glimpse of Millie; we waved at each other and smiled. She mouthed a "thank you". The coach never quite made it to the hospital gates. Sister Morgan stopped it at the Black Horse pub next to the Hospital. We didn't need an explanation. We all piled out and commenced a wild and wonderful party. It lasted from 4.30 'till 11pm. By 8pm we were joined by colleagues who didn't want to be left out. This was before we knew the results. That celebration would be one to remember. During this event we decided to have our graduation party in the Adelphi Hotel in Liverpool and a club night out in the City. The results were due in a couple of weeks.

I was now allocated to the Occupational Therapy unit whist awaiting my results. This was a place where patients did rather menial work posing as occupational therapy. Work such as painting lead soldiers, which did require some skill. In fact I enjoyed doing that myself, but not all day every day. Other work included basketry and sorting goods for packaging. The sort of things nobody else wanted to do. The Hospital sought contracts for this type of work. The problem, to me, was that this sort of repetitive work was not serving any purpose which was beneficial to the patients. It could well be just as institutionalising as sitting around. No real stimulus. Anyway, I hoped one day to be senior enough to change things for the better. This post was combined with the newly formed 'Community Nursing Team'. We were now starting to discharge patients to Intermediate Care in the community. The days of the large Psychiatric Hospitals were numbered. Community Care was now seen to be the way forward. At this stage we were not entirely convinced of the wisdom of this strategy, but ours is not to reason why etc . . . .

As a start we had refurbished one of the former Doctors houses on the main road to experiment with the project. We also had allocated to us a Council Flat in Prescot, with the same idea. This didn't go down well with local residents. It's possible they feared that they would be raped or murdered in their beds by these 'Mad Men.' Our job was to reassure these people that the two very meek and elderly men would hardly be noticeable and would be supervised all the time. We did have to close the flat after only eight weeks due to local hostility. The poor old blokes were subjected to abuse and vandalism. Some folk decided they were "Homos," which they were not. It became unsafe for them and put their treatment back months.

The other Half Way House was not part of the general community and was therefore able to function well with some small success over time.

The Graduation Party at the Adephi was great and we ended up in a club called 'The Iron Door.' I didn't last the night. Too many Martinis knocked me out and I only remember waking up in someone's house, in Everton, the next morning. My Guardian was a male nurse from Fazakerly Hospital who apparently rescued me from the roof of a taxi cab demanding to be taken to London. Together with a few other wayward nurses, I was offered breakfast, which remarkably, I was able to eat and keep down. Others were not so lucky. I didn't know anyone else in the house. They were all from Fazakerly Hospital. Some had never heard of Rainhill and thought I was rambling. Eventually I found my way back to Rainhill via various buses having thanked my host profusely for his kindness.

Later in the month I received the sad news that Vera, my seductress, had died. It appeared that she had been diagnosed with terminal cancer last April. Her fate was sealed and she knew it. Her last fling seemed to be aimed at as many younger men as possible to make her feel alive for a while longer. Some of the girls were quite scathing of her behaviour, even describing her as 'a slag'. Well I don't know. I wondered how I would behave or what I would want to do if I knew I would die within months. I reserved judgement. As with any staff member who had died, we had the whip round and a delegation was requested from managers to attend the funeral. I decided I would go

As was normal practice at the time I put in my application for the post of Staff Nurse within the Hospital. I just had to wait for a decision now. Many of my classmates applied to other hospitals and some were looking to do the extra 18 months General Nurse training, which was also a consideration of mine.

CHAPTER 25

I didn't have to wait long after passing my exams before being offered a Staff Nurse post at Rainhill. I was to be part of the newly formed Community Nursing Team. The job entailed setting up the new scheme to help patients live in the Community, with support from the Hospital. Liaising with other agencies such as Local Councils and Social Services, to help patients gain as much independence as possible. I was also to be available to cover hospital ward duties in emergencies or holiday and absent cover. I was nervous about it. The project was new and everything was starting from scratch. In the light of the previous attempt at settling two men into a flat in Prescot and the problems that entailed, I was wandering what might lay ahead for this scheme

In the meantime, I was invited to attend the funeral of Vera Macintosh, my former seductress and that of several others I believe. The service and burial at Peasley Cross was attended only by close family members and a few Hospital staff. That was a sad thing. During the life overview given by the Vicar, I was quite surprised at the things Vera had done in her 46 years. She had done quite well at school and had a good Civil Service job with passports and immigration in Liverpool. She later worked for Huyton Council as the Deputy Town Clerk and then joined her Husband's Car repair business taking care of the accounts until the business failed a few years ago. It was at this point that she came to work at Rainhill as a cleaner. Such a sad story and a waste of talent. Vera had one teenage daughter at the funeral who was obviously devastated. They must have got on well. The Husband seemed quite controlled and I suspect there wasn't much between them for some time. Two Brothers and two drivers carried the coffin. It made me think of what happened between us. It was really a cry for help and support but perhaps sought in the wrong way. During our encounters the thought that she would have a separate life of her own, which was just like anyone else's; family, friends, a home, never entered my mind. She was purely a sex object. I didn't know how I should feel about that. After the funeral there was the obligatory reception which I didn't attend. That phase was now closed.

Back at work I attended a meeting to discuss the finer points of getting the Community Nursing Project off the ground. There was a lot of talking but I got the impression that real enthusiasm was lacking. The Politicians and Pen Pushers were on a course to close large Psychiatric Hospitals and disperse everyone into small hostels or Community Projects. Fine on paper, but those of us doing the job now considered that things were being rushed. We were assured that the process would be measured and carefully considered at every stage. It would take a number of years to complete and our jobs were secure for several years yet. Such major changes made everyone nervous. When a Politician assures you of something you know it's not true.

For two Months I worked hard as part of a small team to get the project off the ground. The utilisation of the old Doctors houses at the front of the Hospital worked quite well. There was a married couple who had been patients for some years. In the Hospital they had to live separately, we didn't have mixed wards. Now, with support, they were able to benefit from a rehabilitation period and were given a Council Flat in St. Helens. Still requiring support, they were able to reconstruct part of their lives again and live together as a couple. That was very satisfying.

Other than that it was hard work, attending endless meetings with a variety of officials, doing presentations to Local Councils and Social Services Departments, the Police and Charity organisations. We had lots of moral support but little in the way of practical help. The Public were still nervous about having so called 'Lunatics' living near them. Part of the solution was to acquire large houses to use as Community Hostels, which had to be staffed. The scheme became fragmented and difficult to manage but presumably it was a cheaper option to the large Victorian Hospitals.

I suppose we were institutionalised ourselves to a large extent. Having been used to having everything we needed on one site, we now had to fend for ourselves. We had to fight for everything we needed; account for everything we used and everything we did. We performed fewer nursing duties and much more administrative duties. This wasn't what I signed up for. Many of us were becoming disenchanted with the job. I began to look to fresh pastures.

However, not everything was doom and gloom. My duties were shared between the Community Team and the Hospital. As I wasn't attached to a particular ward at this time I was able to move around and gather support for a summer sports day. I contacted other hospitals and Day Care Centres in the North West and together with a member of staff from each location to act as an organising committee; we began to plan the event. Shared funding was agreed and the venue would be Winnick Hospital, Warrington.

Whilst all this was going on, I was summoned home one Saturday morning. My Dad had some news he wanted to share with me. It was a nice morning so I dusted off my trusty motor bike and had a very pleasant, wind—swept, ride to Page Moss. When I arrived there was an obvious air of excitement. With a cheeky smile I asked Annette if she was pregnant. I received the customary smack on the shoulder. I was introduced to her latest conquest who must have been a little un-nerved by my comment, I hadn't noticed him. He was introduced as JP.

'Are you a Magistrate?' I enquired, another smack on the shoulder.

'He likes to be called JP' was Annette's explanation.

Emphasising the letters theme I responded.

'Well I'm LP, JP, and OK? I hold the record. See what I did there?'

Another slap on the shoulder, unabated I continued.

'RA,' then before being hit again I ran into the street shouting 'CU'. I couldn't run for laughing and was soon caught, wrestled to the ground and my hair ruffled. The last response from Annette was 'FO!' Still laughing I continued.

'U2'

'You can't use numbers' Annette pointed as if scoring a point against me. I submitted.

'OL. You win. Now what's the big surprise?'

Arm in arm we returned to the house. JP looked on bemused and possibly confused. For the first time I looked him over. He looked like a skinny John Lennon. Now I smelled food. A buffet was laid out in the living room and a few relatives from various areas of the Pool sat around nibbling or holding cups of tea. Dad beckoned me to the kitchen.

'I've won some money on the Pools' he announced with a slightly quivering voice. 'Not the jackpot, but a tidy sum'.

'Well that's fantastic, congratulations. Is that why we have visitors all of a sudden?' I was told they were invited to the party. For the first time in their lives my parents were able to live a little, splash out a bit. I was happy for them.

I asked had they thought what they would do with the unexpected windfall. Mum joined us.

'We're going to see family in Ireland aren't we Mrs?'

He gave Mum a hug. She began to sob. Annette came in to nosey. Dad proudly announced that he was able to do something for us at last. First, both our catalogue accounts had been cleared. Annette was booked in for a full course of driving lessons and would have a mini on passing. I was handed a set of car keys. My car was outside, but there was a condition. For the first time in their lives, my parents were to have a holiday away. They wanted to visit relatives in Ireland and they hoped I could drive them there. I was stunned for a moment. Annette obviously knew what I was in for. She took my hand and led me outside in company with Mum and Dad and JP. There were four cars outside. Annette took the keys and asked me to walk to the car I thought was mine. I walked to the Ford Cortina. "No"!, then to the Wolsey 1300. "No"! There was only a Mini and a Vauxhall 101 left to choose from. Assuming that perhaps Annette and I were to have matching cars I went for the mini. 'No!' Unbelievably it was the 101. The biggest one of the bunch in Jade Green with lots of chrome trims, a 1966 model. Annette handed back the keys. I sat in on the front bench seat. The gears were column which I had only seen in American Films. It seemed massive. The bonnet seemed as large as a football field. The leather seats were comfortable and the five people now inside fitted comfortably. It was fantastic. After the initial excitement, the visiting relatives left and I offered to take Mum, Dad, Annette and JP to Knowsley Safari Park which was only a couple of miles away. We had never been there.

So, after a quick snack and 10 minutes looking through the manual, we all piled into the car and set off for the Park. We would have considered it quite expensive normally, but as Dad was flush it wasn't a problem this time. We were all impressed with it, never having been up close to wild animals before. The Staff on the gates at each section was armed and had smart safari uniforms with large brimmed hats. Everything went well except in the Chimps Area. Here we lost the windscreen wiper rubbers and the Radio Ariel became a work of art. After a very enjoyable hour we stopped in the rest area at the end to have a cuppa. We thought we would return this summer for the Sea Lions and whatever else we had missed this time. The best bit for all of us was watching all the other cars being raided by the Chimps.

The car was lovely to drive. At last I would be able to say a fond fair well to the old Bike. We stopped at a nearby garage to replace the wiper blades and Ariel. Then home for tea. I dropped Annette and JP off at the Blue Bell Pub on my way to show off the car to James. All his family were at home, including Sandra. They were impressed. Later I took James and Sandra for a ride to New Brighton, a mistake really because I felt like a spare part. The old saying 'two's company,' . . . . came to mind. Still I just enjoyed the driving. The really lovely thing which happened was that both of them now re affirmed their desire to have me as best man for their wedding. For my acceptance I was given a kiss, from Sandra, not from James. I enquired if James wanted me to do the honeymoon for him if he was busy.

'Sod off' was the polite response.

Late in the evening I drove to the Hospital and parked so that I could see the car from my window. Several times before I went to bed, I looked out at it glistening under the lamp light.

CHAPTER 26

April. 1971. After many meetings, thousands of words in reports, begging and manipulating; the Winwick Sports Day was upon us. Everyone was excited about the project. Both patients and staff would take part in a variety of track and field events. As our coach approached Winwick, one of their patients must have decided he was a Traffic Policeman. He was standing at a major "T" junction nearby directing traffic. Remarkably, everyone seemed to be obeying his directions. The coach turned into the site. The buildings were similar to ours but the external spaces were much more open.

We were greeted by senior staff members and directed to the assembly area where refreshments had been laid on. Other groups began to arrive and it soon became a large noisy gathering with lots of introductions, handshakes and even some polite kissing. The events got under way and the day was a tremendous success. No one was lost or injured and everyone had great fun. During the afternoon I was delighted to see someone I didn't expect to meet again; Millie from the final exams day. Actually she saw me first. A voice from behind me shouted, 'Liam?' I turned and immediately hugged her together with a kiss on the cheek. Apart from brief moments of distraction we spent the rest of the afternoon together. She had come alone with only two patients from Grange Hall. We just chatted and enjoyed the day. I agreed to visit her one day at Grange Hall where she was now a resident Staff Nurse.

When the event was over and the prizes were handed out and speeches made, we gathered together our charges and made ready to depart. Prestwich Hospital was overall champions of the day. Thereafter it would become an Annual Event. Before I left I gave Millie another hug and kiss and waved her off in her car. The now Deputy Charge Nurse, Barry Hartley tried to encourage a pub stop on the way back but he was over ruled by the Chief. It was a tiring day anyway and I was glad to get back to my room to put my feet up.

A week later I found myself on the road to Southport to see Millie at Grange Hall. Today was a relaxation day before the busy period leading up to the wedding of James and Sandra. I hadn't quite made my mind up what the situation was to be with Millie. She was a girl with a sweet personality, slightly on the plump side and always seemed to be smiling except when taking exams. I suspected that at this time Millie may have wished to develop a relationship. For myself I wasn't sure yet. I didn't know why.

Having missed a turning several times I arrived at the Hospital. Compared with Rainhill it was microscopic. I was conducted to the staff room and given a cup of coffee. Millie made her entrance looking bright and bubbly. She had changed her hair style from straight to tightly curled. It made her look younger. A little more make up was evident than I had seen before. She wore a cream dress decorated with flowers, very 50s and a belt tied off at the front. The hemline was just above the knee. I thought the tights a bit too dark compared with her skin colour. Nursing shoes completed the outfit.

A nervous laugh punctuated her conversation with me. I felt a bit like I was chatting to a schoolgirl at times but I put that down to nerves. I thought the best thing to do was to get going. A drive might settle her a bit. She linked my arm walking to the car. She was very impressed with it. I opened the door and she sat in, telling me how nice it was. I took Millie to the Abbey cinema on West Derby Road, for the matinee. The film was 'Love Story' which may have given the wrong impression of my intentions at this time. Millie cried a lot during this film and secretly so did I. It was such an emotional tear jerker.

After the film we went walking in Newsham Park. We held hands and enjoyed talking and laughing but I couldn't find a romantic mood within myself for some reason. I think Millie was keen and perhaps she was awaiting my first move. I felt I would have been taking advantage of her innocence. We had tea in a local café and I took her back to the Hall.

We sat in the lounge and I found the words to let her down gently. I told her she was a lovely girl and I enjoyed her company very much. That she had a lovely personality and the ability to do very well in her career. I asked if she would be happy to simply be friends for now. She agreed, but I'm sure she wanted more and was still hopeful that there was a chance that there would be. I could never work out what happened in this case. I liked her, found her attractive, but just couldn't go any further.

I left questioning myself for some time afterwards. We did arrange to meet again, but it never happened. Perhaps an opportunity missed. I would never know.

Now I had several visits with James and Sandra to discuss wedding arrangements. Annette was not to be a bridesmaid as Sandra wanted her own friends to have the honour. I could understand that, Annette however was disappointed to hear the news. In private meetings, James and I decided that Sandra would have a Horse and Carriage and limousines would transport other guests. The Church would be St Luke's and the reception would be decided by John who wanted it to be his pet project. We then had joint meetings with Sandra' and James' and Parents to discuss flowers, dresses, number of guests, food and invitations. Jobs were divided between everyone. We then had frequent meetings to discuss progress or lack of it in some cases. Jane and Mirriame were off on mega spending sprees; John was planning routes and timings for limousines and sorting a photographer. Sandra's Father had died 3 years ago. Her Mother Julia lived in the Family home, a Council house in Woolton, Liverpool. She wasn't well off, so the Cookes insisted on financing the whole wedding. I'm sure that must have been a big relief to Julia. Mirriame was to organise the reception catering and of course John was co-coordinator of the whole operation. Everything was required to be done with Royal Navy precision. Everyone was now looking forward to the big day. For me it would be the big two weeks. After the wedding weekend I had the family holiday in Ireland to look forward to, such an exciting time. I couldn't wait.

CHAPTER 27

This Month, work was a background thing. Setting up the Community Initiative was mainly meetings, paperwork, assessments and supervising the work on newly acquired accommodation for our fledgling adventures into a new independent world. God help them. I was able to use my car quite a lot due to a generous mileage allowance. It was so strange at first driving around for work rather than being in a fixed location. I enjoyed getting around but failed to get any satisfaction from all the official gobbledygook we had to put up with to get anywhere. Often we got nowhere.

The wedding was almost upon us now. I had arranged for two weeks holiday to take in the wedding on the first weekend, followed by the trip to Ireland with the Family. I was looking forward to this holiday very much. The campaign meetings at mission control (Cookes Mansion) under the supervision of John went very well as you would expect with a Navy Officer in charge. Nothing was left to chance. One big secret was kept from everyone the location of the reception. John and Mirriame had arranged it and Mirriame was sworn to secrecy. Even Jane wasn't told.

The wedding was to be at St. Luke's Church at 11am on a Saturday. I took my family to Cooke's mansion at 9.30am. John, James and Jane greeted all the guests who arrived at the house. Most went straight to the Church. By 1015am there must have been 100 special guests at the house and the wine was already flowing. For the first time I was dressed in a posh suit, top hat and tails and I kept looking at myself in any mirror which happened to present itself before me. Poor old James was a nervous wreck and Jane was fussing about everything as you would expect. Still nobody was able to prize the secret of the reception venue out of John or Mirriame. 10.30am. James and I stood in the front garden chatting when Mirriame appeared and kissed us both. I told her that we now knew the venue for the reception and she could now relax and what a great idea it was.

'Who thought of it?' I asked. Mirriame informed me that it was all John's idea, but she wasn't falling for my trickery. She kissed me again and wiggled off into the house.

'Nice try Liam,' was James's response.

2 Rolls Royce Limousines arrived in company with 2 Coaches. There was a lot of difficult manoeuvring in the limited space to get the vehicles sorted and loaded. Just minutes later we all poured out at the Church and filed in to our places as indicated by me and Annette who had promoted herself to church warden for a few minutes. James and myself returned to the front porch for a last smoke before it all kicked off. Quite a crowd of onlookers gathered at the gate awaiting the arrival of the Bride. The sun kindly shone upon us, it was a lovely day. At 11.00am we heard the clip clop of horse's hoofs some distance away. Sandra's Landau was about to arrive so we returned to our seats.

The organist was playing softly in the background. We sat down and James took a few calming deep breaths. When he settled down I asked him had he got the ring. His face paled as he quite calmly told me that I should have it. I looked surprised.

'But why? It's you that's marrying her not me. What do I need the ring for?'

In a slightly angry tone James almost panted.

'You're not bloody serious.' I pulled the little black felt box from my pocket which I had previously emptied. He was visibly relieved until I opened it and pretended to look horrified.

'When I collected it from the jewellers, I just assumed the ring would be in it'

James appeared whiter.

'MUM! There's no bloody ring in the box.

Before Jane executed me I quickly produced the ring. After receiving an Annette type smack on the shoulder the Organ blasted out the introductory chords to 'here comes the Bride' and we all stood up.

Customarily late, Sandra commenced her walk down the aisle at 11.11am. All heads turn to the entrance. I can't see a thing through the crowd. James stares forward, stiff as a board. At last she arrives at the altar. Her Father lifts the veil and a radiant smile greets us, or more likely just James. Sandra looked radiantly beautiful, the best I've ever seen her, but I suppose you'd expect that on a Bride's wedding day. Forgetting for a moment which pocket I've put the ring in, I fiddle for a while and don't find it in any pocket first time around. Trying not to look alarmed I search again, nothing. Now I look around the floor, again trying not to make it obvious. The couple are now at the altar and the ceremony has started. The rules and regs have been announced, nobody has given any reason why they should not be joined and we are on to the vows, still no ring.

'Where the hell is it?' I shout within my head. Then, the thing I have been passing from hand to hand throughout the search is investigated. I open the box. There it is. Phew!

'Do you have the ring?' I'm asked.

With complete composure I hand over the ring.

'I now pronounce you man and wife.'

Rapturous applause follow and the organist blasts out something I don't recognise. The Bridal party go to a side room for the signing of the Register. Then after photographs we escort the Bride and Groom out of the church to the gathered well-wishers and spectators. For the first time I see the wonderful bridal transport, two magnificent, white horses pulling a lavishly decorated Landau. After 45 minutes of photographs, James and Sandra board the carriage and are driven off. The Bridesmaids and immediate family, plus Mirriame and I are ushered into Rolls Limousines and set off for the mystery reception venue. Two Coaches and a Mini Bus follow on behind.

Every few miles we try to guess the venue. We even lay on bets. It becomes obvious that Liverpool is the destination. The popular opinion is the Adelphi. In the event everyone was wrong. 45 minutes after leaving the Church we arrive at the Pier Head. James and Sandra were there to greet us. One of the bridesmaids had a 'blonde moment' by asking how they had got here before us in a horse and cart. After lots of laughter it was explained that the Horse and Carriage had only gone a short distance before the bride and groom transferred to a car for the remainder of the journey. My final incorrect guess for the reception was?, you may have guessed; the' River Room'. However on reflection it wouldn't have accommodated the number of guests. So, where? When John had accounted for everyone he called to us to follow him. A long line of guests followed obediently along the water front and down the bridge to the landing stage. The tide was out so it was very steep. Many of the high heeled ladies removed their shoes to negotiate the incline. Lots of laughter emanated from the crowd as the ladies linked arms in a failed attempt to support each other. Many bums were bruised that day. I asked John if he was hoping to fit us all into his catamaran.

'Not quite' he said with a smile, 'but I must get it down here soon, do you fancy being one of my crew?'

I agreed, but inside I wasn't sure. Then we gain sight of the real venue, 'The Royal Iris', the iconic Liverpool ferry, specially designed for large functions.

Three O'clock. The horn blasts and we set off for a river cruise with commentary and later a dance band would join us for the evening entertainment. The Reception food was laid out in the ballroom. We sailed out to the Mersey Bar and turned for the river again. At this point dinner was served. I was beginning to get a bit nervous. The time for my speech was getting nearer. All too soon my turn had arrived.

'James—Sandra—Family Guests—Ladies and Gentleman. Of all the things I have done in my life so far, this is both the best and the worst moment. The best because I have the honour of being chosen to be best man; worst because I have to make a speech to a few hundred people.

Had I been asked at any time previous to this what special things I would like to experience in my life; skiing, yes? Sky diving, yes. gaining a pilot's licence, yes, walking on the Great Wall of China, yes, seeing the Pyramids, yes, giving a speech to 200 people on board a Mersey Ferry, well not the first thing that would come to mind.

Despite the nerves, I am so very happy to be here on this special occasion.

I have known James since he was knee high to a bull elephant. Our time at school together was great. We would have got GCEs in pranks if there was such a Certificate. We did a lot of overtime due to our sense of humour, not always appreciated by the teachers. We often visited the joke shops to buy whoopee cushions, dog turds, pretend chalk squirty pens, anything to upset the teacher's day. Stink bombs were one of the favourites, although James rarely needed one of them. Nick name farty James. We would go into classes early to swap piles of homework folders between classes, put the dog turds into the girls desks, watch teachers struggle to write on the board with chalk that didn't work. We once informed a class monitor that the classroom had mice and they'd have to wait in the playground until called in. The Teacher sat in an empty room for ages before realising that no one was coming, and then spent ages more trying to find the missing class. We got cained for that stunt. I could go on, but we haven't got time today.

By the time we reached our final year we had learned the error of our ways. James became Head Boy, and I became Head Girl—No—no, Head prefect actually. Thereafter we ruled the school with an iron fist. The staff never stood a chance.

We slipped back a little as teenagers. In the City we would stand looking up at a tall building pointing upwards until a crowd gathered, then leave. We would pretend to carry large panes of glass out of a doorway to see people go around us. In thick fog we would use our car or bike to lead unsuspecting motorists into cul de sacs or even up driveways, then clear off. Using a back pack and tape recorder we would pretend to be radio reporters and interview people about green shield stamps or bus services or whatever was topical at the time. The poor souls actually thought they were on live radio.

Now we are respectable, or at least James is. He now has the beautiful Sandra and I have no one, no one at all. James has deserted me, left me to fend for myself in an unforgiving world. Ahh.

James is now running a clothing wholesale business and I see many of you are already his customers. I'd just like to remind you that he does have some up market clothes too. No, sorry. Of course I'm very proud of my best friend, Very happy to know his family and very impressed by the fabulous Sandra. I've known Sandra for a matter of Months, but already I see a lovely, young ambitious girl who has both beauty and brains, and I'm so jealous. I'd like to assure her that James has now grown up and she can move forward with confidence. Good luck to both of you. All my love, to both of you.

May I also take this opportunity to thank all the Organisers, the Ship's Crew, the Bridesmaids and most of all the Cooke family for making this a special and memorable day?

Ladies and Gentlemen, please stand and raise your glasses, the Bride and Groom." Then moments later, "The Bridesmaids"

Rapturous applause followed, a kiss from Sandra and a joke kiss from James, and at least I hope it was. Then the cutting of the cake and the party slowly took off. The ballroom was cleared and the ferry stopped at Birkenhead to collect the band and singer and a magician. Then the cruise continued into the night. John spent much of his time on the bridge with the captain. He felt at home there. Jane kept telling him off and dragging him back to the guests. The evening went very well, enjoyed by all. At 9pm. We tied up at the Pier Head again. Guests had the opportunity to leave or stay aboard until midnight. Most stayed. Families with children left. The Cooke family and some special guests gathered on the landing stage to see James and Sandra off on their honeymoon. One of the Limousines took them to the airport for a flight to Rome, which James said was Rome antic.

My parents were seen leaving quietly in the background, but spotted by John they were sent home in a taxi. Annette stayed on with me. We danced and laughed together till midnight. The Coaches returned and frustrated drivers tried to scoop up all the tipsy passengers from various parts of the landing stage and bus station. Annette and I joined the Cookes on a Mini Bus and returned home. So ended one of the landmark days.

On Sunday we packed everything for Ireland. We were leaving Monday from Holyhead. James would be in Rome now having lots of sex. Maybe, even some sightseeing.

CHAPTER 28

Everything packed and stowed, family in car. Off we go to Ireland. I've explored North Wales extensively. I frequently took my parents for days out and Wales proved to be their favourite destination. This was our first visit to Anglesey and Holyhead. We didn't have time to visit the Station with the longest name, perhaps on the return journey. After a good rest and a meal on board, we emerged refreshed in the port of Dublin. The biggest problem was getting through Dublin onto the right road. Like any busy City it is not strange driver friendly. After an hour and a half of unwilling exploration of Dublin we were on route to Skerries which was close to Balbriggan, the place of my Mother's birth. We arrived early evening at the Guesthouse of Connie Monroe. Connie was quite small and plump with fiery red curly hair, wonderful smile and a broad Irish accent. She wore a pinney like my mum, and trainers which looked out of place. We were welcomed like long lost friends and immediately given tea to drink. A young lad, possibly a Grandson, took our cases to our rooms. Quite soon after the initial pleasantries we were taken to the dining room and treated to lashings of traditional Irish stew. Before going to bed, Annette and I explored what there was of Skerries, a pleasant little place with a little shopping area in the centre and some cosy pubs, especially along the Water Front. We all slept very well in our cottage bedrooms.

The next day I took my Parents to meet the first batch of relatives. The O'Brien's, my Mother's side of the family, lived in Balbriggan just a short drive away. We had dinner with them, kissed and hugged everyone, and then Annette and I left them to it while we went off exploring. From here on until Friday, the O'Brien's took charge of entertaining Mum and Dad. Annette and I continued to discover Ireland and the wonderful people. Everywhere we went we were treated like old friends. Mum and Dad also did a lot of touring, visiting sites and more relatives. They were driven, mostly at high speed along narrow winding country lanes, by Kieran

O'Brien in his monster Dodge station waggon. An experience with often left Mum drained with stress.

Friday, we moved on to Letterkenny in Donegal. Here there was another selection of relatives. Saturday we rested as guests of the Devlin family. That evening we were due to attend a Country and Western Concert. It wasn't my favourite type of music but I was looking forward to it. Annette and I had experienced a lot of local Irish music and dance in a variety of venues. The Irish loved music, dance and what they described as 'The Craic'. It seemed that there was also a big following for Country Music too. After a lot of snoozing, day dreaming and two enormous meals, we set off to the theatre. The Devlins also had a huge American car which I tried to keep up with on route to the theatre. Speed limits appeared to be only a rough guide in these parts. Fortunately I had one of the locals in my car because I lost the Chevi after the first mile. One intriguing site was a Policeman (Garda) on Point Duty at one of the major junctions. That alone was quite strange these days. However the funniest thing was that while we were stopped and he called traffic across; amongst the passing vehicles was a Robin Reliant with a full size sofa tied to the roof, almost as big as the car, and two boys on a single bike. This didn't seem to register with him at all. It must have been an Irish thing.

We had the tickets for the show but nobody was checking so we need not have bothered. The Theatre, obviously converted from a cinema to a club, was very warm; smoke filled and smelled of Guinness and wellies. A group of school girls were performing Irish Dance amidst the noise of everyone settling in. The customers at the bar were six deep so we decided to wait in the hope that it would ease off later. Many of the audience were dressed for the occasion in Stetsons and Cowboy Outfits. Some even had guns in holsters but I suspect they were not real weapons. There were enough people dressed in regular clothing so we didn't feel out of place. The first act was Kevin O'Leary, who with his guitar sang a selection of John Denver songs. Then another performance of Irish dance by adults. Then a comedian Barry Connor does his bit before the 45 minute Guinness and Whiskey break. I can only remember one of his jokes, so he must have been good.

'If all Brides are beautiful, where do all the ugly wives come from?'

One of our party in the know, pre ordered our drinks so we dashed in and retrieved them before the crush.

After the break, the main turn. This was the quietest the audience had been all night. The main light were dimmed, the stage lighting focussed and the M.C. strode on to the stage.

'Ladies and gentlemen, boys and girls, the time is here for the star of our show tonight. Please give a great Irish welcome to a gorgeous lady from the UK, The fabulous Lacey Jay Black and the Nashville Track.'

A rear curtain lifted to reveal her backing group who were already in place.

The musicians played the introduction to what I later discovered were her adopted signature song, 'Stand By Your Man'. The audience erupted into applause and whistles, many stood up for the entrance of the beautiful Lacy Jay Black. She appeared from the left of stage. Picked out by a spotlight she stopped at centre stage, faced the audience and blew a kiss. I didn't really concentrate on the song at first, I just looked at her. She stood about 5' 6", shapely and slim. Short brown hair lightly curled. Pink and cream cow girl type top with cream slacks and matching 3" heeled shoes. She wore a woven pink and cream belt which hanged down to the knee trimmed with tassels. I was smitten, but not a hope in hell of meeting her.

I remained transfixed as she spell bound the audience with 'Stand By Your Man', 'Your Good Girls Gonna Go Bad', 'Are You Lonesome Tonight', 'Queen Of The Silver Dollar', 57 Chevrolet', 'Harper Valley P.T.A. and 'D.I.V.O.R.C.E.' Then she announced the guitarist, Malcolm Deedy, to do a solo of a fast fingering, Kentucky, medley. Then she finished off, as a tribute to the audience, 'When Irish Eyes Are Smiling.' Not strictly country, I wouldn't have thought, but it went down very well in the club. It was only 10pm. I thought it was early for a show to end. Then strangely everyone bought more drinks and small groups of amateurs sat at their tables and began to do their own songs. Musicians appeared from nowhere. The Nashville track crew also joined in with the community sing song event. Lacey Jay also joined in with the fun.

Feeling tired, I sat myself at a quiet corner of the bar and sipped an Irish single malt whiskey. Much to my surprise and joy, Lacy Jay sat next to me. She asked me how I enjoyed the show. As I complimented her she recognised the accent. The instant connection seeded a long conversation about home. Lacey Jay came from a place called Scholes in Wigan. I did know Wigan; but hadn't heard of Scholes. I was given her itinerary for the week and encouraged to go to at least one more show. I said I would. Having assured each other that it was nice to have met, it was time to leave.

Annette had been watching me and thought I was on there. I passed the comment off as none sense. That evening Annette announced that J.P. was going to join us for a few days. I asked what J.P. stood for. It was Justin Porter. His Father owned a haulage business and laid back Justin helped in the office and did some driving. I was pleased she would have some company besides mine.

Next day I went for a 2 hour walk around beautiful Letterkenny. The Guest house came into view. On the driveway was a beautiful sight, an iconic Harley Davidson motor cycle. Pale Gold with lashings of chrome and all the bells and whistles you would expect to see fitted to a true enthusiast's bike. This heaven sent machine, I discovered, belonged to J.P. for whom I now had the greatest respect. He had travelled overnight and was now flaked out on the lounge sofa, resting his head on Annette's lap. She raised a finger to her lips in a gesture to request my silence. I complied and went through to the dining room for a cuppa and a cake. Mum and Dad had already gone exploring so I relaxed, flipping through the pages of a local newspaper. In the entertainments section was an advertisement detailing the venues for Lacey Jay and her group. I had the contact details for her hotel so I called her. The delight in her voice was obvious. I arranged to go to more concerts or gigs as she called them. I could tell she was tired. She apologised but she had to cut me short due to rehearsals but said she couldn't wait to see me again. I was delighted.

After a while J.P. and Annette joined me. I could see now that this lad was a more serious bet than previous contenders, so I made the effort to get to know him better. His hippy like attitude to life was enchanting but he was no fool. He had a good business head and as an only son was heir to the haulage throne possibly. He was pleased to tell me all about the Harley and he offered me a ride. I of course accepted assuming I would be pillion. He offered me the key and his helmet. I was amazed and told him I'd never ridden a bike so large before. In his typical style he said "Just don't think about it, just ride man". I was advised to mount the monster while it was on the stand, start it up then ease it off the stand to give me better balance. That worked going forward but I was nervous on the turns at first. It was beautiful, so comfortable. The seating and suspension cushioned any bumps. It was like floating on air. On my trip around the Town I noticed many admiring glances. It's possible that a few of them were aimed at the bike. I wanted one. Half an hour later I had to give it back, a very sad moment. I took J.P. and Annette in the car for a pub lunch. Then the three of us explored some more. J.P. had been to Ireland a number of times delivering. He knew his way around and acted as guide. This was the last time we would be together for a while. Our lives took different turns. J.P. returned home after a few days and Annette went with him. Mum and Dad were looked after by relatives. I saw a lot more of Lacey Jay.

Lacey; real name Paula Williams, was working, so it was difficult to find much time together. We met between rehearsals or at the venue before she went on. Even though we had little time together and less in private, the bonding definitely became stronger with each meeting. Lacey had some time off after her return home so we pledged to see much more of each other then.

The group used a converted coach for their time on the road. I got a guided tour of the vehicle one day. It was an ingenious use of limited space to accommodate 6 people for days on end. There was a separate compartment for Lacey Jay and bunks for the lads. It had a caravan type dining room and lounge. The toilet was also of caravan design. There was storage space and even a decent shower unit. The driving area was very plush with swinging arm chairs. There was radio and T.V. and some specialist recording equipment which was beyond me. There was also a trailer for all the gear they needed. I was impressed.

CHAPTER 29

In company with lots of trucks, one of which happened to be Porters; (JPs Company) we arrived about midnight in the Port of Anglesey. The quiet, but tiring drive up the coast was tinged with sadness. Ireland was a wonderful experience for all of us for a variety of reasons. We all agreed that it would be a good idea to go again sometime. Some of the newly found relatives were invited over to see us if they could. My mind focussed on Lacey Jay, the name Paula hadn't computed yet. In any case she liked to be called Lacey. I just wanted to be with her now. Soon it was back to work. There was no such thing as a holiday cover, so two weeks work had to be caught up on. It was a very difficult week and it re enforced my desire to seek change.

It was just over a week before the first proper date with Lacey. I agreed to meet her at Wigan Bus Station, next to which there was a large car park. It wasn't far from Lacey's home and I knew the location well. I dressed in what for me was casual. Light brown trousers and cream open neck short sleeved shirt. The meeting time was 7pm. I arrived at 6.45pm. Lacey arrived at 7.25pm. It was a worrying wait; had I blown it? In the event I hadn't. Lacey wore a black cat suit with light weight feminine leather jacket enhanced by sequins on the back in the form or a treble clef. The outfit was completed with black high heels. She looked stunning. In fact from a distance I didn't think it was my date approaching.

We hugged like long lost friends and kissed with the joy of true lovers. We made our way to the car and Lacey asked to drive. I handed her the keys. She loved the car but struggled for a while with the column gears. After ten minutes she was fine. She refused to let me into the secret of the destination. Lacey talked constantly about her work, who she'd met the songs she'd sung the good and bad times. I could tell she loved her work but there was a lot more to it than I imagined. We ended up on a quiet road through an industrial area behind Pilkington's Glass works in St. Helens. We stopped in front of locked gates to an old mill. I was asked to help as Lacey unlocked the large steel gates and together we pushed them open. My question about what we were doing here was ignored. The car was driven into the yard and the gates closed and locked. The next stop was at a large yellow garage type door but much bigger. Lacey produced a fob from her pocket and pointed it at the door which rolled upwards. We drove into a storage area containing a number of commercial vehicles, one of which was the group coach.

With a beaming smile, Lacey invited me aboard. The Coach was well fitted out for touring. Two large arm chair seats at the front swivelled to make up part of the lounge area. The semi—partitioned area behind was the kitchen. The rest of the coach was fitted with bunks and a separate bedroom for Lacey. It was clean but obviously well used and there was a hint of beer odour. I was asked what I thought. I liked it, and I hoped I would like the reason I was here. The Music centre was switched on and it was no surprise to hear Country Music emanating from the two large speakers positioned at either end of the lounge. As I sank comfortably into one of the 'Captain's chairs' Lacey began to prepare something in the kitchen. After confirming my preference to drink, I was presented with a large Toblerone and a cup of tea. Lacey disappeared for a while, returning dressed in pyjamas, something I didn't expect. She sat on the sofa and patted it as an invitation to join her. I sat next to her, placed my arm around her shoulder and we relaxed listening to the music. Some songs she joined in with. It was lovely. Lacey told me that she had written quite a lot of songs. Occasionally she would try them out on audiences; they seemed to go down well. I asked why she didn't promote her own songs. I was told there were contractual problems with that. At the end of this year she would be free of this contract. She would review her prospects then. I asked if I could see her work. She smiled directly at me.

'I thought you would have other things on your mind.'

We kissed and moved to a horizontal position. The sofa was too narrow and I fell off. We both laughed. Lacey rolled off the sofa onto me and we kissed and fondled some more. She raised her head and looked into my eyes.

"There's a perfectly good bed in my compartment; that's unless you want to get back ache here "?

I elected for the bed. The single bed almost filled the space available. Lacey jumped onto bed face up and stretched out welcoming arms. I joined her and the kissing became more sensuous. She stopped again and pulled back slightly for another question.

'Are you going to stay dressed all night?' All night was the phrase which pleased me most.

I knelt up to remove my shirt. 'Ouch'! I hadn't noticed the wall cupboard above the bed. Concerned but laughing at the same time Lacey asked if I was all right. Shirt removed and head hurting I kneeled astride of Lacey and unbuttoned her top. Easing the garment apart I felt for the first time her firm young breasts, white against the tanned skin surrounding them. She must never sunbathe topless. Whilst massaging her breasts and tweeking the nipples I became more aroused. Wanting to resume the kissing I lay beside her and eased down the pyjama bottoms enough to feel her bum and thighs. Lacey undid my belt and zip, reached inside and fondled me. I was finding it hard, in more ways than one, to hold back. I even amazed myself by doing so. Simultaneously we decided that nakedness would be best now. The remaining clothing was discarded. Now we had the full feel of each other. Now we could express our desires fully and without restriction. During all the manoeuvring petting, feeling and kissing, I found myself in position between her legs. Anticipating my urges, Lacey wrapped her legs around me. Again I held out as long as I possibly could before the snake was allowed into the basket. All too soon my entire body shook time and time again. We were one.

We stayed locked together until sleep overtook us. During the night I wanted a pee. Disorientated in the darkness I couldn't find anything. Light switches, the position of doorways, my clothes; everything eluded me. Eventually, on the verge of wetting myself, I found my way outside and had a pee against the mill wall. It was a mild night so my nude excursion wasn't uncomfortable except for the odd stone or other little objects on the floor. I found my way back to the bed easier as my eyes accustomed themselves to the dark. Lacey had woken up.

'Where have you been?'

'For a pee, couldn't find anything, so I went outside. It's not cold

'Didn't you put anything on?' She giggled.

'No, I couldn't find anything in the dark.' Lacey laughed heartily.

'Well I'm sure Security will have found it good viewing for a change.' I was mortified.

'There are cameras?' Again in, fits of laughter.

'I'm sorry for laughing, hopefully they were asleep. Don't worry, and they've probably seen all sorts at night'

Then I had another horrible thought. 'They'll know we are here won't they?'

Lacey laughed again. 'Don't worry; they're after thieves not lovers.'

It took me a while to get back to sleep. We kissed and cuddled a while but I wasn't at ease enough for sex after knowing about security. In the morning I was aware of my forest like stubble. I didn't think Lacey would like being passionately kissed while having her face sand papered. I was ordered to stay under the covers until she had put her face on and done her hair. I obeyed. When it was my turn in the bathroom I found and used the electric shaver which must have belonged to one of the group. I was a wet shaver and I wasn't impressed by the electric model. Returning to the living area I found Lacey preparing breakfast. It smelled good. I hugged her from behind and kissed her neck. I was becoming aroused again but made no further advances.

Breakfast was eaten mainly in silence with occasional furtive glances and shy smiles. Lacey was still in pyjamas. I washed up while she got dressed. In the lounge I listened to the radio for nearly an hour before Lacey emerged carrying a guitar. I received a good morning kiss and she sat opposite me to give me a private show. She was great on the guitar. I was treated to a medley of 'Rose Of My Heart', 'Rocky Mountain High', 'If I Could', 'Kilkenny Blue Eyes', 'Everything That Glitters'. It was a great way to start the day.

Lacey had rehearsals after dinner. We kissed and cuddled some more and then we left for a bit of shopping in Wigan Centre, dinner in a café in one of the quaint arcades and I dropped her off at the end of her street. Not time for parents introductions yet.

On two occasions, whilst driving back to my hospital digs, I found myself going off route. My mind was in Lacey Jay Black mode. On the second occasion I had almost reached Salford, on the East Lancs Road, before I realise I was on the wrong track. Still, I was a very happy man. I pulled off at the Carr Mill café for a drink. It was quiet, so I sat at a window with a view and watched the traffic for a while. I thought I'd visit James and Sandra later to tell them about Lacey and get a full report on the honeymoon. Well perhaps not a full report, just the bits they could tell me about. I left the café to discover that I had left the keys in the car and locked it. It had quarter lights with internal twist locks, so I went back inside and asked to borrow a fork. Returning to the car I inserted the fork handle between the rubber seals and flipped the lock forward, reached into the door handle and opened up. Having made sure I now had the keys in my hand I returned the fork and went on my way.

10 minutes later while driving along Burrows lane I was aware of flashing lights behind me. One of them was blue. I pulled over and awaited the reason for the stop. Rolling down the window I looked in the wing mirror to watch the slow determined walk of a 6' Traffic Policeman as he inspected my car.

'Is this your car, Sir?' He crouched down to peer inside.

I confirmed that it was.

'Do you have your licence with you?' I produced my licence. He looked at it like I had presented him with a turd.

'Can you tell me the registration number Si?'

I responded at once. "HKA 838 D". He seemed disappointed.

'Just give me a moment Sir.' He strolled back to his car.

Passing motorists looked at me like I was a criminal, I felt embarrassed. After a short period of conversation on his radio he strolled back.

'It seems that a member of the public called in after seeing you break into the vehicle Sir'

I explained the circumstances of my seemingly criminal act.

'I see, of course, I can see how that would look suspect. Right, I'll just have a quick look round the vehicle and you can be on your way.'

He walked slowly around the car, bending to check the tyres. He called to me to press the brake and switch on the lights. Having exhausted his checks he seemed disappointed again to let me go without a booking. He followed me for about three miles before calling it a day. I was so busy watching him that I lost track of my route again; I had gone past Knowsley Safari Park heading home instead of to the Hospital. I wasn't on duty 'till next day so I continued home.

Annette and Dad were still at work so I spent time with Mum talking about the Holiday. She had loved it. First time away, anywhere. She wanted some shopping from 'The Village', that's Huyton, so I took her in the car. The newsagents had lots of advertising cards in the window. It was cheap to put a postcard in so I advertised the motorbike for sale. I had tea with the family. Everyone quizzed me about Lacey. I didn't tell them everything. Annette kept teasing me to tell all. It seemed that J.P was also a serious issue. I was pleased now that I knew him better. Later I called at Cookes

Mansion. James and Sandra were staying there pending the purchase of a new love nest. It was wedding photographs and cine film time. My speech was on film, I was delighted. It seemed strange hearing me like this. I didn't like my recorded voice much. Mirriame also appeared about 8pm. She tried to look pleased about Lacey Jay, but she definitely wasn't.

Later in the kitchen Mirriame cornered me saying; 'I bet she's not as good as me' I smiled. 'Nobody could be as good as you gorgeous.'

She patted my bottom. 'That's my boy.'

That seemed to do the trick. She was happy; I was still on the Christmas Card List. Happy Days.

CHAPTER 30

August 1971. James and Sandra move to a new home near the Priests' College, Rainhill stoops. I got to know 'The Nashville Track better.' The group manager, Jim Henderson, was a man I didn't like much. He was about 20 stone, ignorant and seemingly a bully. People rarely argued with him when angry, which was often. He had a foul mouth. The guitarist, Malcolm Deedy (Malc), was a hippy type. He would have got on well with J.P. He was a talented, mild mannered bloke whom I quite liked. He thought deeply about things and had tremendous knowledge about everything. In Music he was a perfectionist. On keyboard was John Murray. He was the only one with glasses. He was bald and thin with long fingers which were very pliable. He often had big arguments with Jim. Jerry Cole, the drummer was brilliant and energetic despite being overweight like and Jim. Heavily tattooed and a bushy moustache . . . Always wore a tatty brown cowboy hat. Lacey said he even wore it in bed. Kenny (sparks) Milligan; Driver, Engineer, Electrician, trouble shooter. Kenny was always calm and didn't know the meaning of the word crisis. Just 2 years ago he was in a red and black uniform outside Buckingham Palace in the Coldstream Guards. I met them all properly when I was invited to the next gig at 'The Owl Club' in Warrington.

However, before that event I went to visit James and Sandra at Rainhill stoops. The house was a 1930s style semi with traditional bay windows. In the drive was a white Austin 1300. I couldn't believe that James had changed to that car, he like big stuff. I was greeted by Sandra and discovered that the Austin was hers. I was asked to remove my shoes which were a first for me. Then I worried that my feet might smell and there was a hole in one of my socks. I was directed to the sitting room at the front of the house. James was kneeling at a cupboard getting out lots of folders. I made myself comfortable on the new Chesterfield Suite and began answering questions from James about Paula. Sandra went to get drinks and some

Crawford's Shortbread biscuits. James arose from the cupboard with an arm full of albums.

With a little laugh he said, "Right you've got 3 hours 40 minutes to get through the wedding and honeymoon photos starting now"! Sandra returned with refreshments. Luckily I liked shortbread.

I asked Sandra about the job. I didn't realise how much was involved in being a holiday rep. Many amazing stories were told. She had now changed her roll from being a resort rep. to working in the travel shop for Thomas Cooke; no relation to James. This enabled her to be at home most of the time, with only an occasional trip abroad. Then it was time for the albums. I enjoyed the wedding photos, and I was in many of them. I was invited to view the films at Cooke's mansion at a later date. By the time we got to the honeymoon I was trying hard not to yawn. There were lovely scenic photographs of Rome and area of Southern Italy, but all these photographs to view at once made it hard work. Then I was treated to a lovely tea of stew and dumplings, followed by a tour of the house. The ground floor was very homely and inviting. Upstairs was a 'work in progress.' When we got to the garage I found that James had changed cars to a Jaguar XJS, in midnight blue, very nice. Then we went through the conservatory to the neatly manicured garden. A central garden table was surrounded by wooden folding chairs. Sandra brought a tray of drinks. We sat and talked 'till dusk.

At work, a long standing request to get a Hospital post was realised. I took up the position of deputy charge nurse at the Benedict Clinic. I was happy again in my institutionalised state. Vince Hall was still Charge Nurse but the rest of the staff had changed. I was extremely lucky to be elevated to this post so quickly. I must have made a good impression when I was last here as a Student. It seemed only five minutes ago. A few of the older applicants were not pleased at being beaten by 'an upstart'. I wasn't bothered; I had a big task ahead of me. This was a busy unit with many and diverse problems to deal with. My first Monday morning consisted of an hour long meeting with Vince to ensure that I was up to date and in line with his policies. He was friendly but firm in his dealings with both staff and patients. Then we had a staff meeting. I was introduced to everyone and was asked to introduce myself with an outline of what the staff could expect from me. This was unexpected, but I give it my best shot.

'Thank you Vince for the introduction, and putting me on the spot with this talk.' There was some polite laughter. "We have here a new crew.

Only two of you have worked in this unit before. My job will be to ensure that the policies and procedures formulated by Vince are carried out properly and to make sure that the priority at all times is the welfare of our patients. Likewise I am also here to look after your interests. Whilst Vince will be taking an overall view of the running of the unit, I have been given specific responsibilities in the areas of patient and staff social events and I will chair all patient and staff meetings from now on. I am also the unit administrator, so if you have any issues with your employment or requisites or anything which requires paperwork generally, I am your first port of call. When Vince is away I am in charge, and I will be carrying out my duties in accordance with Charge Nurse Policy. I look forward to working with you as part of a great team this is by far the best and most progressive unit in the Hospital, and we will have to work well together to keep it that way." For some reason I got applause for that. It was all off the top of my head, but it seemed to go down well. I got a 'well done' from Vince.

Another new phase, another new challenge. I was happy and proud. Lacey Jay was also delighted and organised a surprise party for the following weekend. I was a little bit dismayed during the week because everyone at home and my friend James didn't seem very excited about my promotion. They all planned between themselves to keep a low profile until the big party. I had been asked to give up my room at the hospital so I was now living at home again. Annette had moved out to live with JP. They had a house in Netherton. I was concerned about Dad. His chest was getting worse and energy was not what would normally be expected. I suggested he see the Doctor but he insisted it was only Flu. I knew it wasn't.

The first week in my new post was hectic. Most of the time I was getting to grips with ward administration, from patient records to medication records, patient finances staff rotas, down to the ordering of food and toilet rolls. The store room had to be kept full of everything needed to run the building cleaning materials, tools, paint, linen, light bulbs, and all manner of things for day to day use. I had to ensure that the building was properly secure and safe. I was the first person to institute fire drills on a weekly basis and I invited the fire service to train staff in the use of fire equipment. The Hospital had its own staff fire brigade and even an old fire engine, but I considered every second vital in tackling a fire. Then of course there was the operating theatre section to look after, but my previous time there proved to be an asset in supervising that area.

The patients meeting on the Thursday was the continuation of the meetings I had initiated as a student. I was so pleased that they were still going. One interesting thing to note here is that the questions were never about quality of care or attitudes of staff; rather they were about small practical things. A toilet that failed to flush or some forks were missing from the kitchen or a light bulb was out. I put forward the idea of day trips or even holidays both for leisure and perhaps an aid to treatment. This idea was enthusiastically welcomed but I had to make it plain that we had to find out about resources, and I asked who might be able to at least part fund their place on such schemes. To some, the prospect of paying towards something went down like a lead balloon. Still, it was food for thought and further research.

My next project was to organise frequent meetings between Nursing and Medical staff, Psychiatrists and Clinical Psychologists. Until now a patient would be seen by one of the latter, the prescriptions or regimes for treatment set out, the Charge nurse or I would instigate the treatment by passing on the details to staff. This system didn't involve nursing staff much in the reasoning behind the treatment. So I sought agreement to start having case studies after consultations were completed. Everyone would then be involved at every stage, and know the reason why certain treatments were prescribed. It improved knowledge and made us a better team. The suggestion was adopted and the case studies were set on a weekly basis. I was very pleased.

Saturday. Tonight it's the gig at 'The Owl Club' Warrington. I'm enlisted to help get all the gear ready and loaded into the trailer. 'Sparks' and I work together under his direction. There's loads of cable, lighting units, heavy speakers and mixers and sockets, tools, the list goes on and on. I was amazed at how much gear was required to get the band on the road. Lacey and the band were rehearsing inside the warehouse until it was time to go. I barely had time to greet Lacey. A lot of work went into preparation. We boarded the coach and set off to the venue. I had to share Lacey with everyone else which was a bit frustrating. We arrived at 'The Owl' just over an hour before start time. Everyone helped unload the gear then I tried to help 'Sparks' set it all up. I don't know whether I was a help or hindrance but he was polite about my efforts. Then there were sound tests, lighting tests, adjustments and more adjustments. Then we had the tune up session during which there was a few crossed words flying around as the tension built up. The Manager arrived when all the work was done.

He moaned and 'nit-picked' about things. 'Sparks' told him to 'fuck off' and mind his own business. He told me that if Henderson had a brain he'd be dangerous. I went to see Lacey in the dressing room. She was hyped up like a racehorse and raring to go. With a kiss and hug I wished her luck and off she went to greet her audience. I went to the back of the hall and joined 'Sparks'. It was fascinating watching him do all the technical bits.

I was given command of the spotlight.

'Here, keep that trained on your girlfriend' was Sparks' casual remark.

I had never been so nervous about anything in my life. I was so busy trying to do that right I didn't know what songs were sung. It took all my concentration to do that one thing while sparks did everything else. There were no supporting acts. The group did the whole show with one half hour break. During the break I helped sell tapes and give out information about future venues. The little country music stall took over £200. I was amazed. It was a wild, happy occasion. At the end of a brilliant gig we all pitched in to collect and stow all the gear. I managed a few precious moments with Lacey in the dressing room before we left. She was absolutely drained of energy. We sat on the coach arms around each other on the return journey the lads drank beer and joked with each other. Lacey and I made arrangements to meet next day for my promotion party. She wouldn't let me in to the secret. It was 2am before the coach was secured in the warehouse it was at this point that I was let in to one secret. The site did indeed have security guards and cameras, but the cameras were only external. My nude expedition was not observed.

CHAPTER 31

Sunday, Promotion Party day. Late afternoon the family was picked up by minibus to a mystery destination. On the way we stopped at James's house to pick up James and Sandra, then Cookes Mansion to collect John and Jane. I tied to trick the driver into telling us the venue, but he was in on it. We stopped in Platt Bridge to pick up Malcolm Deedy, the group guitarist, he wouldn't tell us either. We arrived at Wigan Athletic stadium where we were met by Lacey. After receiving a lingering kiss, I was taken with guests in tow to a large hall which had been set out like a dance hall. Chairs and tables around the perimeter and a temporary stage at the far end. There were banners and balloons proclaiming my success and a row of buffet tables full of food. Plus of course there was a bar.

I was then introduced to Laceys', or Paula's, parents. They would only call her Paula so I had to think carefully when addressing them about Paula, and others when talking about Lacey Jay. Paula's Dad, Jack was a miner at Bickerstaffe Colliery. Small but muscular and wearing a nice suit and the cloth cap. Seemingly the cap went everywhere. Her Mum, Marjorie, worked in one of the Wigan Market cafes. Marjorie was taller than Jack. Black curly hair, probably dyed, no makeup but she didn't need it. She was attractive for her age, perhaps 50. She wore a white blouse and dark blue calf length skirt. They were both nice people and very down to earth Wiganers. Marjorie congratulated me. Jack simply wanted to know if I supported Wigan. When I told him I didn't follow sport he thought I was from another planet.

Now other guests began to arrive, some colleagues from the Hospital, more of my relations from Liverpool and some of Laceys family. Equipment was being set up on stage for a DJ, and Lacey promised me some music by herself and Jim later. Everybody began settling down. Drinks were flowing; James mounted the stage to propose a toast to me. After the applause, a MC appeared to get things under way. He too congratulated me and then it was on with the show. I was quite taken aback with all this attention. I learned that Lacey and James had pooled resources to organise this event. I wasn't used to people doing things for me; it was usually the other way around.

Having been introduced to everyone, many for the first time; the show started. First up was a comedian from Wigan, Bobby Hall. He went down very well, mostly sporting jokes which I wasn't up to speed with. Then we had a magician, 'The Great Messuply' after the style of Tommy Cooper in which everything went wrong. Later he would wander around all the tables doing proper close up magic. He was great, then the buffet. This was a chance to go around chatting to people. I enjoyed that. Jack and Marjorie asked me to visit as soon as I could. According to Jack, Marjorie did a mean plate meat pie. That clinched it. Sandra was getting giddy and embarrassing James by getting over amorous. Annette was deep in conversation with JP most of the time but got more energetic when the dancing started later. My Mum and Dad sat with Lacey's parents which was a good sign. They got on well. Barry Hartley, the joker from the hospital, handed out tickets for the buffet. Each one had written on it 'you are behind—followed by a random made up name,' so everyone started to look for the person they were behind. This caused some amusing confusion for a while.

Buffet over and the DJ began his stint. He was quite good with the chatter but the music was so loud it made conversation almost impossible unless you had been a mill worker. After about half an hour we had a break when the MC announced Lacey Jay Black and Malcolm Deedy to give us some Country Music. There followed rapturous applause and whistles. Lacey and Malc walked calmly onto the stage. I noticed they both carried guitar and banjo. I hadn't heard Lacey play the Banjo. When she could be heard lacey began her introduction.

'Hi, everybody, great to see you all enjoying yourselves. First I want to congratulate my Man Liam on his success and to celebrate I'm going to sing you a song you won't have heard. It's one of the songs I have written myself and I'd like to dedicate it to my Liam" For the first time since school, I blushed. Here are the words.

Chorus.
I love you my darling
I love you so much.
I live for your kisses
And yearn for your touch.

With you I am happy
To be free as a bird.
You're in every love song
That I've ever heard,

Sometimes we're unhappy
Lonely and sad.
But let's count our blessings
And try to be glad.
As we have each other
And a love that's so true.
You give that to me
And I give back to you.

Chorus.

One day destiny will turn around
And allow us to enjoy.
This endless love we have found
With you my wonderful Boy.
I love you today, tomorrow, forever
Always be with me
Leave me never.
Yes mine you'll always be.

More applause, more blushing. She blew me a kiss and went immediately into a local folk song. 'The Martians have landed in Wigan,' Not exactly Country but it went own well and everyone joined in. Then the banjos came into play. Lacey clarified the change of mood.

'And now for something, completely, different folks! We've been practicing this for ages. Hope it goes well and hope you enjoy—' Tuning Banjos' Lacey started the sequence, Malc followed. Everyone recognised it and began stamping feet and clapping. As it got faster and faster the room rocked, everyone just went crazy. They did a great performance and at the end the noise of appreciation must have been heard at the Pier Head. Lacey rushed to me and gave me a hard excited kiss, and then she turned and gave Malc a hug and kiss on the cheek. The DJ completed the evening and there were lots of dancing and lots of drinking.

At midnight Lacey and I stood at the door to thank all the survivors as they left. Everyone enjoyed the event, but I suspect some had no idea what event they had attended. Lacey prevented me from boarding the mini bus for home. I was enticed into a taxi which ended up at a hotel not far from the stadium. She had booked us a room, telling me that our celebrations were only just beginning. (Reluctantly) I played along. We were Mr. and Mrs. Black for tonight. Lacey must have been to the room already. I was whisked straight passed reception into the lift and taken along the third floor corridor to room 312. The room was lovely, colour scheme maroon and white. The bed was most inviting. We bounced onto it enthusiastically and had an Ahhh1 moment.

It wasn't long before we began to cuddle and kiss. We even talked in short bursts between the kisses to relive some of the evenings best moments. I told her I loved the song and she embarrassed me again by telling me she saw me blush several times, she thought it cute. I was asked to make myself comfortable while Lacey went to the bathroom; however I needed to go first after all that fluid earlier. I looked at myself in the mirror and smiled. I washed my face and concern arose about not being able to shave again. I was a bit stubbly. Now I stood, arms outstretched and leaning on the sink. and looking once more at myself. In my mind I asked was I ready for this? I took a deep breath and decided that I might be. My mouth had the after taste of alcohol. There was no sign of toothpaste. There were plenty of smellies, so I opened my shirt and squirted some under my arm pits. Then I ran the cold tap and vigorously rubbed my teeth with my finger and rinse out my mouth a number of times. I made sure my bladder was as empty as it could possibly be so as not to interfere with the main event. Then returning to the mirror again, I questioned and inspected myself one more time before re-entering the bedroom.

Lacey thought I had fallen asleep in there. As we passed each other I received a brief kiss. Lacey entered the bathroom pulling a suitcase. Perhaps we were sleeping separately. The bathroom was actually plush enough to sleep in. Assuming the best, I undressed and slipped in between the pristine sheets. I lay on my back, hands behind my head, and peered at the ceiling. It was a lovely bed. I slowed my breathing and thought of a quiet beach and warm sun. After a while I heard the bathroom door open. I raised my head a little to see Lacey appear dressed in a sexy cow girl outfit. She wore a black Stetson hat with fur rim and a black tight fitting top with glitter pattern on each shoulder, a very short black skirt with fur trimmed hem and white calf length boots. She looked stunning. Walking first to the dressing table, she leaned forward and bent to rest her elbows on the table top to look into the mirror. This revealed her gorgeous smooth shapely bottom and lack of under ware. I rolled onto me side to observe more closely.

'Do you like what you see cow boy?' I began to move from the bed. 'No no, stay there honey. Room service will be with you shortly.' I obeyed.

Turning towards me Lacey walked slowly to the pillow end of the bed. Gently, she pulled down the duvet until I was laid bare. She did one side at a time, making me wait. So far I managed to stay quite calm and fairly relaxed, but that was about to change. Slowly walking once more around the bed, she smiled and removed her Stetson and placed it over my dick. Then she climbed slowly onto the bed from the bottom and walked on her knees past my feet, ensuring that her legs were astride of mine. When she arrived at the Stetson she removed her top to expose her firm young teats. She brushed up and down them a few times and then took the Stetson and tossed it aside. I was now aroused. She bent down and kissed my dick, sucking it just a little bit, and then she moved in for the kill. I was mounted and Lacey began to ride me like a Horse. She even shouted 'Yee Haaa!' To add some authenticity to the effect I pulled hard on her bottom to gain full penetration. She was hot and wet and gorgeous. I pushed her to the one side and dis connected for a moment, then turned the tables and mounted her. The thought of more fore play flashed through my mind but it was impossible. We were at the height of our sexual excitement. We screamed at each other as I filled her with what felt like gallons of love juice. We collapsed like jelly when it was over. We were completely spent. No energy even to speak for a while. We turned to each other, gently embracing, with light kisses. I asked her did she come here often. "Depends how much energy you've got in you honey. I can keep coming all night if you want me too". I must say, that un nerved me a bit. I had a Tigress under the covers. I was on duty an 9am in the morning, but decided that it might not be a good idea to mention it at this stage.

We held each other tenderly and began to talk. It occurred to me that we hadn't taken time to just talk before. Our meetings were too public, too busy or too sexy to converse much. She told me about some future tours which may interfere with our love life. One to Belfast for a week entertaining troops on duty there during these troubled times. Then after a short break, to Germany to do the same thing, for both British and

American troops stationed there. I was concerned about Belfast. I didn't say anything about my concerns, but it was obvious that Lacey didn't realise that it was an active conflict zone. I didn't want to worry her. She had now written quite a few songs and guitarist Malc had helped with the music. She was looking forward to trying to go it alone. She asked if I would like to be her Manager. I said I would help in any way I could, but probably wouldn't make a good manager without music industry experience. She said she thought it was easier than 'the fat bastard' made out and that they were being screwed out of much of their earnings by a bad contract. I promised I'd look into it.

More of Lacey's background came to light. She knew a lot about me. I knew little about her life before Liam. She had been brought up in the house where she lived with her Parents. Wigan was recovering from a period of heavy industry and Pits. The almost permanent fog blanketing the valley in which the Town centre was situated was showing signs of improvement, but as a child Lacey called it 'smogtown'. Her schooling was all local and she left senior school with 3 A levels and 8 O level G.C.E.s together with City and Guilds Music. She wanted to go to University to study music, but parental influence made her seek immediate work instead.

After such an intense sexual experience, I didn't expect to be laying together quietly like friends hand in hand, listening to a brief life story. But, here we were, doing precisely that.

Straight from School, Lacey, then Paula, got a job with a Solicitor doing general clerical work. That being making tea and distributing mail, going to the Bank or Post Office and collecting lunch orders. That got her some funds and times to get the Country group together which was her first love. As they got known in the North West Labour and Working men's clubs, they were swept up by John Henderson who offered to get them lots of work and fame and fortune. So far it was lots of work.

I was amazed and a bit stunned to be told her big secret at this early stage in our relationship. With hindsight it was the right thing for Lacey to do, and then she knew exactly where she stood. In her desire to climb the office ladder, she was seduced by and slept with one of the Solicitors, a senior partner. He was married and she admitted to being foolish. Thinking there was love there, she became pregnant at only 17yrs. old. The Solicitor lost interest. She never revealed his identity to her Parents who were furious with her. Due to extreme stress and no support, she had an abortion. She's never forgiven herself since. I held her to me. I told her I was so in love with her and that I fully understood. I kissed her wet cheeks as the tears streamed down. I held her tight to cushion the sobbing motions. Just now I felt so much love. I wanted to make everything right again. Nothing more was said as we drifted off to sleep. Recovery time was needed.

CHAPTER 32

A few days later I was invited to a band get together. No rehearsals, just a relaxation evening is how it was described to me. As I was now part of the scene I was allowed into the inner workings of the group. We met at Jim Henderson's house. Even though he was a bit of a 'Pig' most of the time, this was an occasional glimpse of his softer side.

I collected Lacey from her house about 6pm. After a brief chat with the Parents we set off. I stopped at the end of the street. Nothing was behind so I just waited and looked at her.

She smiled. 'What's up?' I waited. The smile became a giggle. 'Whaaat?' I continued to stare. 'Tell me!' After a punch, which hurt, to the shoulder. 'Where are we going?'Oh, I see. 'You've never been to Jim's house have you"?

I was directed to Standish. The House was on the main road between Standish and Wigan. It was an old detached house with its own drive and scruffy garden. One car was already in the drive, probably Jim's, a Daimler Sovereign, Rubbish, all over the dash and it hadn't seen soapy water for some time. Shame, it was a nice car. We parked behind it. I rang the 'Avon calling' bell. Jim answered the door. Through a cigarette he coughed a greeting of sorts, turned and led the way in. I immediately smelled the distinctive aroma of Cannabis. As we entered the hallway my Benedict clinic experience kicked in and I began without thinking, to look for other signs of drug use. I hadn't been told this but I could see that Jim lived alone. The house was much lived in. He wasn't over keen on cleaning. The Carpets, furniture and curtains were held together by nicotine stains. Newspapers and sheet music lay everywhere. He had made the effort of putting his latest take away cartons into the overflowing pedal bin near the T.V.

The fag was stubbed out so he could speak more understandably.

'Sit yourselves down' he invited, as he wacked the ginger Tom from the sofa with a newspaper. The cat, who appeared to be called 'bollocks,' yelled as it found a place to land. As soon as we sat down, the cat made a u turn followed by a majestic leap onto Lacey's lap, where it curled up and purred constantly for the rest of the evening.

I whispered into Lacey's ear. 'It's not the first time you've played with bollocks in your lap then?'? She had a fit of laughter which she declined to explain to Jim. Basic pleasantries were exchanged, and then we were asked would we like a drink. I expected tea of coffee but was dispatched to the fridge in the kitchen. It was a large American style fridge freezer. I opened the door to find it fully stocked with lager, nothing else, just Lager.

I yelled back to the lounge. 'Do you want Carlsberg or Carlsberg?' I was instructed to take a handful to the lounge.

Soon the rest of the group arrived. Remarkably, everybody chose Carlsberg from the fridge. One thing I found strange; well I found it all strange really. No music was played, just conversation. Bit by bit I discovered more about each member of the group. In his younger days Jim Henderson had first been a bouncer and then a Professional Wrestler until a serious knee injury took him away from the sport. He had made some money out of the sport and put much of it into the music business, first on Paddy's Market in Liverpool as a retailer, and then he became a small time group manager. The Nashville Track has been his biggest and best venture to date. He was divorced; no surprise there and he had two daughters, Sandy and Cilla. They were both at University. Overall. Jim had let himself go a bit. He ate too much, drank too much and dabbled in drugs. A laying out trolley wouldn't have looked out of place.

Jake Miller, driver and handyman. Nick name 'Sparks', Ex-Soldier, and Served in Northern Ireland at the beginning of the troubles in 1969. Single. No Girlfriend, but liked to play the field of available groupies from the Gigs. He loved gadgets of any kind and was quite adept at building his own weird and wonderful devices. He could even build or defuse bombs. I'm not sure how useful that was to the group. He was a handy man to have around. He would never start a fight, but he would be the one left standing at the end. He would do anything he could to help anyone.

Malcolm Deedy, Instrumentalist. He played guitar with the group but was equally at home with many other instruments. Malc had toured the world doing all sorts of jobs to fund his travels. He had worked for a year as a wheel tapper and shunter for Indian Railways. He conned his way into the job without any experience or qualifications. He got away with it. He assured us that after the first few weeks he did know what he was doing.

Anyway, no one died as a result of his efforts. In Africa he bought an old Land Rover, rented an office In Borxtown and set himself up as "The Safari King". He made $40000 in a year driving unsuspecting tourists through the animal reserves before the Authorities caught up with him and he had to leave. He drove yellow cabs in New York and was a Bull ring Clown in Spain. I could write a book just about him. He was a great bloke and I could imagine never being bored if marooned on a Desert Island with him. Malc was a confirmed bachelor boy.

John Murray, keyboard, married with one Son, Garry and two Grand Children, The old Man of the group. Keyboard was his life. He had been a soloist, a busker and spent time with a number of groups. At heart he was into folk music, but he could turn his hand, or rather his fingers to any type of music. John was of a quiet nature, perhaps even a bit introvert. Conversation was brief and he tended not to confide in any one. He was neither friendly nor unfriendly, but neutral, boring perhaps, but an excellent musician. Remarkably, he would be the most likely to have big arguments with Jim. The others tended to keep a low profile.

Jerry Cole, overweight and heavily tattooed. If he said it was Wednesday, then it was. Jerry had been a Cook in the Royal Navy, but I think he only fed himself. He was actually a very good cook as I discovered later in the evening. He bought in some food from the local supermarket and served up a very pleasing steak with all the trimmings at about 9pm. Jerry had played drums since being very young. He was also a Bandsman in the Navy, playing a range of percussion instruments. Jerry was married with a Son, and a Daughter. His Son, Dan, was in the Navy and his Daughter, Helen, was a Nurse at Billinge Hospital. His Wife Lora worked for Poole's Pies in Wigan. She obviously brought her work home and shovelled it into Jerry every night. Jerry was one of those people who retained an encyclopaedic knowledge of popular music. He would have done very well out of one of those game shows on TV.

The evening was a sort of relaxed business meeting over a number of card games and everybody partook of the Cannabis except me. Despite much encouragement, I politely declined. Jim made a number of announcements. The Gigs he had arranged over the coming months were. A week in Belfast entertaining Troops inside their barracks. That sounded like fun. Jake asked if he was mad. The situation there according to Jake, was far from stable and we had only recently had 'The Ballymurphy Massacre' with the blame resting with the Para's. Perhaps not the best time to go. Jim insisted that he had been assured of the group's safety by the military. Jake retorted that there were a lot of people who had been assured by the military who were now six feet under. Jim said he was over stating the dangers. Then there was a two weeks trip to Germany, also entertaining troops stationed there. Hopefully there was one more. Jim was awaiting a fax to confirm it. He seemed both excited and on edge. He wouldn't reveal the venue until he received the fax. The evening continued with Jake still questioning the wisdom of a Gig in Belfast. Jim calmed the tone a bit by fishing a large wad of notes from his pocket and began sharing the spoils from the previous month's work. I put my hand out but was told to 'fuck off'.

Then the crackle and rattling of the fax machine made everyone hold their breath for a moment in anticipation. Jim quickly took up station to retrieve the news he had been waiting for. There were a few brief pauses between paragraphs, then the 'beep' signal at the conclusion of the fax message. Jim tore off the sheet and read it to himself at first. Then his eyes lit up and a beaming yellow toothed smile radiated around the room.

'I've got it! I've fuckin' got it!' Jake interrupted.

'What's that then, Syphilis?'

'No you cheeky bastard, I've got us two weeks in your names sake; Fuckin Nashville—That's Nashville Tennesey you lucky arse holes. Nashville, Tennesey. What do you think of that then?'

Every one stood up to cheer or hug or kiss. Poor old bollocks was once again ejected to the floor and ran out of the room in panic. Jim passed the fax around and every one checked it again. It was a moment of sheer joy.

At this point the details were sketchy, but the trip was a fact. We were all so excited about it. The fact that Nashville Track was a supporting role to the big stars made no difference. This was a potential big break. It was quite late in the celebration that Lacey cried out

'The Grand Old Oprey; it's the Grand Old Oprey!'

I didn't understand the meaning of this moment of excitement. I was told then how important and famous this venue was to the Country singing fraternity. It took some time for everyone to settle down again. Until it was time to go, I felt a bit left out. This trip I knew was a great thing, but I couldn't fully share in the joy of the Grand Old Oprey, which I'd never heard of.

The evening drew to a close. I hadn't had much to drink, but everyone else was fully loaded, and the others were driving home. Luckily the reversing out of the drive went without incident; I hoped it would stay that way for every one until they got home. On the drive to Lacey's house I broached the subject of the cannabis. Lacey didn't see any harm in it but I tried to explain the possible hidden dangers. I was told I sounded like her Mother. Perhaps it wasn't the best time for this discussion. Lacey was so excited, so 'over the moon,' we did no more than kiss before entering the house. The big announcement was made to her Parents in a screaming voice and she hugged them tightly. So tightly that her Dad lost his cap for a moment. Again, I felt like a spare part, so I left quite soon to allow Lacey to calm down in her own time. When I got home my parents were in bed, and soon after so was I. It was quite a night. I had concerns about how to tackle the drugs question without upsetting the apple cart, if that was possible.

CHAPTER 33

The remaining months of 1971 went quickly. It was such a busy time for the group. At work there were still concerns about the future of the Hospital. Discharges to the community continued, though slowly for now. We were entering the busiest time of the year for short term admissions to the clinic in terms of drug and gambling problems. We were constantly at capacity now. Funding was being cut year on year and morale was taking a hit on the staff. Despite less money being around I did manage to arrange some day trips until mid-October, but as yet no holidays. I hoped to put that right next spring. It was suggested by one of the senior members of the team that there may be funding available to send me to University to do a Psychology degree. I liked the idea, so enquiries were commenced. Subsequent events in my life dissolved this idea so it never happened.

The Belfast trip for the group was upon us. They were leaving on a Friday evening. I could go, but only for the weekend. The Coach and trailer were packed and off we went to Fleetwood to catch the midnight ferry to Belfast. I was amazed at how many trucks, cars and Coaches were crammed into the ferry. It didn't look that big. The crossing was calm and without incident. Lacey and I cuddled and kissed in a quiet corner. Everybody else dozed their way across.

We docked in Belfast early next morning and had breakfast on board. Manx Kippers. Delicious flavour, but the bones were a nuisance. Jake came back to the dining room late, after being required to unship the Coach and trailer. We sat around his table and teased him into rushing his kippers, poor lad.

Normally we would have simply driven out of the port and into the City without formalities. However we were immediately aware that this time would be different. We were stopped, as was everyone else, at Police check point. The vehicle and trailer were searched by armed soldiers and documents were checked. This seemed very strange and un—nerving to us. Jake eased us through the process, being familiar with the requirements.

The fact that he had served there gave us some advantage, so we weren't delayed long. A heavily plated Land Rover escorted us to the barracks. There were soldiers everywhere; troop carriers and Police Check Points. It seemed like another country. The barracks was an ugly corrugated inner city. The large gates opened and we moved inside. It was like entering a prison. We unloaded the gear and stowed it in a small warehouse. Everything was dark green or grey, really depressing. Despite that, everybody was seemingly happy with their plight. Jake was happy. He recognised some former mates.

We were accommodated in a dormitory hut which reminded me of some of those films about prisoner of war camps. We were told that this unit was reserved just for us. A curtained area at the far end was for Lacey. Lacey wasn't happy and told Jim she thought we would be in a Hotel. Jim said he was advised that we would be safer within the camp and that our Coach in particular may be targeted by anti-British factions in the area. We settled in as best we could. No concert today. Today was a rest day. There were some rehearsals during the afternoon. The evening was ours. Lacey and I decided to go out to a local pub. The food in the NAFFI was very good and everybody was very welcoming. Lacey got a lot of attention from the lads. After tea, Lacey and I decided to explore the City

At the guardhouse we were stopped and given advice about where not to go. Polaroid photographs were taken and put up in the guardhouse to aid identification on our return. The forms of ID we had with us were noted. A small door built into the larger gate was opened. Two soldiers went out first to survey the area, and we were set free. We walked around for a while looking for a nice pub to settle into. All the Civilians seemed to be getting on with life as normal. The only unusual thing to us was the constant presence of armed troops and one burnt out bus.

We arrived at a pub called 'The Welcome Inn.' It seemed like an appropriate name so we decided to give it a try. It looked like a Victorian design with quality brick and large multi panelled windows. It was a busy place and there was live music going on. We entered the smoke filled lounge and squeezed between groups of people to eventually find a couple of seats, most seemed to prefer to stand, for some reason. We could hear what seemed to be a local group singing Irish folk Songs somewhere across the room. We removed our coats; kissed, smiled at each other and I squeezed my way to the bar for a Guinness and a Pony. The barman told me he didn't have a Pony, but he did have a Cart Horse out the back if that was any use. I settled for a Bacardi and Coke. I got back to the table with most of the drinks left, it wasn't an easy journey.

We sat with our two drinks for nearly an hour, just enjoying the music. Then we decided to try and find a quieter pub where it might be possible to move around easier and perhaps get more drinks. So, time for a visit to the toilets and meet at the main door. With some difficulty I found the gents. The smoky room had made my eyes dry, so before I left I swilled my face in lovely cold water. Lifting my head from the sink, I wiped my eyes and looked into the mirror. Two men stood behind me. They looked like brothers. Both wore leather jackets, were clean shaven and had identical haircuts. The one at my right shoulder spoke to me in his distinctive Belfast accent. I was asked very calmly was I military. I assured him I was not. I was nervous. This wasn't a social visit. The man on my left shoulder, equally calmly, informed me that I had been seen leaving the barracks. They had followed me here. My right shoulder man offered me a towel. As I dried my face I was turned around to face my visitors. I noticed that one of them had a pistol in his belt. I needed the toilet again but thought better of asking. I was asked what I was doing here. I explained about the group, and pointed out that some community gigs were also planned. I was asked to present my wallet. I knew I couldn't afford to be reluctant. I gave it over. Everything was carefully scrutinised. One of my new found friends announce that I wasn't military. A woman popped her head around the door.

'Rory, the Girls, OK, There's soldiers coming down the road. Routine patrol'

My wallet was returned.

'Enjoy your stay' one said, and they left.

With a sigh of relief I had that other pee I'd been wanting. Concerned about Lacey I hurriedly went to find her. She was just inside the front door. I could see she had been crying.

'What did they do to you, are you ok?'

Lacey had a similar experience but the two women weren't so polite her search was rather more vigorous than mine. The contents of her bag were thrown into a sink with the water still in it. She had to dry it all out. One of the women kept her money, calling it a service charge.

Rather shaken up by our experience we began to walk back towards the barracks. The patrol which had been announced filed past us, taking no notice of us but constantly looking around for danger and stopping at each corner before being waved on by the leading soldier. This wasn't a film or T.V. drama; we were in it. As the patrol melted away I was aware of being followed again. A man quickly caught up with us. He wore civilian clothes but announce himself as Captain Milligan. He produced an ID card but it could have been anything. I had never seen a military ID. So I didn't know what I was supposed to be looking for. Moments later an army land rover pulled up alongside and we were asked to get in to return to the barracks. Once inside he asked how we were. He had been in the Pub and seen what had happened. He asked us if we wouldn't mind telling an intelligence officer about our experience in detail back at the barracks. The only incident on the return journey was a group of Children throwing eggs at the vehicle. Two hit the windscreen followed by much cursing by the driver. Eggs make a terrible mess which wipers cannot cope with. Luckily we made it back without hitting anything. How I don't know. From the back seat I couldn't see a thing through the grease.

Once inside we were interviewed by an Officer, asked to view photographs and write statements. He suspected that Rory was the brother of Dermot McAvoy, two prominent characters on the wanted list. He thought they allowed themselves to be identified deliberately to let the army know that they were watching them and could do as they wished in their area. It was a message. We were advised to stay in the barracks for now. We were not confined, but simply advised. I couldn't comfort Lacey properly; there was little or no privacy here. Next day we both felt better. The gig was to go ahead and Lacey was full of confidence. I couldn't stay for the gig; I had to make my way home. I was worried about her though. Jake was right. This was no place for us at this time. I was taken back to the Ferry Port in a troop carrier together with soldiers going on leave. They recounted stories of their duties, the nervous patrols, not knowing who the enemy was, Suspicion even of children, laying in hedgerows and derelict buildings doing observations, brief exchanges of live fire at border points or at public events and the feeling of being hated by everyone. Some of the lads appeared to be brainwashed into viewing Belfast as a war zone, giving them nervous itchy fingers, a very dangerous situation. I was only hearing one side of the story here. I'm sure the public in England had no idea of what it was like in Northern Ireland at this time. Until now it had just been sensational news headlines. Now I had felt a little of the atmosphere. It wasn't good.

I felt relieved as the ferry docked at Fleetwood. Annette and JP picked me up in the mini. We went for a meal at a local pub before continuing home. Annette told me that they were to be engaged soon and there would be a party. I congratulated them. I was looking forward to the party. My description of events in Belfast was greeted with amazement. Annette, like me was concerned about Lacey, s safety. JP had delivered goods to Belfast without any problems, but he too found it strange to see all the troops there and armed Police which we were not used to. On the journey home we got carried away with conversation. Neither I nor JP noticed that Annette had got lost. It was me that first recognised the deviation in course when I recognised Lancaster City centre . . . After laughing it off, JP took over the driving. We arrived home an hour later than expected. Mum and Dad were very worried about our lateness but settled down to enjoy the joke when we explained about Annette's poor sense of direction. Again I had to go over the Belfast experience. I got a telephone call from Lacey about midnight to reassure me that all was well and that the gig went very well. My mind now eased, I slept well.

My hope that work would be more relaxing was dashed on the first day back. The Charge Nurse had called in sick. I had just completed my paperwork and escorted the Psychologist on his rounds. We sat together with a cup of tea for a general discussion when a Nursing Assistant came into the office looking quite distressed. She was very nervous. What she had to tell me was obviously difficult. The Psychologist diplomatically left the office. The Assistant, Claire, began to tell me the problem she was struggling with. One of the Male Student Nurses had assaulted a patient during a confrontation about hidden drugs. Such confrontations were common in this unit, but a physical response by staff was not acceptable. Claire began to cry and became apologetic for bringing the matter to my attention. I gave her a drink, calmed her down and assured her that this was the right thing to do. I also assured her that she would not be identified to the Student, her report was confidential. When she was sufficiently recovered, I took a pad and asked her to accompany me to a vacant office on the Theatre side of the unit. I requested that she write a statement about the incident. She was to remain in that office until I returned later. One again reassuring her, I returned to the main office. On the way I called in the Staff Nurse on duty. I told her to consider Claire off duty for a while and to bring in Student Nurse Chris Waldron.

In the meantime I looked at Chris Waldron's file. He was in his 4th. Year, having failed his final exams. He was due for re exam soon. In the past he had been interviewed regarding his attitude to Senior Staff. It seemed he had anger issues, but no recorded assaults on patients. After a brief look through his file he was escorted into the office by the Staff Nurse. I asked him to sit and requested that the Staff Nurse stay. I didn't' beat about the bush'. I told him that a complaint had been made of assault on a patient during an argument about hidden drugs. Much to my surprise he freely admitted it saying.

'You know how these bastards are, these druggies, you try to help them and they just spit in your face. I knew he had a tobacco tin with drugs in; I was told about it, but he insisted he didn't and wouldn't hand it over. We got into an argument and he tried to leave, so I held onto his shoulder and we struggled I got him on the ground and he kept punching me. I lost it and punched him back.'

Chris was obviously still angry. He was a red head, and perhaps the scientific evidence would not be on my side, but I'd always found red heads, both men and women, to be bad tempered. However that wasn't to feature in my response. I thanked him for his honesty went over the reasons why this behaviour was not acceptable. I suspended him from duty immediately pending an enquiry. I told him he must leave the premises straight away and await contact from the Hospital informing him when his disciplinary interview would take place. Lastly I told him that he would be entitled to have representation at the disciplinary, and then I asked the Staff Nurse to escort him to get any belongings from the staff room and then off the premises.

I then went to see Claire to get her statement and informed her that Chris had been suspended pending enquiry. She then returned to duty. I then went myself to find Joe, the patient. We sat in a quiet corner whilst I got his side of the story. He confirmed the confrontation but asked me not to do anything. I told him we couldn't have this sort of thing happening and it had to be dealt with properly.

'We are not Police or Prison Warders, our job is to take care of you and try to ease your problems.'

Now I had to inform the Chief who called me to his office. I then had to go over everything with him. He was satisfied that I had followed the correct procedure. He would now inform the patient's relatives. I was warned that either the patient or the relatives could bring charges in relation to this incident. That was something I hadn't considered. So I had to write up a very concise report on the matter. I was also told to refer any press or media enquiries to his office and not to comment under any circumstances. The disciplinary interview was set for the following Friday. When I got back to the unit the Chinese Whispers had been at work. It was blown up out of all proportion and everything exaggerated. I suppose that was to be expected. I organised a Patient/Staff meeting for that same afternoon to quell any ill-informed stories . . . It seemed to do the trick. Quite, a day. Now my concerns returned to how the Belfast job was going on. In the evening I received a call from Lacey. Everything was fine.

CHAPTER 34

Henry Alder, the Clinic Charge Nurse returned from sick leave on Thursday. In the meantime I had fended off several press enquiries and one from Granada Reports. He seemed a bit bothered about my not keeping the incident within the Clinic but that was only a feeling. There was no discussion on the matter. The disciplinary meeting on Friday resulted in the dismissal of Mr. Waldron, so that was an end to the matter. A piece on the issue had appeared in the Liverpool Echo. Thankfully that was the extent of bad publicity. The issue blew over after a few weeks and we were able to move on. I must admit that my own morale had taken a beating as a result of this. One journalist was particularly nasty on the phone. Another posed as a visitor to try and get more information from patients. What was in the press was not balanced. They were only looking to discredit the Hospital. Nothing was printed about all the good work that went on. I've never liked or trusted journalists since, save for a very special one I met some time later.

At long last, after many romantic telephone conversations, I was again able to hold Lacey in my arms. The only incident in Belfast was some vandalism to the coach, but it wasn't disabled. Our meetings now were very intense, with long deep conversations and meaningful love making. Our bond was strengthening all the time. My proposal of marriage was accepted and we decided to get engaged in Nashville. I booked holidays so I could go with the group. Excitedly we informed both sets of Parents, Annette and J.P. and the Cookes. Everyone was delighted but none more than us. All too soon we were parted again for the group's trip to Germany. Again it was back to telephone romance. Sandra Cooke was pregnant and I was asked to be the God Father. I questioned the wisdom of being an Atheist God Father, but they were insistent, so I agreed. That event was expected to be in June.

While the group was in Germany I felt so lonely. I spoke to Lacey every day by telephone, but the evenings were spent on long walks, sometimes around the rural area of Cronton, sometimes in the City and on the waterfront, sometimes at Otterspool. My thought was cantered on the future with Lacey. I wondered what would happen when her contract ran out at the end of March. We hadn't fully discussed if she would go it alone, renew the contract with Jim or find another manager. Also there hadn't been any plans made for the group. Would they stay together or split up. Also, I had intended to ask Lacey what her Tax situation was. Had Jim been doing proper Tax returns? Had he been paying the National Insurance for everyone? They were things to be addressed before the contract ended. Where would we live? I could apply for a Hospital House. There was a small estate of Hospital Houses near the Black Horse and there was also an agreement with St. Helens Council for the allocation of some housing for Hospital staff. What would we do about managing money? I didn't even know what Lacey earned. Would she want children, or would career come first? What would it be like being married? Our meetings now were so intense and the sex was great, but does it wear off when you're married? If Lacey kept working like she is now, would we have much time together? Should I actually become her Manager so we could always be together? Could I do that job? Questions, questions, questions. At the end of each thinking period or walking session, some of which would last four hours; I convinced myself that it would be fine. Then it would all start again the next day. I realised that far from being happy at this time, I actually felt depressed. At work I consulted one of the Clinical Psychologists, John Vernon. He was more of a friend now, so I asked him what he thought about my feelings

I was assured that these feelings are quite normal. Marriage is one of life's major events. The pressure to make them bigger and better year on year adds to the pressure. You begin to wonder if you can handle the extra responsibilities, the finances, the housing. Then there is the prospect of children and how to cope with that. You ask yourself over and over again if it's the right decision. The issue of love is complicated and means different things to different people. How much is love and how much sex; or are they interlinked. You can certainly have one without the other. At the end of the day, only you can decide if it's right for you. I was advised to discuss all these issues with Paula. It was likely that we each had similar concerns. The last bit of advice seemed to cut to the core of the matter. Discuss everything. When Lacey returned I would definitely do that.

I felt better for having the chat. I would also talk to James about his feelings prior to the wedding. We never talked about it before. My next port of call was James and Sandra. The house decorating was now completed, so a visit and tour of the new' look' house was in order. I arranged to have tea there one evening. I was looking forward to it. On arrival I noticed that the driveway was now Tarmac rather than the original gravel. The garden had been converted to low maintenance flagging with pots and troughs for plants. All the woodwork had been painted and all the pointing had been done. James must have been doing well. Also the inside had a makeover. Again all the woodwork had been painted and the seating was now leather. A giant 24" T.V. almost dominated the lounge. The back room served as an office come dining room, and the Kitchen was revamped since my last visit. Upstairs was a beautiful master bedroom, as tidy as any hotel. There was a guest bedroom and toilet with bath and shower and what they called a box room. This was to be refitted as the baby's room. It was lovely and I hoped I could do something similar with my future house. James and Sandra were obviously very happy and this eased my mind a lot. After a fantastic tea cooked by Sandra, I spoke to both of them about their pre wedding experiences. It seems that they were exactly the same, but it all washed away on the wedding day. They also told me that they had no problems setting in together; it just seemed to happen without any fuss or problems. They did have full discussions on how everything would work before the wedding. What there wishes and desires were and what basic plans they had for the future. This they said made the transition much easier than some couples they knew who had not planned anything, who just went with the flow. Sandra was very excited about the prospect of our wedding. Even though the date had not yet been set, she was thinking about what to wear. James told me he was happy that I too would join the ranks of 'Hen pecked' men and that I would no longer have the freedom to make my own decisions. He said he was still jealous of that. But he said it with a smile. I left that evening with an uplifted mood. I had a plan now and I was happy with everything.

After what seemed like an eternity, the Germany trip was over. I went to Manchester Airport to meet the group on their return. Manchester airport seemed to be growing like a fungus. I had visited several times to view the planes and each time the place had expanded or changed in some way making it ever more difficult to navigate. Anyway, I found a parking area and made my way to arrivals to await the arms of my lover. It was very busy, but somehow amongst the mayhem, our hormones homed in on each other and we held each other for ages before being prized apart by Jake who wanted help to gather up the luggage. There was a lot of it. We filled 12 trolleys and pushed them all out to a hired van. Everyone in the group was visibly exhausted, but Lacey managed to be a bit chirpy just for me. Lacey and I travelled back to Wigan together in my car. The others made their own arrangements. I expected a full report of all that had happened, but within minutes of leaving the airport, Lacey was fast asleep. At her home I took in her luggage, had a brief talk with her parents and allowed Lacey to go straight to bed to recover. We arranged to meet the next day.

CHAPTER 35

We met the following evening. Lacey was still tired but happy. I took her to 'The Waterside' at Carr Mill. It was early November and a bit chilly, but the dusk walk around the lake about 7pm was peaceful. Hand in hand we walked and talked. The wedding was the main topic of conversation. I couldn't quite believe we were talking about it. Lacey didn't intend to renew her contract with Jim Henderson at the end of March, so she suggested April as a good time for the wedding. She would then be relaxed and able to take time out to settle in to being a married woman. The group wasn't to be told until after the Nashville job was over and just before we returned home we would still officially announce our engagement there; it was a dream of hers to do that. It seemed extra romantic. Fortunately, as I was now a confirmed Atheist, and Lacey wasn't religious either, we decided to marry in a Registry Office with just family guests, and then have a giant bash afterwards.

'And probably a reception too' I remarked.

Lacey smacked my back and we relaxed a bit with the laughter. So the basic plan was formulated and we went inside for a nice meal. Now I got the full report on Germany. It seems it was all work and no play. The tourist bit wasn't practical because the winter had hit hard there and the temperature rarely got above freezing, so a lot of time was spent in the NAFFI playing games with the soldiers and rehearsing each afternoon. They had the best time with the American troops who seemed more able to let their hair down. The also appreciated the Country music more.

The trip was exhausting though and she confessed that she didn't really want to work at that pace all the time. For the next few weeks I spent time with Lacey every day. We talked a lot to both sets of Parents about the wedding arrangements and I suspect that they spent a lot of time talking between each other about it too. It was a great time. We could relax and just be in love with no outside pressures. At the monthly group meeting it transpired that Jim had miscalculated the enormous cost of attending

Nashville and his deal meant that the group members would not earn much out of it, possibly even anything except from record and cassette sales. I was paying my own way except for accommodation, so I offered to help by doing as much as I could on the promotion and sales side as my contribution. I wasn't impressed with Jim's management and I suspected that he wasn't going to lose out himself. However, the group had earned decent money over the year and were seemingly happy to go along with this arrangement for the thrill of playing at "The Grand Old Oprey"

Soon the day came, the trip of a lifetime for 'The Nashville Track'. The excitement was boiling over. The only member to be fairly calm about it was the keyboard man John Murray. John had lived and worked in the U.S. for eight years. He had worked for a T.V. company in Washington as an outside broadcast engineer. He would be our advisor and one of the drivers for our expedition. We first went to London by train and on to the Airport for our U.S. flight. Most of the gear was sent ahead of us by air freight. All the stress of getting ready for the trip was now over, all the paperwork done and dusted. No body forgot their passport, and for me, my first ever trip in a plane, and it was to be a long trip. As we walked through the glass fronted area towards the aircraft I wondered first how on earth such a massive plane would get off the ground. Then I couldn't get around the fact that this thing was going to get us all the way across the Atlantic. I began to wish we had booked on the Queen Elizabeth. Yes it would take much longer but if anything went wrong it had life boats. If anything went wrong with that big metal tube we were getting into, it's curtains.

We were welcomed onto the plane by a pretty, but over made up, Hostess and the general area of our seats pointed out. It seemed a lot larger from the inside and perhaps more comforting. I was pleased to have a window seat just to the rear of the starboard wing. More and more people filed in to the passenger area; all of them stuffing bags into overhead lockers. Outside I could see the baggage being loaded into the storage underneath and a tanker moving away. I began to make myself nervous again by thinking about how much weight we were carrying all together and wondering again how on earth all this gets off the ground and stays aloft. Soon everyone was seated. There was a 'ping' and a fasten seat belts sign illuminated. Hundreds of clicks replaced the talking for a moment. The pretty, over made up, Hostesses patrolled the aisles to assist anyone who required it and ensure we were all belted in properly, and there was a performance by two hostesses concerning the matter of emergency procedures. I just realised that the engines had started and the Captain began his introductions and essential information. As the plane was being pushed back the flaps were being manipulated. When we were parallel with the terminal buildings we stopped for a moment. The engine roared to get us moving then settled to a purr as we rolled towards our runway. It seemed to take a long time. I asked Lacey if we were going by road instead. Then out of my window I saw the runway lights to my right. We waited again for a few minutes while another jet came in, then we turned to our starting position. I slowed my breathing and Lacey squeezed my hand. I looked into her eyes and we briefly kissed as the engines powered up again. The engines once again roared, the brakes released and off we went. The acceleration was hard to judge but I didn't think we were going fast enough to lift off, but lift off we did. The climb was steep and we quickly entered a cloud base. I could only see cloud for a while, and then we burst out into clear skies leaving mountains of cloud well below us. The climb continued for what seemed to be a long time before we levelled out, the engines eased to a gentle hum and we were allowed to unfasten our belts. I was still in contact with Lacey by hand but I was irresistibly fascinated by the scene outside. It was wonderful.

Lacey shook my hand. 'I'm still here' she said with a smile.

I apologised and we started to chat about things again.

The long flight was made easier with games of cards, conversation, sleeping and reading the inflight magazines. The Emergency Procedures card was a little un—nerving. There were frequent visits from the Hostesses with a variation of trollies full of either snacks or gifts. The catering was very good, I enjoyed the meals. As we neared the American coast the Captain announced that we would encounter poor weather conditions in about 15 minutes. We were to settle into our seats by then and fasten seat belts. He would make a further announcement when the weather front was imminent. We were told not to worry but there would be some turbulence lasting about 10 minutes. The Hostesses gradually settle everyone down. The trolleys disappeared and the expected announcement was made. I could see the dark angry band of thick cloud ahead. The Captain said he would change course to avoid the worst of the storm which would result in us arriving a little late at our first destination which was Atlanta, followed by a short onward flight to Nashville. The plane banked quite steeply to port then levelled out again. Soon we entered the cloud bank. There was some minor buffeting at first then it got a lot rougher. Hailstones battered the body of the plane. It was very loud for a while. I looked around and everyone had gone quiet except for a baby crying. The body language showed fear. People sat rigidly in their seats. The buffeting got worse and the tension was heightened with the arrival of lightening. Each shaft of lightening lit up the interior like a camera flash. Many people pulled down the blinds. Lacey gripped my hand tightly and put her head on my shoulder, wrapping her other arm around mine. As predicted, the turbulence subsided after about 10 minutes, but it was a very tense 10 minutes. Once more we were in clear skies. The Captain apologised for the rough ride but asked us to keep seatbelts fastened as we were soon to begin our descent for landing at Atlanta International. The Hostesses patrolled again to make sure everyone was ok and reassured anyone who was still nervous.

As we reduced height we once again entered dark cloud. This time there was no buffeting. After a few minutes we dropped out of the cloud base but we were now in heavy rain, then suddenly the bump which signified our return to earth. How we got here I'll never know, I couldn't see much at all except the runway light whizzing past then slowing down. Overall I did enjoy the flight. The hairy moments made it something to talk about when I got home. The extended flight to Nashville was un—eventful and in clear weather. We reached Nashville in the dark and the City lights looked wonderful from the plane. As we approached for landing all the buildings, streets and cars became clearer. We passed over a road very low before landing at which point I wondered had we reached the runway. Then the very welcome bump as we did meet the runway. The reverse thrust brought almost to a standstill as we turned off to our disembarkation point. We were told to stay seated and belted until the aircraft came to a standstill, but just as it happened in Atlanta, most took no notice and the clicks started 50 yards from the stand and a mad rush commenced for the lockers. Why I couldn't understand, nobody could get out until the door opened, and we had to leave in line anyway.

Our trip through the enormous terminal went quite smoothly. All the Officials were both fat and armed to the teeth. It seemed to be the main qualification to work in Passport and Immigration to be at least 20 stone and look good with a gun strapped to your waist. After retrieving our cases we gathered in a group to hear the arrangements for the next phase of our journey. Jim had organised the hire of 2 Dodge vans with 5 seater crew cabs. It took us ages to find the office for the Hire Company.

There were loads of them and not all in the same area. We flopped down on benches while Jim and John sorted out the documentation. Lacey kept telling me how excited she was, almost squealing with delight. The lads seemed calmer. Documentation sorted, we were escorted to our vehicles by a smart red—headed lady in a business suit. She introduced the drivers to all the controls, showed us how to adjust everything, gave us a copy of the U.S. equivalent of 'The Highway Code,' wished us luck and wiggled her way back to the terminal. With all the excitement we realised that the trollies had been left behind. Half expecting them to be gone, we panicked our way back to where we had left them, it was fine. Phew!

The first stop was the freight part of the airport to collect the rest of the gear. Having got lost several times on the un—familiar roads, we arrived at the freight terminal one and half hours later. It was only three miles away from the passenger area but our drivers kept missing turnings. Jim, the inexperienced U.S. driver, insisted on leading. We were in John's car in which the air was blue much of the time. Jim admitted defeat and agreed to let John lead thereafter. Our troubles were far from over when we reached the freight area. At the security gate we were allocated an area to park to collect our goods and the name of the person to deal with. So far, so good. On arrival at unit 7G, we were met by four fat uniformed armed men. They didn't look very sociable. Having established who the party leader was, they took Jim inside. Two officials stayed with us and conducted a search of all of us and the vehicles. We were informed that sniffer dogs had detected the aroma of drugs on the equipment packaging and the instruments themselves. No drugs had been found but they remained suspicious. The suspect substance was Cannabis. It was hardly surprising that this should be the case as the entire group used Cannabis at home. After a further hour delay and lots of questioning, we were allowed to continue on our way. One funny thing, at least to me, was that the guard on the gate was the first official I had seen who was about the right weight for his height, and he seemingly had the least exercise.

I enjoyed the drive to the suburbs of Nashville. I loved seeing all the massive American cars, the different buildings and signs, the easier pace of life. It was November but much milder than at home. It had been a showery day and now the rain was heavier and the temperature had dropped significantly after sunset . . . The Dodge vans were smooth and comfortable and John was very competent on these roads. He kept an eye on Jim behind. At one of the traffic lights junctions John just scraped through. Jim was anxious not to lose us so he followed through the junction, big mistake. As if by magic and out of nowhere the Police were on to Jim like a fly to a turd.

The first we knew was when John said, 'Oh fuck me, Jim's been stopped by the Police.' We pulled over and reversed back to the scene of the crime. The rain had stopped now. There were two Officers. One stayed by the Police car, hand on gun. The other walked slowly to Jim's window, also hand on gun. We were ordered to stay where we were. Jim got out of his vehicle and presented documents. The second officer moved in when there was obviously no threat. There then followed a search of both vans. The Leading Officer was asking about the band and where we were going. He was so impressed that he simply asked for Lacey's autograph and told us to have a nice trip. As they walked to their car a woman driving in the opposite direction was so engrossed in what was happening to us that she ran into another car stopped at the lights. The officers simply changed direction and strolled over to the accident. We moved on without any tickets.

At last, without any more complications, we arrived at a Motel which was pre—booked by Jim. It wasn't luxurious to say the least. It looked like several rows of Butlin's Holiday Chalets stuck together. It was situated at one end of a lorry park, so it was obviously used by Truckers as they called them, Wagon Drivers to us. Much to my surprise, and my delight, Lacey and I were in one room. I asked Lacey did she request this. She said she hadn't but wasn't objecting. Neither was I. Jim was probably not thinking of doing us a favour; it was likely to be simply down to cost. We gathered our luggage and put the group's gear in a lockup for security. The room was basic. A double bed, table and a few chairs. There was a small portable T.V. a wardrobe and a few wall mounted pictures of Peterbilt Trucks. Oh, and just in case you weren't into trucks, there was a picture of a naked lady on a Harley Davidson. The washroom was quite small. It had a flushing toilet, a hand basin a shower for a midget and a smoke effect mirror in which you could just about make out your face. The heating and air con was coin operated. The first priority was to feed the meter. It was freezing. The one double window in the lounge/come bedroom was tastefully decorated with a well-worn, tobacco stained set of curtains. The window opened onto a magnificent view of the lorry park. Still, the view inside was getting better as Lacey was now down to bra and knickers and lying on the bed. I needed a wash and shave. I felt tired and sticky. When I returned to the bed

Lacey was asleep. I lay down with her, kissed her on the forehead and was soon asleep myself in the 'spoons position'. As I drifted off the realisation dawned on me that we hadn't spent a full night together. Now it was to be two weeks sleeping together. I smiled to myself and wondered if I could keep up the pace sexually.

CHAPTER 36

In the early hours I was awoken by the sirens of an emergency vehicle passing by. I decided it might be a good time for a pee. I eased gently out of the bed trying not to disturb Lacey. When I returned she too was awake. We settled into the cuddle position and I was immediately aroused. The passionate kissing was accompanied by vigorous exploration by all four hands all over both naked bodies. She felt wonderful. I felt her firm young breasts and sucked her nipples, and then I massaged them until she shivered with orgasm several times. I explored her soft smooth skin from her shoulders down to the bum. This was another erotic area for me. The shape and firmness was gorgeous. I manipulated my finger in the upper bum crack in a sensuous and suggestive manner. The kissing remained uninhibited and included the use of tongues. No longer able to resist I rolled onto her and rested between her legs, both of which wrapped around me like a bear trap. My first thrust engaged the heat and moisture of her succulent fanny. The need to fill her became more and more urgent. Her orgasm gripped me so tightly I thought she was going to keep her trophy penis inside her . . . Being aware that the walls were thin we tried hard to keep the sound to a minimum, so it was controlled groaning and panting until the excitement had calmed to a collapsed flatness. It took a while for me to recover enough to return to my side of the bed. We were both soaked. It was a warm sweaty type of night. I retrieved a towel from the executive bathroom and rubbed us both down like horses after a race. Not a word was spoken throughout this experience. Now we drifted off again, content and silently in love. Several firsts here, the first full night in bed with Lacey, The first love making for us in the USA. The first time in a Motel and the first time I had rubbed a woman down with a towel.

We were awoken again at 6am; yes that's 6am, to the sounds of trucks starting up and moving out. This went on for an hour. It was obviously not going to be quiet enough to get back to sleep. Just after 7am I got up and walked to the window. I slightly parted the Tabaco curtains to see an almost empty truck park. Perhaps some peace now. As I turned back to look at the bed, Lacey had started to get up but rested back onto the bed, her legs dangling over the side nearest me. I admired the lightly tanned skin from her face to her toes which was punctuated by a white bikini bottom line which accentuated her thighs and fanny. I was turned on again. I bent over her, my arms holding me above her. I bent to kiss her once and then proceeded to insert myself again. This time it was just sex for fun. Not love making but just sexy fun. As I pushed and pushed I enjoyed watching her face, the expressions of joy and excitement, the licking of lips, the closed quivering eyes. This was raunchy and mad and Lacey responded with thrusting hips and nails dug into my bottom. This didn't last long. It was intense and forceful for both of us. Now we slept another hour. Then reluctantly we got up, used the midget shower; impossible for two. Then we dressed and left for breakfast in the silver diner.

We made our way to the Diner. We were the only members of the group there at that time. Other patrons included a family of 3. Two men in suits at the bar drinking beer at this time of the morning which I had never seen before, plus the few remaining truckers. A mini skirted young girl attended us with a menu. It was several pages long and just listed the breakfast options. We asked for the regular American Breakfast. Her chewing gum stopped between her teeth as she contemplated what that meant.

'Yeah, I get it' she said knowingly, She walked briskly to the bar shouting an order at the cook.

I didn't understand most of what she said it was local slang, I think. Now we waited for the surprise breakfast. The other members of the group arrived and sat at the nearest tables to us. Our young friend returned with more menus and chewing much faster, in fact you could hear her teeth gnashing. John advised the others on what to order, and then he spoke to the girl in her own language. She was impressed. Our breakfast was the first to arrive. Well actually it nearly didn't. It's possible that the girls shoes were a little too big for her and she fell out of one of them, nearly dropping our breakfast on the floor and her chewing gum shot out of her mouth, hitting Jake on his left ear. He didn't see what had happened and just flicked his ear, perhaps thinking it was just a fly.

The plates now in front of us displayed a mountain of food. It included eggs, hash browns bacon, steak, beans, salad and chips, which they called fries. 2 large bread rolls each and 2 large Cokes. We both stared at it in amazement. The waitress recovered her shoe by flicking it up and catching it in her hand. Then supporting herself on a chair back she applied the shoe to the bare foot. Similar mounds of food were served to the lads who eagerly mopped it all up. I also finished mine, but Lacey ate only a small portion of hers. Then we had an impromptu group meeting about what was to happen next. The actual time spent in Nashville was 12 days. 10 of them would be work and 2 days off, one on the Wednesday of each week. The Motel was our home because it was the cheapest that could be found. No surprise there then. Today was set up day. We were to go to 'the pry' at dinner time and meet the manager for the induction. Having had enough food to last us a week, we returned to our rooms to make ready for the trip into the City. The vans were loaded from the lock up and off we went. The roads were quiet and we were able to take in the sights. All the houses seemed to be much larger than British houses. They varied in design and they all had front lawns. No terraces here. Each one had a post box at the front edge of the lawn, much easier for the post men. The houses had drives and garages and no one parked on the street. I didn't see any new buildings. They all appeared to be traditional in style. In the City, again there was an interesting mix of building styles. The main streets appeared well established over many years. Very little construction was going on. The streets were very wide and very clean, some of them tree lined which gave them a freshness. The shops looked old fashioned in style. There were People about but it wasn't busy. Lacey kept shouting 'Oh look at that' whenever anything interesting appeared; then a yell of 'Wow,' when the Grand Old Opry came into view. John stopped and asked a passer-by where we could park. There was a car park next to our destination. Jake and Jim went inside to find the Manager. Two men in overalls came to greet us and offered to help unload the gear. A large roller shutter began to lift and we reversed into a storage area. Just in time as a heavy rain storm dropped onto the area.

All the gear unloaded we were taken to the main office where Jake and Jim had completed the business with the manager. A lady called Ellie showed us around the building. Beneath the main building was a labyrinth of storage and utility rooms with loads of stage scenery and lighting equipment. Upstairs were the dressing rooms, large ones perhaps for dancers and small ones for other performers. Here there were hundreds of costumes and rooms for hairdressers and makeup artists. On the first floor were management offices and administration. There was a plush conference room. Above that were empty rooms on the second floor from which there were good views of the City streets and beyond. The auditorium was vast, as was the stage. I expected it to be much smaller, but then that wouldn't be American would it? Jake spent a lot of time inspecting the power sources and he was able to perform some sound tests. The group was asked to do some songs to test equipment. Publicity pictures were taken. I accidentally got onto one. Jim discussed various things with the stage management team and some members of the local press arrived to do interviews and take more photographs. Then after all that we had to attend an interview at a local Radio station and they asked for some of the groups' tapes. So the publicity wheels were rolling. There was so much to do that we didn't get to return to our luxury hotel until 9pm. We were treated to another massive meal and we had a few celebratory drinks at the bar. American beer was rubbish. A local advised us that there was an Irish bar on Printers Alley in the City for future reference. What a day. And the real work hadn't started yet. Lacey was ecstatic. She just couldn't wind down until about 3am. Tonight was just sleep. We were exhausted.

Next day we didn't arise for breakfast. The group met up for lunch at the Diner. We were delighted to hear the group on local radio together with recorded interviews. In the paper was the group photo, Lacey Jay Black and the Nashville Track, Jake Miller, Jim Henderson, John Murray, Lacey Jay Black, Jerry Cole and Liam Parry. 'Oh shit'. There would be trouble now. I didn't know I was on any group photos. Now we were famous, we got our enormous dinners free. The manager asked for a copy of the photo so he could display it in his Diner, So, another first, my photo in an American Diner. Remarkably, no one was upset about it thank goodness.

Now it was back into the City to get the technical gear together in the Opry. The group had a supporting role to play so they had to work around the requirements of the better known performers. I stayed around on the first afternoon to see if I could be of any assistance. Marty Robbins was top dog here at the moment so we met him, and also Bill Monroe who was a famous song writer. Everybody was so busy. I was amazed at how much there was to do to get the shows together. There were meetings between Managers of each department, Producers, Agents, press, TV. Staff, photographers, sound engineers, electricians, porters, scenery men and security companies, the place was alive with cleaners, painters, advertising people and visits by various company representatives. There was even a visit from a Congressman. I helped Jake with the gear set up for a while, and then Lacey and I hit the Town with leaflets and shop window stickers. We must have walked about eight miles. It was such an exhausting day. The group met up at 5pm, for a treat set up by Marty Robbins. He'd bought us all a meal at 'The Hard Rock Café'. There was a giant model of a guitar outside. He was a lovely man, great personality and no snobbishness. It was another enormous, but very welcome meal. I thought we had done for the day, but at 8pm it was back to the Opry for sound tests and photo shoots. Lacey showed some of her own material to Bill Monroe. He was impressed and offered some advice and contacts information. He was a nice person too. At 1am. We set off back to the Motel. It was busy tonight, there must have been 40 trucks parked up. I wasn't looking forward to 6am, again.

We took the opportunity of a quiet moment to make love again. The room left a lot to be desired but Lacey made up for it. This time was love making, slow and sensuous with lots of whispers in the ear and kissing areas which would not normally be kissed. It was a beautiful time. I hoped they would all be as beautiful, always. Sleep was deep and we were wrapped around each other drifting off. I felt wonderful. We were not awoken at 6am. It was 5.15am when the first monster engine burst into life. Of course it was the one nearest us. There followed a period of nodding and waking constantly until 7.30am, when I was the first to give up and get up. I left Lacey struggling to get some more sleep while I went for a walk. The pattern was much the same for the entire stay except for Wednesdays, our day off. I attended every show, but tended to sneak off during rehearsals in the afternoons. I began to get to know some of the shop and café owners in the City. My English accent got me a lot of attention and a lot of treats, including one offer of a freeby from a prostitute, which I politely declined. Still, the offer remained open anytime. Each day I used my time walking the streets to promote the group, For Wednesdays I discovered a cheap and cheerful car hire place. I hired a Chevrolet Impala on each of the Wednesdays, and Lacey and I went exploring the area. It was rich in History, in particular related to the Civil War. I couldn't spent as much time as I would have liked looking at that area because Lacey thought it was boring looking at graves and Museums. She just loved riding in the car and looking at the world go by. We were lucky with the weather on both Wednesdays. The sun was shining and the temperatures were not bad, so we had the top down much of the time. The large screen kept the wind at bay.

Now it was a lot of work and a lot of love making. I spent a lot of the time in a daze . . . It was a very hard two weeks, but a very rewarding period too. Despite all the pressure and tension from time to time, Lacey and I got on very well. However, there were a few moments of strain between us when I noticed the signs of stimulants being used to help her through all the mayhem. When I brought up the subject and told her I could see the signs, she always asked me to leave it for now. It was only for now and they all used them. It was a big event with lots of pressure and she needed something to help her through. Of course I had heard all these 'fob offs' at the clinic, but it was difficult for me to stay detached from the situation. I gave her all the proper advice about what the dangers were but stopped short of recommending treatment for now. I knew I would have to tackle the problem head on very soon.

The Wednesday drives were a relief. I knew that while Lacey could relax and be with me all day she would be able to refrain from stimulants, though I still remained suspicious based on me experience working with drug dependency. I hoped it wasn't serious and that I could handle it with diplomatic intervention. Near the end of the second week, I could see that events were getting the better of Lacey. She had a slight quiver with her head and hands and her eyes became pointed. I didn't want to face it but this was now getting serious. During one of the shows I noticed Jim Henderson nip out of a fire door into the alley. I gave him five minutes then followed him. It was raining again. In the dimly lit alley I saw Jim talking to a man who looked Chinese. Money and packages were exchanged and the Chinese man left. I approached Jim and grabbed his collar.

'Are you giving your people drugs you stupid Bastard?' Lacey's started trembling with the effects. You're ruining her life and her future to line your own pocket!' I was trembling too with anger.

He turned to me. 'Mind your own fucking business; it's nothing to do with you. Do you think because you're a nutter nurse you know all about it, do ye?' I held his collar with two hands.

'"Leave her alone you Bastard, she doesn't need this crap, I'll get you arrested shall I?'

Big mistake. I felt the pain as the former boxers head connected with my nose, then a couple of punches and I was out of it. I fell to the ground and lost consciousness for a while. When I come around, wet and cold, I heard sirens quite close. Just in case it involved me I tried to gather my thoughts. I didn't want the group involved or Lacey to know what happened at this stage. I thought I'd stage a mugging. Fighting the pain I reached for my wallet and removed the notes, putting them inside my handkerchief, and then I replaced my wallet. My head and chest hurt a lot. I couldn't breathe very easily. The lights went out again. Next time I came around I was in the Ambulance. The attendant asked me my name and date of birth. I answered. She then asked me what happened. I almost told her when I noticed a Policeman sitting near the door. I told her I had gone into the alley from the theatre to get some fresh air and I was mugged by a Chinese guy. The Police officer repeated to me what I had said. Then he continued.

'So this Chinese Guy, can you describe him Sir?'

I described what I had seen of the drug dealer I saw with Jim, without including the circumstances of course. The Police officer thought for a moment.

'OK sir so a Chinese Guy just happened to be in the alley when you exited from the fire door, he pounced on you and robbed you; is that how it happened?'

I answered 'yes.'

'And so after he robbed you, he returned your wallet to your pocket after taking the money out of it, leaving your cards and other stuff inside. Is that correct sir?'

I confirmed that that's what must have happened. He asked me how big this Chinese man was. Of course I described the puny figure I had seen.

"Well he gave you quite a beating Sir. OK I'll make a note of these things. But I must tell you, I think something else went down here that you're not telling me. Still, if you don't want to file any charges, then it makes my life easier. I suggest you sort out whatever with whomever and we don't see you again in this beaten up state.'

I was then given gas and air for the pain and spent the rest of my ride feeling dizzy. I heard no more from the Police.

Lacey visited me in Hospital about 1am. I persuaded her to go back to the Motel to get some rest. I would be out in the morning. I never told her what happened to avoid disrupting the programme. I was kept in for observation overnight. In the morning I had minor surgery to fix my nose. Then I was given pain killers and discharged. I was told I had two cracked ribs but there was nothing they could do for that except recommend that I take it easy for a couple of weeks. John and Lacey picked me up at mid-day and I was returned to the Motel to rest. I didn't attend the rehearsals or the show that day.

On the evening of the last performance we announced our engagement to the group. Everyone congratulated us and was very happy. Jim Henderson made sure he was absent for this occasion and also for the celebration at the Irish Pub later Opening hours didn't seem to exist here. We were at the pub 'till 3am. Our return flight was 4pm the next day. The Motel owner arranged a group photo and gave us each a framed copy. It seems we were welcome to return any time at favourable rates.

Much of the return flight was spent asleep. The periods when we were awake were spent going over our experiences again and again. I had a lot of film to be developed when we got home. London was freezing. The trip back on the train took us through areas which had been covered in varying degrees of snow. Welcome back.

CHAPTER 37

Much of December was time off for Lacey, resting before the busy festive season gigs. We visited as many friends and relatives as possible with tales of our American adventures and lots of photographs. The Month went by quickly and it was time for our official Christmas Day announcement. JP and Annette arranged with us to make it a dual announcement and we also planned to make it a dual Wedding into the bargain. The Weddings were to take place on a Saturday early in May.

Planning for the big engagement event went well. Everyone wanted to be involved. Both sets of Parents were very excited about it. The event was to take place at my home in Liverpool. It was quite a big house with gardens front and back, so room for guests wasn't a problem. My Parents would prepare the house for catering and possible overnight stays. Laceys parents were put in charge of pies, as they were from Wigan. This actually meant all the supplies for catering. The Porters were in charge of all things transport and extras required such as chairs and tables for the garden areas. Lacey of course was in charge of being beautiful and I was in charge of administration such as invitations, press releases and the like.

The planning for this was hard enough. I wondered what sort of nightmare the weddings planning would be. Christmas Eve arrived. JP turned up with a truck full of garden furniture, lighting and heating equipment. I was at work during the day. When I arrived home the lighting was being tested. The front of the house was festooned with coloured lights. There was arc lighting for the garden and large outdoor gas heaters. In the evening a van arrived from Poole's Pies of Wigan. Excess unsold stock from some of the shops was delivered, sixteen trays of all sorts of goodies. The influence of Laceys Mum had paid dividends. Before going to bed, we put all the equipment from the front garden into the back garden or inside the house. It may not have been there in the morning.

Christmas Day, The party was to commence at 1pm. Harry Porter had organised a Coach from Smiths Happyways to pick some of the guests up from around the region. Others arrived by car and taxi. People with Children arrived later in the day having sorted out all the presents and allowed the first new cycle ride or the playing of new games, trying on new clothes and the like. By early evening the house was crammed full. We decided not to bother arranging live music or a DJ on Christmas Day. I used my 8 track, but even at full volume it was useless. It didn't seem to matter. Everyone had a great time. Lacey and I, JP and Annette shook more hands and kissed more babies than a Politician at election time. We met members of our extended families and friends, and their friends and possibly some gate crashers. We knew all the neighbours from our side of the road, but tonight we got to know many people from across the wide dual carriageway. It was a major dual carriageway and we simply never met anyone from 'over there,' strange.

By 4am Boxing Day we were down to the last few guests. Eight people stayed over. We had regular visits from the Police, not due to any problems but word got around that they were all welcome to have some food and fags or cigars on the house. We even had a Fire Engine call at about 2.30 am on its way back to Huyton from a call. Annette thought they were strippers. She was disappointed. It was an exhausting night but well worth the effort, the best Christmas ever.

The following Months were dominated by wedding plans. The venue for the ceremonies and reception was to be Haigh Hall near Wigan. Not many venues could cater for the anticipated 200 or so guests. Laceys contract with Jim Henderson expired at the end of April so we looked around for another agent/ Manager. The group was to disband. The Musicians who were to stay with Lacey were, Guitarist Malcolm Deedy and Keyboard John Murray. Also Jake (sparks) Miller would help with technical stuff. They decided to re-launch themselves as "Lacey Jay Black and the Confederates".

After much research and lots of meetings they decided to go with a company called "Sounds Fantastic" run by Harry Shaw, with plush offices on Deansgate, Manchester. I accompanied the downsized group to the first meeting. Harry Shaw was a breath of fresh air compared with Jim Henderson. He interviewed the group in depth about their careers and the venues at which they had performed. He knew Jim Henderson and he was not impressed. After a while he asked us to wait in reception while he made some calls. Then he called each member individually into the office again. Jake was asked to be company technical engineer as they didn't have one at that time. I went in with Lacey. The only concern he had was that on commencement of the contract, Lacey would be newly married, and he sought a firm commitment that she could devote 100% to her career. He also asked me if I would fully support her and that it could be difficult for a spouse at times when tours were in progress. I gave my assurance, but inside I was concerned about exactly what that would mean in practice. Still I wanted the very best for Lacey. Everyone else seemed very happy with the contract. Before we left we were given a briefing about the company and its achievements and some notable personalities were on their books, no body major, but everyone was working most of the time. Their main business seemed to be holiday camps and cruise lines with some seasonal work in the Spanish resorts. So it was looking good for the future of 'LJB and the Confederates.'

The next big item which was to be addressed, which I hadn't thought about, was the Stag and Hen nights. The Girls had already decided to go to a night club in Manchester to ogle at male strippers. When JP and I were asked what we were planning, it came as quite a surprise. It made me realise that I didn't have a large group of friends, or even a small one. My Life was my work. There were colleagues but I didn't class them as proper friends. I only had James really. JP was in a similar position. He spent most of his time helping to run a haulage business and he too only had one real friend. So we decided to make it a foursome and go for a weekend to Amsterdam. This went down like a brick in a swimming pool with the girls, but they were going to see strippers after all and saw nothing wrong with that, it was only a bit of fun. Apparently we were on a sex tour. Lacey said she would put a lock on my zip. I asked how I would pee. She told me I could pee when I got back.

The Hen night became a Friday night strip club and a stopover at 'The Midland Hotel' for some of the girls, followed by some serious City Centre shopping on the Saturday which would include a visit to a wedding exhibition at the University. The Amsterdam 'sex tour' went ahead. The group consisted of J, Joe Ball, one of his drivers, James Cooke and me. The City was beautiful with its canals and tree lined streets with quaint old buildings. You needed a second mortgage to buy a snack and they didn't know how to make proper bacon sandwiches. The bacon was pale and fatty. But it was a lovely place to explore whilst avoiding the bicycles. Of course we couldn't resist looking at the red light districts in the evening. It was fascinating to see lots of legs and teats on show in shop windows with some attractive and some not so attractive women attached to them. At one point we were reluctantly ushered into a strip club. It was in a cellar; dimly lit and full of smoke. A topless girl danced on a central stage. We were guided, or rather pushed to two tables next to a wall fronted by red leather seating. We were quickly joined by scantily dressed girls who requested many overpriced weak drinks. We got flashy eyes and a bit of slap and tickle until we had only loose changes left, at which time they lost interest. I was actually very nervous throughout this experience. Joe Ball was on a promise to the tune of several bank notes. His date, arranged for a time after the show in a side alley, but it never materialised, an expensive lesson. Apart from being ripped off at the club we did enjoy our time in Amsterdam. Quite a few men did avail themselves of the goods on offer in the shop windows. I would have been too embarrassed to enter one of those places in full view of everyone. I could have stayed longer than a weekend. I hoped to return some time in the future for a holiday and explore more of Holland. The People were very friendly and anxious to help in any way they could. They seemed to like the English but were still stand offish about the Germans.

On our return we were grilled about our Amsterdam experience with great suspicion. Annette and Lacey questioned the word 'ushered when describing our strip club visit. Then we got the full report on the Hen Night. Then Somehow Jake Miller wangled a seat on the Hen night coach as a sort of chaperone or body guard. Of course he was only interested in possibly getting his end away with one of the girls on the trip when they were suitably sloshed at the end of the night. However, his trip didn't turn out quite like that. A few of the girls took the option of staying at 'The Midland' overnight. Jake returned on the coach with those who managed to make it. Whilst trying to get it on with one of the girls; well actually one of the girl's mums; he was set upon by the party, stripped naked and ejected from the coach 2 miles from home. We couldn't wait to find out about his naked adventure when we next met.

The final total for wedding invitations was 230. I had a standard invitation printed and arranged a signing evening for the four of us. The signing evening took place in 'The Blue Bell' at the corner of Blue Bell Lane and Liverpool Road. When we left I discovered that my car had been stolen. JP had arrived in a pickup truck, so we squeezed into the cab and went to Huyton Police station to report the theft. I was very upset. I loved that car. JP then took everyone home. 3 days later I recovered the car from Kirkby. Jake gave me a lift to the recover it. On the way he told me about his naked adventure. Having been forced from the coach his first concern was to hide. He sheltered for a while in someone's garden until he could formulate a plan of action. There was a row of shops nearby so he made a dash for the rear of the shops hoping to find some cardboard to cover his vital parts. It was about 4am and fortunately very quiet on the roads. He found a box into which he could fit and held it around hid middle. This provided some dignity as he set off towards home. He got the odd horn blown at him; some whistles and cheers, but no assistance. After he had gone about half a mile it started to rain heavily so the box which was lightweight and thin began to disintegrate. One again he found himself in a garden behind hedges. Fortune was with him again when he spotted a Police car on patrol. He stood at the gate and waved it down. The box was almost gone now and he held the last useable piece in front of his tackle. His good fortune was dampened somewhat when a WPC exited the passenger side of the car to assist him. The male officer took his time leaving the vehicle, no doubt to give his colleague the best chance of some amusement. Having explained the circumstances of his plight, the officers gave him a lift home. The WPC couldn't stop giggling for the whole journey which seemed to last forever. Having got home, the WPC kindly lit up his way down the path, or more likely lit up his bottom and gonads. He could laugh about it now, but he wasn't amused at the time.

My car came into view. It looked ok. Fortunately, though it was unlocked, nobody had noticed that it was abandoned and no vandalism had been done. The thief had gained access via the quarterlite window as I had done before. It was so easy. The wiring had been ripped from the ignition and the car started using the wiring. Jake showed me how to start it, but the battery was flat. Jake, being ready for anything, jump started it. I was so relieved that I only had to replace the ignition. The other bit of good fortune was that there was a lot more fuel in the tank than when it was stolen, so the thief must have fuelled up too. How nice of him. The Police informed me later that the thieves had intended to take the car to London but had been spotted by a patrol and stopped. They arrested them for several offences including theft of fuel from a filling station.

CHAPTER 38

There was frantic activity leading up to the big day. We had several family meetings to ensure things were going according to plan. The Hall was booked. The Registrar was sorted and the special arrangements for the double wedding ceremony sorted out. The Catering was organised. The Bride's dresses were sorted, although there was a brief period of panic when the addresses were mixed up and each Bride received the others dress. The cars were sorted by Harry. Everyone including the Bridesmaids had been measured and trial fitted. The Honeymoons were booked. Ours was to be Malta; JP and Annette were going to Switzerland on Railway Tours.

On the day before the weddings, JP stayed with his parents. Annette stayed at our house. I stayed with the James and Sandra who was now heavily pregnant with only a Month to go, and Lacey stayed with her parents. The big day came. I awoke at 7am. The wedding was at 11am. Surprisingly I wasn't nervous. According to James 'The condemned man ate a hearty breakfast.' After a light hearted chat which was meant to settle my nerves; actually I spent the time settling theirs. I returned to the guest room to put on the posh suit from Moss Bros. It didn't feel as comfortable as when I tried it on at the fitting, I think this was down to the starched shirt which was so stiff I felt like a stuffed dummy at first. With everything now on, and having tried my very best Windsor tie knot, I stared at myself in the full length mirror. I didn't look or feel like me. It was like looking at a photograph of someone else. I looked at my hair and re combed it. Then I thought my eyebrows were too bushy. I found a pair of scissors and began to trim. No, that's not right. Trim again. Now one's wider than the other. Trim again. Oops! Shit! Now the left one has almost gone altogether. Now I have to trim the right one to match. Now I look like a cancer victim. My eyebrows now emaciated I think it's time to stop and hope nobody notices, perhaps if I borrowed Sandra's eye liner, perhaps not. I'd look like a clown then.

James and Sandra were also dressing for the occasion. We met up again downstairs. Sandra smiled.

'You look fantastic Nurse Parry; what happened to your eyebrows?' Now I'm in trouble. The first person to see me has noticed the bitched job. James didn't make it any easier by pointing and laughing. Sandra sat me down and reshaped by diminished eyebrows. Now they were very thin, but straight and even.

Sandra stood looking out of the window when the car was due and excitedly announced its arrival. It was a beautiful grey on cream Rolls Royce with immaculately uniformed Chauffeur. We settled ourselves into the soft kid leather seats and floated as if on air to the venue. Now the nerves started to tingle about my body. James brought me up to date with the business in an effort to divert my mind. Sandra told him off for talking about work and she began reminiscing about their wedding and my lovely speech. We arrived at the Hall, and parked behind a, matching, Rolls which had brought JP. This part of the proceedings was family and close friends only and guests were arriving. James, JP and I paced up and down outside for a while, chain smoking. It was a lovely sunny day and the sweat was building beneath my starched collar. We all took off our jackets until we were called inside. The Bride's cars were on their way.

Once inside I settled down a bit. The Grooms and Best Men standing as if on parade, transfixed by the large window behind the registrars lectern. The flower display, on the window sill, and the ancient Oak outside, moving slightly in the breeze, then some movement of doors and shuffling and whispering from the rear. Everyone was asked to stand and 'Here Comes The Bride' boomed through the wall mounted speakers. I could see JP and James looking back, but I couldn't. In a few seconds she was at my side. I didn't take in the dress at first, just her face, the soft gentle skin tones and bright wide eyes. The feminine smile circled by soft pink lips. This face I had never seen before in quite this way. There was a peaceful, relaxed and loving look which said' I am yours, you always knew it. I'm here now my love' Hands, drawn by the magnetism of love, gently joined and squeezed for a moment. We almost kissed but realised that we must wait until invited to do so.

Now I was to drink in the entire view of my Bride to be, the long veil was enhanced by a diamond headband from which protruded curls of lush brown hair. The pristine while full length dress embossed with intricate embroidery and pearls hugged that figure which I adored so much. Just the points of white shoes completed the stunning outfit. I didn't look across to Annette at this stage. I didn't notice the Bridesmaids or James or the Registrar; just Lacey. We had agreed beforehand that from the moment we were married I would call her by her own name, Paula. I felt that Lacey was a name for everyone. Paula would be mine. I didn't want to share her with the world.

The Registrar began speaking but I wasn't listening. James eased me forward at the right time for the main part of the ceremony. After a short while I got a nudge from James. I looked at him. He pointed in the direction of the Registrar. She had said the first line which I was to repeat. I didn't take it in. There were a few giggles from behind. This mistake shocked me into concentration and I followed the words as I was supposed to. Then it was the turn of JP and Annette. Now I looked over to the other couple. JP had got rid of his pony tail and to look the part, Annette wore a full length veil with similar headband. Her dress was not as elaborate but appeared silky and plain and flared out more from the waist down. I was so proud of my beautiful Sister. I loved her very much and today she looked like an Angel from Heaven. Now both couples were asked to give the rings together, which was such a moving moment. Both Mothers cried and the guests spontaneously clapped and cheered. Then we were pronounced Man and Wife or rather Men and Wives, and the long awaited kisses could take place.

Then the Brides, Grooms and Bridesmaids walked out in procession, followed by weeping Mothers and smiling Fathers, to the reception hallway and outside for photographs. We hired two photographers. They had already used possibly 2 miles of film inside. Now the flashes and organisation of the families and friends went on for another 90 minutes. I was knackered already. Our photographer wanted some special studio photos so we had to use the Bridal Limousine to pop into Wigan. This car was a beautiful classic Rolls Royce Silver Shadow. Smooth as silk. You could balance a threepenny bit on the grill and it wouldn't even shiver. We just sat hand in hand and used the drive to recover. Not much was said we just glanced at each other from time to time, kissed now and then and talked a bit about the ceremony which seemed like a dream now.

The studio visit was another 90 minutes, then it was back to Paula's house for a little rest and freshen up before returning to the Hall for the main reception. We had to remain in our wedding clothes to greet guests and start the dancing. Paula and I would return to the house later to change into casual outfits. JP and Annette, not having any studio photos done, stayed at the hall in a private room until it was time to greet all the guests.

Then, the meal. We decided not to have speeches. Too many people would be involved and it would go on for ever. We hired one of those professional after dinner speakers, Roy Mitchel, who was just fantastic. He had the perfect balance of official tributes coupled with copious helpings of humour. The meal was excellent and I enjoyed being on the top table like Henry the Eighth surveying his subjects. The Wedding Cakes, yes there were two, were in the shape of a guitar and a truck. After the cutting they were gone and devoured within minutes. My eyes tired with the constant attack of flash bulbs. Now I had an idea what it felt like to be a celebrity. I kept glancing at Paula. She was having a wonderful time. She was constantly chattering to Annette. They got on very well together. All too soon the children in the room began to get restless and run around or crawl under tables. They became very disruptive and one or two had minor accidents and began to cry. It was time to move on.

6.30pm. the guests start arriving. The four of us stood at the entrance to greet our guests. We shook all the hands. The Bridesmaids organised the presents, the parents took in all the cards. After 45 minutes we retired to the main hall. Remaining guests could find us after that. The live band was setting up, a relatively unknown group who were friends of Paula's, 'Jerry And The Pacemakers'. Just joking, of course they were very well known and a great surprise to me; a surprise to everyone. She kept that secret well. I went to the restroom to freshen up. I was very tired now but I had to keep up with events. JP joined me. He was in the same condition. The evening was electric. That's the only way I can describe it. I had never danced so much in all my life. The music, the singing, lighting and the smoke was draining, but somehow adrenaline overcame the entire atmosphere and produced copious energy as if from nowhere. I decided to stay on one type of drink, white wine. I thought mixing drinks would speed up the effects of alcohol. I needn't have worried. Just dancing with the principal female guests kept me very busy all night. I may have managed only 3 glasses I think.

From 9pm. guests with children began to disappear. By Midnight the Band was all done and piped music completed the wind down. Soon after midnight, Paula and I went round the hall saying our goodbyes to everyone, again lots of hand shaking and kissing. I must have tasted 40 brands of lipstick and smelled the dying effects of a similar number of perfumes. Finally we got to the Parents with a much fonder farewell and more tears. The Rolls was still available to us. The address was our new home at Rainhill. We arrived at 1.30am. Presents would follow us later in the day by courier. We got out of the car. I gave the Chauffeur his tip and away he went. We kissed a long loving kiss. Then, standing at the gate we admired our house. It was a semidetached with garden and privets and an old wooden gate. We walked arms around each other, to the door. I pretended to have lost the key. Paula watched me anxiously as I fumbled from pocket to pocket with a worried expression. Then I produced the key. She was visibly relieved. I opened the door; then accompanied by fits of laughter I gathered her up, with some difficulty because of the dress, into my arms and carried her over the threshold. Unfortunately I lost my footing and ran along the hall leaning further and further forward until we landed in a heap at the foot of the staircase. After checking for broken bones we recovered our posture and giggled our way upstairs.

The house was very warm. We entered the bedroom and I opened a window to let in some fresh air. We kissed for a while and once more declared our love for each other. Zips and buttons were found and surprisingly shyly we combined the undressing of ourselves and each other in silence whilst ensuring that enough reassuring kissing was maintained. Soon we were in bed. The covers not required at this stage we began a form of limited foreplay before joining completely in love making. Tonight it was an expression of love and commitment, the joy of having each other without reservations. We were now together properly. We didn't have to check in or out. We didn't have to use the car or a grassy meadow. We were where we wanted to be, where we needed to be. It was so strange. It wasn't secretive. It was o.k. No problem. I wanted to feel the edge, that guilt, but it wasn't required any more. I have to admit also that there was an element of duty. It was our wedding night. We were both absolutely knackered after what was probably the busiest and most demanding day of our lives so far; and what do we feel we have to do? Be brilliant at making love. Well, under the circumstances, we were brilliant. It was great and wonderful and gorgeous and very loving. We kissed our way to sleep. As I drifted off I couldn't quite believe that this would be us for good now.

Sunday morning. I was first to awake to the sound of birds and the odd vehicle passing by. I looked at my Bride, peaceful, gently breathing. Smudged lipstick and destroyed eye shadow. She was still beautiful though.

She still had her glittery headband on. I decided to sneak away and make a surprise breakfast. I put on a bath robe and went down stairs. The front door had been left wide open all night. The threshold incident made me forget the door. We had remembered that we would need to eat. The fridge and cupboards were well stocked. I managed to prepare bacon egg and toast with tea for me and coffee for Paula our first breakfast in bed. Ahh. Being well organised, I carried the breakfasts upstairs on one tray with the spare tray underneath. Paula was awake now. She was pleased with the attention. Whilst this was a lovely idea, we found that it wasn't easy to actually have breakfast in bed. Great care had to be taken not to spill anything and once in position it wasn't wise to try and move at all for fear of accidents. Still, we enjoyed ourselves. We revisited our experiences of the day before. Paula was so very happy with how everything went.

At dinner time the van arrived with the wedding gifts. We placed all the boxes and cards in the front room. We were leaving for the Honeymoon on Monday morning so the sorting had to be done today. Fortunately not too many items were duplicated. We had 3 toast racks, 2 kettles (3 with the one we already had) 4 sets of cutlery and 7 sets of place mats. Otherwise there was a good mix of mainly domestic items. James sent me a box of 100 condoms with a note saying I may need to top up after the first week. Well, I hoped so. He also sent me an Omega watch of good quality, again with a note saying this was to time my sexual performances as well. Paula seemed in favour of trying. She suggested we telephone him from Malta after 3 days and tell him we've run out. It took us much of the afternoon to sort everything out and the bin was mow full of wrappings and boxes. When's bin day? Just one of the things we have to think about now. There's electricity, gas, telephone, rent, rates, gardening, cleaning, washing, which T.V. programmes to watch, how the money will be sorted out, Bank account. Oh forget it. We've got a Honeymoon to sort out first. When we've used all the condoms we can talk about all the practicalities of living together. Up to now both of us had been looked after. Household matters were dealt with by others. I was fully institutionalised by living in the Hospital; everything was done for me then and also at home. Paula was a lot more independent having spent a lot of time on the road with the group.

I telephoned JP and Annette to find out how they were getting on. Again there house was ready and they just had to move in like us. They were also off on Honeymoon on Monday. Today, like us was presents sorting day. We forgot to have dinner, but we went to a Chinese restaurant in Prescot for tea. I didn't like foreign food so I selected from the English menu. Paula was more adventurous.

In the evening I took Paula on a tour of the Hospital. She was a bit reluctant and fearful but she soon settled after meeting staff and some of our more entertaining residents. She had never seen inside before. Now, after an ordinary sort of day and no problem sharing the T.V., we were able to concentrate more on each other in bed. Tonight it was Paula on top, complete with Stetson. The condom status remained the same. Paula was on the pill. I liked this position. I could see all of her gorgeous body, feel her when she leaned over me to kiss and the penetration was deep. The advantage was of course that Paula did all the work and I just had to fill up the tank with premium sperm. I did have one annoying moment of distraction when I wondered if I'd closed the front door.

CHAPTER 39

James and Sandra took us to the airport for our flight to Malta. We were flying from Manchester Airport and as I had only been there once before I very was not familiar with this vast airport. We decided it would be easier to be taken there. Getting to the airport was easy, the last quarter mile finding our way to International departures drop off point was a nightmare. Fortunately we allowed plenty of time. Having said our fond farewells to the Cookes, we made our way to check in with seemingly 10 million others in the same queue. At last we flopped down into seats in the waiting area and dreamed of things to come. It's at this point that you ask yourself; have I switched everything off at home? Have I locked the doors? The travel agency documents re checked over and over and the pocket is constantly tapped to see if the Passport has escaped somehow. Then your flight is announced and the nerves change tack to excitement as you board the plane. The flight was uneventful but seemed to take for ever. At last the Island came into view. The rich turquoise sea glistened in the early evening sun. The Pilot announced that it was 28 degrees. I didn't know what that meant in English, but I just knew it was beautiful. A few hours later we disembarked from the coach at our Hotel. Then there was the sound of lots of suitcases mini wheels trundling along the pavement and up a few marble steps to reception. Fortunately there were only eight passengers for this stop so we were quickly processed and directed to our rooms. The Hotel was so lovely. A lot of marble and air conditioning made it a very pleasant place to be. I was quite surprised at how hot it was outside.

Paula immediately explored the en suite room with lots of Oohs and Aahs and come and look at this! at each new discovery. I just flopped down on the bed and took a deep breath. The Hotel was wonderful; the Staff was wonderful and the food good. However, just like America, they didn't understand the concept of lean quality bacon. It was weak thin strips with lots of fat. That was my only criticism. The Hotel was set out in a semi-circle partly enclosing two large pools. We spent most of the evening there and went out for a meal late in the evening.

I loved Malta. There was lots of history, and my membership of the St. John Ambulance gave me an insight into the history of The Knights Of St John, whose historic presence was all around the island. We hired a car to explore, both of us having our first experience of driving on the right. After a little practice we were fine, but you couldn't let your guard down; local drivers were a bit care free, and of course there were also lots of tourist drivers to look out for. It was a wonderful honeymoon, full of sand, sea and sex. We made a point of travelling on the old buses, they preserved, which were in normal use. The main tourist areas could sometimes be a trial due to people trying to get us into restaurants or giving out leaflets or trying to sell us time share apartments. Shopkeepers could be persistent and pushy, but it was all part of the experience. There was one incident which inspired me to poetry. It was dedicated to Thomas, a chap who looked like he was from Wigan with his flat cap, wrinkly skin and uneven yellowing teeth. He was an old man with endless energy and enthusiasm. He owned a Horse and cart which was used to take tourists on guided tours of the area.

THE MALTA EXPERIENCE.
Ode to Thomas and his Horse.

At Valletta there's a little man
His fame it is worldwide.
His life revolves around the need
To take tourists for a ride.
He speaks in several languages
Including that of Morse.
He stalks the streets in every way
Does Thomas and his horse.

An Exhibition visited
Above the Harbour Grand.
We set about our entrance
Walking hand in hand.
When all at once he set his course
Did Thomas and his Horse.

He asked us did we want a tour
Of a City full of treasures.
Did we want to go with him?
Partake of all the pleasures.
We said we didn't want to go
Around the tourist course
We're surrounded, pinned and held there
By Thomas and his Horse.

We left him; striding down the street
As fast as we could go.
Thomas jumped aboard his cart
His face was all aglow.

He chased us down for many miles, stopping frequently.
We didn't even have the time
To have a cup of tea.

Escaping to a toilet block
To rest our weary bones.
I heard a funny clonking sound
Like someone throwing stones.
On opening the toilet door
I had a frightening start.
For there before my very eyes
Was Thomas and his cart.

The price it started fairly high
At 15 Maltese Lira.
I asked that if for that high price
I could mount the Horse and steer her.
As he chased us here and there
At speeds both high and low.
Insisting that upon his tour
We must surely go.

At length, and after 3 long hours
We were barely left alive.
For Thomas and his Horse drawn tour
The price had dropped to five.

We found a bus to take us back
To the Hotel clean and white.
And there inside the swimming pool
We saw a funny sight.

You've guessed it what doth greet us there
You'll know it, yes of course.
For waving at us from the pool
Was Thomas and his Horse.

All too soon, the sun, sea but not the sex I hope, was over. The memories of Malta melted into history and it was back; well I was going to say normal, but things were far from normal. We were now a married couple and thinking for two, as a team. We had to organise our own lives. Paying bills, who does what, how the money matters would be dealt with. Everything was now joint, nothing separate. We still needed two cars because of our jobs. I did the manly things mainly like botching up the DIY and being ready to fight off burglars. We shared cooking and cleaning and I looked after the fish, which was easy because we didn't have any. Lacey Jay Black and the Confederates were booked for a season with the holiday camp companies Butlins and Haven, so this would mean a lot of travelling for the band this season until the end of September.

At work everything was fine. The only background issues were concerns about the future of Psychiatric care, concern over the future of the Hospital and year on year cost cutting measures. The old Victorian place was very expensive to run. Also I couldn't see any prospects of further promotion for a long time unless I had somebody assassinated. Still I loved the work and I was content for now. As Paula was away a lot now I tended to spend a lot more time at work just to pass the time. I would spend many evenings playing snooker with the night staff. I became an expert.

In June I became the Godfather of Christine Cooke. I visited Sandra soon after the birth. Sandra proudly presented the bundle of joy for my inspection. Of course I said she was beautiful, but in reality I saw a soft pink bundle of wrinkles which smelled of milk and powder. I could never see any resemblance between babies and their parents so I didn't comment, not knowing who she was supposed to look like. Soon after Annette was also pregnant so I would soon have a Niece or Nephew to contend with. I hoped He or She would like Trucks. My Dad had to retire due to a chest condition having worked for years mixing paint. Mum and Dad could now spend their time getting in each other's way. Paula's Dad was promoted and given a surface job at the colliery. Her Mum was now a shop manageress. So on the whole things were looking good.

My first summer as a married man was difficult. I felt like a bachelor most of the time. My days off would be spent chasing after Paula wherever she might be performing. The up side was I got to know the country very well. Paula managed to get home only three times that summer. I was also able to vastly improve my DIY skills and I was persuaded by a neighbour to get a greenhouse and grow tomatoes. I also got a fish tank and became keeper of the fish. I killed the first half dozen by putting ordinary gravel into the tank from the garden. It seems that it could have been the lime content that turned me into a murderer.

I was very impressed with the standard of caravans at the holiday parks. The bedrooms were always tight, but the living areas were spacious and well appointed. I never imagined that I would ever spend so much time in them. Paula was working very hard and seemed less able to cope with the vigorous schedule than the lads. I knew she was taking supplements to increase energy and sleeping tablet to help her rest. I persistently warned her of the dangers, and while I was with her I didn't see any evidence of the abuse; my experience told me that I had probably driven the habit underground.

The stress and tension of the busy season was showing with Paula. Although the band was doing really well with popularity soaring, Paula was never happy with it. She constantly complained that she never looked right, that her performance was not as good as it should be. She began to have arguments with the lads about insignificant things and even I began to irritate her at times. At the end of the season I took Paula on holiday to Ireland. We rented a country cottage in Donegal in the hope that the peace and relaxation would help to settle nerves and reinstate some sense of reflection and a more sensible plan of action for the future. It took several days to calm Paula down. She was hyped up so much at first. During the holiday we went for long walks and talks. I tried to make her realise her true value to everyone, me, her family and friends, the band and her fans. For four days I was more like a carer than a husband but then things settled down and we relaxed and found love again. In my heart I knew this would not be the last time we would go through this. Another busy period loomed over Christmas and New Year with weekend gigs in between. There was indeed plenty of work as promised; perhaps too much. A recording contract also added to the potential stress.

I arranged a private meeting with Harry Shaw on our return to discuss all the issues of concern. But for now it was peace in beautiful Donegal. We spent the evenings sat in front of the log fire, the light of the dancing flames playing with Paula's skin tones. She had just had her hair cut to shoulder length and tightly curled. Her eyes glistened and her smile was warmed by the soft glow. She was so beautiful. There was a T.V. but it was rarely used. We played scrabble or Monopoly and I taught her to play Chess. Paula started teaching me guitar. We sang songs together, laughed and joked. We even played hide and seek in the woods which sometimes ended up with making love on a grassy bank. David Attenborough may have been interested to know that intense love making attracts millions of Midges. I made a play of being David making his commentary on the scene for Paula's amusement.

'And so, the male having spotted his potential mate hidden in the undergrowth, makes his move. The female, pretending to be stuck, makes giggly mating calls and crawls backward out of the bushes accentuating the shape of her sexually attractive bottom. The male, now fully aroused reveals his hard won prize and mounts her. The mating is over within ten minutes, interrupted by the arrival of 40000 Midges which begin feeding on his buttocks. And so the pair retreat to their den where the female rubs ointment onto the males reddening arse.'

Paula fell to the ground with laughter. 'You're bloody mad you.' was the eventual response.

We spent two wonderful weeks enjoying each other and enjoying Ireland. It was over far too soon and here we were driving along Nut Grove Road just a half a mile from home. How time flies, especially when you're having fun as the saying goes. How true that is.

CHAPTER 40

On my first day off after the holiday I went alone to meet Harry Shaw in Manchester. I told him about my concerns on the drugs issue and the strain Paula was obviously feeling. He responded by assuring me that it was not his company's policy to condone the use of drugs and he would talk to Paula about it. However he was also at pains to point out that he was dealing with adults who were responsible for their own actions. He was not a Priest or a Social Worker but he liked Paula and would try to help. There was, a but, though. He was there to run a business at the end of the day. The band had a contract to fulfil, and if they kept that in mind they would make good money. The Recording Contract had significant value in itself, but the expected increase in work resulting from it would need a lot of commitment. He could only promise more work rather than less. He would tell the band what to expect and advise them how best to deal with it. It was in his interests to ensure that they performed well and stayed fit for the task.

Was I reassured? I'm not sure. I could see nothing but hard work ahead. I decided to talk to one of our clinical Psychologists and seek advice on how best to deal with the forthcoming difficult period. Paula was able to relax at home for a while awaiting the next gig. It was lovely being together and my guitar lessons continued. I very quickly became a reasonable basic guitarist and I could accompany a singer without much difficulty. I found Beatles music very challenging. Their music seemed simple but it wasn't. Paula became partly domesticated for a while but she was less adventurous than me. Ready meals were her preferred method of catering. I liked to prepare as much as possible myself and experiment.

I accidentally found a stash of pills one evening and challenged Paula about them. She told me they were left over from the holiday season and she didn't use them now. I wasn't convinced. My suspicion was confirmed by her mood when I flushed them down the toilet. Although trying to conceal it, she was agitated for several days afterwards. It was then like being at work for a while, the cat and mouse drugs game continued until the band was away again around Warner Hotels for the lead up to Christmas. I didn't see Paula from mid-November until a few days before Christmas. We spoke only on the phone every few days. During this period I visited James and Sandra quite a lot, and JP and my Sister. I spent a weekend with Annette and JP at their haulage yard house. I got to drive a big truck within the site. That was quite exciting. I was also allowed to have his beloved Harley for a full day. Even though the weather was now cold, the large Harley screen made it a pleasure to ride. I took it to Liverpool City Centre where it got plenty of admirers. Fortunately it was dry and the sun tried hard to stay out. I loved it. I also spent time with the in—laws, both of whom were also concerned about the pressures Paula was experiencing. They seemed to think that I was in the ideal position to deal with the situation because of my job and because I was her husband. I only wished it was that simple.

I attended one concert given by 'Lacey Jay Black and The Confederates' at Blackpool, the last concert before returning home. Much to my embarrassment, Lacey Jay wrote a special song which was to be performed in my honour. Lacey announced my presence to the audience, pointed me out with a spotlight and sang her special song to me. I remained in the spotlight for the duration. I was pleased but uncomfortable at the same time. Lacey had written the song for me. These are the words.

I love you my darling love you so much.
I live for your kisses
And yearn for your touch.
With you I am happy
To be free as a bird.
You're in every love song
That I've ever heard.
Many times we're unhappy
Lonely and sad.
But let's count our blessings
And try to be glad.
As we have each other
And a love that's so true.
You give that to me
And I give back to you.

One day destiny'll turn around
And allow us to enjoy.
The endless love we have found
I love you today, tomorrow and forever
Always be with me, Leave me never.
This song is for you, my wonderful Boy
My darling Liam, you're my endless joy.

It was a wonderful moment. The audience erupted. I was patted on the back, my hands shook by many enthusiastic fans, and Lacey Jay came down from the stage and gave me a long loving kiss. My heart was pounding, my face exploding my smile as wide as the ocean. I will never ever forget that. That night in the Castle Hotel was wonderful. We spent a long, loving exhausting night making love like the world was about to end. Our emotions, our passions had been built up for six weeks and were expended in one 'Volcanic Eruption' of a night. I'm sure Paula was high again, but on this occasion it seemed to be for a good cause. I'd argue about it another time.

Christmas Day was shared between both sets of parents to make everyone happy. Between Christmas and New Year we visited friends to keep them happy. New Year's Eve was spent by me at the Hospital. Paula was working again at 'The Castle Hotel' and was due back home New Year's Day after dinner. Now we had some more time together to catch our breath.

The big event for 1973 was the birth of my first Nephew in June. John Paul Porter, was born on the anniversary of 'D' Day,' June 6th. Annette wasn't impressed with the significance of this. Again I was presented with a bundle of wrinkles which this time smelled of milk, powder and for some reason oranges. John had decided to be very noisy and like me was never very happy unless he was sucking a teat. My Mum insisted the baby was the image of JP, but I honestly couldn't see it. He looked more like Churchill to me. So another big family day goes down in History.

The Paula situation was getting more difficult for the next five years. Paula doing frantic period's away working and me coping as best I could. I got used to it, but it had it's difficult times. Paula never quite kicked the reliance on pills and potions. I never quite found the answer to this problem which was getting worse. The discussions about drugs became more frequently rows and at times Paula would walk out and spend a few days with her parents to calm down. I felt I had failed. I was very good at my job dealing with the same problems, but couldn't translate that skill to home for some reason.

September 1979. Paula had left for s weekend of gigs in Portsmouth, aimed mainly at Royal Navy establishments in Portsmouth and Dartmouth. I wasn't unusual by now that I wasn't given precise details, and it wasn't often I could get to the distant places to support her. Paula left on a Thursday morning to get in some rehearsal time before the shows. Later the same day I was informed by the chief that I had 5 days holiday left over from the previous year and I was asked to take them now if possible before an anticipated busy period. I was pleased to do so and finished for five days at the end of duty that day. I decided to go to Portsmouth for the weekend and join Paula as a surprise for the weekend. Even though she was working, we could still find some time to go for meals or a bit of sightseeing. I phoned Harry Shaw to ask for details of the venues. He told me he had booked the group into the "King George Hotel," in Portsmouth and that rehearsals started on Saturday. When I told him Paula had already left he assumed she needed some quiet space before the busy weekend. I could understand that. I also thought a private quiet rest may help her to prepare better than a rush down and rehearsals within a short space of time.

On Friday I took the drive to Portsmouth at a leisurely pace, stopping frequently at places of interest. I went through London which was choked up with traffic as usual, but I liked London. I liked the challenge of driving through it. As I left the City heading for Portsmouth, I had to stop for petrol. I first used my Access card which was declined. I knew there was plenty of money on it, but several attempts proved negative. I assumed it was a problem with the chip because my savings account card did the trick.

I arrived at Portsmouth about 6pm. Having found "The King George," I parked up and walked with a slightly tired stoop to reception. I announced myself as being with the Band and asked what rooms they were booked into. The receptionist told me that 2 of the group had signed in. She wisely didn't give me the room numbers but said she would call to see if anyone was in at that time. Perhaps unwisely I could see that she dialled room 113; telling me there was no reply and would I like to leave a message. I said no thank you, and that we would be meeting up anyway later. I then sat in the lounge for a while. The receptionists changed over and I took the opportunity to go up to the room myself. The door wasn't even locked. I walked in on a scene which although I half expected it, the shock was devastating. Paula was stretched out on the sofa fast asleep and snoring which I had never heard before. On the coffee table were foils, some scorched and small mounds of white powder. I roused her. She hardly recognised me for a moment, and then she just smiled and asked me where she was. I demanded to know why she was in this state, I kicked over the table and roared at her which I had never done before, but it went nowhere. She was in another place. I realised that I would get nowhere. I established that she was in no danger of any further deterioration. I searched for more drugs and found them. I flushed it all away. I decided to find out who else had booked in from the group as the receptionist said 2 people had booked in. I was about to leave the room when I heard a noise from the bathroom. In there I found Malcolm Deedy, the keyboard player. He was stoned too and sitting on the toilet. I pulled him to me, trousers around his ankles. I demanded to know what was going on. Vaguely he explained that they were just chilling out and not to worry. He wasn't worried; he was in the same world as Paula. I threw him into the empty bath tub and left him being sick over himself. I hoped he choked. At reception I asked was there any mail for Mr. Deedy. The receptionist checked the box for room 220. That eased my pain a little, but not much.

I decided not to stay and deal with this situation now. I booked into 'The King's Alms,' a few blocks away and returned home next day. I'd deal with it when Paula got home. I didn't even mention it during telephone calls. Paula acted as if everything was normal and ok. She even said she dreamed about me, but she probably got confused with our actual meeting in the Hotel room.

The fateful day came. Paula arrived home on Tuesday. I allowed her to settle in and asked about the trip. I said I had spoken to Harry and he wondered why she had gone down a day early, though perhaps she had the date wrong. She said she just wanted a day shopping. Then I dropped the bombshell. I told her what I had discovered on my Portsmouth trip. She blew up. Said I was spying on her, why didn't I stay. Why did I sneak off? I explained that I didn't want to ruin her concentration for the shows by having a row about drugs. I described the state I found both of them in and what was he doing in her room anyway. The row got worse and I brought the lack of money into the argument. The Access account down from £2000 to £8 and our Joint Account down from about £5000 to £80. Where had all the money gone, on drugs? We were now holding and shaking each other with rage. I remember her pulling away and Paula turning. The crash of cutlery from the draw as it fell to the ground, then the brief sight of the knife. I stepped away but she lunged at me. I felt the sharp pain in my left shoulder, then again around my left hip, then nothing.

I awoke briefly in the ambulance and quickly out again as the mask was applied. The next memory was casualty at Whiston. In casualty I drifted in and out of consciousness. I was aware of the presence and expressions of concern of Mum, Dad Annette and JP. I tried to say something but was unable to form words, I was dazed and my head was buzzing. Then I was out for a while dreaming of a journey on a bus which had a platform made of milk bottle tops and walking on muddy banks in the Mersey when the tide was out. I smelled oranges and had a ride on an Elephant. I was enjoying my unreal world. Then I began to come around. I heard a jumble of voices and the clattering of metal dishes or pans. Then I focussed on a neon light in the ceiling above me. A female voice, at first muddled, became clearer.

'How are you Mr Parry, are you with us yet?' I think I just said 'Hmm' as my brain began to make sense of my surroundings. A nursing Sister stood over me. She was in the process of doing my pulse, respiration ant temperature. She looked satisfied at what she saw and when I was able to converse better she left. Judging by all the noise I was now in a ward. I didn't want to explore further at this point. I fell asleep again.

I was woken up by a Nursing Assistant who wanted to know what I would like for tea. I could smell food and I heard the rattling of cups and saucers. I felt numb and my mouth was very dry. I lifted my arms to rub my eyes which felt itchy and crusty and noticed that I had a drip connected to my left arm. The Nurse assisted me to sit up and placed pillows behind me. I requested 'T' bone steak with creamed potatoes, mixed vegetables, gravy and half a Lager, followed by Black Forrest Gateau and fresh cream. 'Well you're feeling better aren't you; now what would you really like?'

I settled for Shepherd's pie, then Banana and custard. As she walked off to get my order I noticed she had nice legs. I was feeling better.

I was in for ten days. My wounds were quite serious but not life threatening. I had many visitors who kept me informed about events, including the fact that Paula had a history of drug related problems and up to a year before she met me, she was no stranger to the judicial system. I was amazed and disappointed that she felt unable to tell me about these things. Paula had been arrested. She had been to a hearing and remanded in custody. For now I had no idea what I was going to do. My Family had engaged a Solicitor. I had given statements to Police and to Legal Teams, my own and Paulas. I was questioned and re questioned, a Medical Photographer was brought in to take pictures of my injuries. I was very tired and fed up most of the time. As a self-diagnosis I began to have severe bouts of depression in Hospital. I had very dark thoughts of self-destruction; I blamed myself for letting Paula down. I should have known how to deal with her problems better.

The standard of care was much as I expected from when I had my brief period of General Hospital experience during my training, I got the impression that in general nurses were more interested in paperwork and chatting than getting involved with the patients. My impression was confirmed during my stay as a patient. It was often difficult to get attention except during scheduled visits when doing charts or medication rounds or when it was Doctors rounds . . . At any other time you were often wasting your time calling for assistance. I spent much of the time during the first six days in pain. I once asked to see a Senior Nursing Officer but only got the Sister who told me I wasn't the only person they had to deal with, they were doing their best. At night it was difficult to get a good sleep due to the number of patients trying to get the attention of the staff in the nurses' station near the ward entrance. Often the requests would have to be passed up the line to the bed nearest them. This was a trauma unit were patients had been injured in car accidents or industrial accidents. There was only one other stab victim, a Police Officer across from me and someone who had been shot. I never found out who or why. The Bed to my right was occupied by a variety of short term cases; the bed to my left was occupied by a bloke who found everything wrong with everything in the world. He didn't help my depressive periods at all. I wanted to strangle him.

At long last I was able to leave, with instructions to attend physiotherapy for a while. I contacted the Chief at Rainhill. I was assured that I could take all the time I needed to recover. That helped ease my mind about work but the guilt about my failing Paula continued. My time at home was lonely. I had too much time to think. I continued to receive Solicitors letters to clarify this or confirm that. I decided I must visit Paula at Risley to discuss things we needed to discuss if possible. Before I could arrange that, I received a letter from her.

CHAPTER 41

'M_y darling Liam,

How do I begin? How do I have the right to even attempt to say that tiny little word? That word that hasn't a chance of repairing the love we've had, that I've torn apart and scarred it forever.

Well I will say it anyway. I am so so very sorry my darling. If I could turn back time I would, and take the hurt myself, even end my life so that I could never hurt you.

I hate myself. I hate what I have become, my lovely Liam. You deserve so much more. You've been so wonderful and loving to me. You've been right from the start about the drugs, and now I confess and admit that I have a crazy uncontrollable addiction to these soul destroying drugs.

It crept up on me darling. I thought I could control it. I told myself it would never get to this stage. My darling, I knew you could see this coming, and now I see how right you were my love. You must hate me. You have every right to. I would understand if you were to rip this letter into tiny pieces and forget it ever arrived.

If that is what you want my darling, so be it, but always try to remember these words, maybe my last words to you. I love you, I love you more than life itself, and if these are my final words to you, then my life is now over and all the happiness gone forever.

Now another tiny word, IF. If there is the slightest chance that you will have me back, I will do anything and everything to try to be the girl you loved. The girl you laughed with; the girl whose eyes you looked into on that beautiful day when we said 'I Do'. To each other, the love and tenderness we have shared.

Please don't let it be the love we have lost my darling. I ask you, I beg of you my one and only love. Please, oh please give me a second chance to repair the damage I have done to us and our lives together.

I ask only once my darling. If you don't reply then I will understand, and I will know I've lost you forever. If that is so my darling, I will never forget you and never stop loving you. I will be eternally yours, always until my hopeless life has ended.

Your Paula. XXXXXXXXXX'.

That was so emotional. Paula poured her heart out and was obviously sincere at the time. Her mind would be clear now without the influence of the drugs, but she must also be feeling like shit for the same reason. She needed proper treatment and with the court case looming we might at last be able to make proper arrangements to sort the problems out. It wouldn't be easy. My experience told me that. I was nervous about visiting Paula. My Solicitor thought it was a bad idea, but she is my wife after all and she needs to tell me about what happened from her point of view. I didn't reply to the letter in full. I let her know that I would see her in person very soon. The day came. I drove to Risley, a place I had heard of but never seen before. When I arrived I was stunned. My wife, my Paula was kept behind that horrible wall with barbed wire mesh on top. I was chilled with fear. I parked up and made my way to the visitor's entrance in company with quite a lot of people. Most of them seemed quite happy, like it was a day out, I couldn't understand that. Everyone was checked in and we had all our bags searched and personal items checked, rather like the airport but more miserably, if that was possible. We were then escorted to a large hall with tables and chairs set out. Even though I wasn't a prisoner I felt terrible in there. We were escorted by a small, fat, red haired warden who looked like she would kill you if you stepped out of line. Red heads always seemed bad tempered to me. We could sit wherever we liked and awaited the appearance of the inmates, rather like awaiting the arrival of an inbound flight at the airport, except that you wouldn't expect the same smiles and hugs. Amazingly though, that's exactly how it was. It was on the whole a jovial occasion. For a few, like me it was a lower key and emotional meeting. The prisoners, all women in this area, hurried to their respective visitors. Some were greeting families; even children. I couldn't imagine how stressful it must have been for children visiting their Mothers in jail. Well technically it was a remand centre but the distinction would be lost in the eyes of a child. No one here had been convicted of anything yet.

All the tables were now occupied. Mine was still vacant. I looked towards the entry point for prisoners. There stood Paula. She looked drained and lost. The Warden pointed me out and encouraged her to take a few more steps. I stood and walked towards her. She was a broken woman. I had never seen her hair untidy and she wore a standard issue garment which made her look like a cleaner. Her face and legs were white as death, her lips pale and no makeup. I hardly recognised her. As I approached she again halted, her cheeks glistened with tears. She almost seemed to look through me. I hugged her to me. She was stiff and cold. Her curves had disappeared to make way for what felt like a bony wreck. I walked her to the table and sat her down. My chair was situated opposite. I moved it to the side.

I didn't know how to start the conversation.

'Come on now love, I'm here now, don't be upset. How are you?'

I immediately regretted that stupid statement. Of course she knew I was here, of course she would be upset and I could see how she was. I noticed that everyone else had brought things in, rather like a hospital visit.

'"I'm so sorry, I haven't brought anything, and I didn't know I could. Thanks for the letter. I know you feel terrible about what happened. Don't worry, we have to sort things out now and try to make it all better.' Paula managed to stop crying.

'We can't make it better, I almost killed you, and don't you hate me?'

I held her hand. 'It was your use of drugs which put you in that state love. If you agree to a course of treatment it will go down well in court. You must show you're serious about it though.'

She started sobbing again and between sobs she said 'No, I'm done for. They say I'll go down for this, all the girls here know what's what; they say I'll be seeing them later, and they laugh. I've been in trouble a few times before you know. I didn't tell you because I didn't want to put you off. I'm so, so sorry.'

I wiped her cheeks with my thumb. 'Nonsense, they're just winding you up. Don't take any notice'

The conversation continued in that vein. Paula denouncing herself and me trying to be positive. I noticed that I couldn't bring myself to use a more endearing term than 'love'. It made me question how I really felt. I was ashamed at my poor performance on the visit. I had no impact on her mood, perhaps even made it worse. Her Mum and Dad had visited but none of the group as yet. She didn't think they would because they would probably be out of work for a while. I said I would enquire about the situation there.

Our time was up. The detainees sauntered out of the room and disappeared. There was the sound of a bunch of keys turning in the lock like a final goodbye. The visitors were escorted out. In the car park I stood once more to gaze upon the chilling sight of the high grey wall. I stood for some time. Everyone else had gone. I stood alone, just looking at the wall. My optimism about the outcome of the court case was now deflated. Perhaps the other women were right. I just couldn't imagine how Paula would cope with that. Also, I couldn't imagine how things would be if she returned home. I was lost in a jumble of thoughts.

There was a gap of two months before the matter came to Crown Court trial. Between times I worked rather like a robot at the hospital. I just did what I had to do and went home each day to my own cell. The routine was broken occasionally by family and friends; thank goodness for them, then came the day of the trial. In addition to me there was rather tense contact between the two families; it was nervous rather than confrontational. We were then separated for a period just prior to going in to court. The Solicitors pre-trial pep talk went in one ear and out the other. I was as nervous as if it was me in the dock. When the Defence Lawyer laid into me I did feel like the accused. She tried everything to trip me up, confuse me and make me angry. I was so deflated; nothing could have made me angry. I just wanted to fall through a hole in the floor. Other evidence drifted over my head, I didn't want to listen.

Paula looked pale and drawn. She kept her eyes to the floor. My Lawyer laid into her too and I felt for her. At one point I jumped up and shouted. 'Leave her alone, hasn't she had enough?' I was immediately rebuked by the judge and told I would be held in contempt of Court if there were any more outbursts. The Court was adjourned for 15 minutes to allow my Lawyer to instruct me. I was pleased. It let Paula off the hook for a short while. The rest of the proceedings were hard to bear. After what seemed to be an eternity, the Jury retired to consider their verdict. After only 15 minutes they returned a verdict of guilty. It was expected but felt like a sword going through my chest. There was then a period of submissions by experts and Lawyers, Social reports etc. Previous offences were then brought up which did nothing to help her cause. Paula was sentenced to 3 years detention. The judge stated that Paula would now have the opportunity to receive proper treatment for her addiction. She was escorted to the cells. Her Parents broke down in tears. I fainted. A Court Usher helped to bring me around again. I was given a cup of sweet tea.

We were allowed to visit Paula in the cells before she was taken away. My Solicitor told me that the sentence would actually be 18 months, less time already spent in remand. She could actually be released in a year if all went well. For the time being she would be returned to Risley until a place could be found in a Prison. This could be anywhere in the Country. At the cell I joined Paula's Mum and Dad. They were ok. All three of them were apologising to me which made me feel awkward. I was able to kiss Paula through the bars and hold her hand for a moment before giving way to her Parents. Then we left.

In the car park I met my Family together with James and Sandra. We agreed to meet at my Family home in Page Moss, rather like a gathering after a funeral. That's what it felt like we were doing. Everyone left. I stood by my car and looked blankly at everything. I watched traffic and People, Lawyers in gowns wandering in and out. Then my heart pounded again. The prison van edged its way out into the traffic. I watched it disappear into the distance. It began to rain so I sat in the car. A sort of Paula ghost appeared next to me where I was used to seeing her. I began to shiver and switched on the engine to get some heat into the car. It wasn't a cold day, but I felt cold. The evening at the Page Moss house was a nice diversion from events. I wondered how many more diversions I may need.

I arrived home about 11pm. I had some drinks in the dining room which I looked over in consideration of which to use. I settled on a single malt Irish whiskey and drank enough to make me dizzy and aid sleep. It worked.

For several Months I would use this method for getting to sleep, reminding myself not to do it too often. Paula spent another six weeks at Risley before being transferred to Holloway for twelve weeks then Askham Grange for eight weeks and finally Styal in Cheshire for the remainder of her sentence. I visited frequently at every location. Many letters flowed to and fro, and Paula seemed to be improving all the time. There were some worrying incidents with other inmates from time to time. At each location there was a status pecking order in which Paula found it difficult to adjust. Fortunately nothing of a major nature occurred in her case, but there were some serious incidents in which people were hospitalised due to disputes. I was disturbed also by the knowledge that drugs were also available in Prison and fags, gifts from visitors and almost anything else were commodities inside. Some women it seems could be very aggressive to each other. Paula managed to create a niche for herself as a Music

Tutor. The Governor at Styal was delighted to use her skills for the benefit of about 12 prisoners; three of whom formed an internal pop group who called themselves 'The Stretch.' They even did a gig at Strangeways for the men. It went down very well.

Paula stuck faithfully to the treatment regime and by the time her release was due, her spirits and general wellbeing had improved considerably. We were both ready to try again and put it all behind us. There would be remaining issues to deal with, but the worst was behind us. I talked to neighbours who were very supportive, so I was less anxious about her return home. Family and friends were still nervous about it and wondered if I was doing the right thing, but the decision was made and the day of release came.

10am, on a Friday morning. A pleasant, autumn morning, October 1973, my final visit to the prison car park as a visitor. Several people awaited friends or loved ones being released that day. The Main gate opened to allow a prison van to leave, followed by six women, one of whom was Paula. Two groups of delighted people merged to form a hugging and kissing convention before fanning out to their respective vehicles. I hadn't seen Paula dressed in nice clothes for what seemed to be an eternity. Still no makeup but she had managed a touch of lipstick. She had put on about two stone in prison, a fact which I was very careful not to mention. I didn't drive straight home. First I went to St Helens where we had dinner and did some therapeutic shopping. It occurred to me that her clothes at home probably wouldn't fit now. Again I said nothing about my reasoning behind this. We had a lovely couple of hours walking around the shops. Paula was obviously ill at ease most of the time. Next stop was Taylor Park for a romantic walk before the sun went down and the temperature dropped. We walked hand in hand shuffling through occasional small mounds of fallen leaves. The now horizontal shafts of sunlight enhanced the blazing reds and gold's of the remaining leaves on the trees. The evergreens looked richer and perhaps smug amongst their deciduous friends. There were flocks of birds swooping between clumps of trees and very few people about. There wasn't much conversation but the walk was punctuated with stops to kiss briefly. Before we returned to the car there was a long hug with some tears and reassuring words from me. The air got noticeably colder suddenly. We returned to the car for the slow drive home.

CHAPTER 42

The return home was both happy and tearful for Paula. We sat in the lounge and I switched on the T.V. She seemed lost, but that was to be expected. She was waiting to be told what to do.

'This is your home, you do as you wish, you don't need me to tell you when or what; just do anything.'

I made a cup of tea and began unloading the shopping from the car. Excitedly we looked through all the new clothes and I requested a Fashion Show. Shyly, she agreed and for an hour I got a parade of different items of clothing. Eventually we settled in to watch T.V. sitting together on the sofa hand in hand. Paula fell asleep. I wondered what my approach should now be. Would she like to just relax and sleep tonight, or would she like to be appreciated as a beautiful woman and be seduced. Would she be feeling under pressure to perform sexually or would she feel better being allowed to settle in to her new freedom first? This was a new situation for both of us and there was no 'newly freed prisoner help line' to phone. The situation was decided for us when at bed time Paula apologised for being on her period. So it was just cuddles for a few days. In a way I was pleased, the pressure was alleviated.

After initial nerves, like the first time together, we got into bed. The strange thing was that Paula now wore a nightie that was a new thing, before we were always nude, still, no problem perhaps that would change soon. Domestic life returned to near normal quite quickly and the first week saw much progress, except for the nightie and the early morning rising, followed by bed stripping and neatly folded bed clothes at the foot end of the bed. There was also a need to be obsessive about cleaning and tidying for a while, no doubt the influence of institutional prison life. On the evening of the fifth day the skies looked quite gloomy as I left the hospital on the ten minute walk home. Storm clouds were brewing and distant thunder could be heard. I counted the seconds between rumbles which I understood gave an indication of the number of miles away the storm was. The count reduced from 10 to 4 by the time I turned the key in the front door. As I walked into the lounge I announced my arrival. There was no response. I looked in all the rooms but they were empty. From the back bedroom I looked at the angry sky and was momentarily surprised by a flash of forked lightening. Just before I turned something drew my attention to the garden it was Paula sat at the wooden garden table. It had started raining and she didn't make her way inside. I went down to meet her to discover why this strange behaviour was happening.

As I stepped into the garden, Paula turned to look at me. She was dressed in a bath robe and seemed unconcerned that the rain was getting heavier and the thunder and lightning was all around us. I was soaked before I realised that I was in shirt sleeves. Paula smiled at me without answering my question about what was going on. I reached to take her hand and escort her inside when she pulled me to her and kissed me. I leaned back a little and looked into her eyes. She was smiling; a genuine happy smile. I took a pace back, now smiling myself.

'Aren't you coming in?'

'No' she said and opened her robe to reveal her curvy body. She ripped open my shirt, pulled down my trouser zip, pushed me against the high privets, pulled me to her and we kissed again. The thunder clapped again as she mounted me, wrapping her legs around me I sank a little into the firm hedge as I became fully aroused. Suddenly I was inside her and she rode me like a horse. As she leaned back a fork of lightening lit up her wet face and large raindrops entered her mouth and covered her face. The rain became so heavy now it was like having sex in a shower; well of course it was a shower, but not a comfortable bathroom shower. We weren't cold just very wet and steamy. Paula began screaming with passion. Fortunately the noise of the massive storm drowned her out from neighbour's ears. This wasn't love making, this was wild, unbridled shag. It was sex for the sake of it, for the fun of it. Paula was at last free. Every emotion went into this, love, sexual expression, fantasy, anger, rage, domination, although I'm not sure by whom. It was mad, spontaneous, or as I called it sponktanious. It was desire, urgency and crushing Also Paula's extra weight nearly killed me. The rain eased, the tension eased and my legs gave way. We fell to the wet muddy grass laughing, kissing, and feeling. It was just the most magnificent shag of my life. I hoped it wouldn't be the last.

We soggy pair made our way inside. When I first got home I had fortunately switched on the gas fire. We lay together, now nude, on the rug to dry out. Paula had several grazes to her legs and I felt some cuts on my back, but we could deal with them later, much later. The light of the flames danced on her cheek and lit up her eyes. The fire made everything feel good and natural. Fire can be man's best friend. It's what made us what we are. The flames were relaxing, warming, comforting. From now on there were no nighties.

After some time relaxing, we made our way to the bathroom to stand together in a proper shower with clean warm water . . . We fondled, kissed and soaped each other, again becoming aroused. At the point where I knelt and kissed her vaginal lips I sensed some nervousness. I began to play with her and as I inserted a finger she flinched. Asking if she was alright I was helped to my feet to be met by a concerned expression. I left it at that until we lay together on the bed. She had loved the sex session in the garden, it was just wonderful. The playing with the fanny brought back flash images of being forced to have sexual relations with a bully lesbian at Holloway. There were a few butch lesbian women there who ruled the place, selecting anyone they wanted for sexual abuse. Any women who resisted were beaten up or in one case stabbed in that area. I was stunned. I asked how it could be allowed to go on. It was a regime of fear with serious consequences for noncompliance. I was angry, but asked to forget it. It was in the past and we could work it out together.

The subject was never mentioned again. Sex became normal and routine, rather like a duty than a spontaneous pleasure. Normal sex was fine, but sex play with the hands was out of bounds. She never got over it.

Friends and family accepted Paula back into the family circle, at least on the surface. We took part in all the family occasions and Paula began to help out at the clinic with music sessions and lessons for the patients. Christmas and New Year went before Pula had the urge to get back into the music business The Agencies rejected her for now and she began to get depressed about it. I suggested she try busking in the City. She laughed it off at first but one Saturday afternoon in the spring of 1974 I persuaded her to take the guitar into Church Street in the City and give it a go. I said I would stay with her and give support. The trial went very well. Paula was good at what she did. Her enjoyment was written all over her face. Paula dressed in her glittery cowgirl outfit which was picked out nicely by the sun. She sang Country songs and many people lingered on the benches and the spare ten gallon hat upturned on the pavement began to fill with coins. We set up at 11 am and by 2pm the coin collection was looking very healthy. At this point we were approached by a Copper who was wandering if we had a licence to perform on the public highway. I had no idea a licence was needed. He could tell that our surprise was genuine. He said he thought Paula was great. Some old ladies rebuked him and told him to leave us alone. With a smile and in his broad Liverpool accent he said.

'All right girls, keep ye air on, am only advising dem. Keep jigging away.' Turning to us he said quietly . . . Am not arguing with dem owl girls, dey'll tear me te pieces, ye no warra mean like? Get the paper please will ye?'

We agreed and he had a little dance with one of the owl girls before moving on. At three we packed up and counted up the bounty, £30. Wow! The next step was to get legal.

All that summer Paula went busking, weather permitting. She earned more than me. However the bug for the gigs remained strong. One rainy Saturday in November we were browsing around the Walker Art Gallery when we met an old friend. Sitting on a couch and dressed in a track suit was Jake (sparks) Miller. He was delighted to see us and gave Paula, whom he still called Lacey, a big hug and kiss on the cheek. I got a firm hand shake; I didn't really want the kiss. We were invited to have a drink in the café to discuss some information he had for us. During our chat we were given details of a man who was in the industry, Andre Belvoir. Andre was a record producer, known more on the continent than here in England. He had lots of contacts and was well known by entertainment managers on all the cruise lines. Andre was also a well-known pop singer in France and Jake thought he may be useful to get to know. Jake had done a lot of work for Andre in the past year which took him all over Europe. He offered to arrange a meeting with Andre if we wished. Paula was keen to have such a meeting. Jake would get back to us. Now Paula was excited, but I urged caution in her expectations. Andre was obviously a high flyer businessman and may not be able to do anything for us.

It was January 1974 before the meeting took place between Paula and Andre Belvoir. I was not able to attend but Jake was at the meeting which took place at The Adelphi Hotel on a Friday evening. It was late when Paula got home to report on progress. She was so excited. Andre agreed to get a contract together and advised Paula to seek the advice of a Solicitor on the detail. If she was satisfied, a recording contract could be in place soon together with a season of work for Princess Cruise lines out of Florida. It all seemed like a massive storm of change which was about to hit our lives. I was happy to see Paula so enthusiastic about opportunities again. More meetings were to take place to iron out all the detail and I was also encouraged to join in with the process. I was comfortable with all this because Paula was advised to get her own legal team to help her. This I believe made the potential deal above board.

By April 1ˢᵗ. a 3 year contract was in place. Paula became more excited as each day passed. She wanted to start afresh with a new name but Andre advised against it. His wish was to retain the Lacey Jay Black brand which already had a reputation. He started looking for candidates to form a new band to back her. There were over eighty applicants, all of whom were carefully scrutinised at lengthy auditions over a two week period. I was invited to put my opinions forward. What a difficult job that was. There were a lot of great musicians out there. Finally we sorted out the best of the bunch that would be offered contracts.

Jimmy Kelly, 22yrs old, married, 2 children, lived in East Sussex, guitarist, described as a session man. He had played backing for a number of famous groups. He played all string instruments, even the harp. I thought he had magic fingers, I loved listening to him

Damion Shell, Single, 29yrs old, played all things keyboard and he was an established music composer as well. When he played classical music on the piano he just blew me away.

Henrik Bushkart, from Germany, divorced, 38yrs old, now living in Birkenhead, drummer or anything you hit with a stick. He had boundless energy and precision. His solos were transfixing and sometimes ear splitting.

Valerie Walker. 21yrs old, backing singer, violinist of distinction, bass guitarist and song writer. She had orchestral experience with the Liverpool Philharmonic and was single, thought to be Lesbian. I wasn't convinced, perhaps just dedicated and unavailable for now. That was my impression. Women who didn't fall over themselves to go out on dates could often be wrongly labelled. Time would tell if I was right. Valerie lived in Warrington.

So now the new band was formed,'Lacey Jay Black and The Jetstream.' Now the hard work began. Andre was well versed in bonding new artists. He was a hard task master. For a month I saw little of Paula and when I did see her she was exhausted. I was able to attend some of the rehearsals and watched the group develop. I could tell that the style and quality being produced was far superior to 'The Nashville Track'. In June they were off on their first assignment with Princess Cruise Lines from Southampton to the Red Sea and Egypt, a four weeks period away, apart from just two day turnaround at Southampton after the first two weeks. We arranged to spend that time together in Southampton.

This was the way life was now. Lacey Jay was in her element again. The regime didn't seem to be as demanding as before but the travelling was relentless. Judging by telephone communications and letters and the great relaxing times we managed together, Lacey stayed away from the drugs. She dieted frequently to keep her figure which had slimmed down to her pre prison weight quite quickly.

There were a number of changes over the term of Paula's 3 year contract. Sandra had a second child which they named Lorna. Annette also had a second baby which they called Sarah, a lovely little niece this time. Jack and Marjorie, JP's parents were still in the same jobs and The Cookes still happily messing about in boats on the Isle of White. My Parents Moved to a bungalow on Tarbuck Road Huyton. I was looking for a new job, possibly in Social Services. The atmosphere was changing at Rainhill, budgets were being squeezed and I needed a change and a challenge.

CHAPTER 43

March 1977. Paula's contract had come to an end but was to be renewed. Valerie Walker left the band to be replaced by Juliet Muttabe, an African girl with a soft soulful voice, a talented instrumentalist across the board into the bargain. The group had enjoyed a great three year's work on the Princess line. They travelled extensively and Paula had a great tan and model figure. There wasn't much married life to speak of and I was hoping for more home life, but that was not to be. We had a month off, 3 weeks of it spent on holiday in France. Andre stayed with his family in Burgundy and we stayed in his villa near Paris. On a couple of occasions he visited us to take us on trips around areas he knew well. It was a wonderful relaxing time, but I could tell that Paula's mind was often somewhere else. Her first love wasn't me, it never was. She wanted to be touring all the time. Still I was enjoying the moments we had.

Paris was a lovely City. A great mix of cultures and traditions dripping in History and culture and many very poor areas were evident. Many of the less expensive cars were damaged and parking regulations seemed non-existent. Drivers of large vehicles could often be seen enlisting help to bounce double parked cars out of the way in the narrow side streets. Pavement Cafes were everywhere and there was a strange mix of frantic rushing around and sitting around in cafes and bars as if time didn't exist. Many French ladies carried poodles either in bags or in their arms like a sort of fashion accessory. Women were always perfectly groomed and proud. The men on the other hand tended to be scruffy and careless in their appearance. French men had a reputation of being romantic. I thought they were scruffy and arrogant.

I found the driving great fun and often a real challenge. The Periferique or ring road had a strange system for filtering on and off. Whereas we have definite on and off slip roads on our motorways, this road had the on and off slip road combined into the same stretch which made it rather hazardous at times. This was a high speed road and decisions had to be made quickly and accurately if you wanted to live a bit longer. In the centre core of the City it was very much every man or women for themselves. I thought London was a 'Rat Race,' but the race was invented here in Paris. I remember at one intersection being confronted with a junction with about six exits. In England there would have been a roundabout. Not here. You stopped briefly and chose your intended route, then dashed, many I think, with eyes closed, towards your intended exit. My mind was blown for a while and I got stuck in the middle of no man's land with mad French men buzzing around me with hands welded to the horn. Eventually I found an exit. It was the wrong one, but I was just pleased to be still alive.

On another occasion Paula and I were sitting at a pavement café on the Champs—Elysees, near the Arch De Triumph. Several lanes of traffic raced around as if on a fast merry-go-round and changing lanes in a spaghetti formation. 2 Policemen stood on a white spot at the head of the Champs-Elysees. They casually watched the mayhem. Then one of them pointed at a hapless women driver and indicated that she should pull over. She was a couple of lanes over and had to risk death by forcing her way suddenly across the lanes of fast moving traffic to meet the Police. Having made it without a major accident, the Police commenced their inspection of the little fiat, one interviewing the woman, the other walking around inspecting the vehicle. Whilst doing this, a young lad on a scooter lost control of his mount and crashed into the back of the Fiat being inspected. He fell off and his helmet fell off and rolled down the centre of the road. The young man then having retrieved his helmet, re mounted his scooter and rode off. The Police meantime took absolutely no notice of this incident and continued with their inspection of the car. After 5 minutes they simply waved her on again.

I loved just walking hand in hand with Paula and exploring this wonderful City, sitting in the street cafes and 'People watching' or taking a bus ride or a River Boat trip. Paula was more interested in shopping and eating than visiting Art Galleries or Museums. Lots of wine also flowed and much of the time I was either merry or slightly dazed whilst exploring. Once, in a department store I stopped to look at some perfumery. I let go of Paulas hand whilst I inspected some bottles as the French assistant told me all about the items in sexy French. I didn't understand much of what she said with my school French. I walked on taking Paula's hand again, discovering after a minute or so that it wasn't Paula. Fortunately the lady was amused rather than angry. She made no effort to point out my mistake until I noticed myself. It took me some time to find Paula again walking a grid system around the counters until she reappeared. She thought the taking of the wrong hand incident so funny she frequently laughed about it for the rest of the day.

The Parisian nights were as expected very romantic. We would go for an evening meal washed down with great wines. Then we would giggle our way back to the hotel. The receptionists didn't quite get why we would ask for the key for Mr. and Mrs. Smith every time. They just assumed we were mad English people. They were right. We would giggle our way to the lift, at which point Paula had lost at least one shoe. It cost us a fortune in shoes. We would giggle our way up in the lift, often to the wrong floor. Each floor had identical table and flower display across from the lift door and identical yellow wallpaper, so it was difficult to know what floor we were on. Even sober people made mistakes, so there was no chance for us. At times it took us up to 40 minutes to find our room. The nights were warm so we would throw open the French Windows; this time they were actually in France. Then we would make love in the reflection of flashing lights from the street and with the background noise of traffic and constant horns blowing. I remember after one very hot sex session, Paula went out onto the balcony to cool off in the breeze, forgetting that our room was at the front of the hotel above the main street, the horns were then joined by clapping and whistles. Next morning we had a visit from the Gendarmerie and the Management with a firm warning.

All too soon France was a distant memory and it was back to the day jobs. We visited family and friends with all the news and photographs and I became a part time Husband again. The band got into the charts top 100, in fact to number 45 with a song written by Paula called 'Chances'. We had money in the bank, Paula was happy and without the need for drugs; although she could knock the wine back. I had a Mercedes 500 and Paula had a growling white Beetle Convertible. Financially it was our best period to date and getting better.

This year the Band toured the U.K. resorts until October. Then a brief rest until the Christmas and New Year gigs started. There was talk of a U.S.A. tour for 1979. I wasn't looking forward to that. I would virtually be a Bachelor if that came off

The U.S.A. tour did indeed materialise, a three month tour from April to the end of June 1979. Then after a short break it was Cruise Lines again until October and so it went on and on. I had the occasional treat when I was able to fly out to more places in the world than I had ever been to before I had a good tan but a not so good marriage. Paula drifted further and further away. There were times when she could have returned home for periods of leave but decided not to. We didn't argue we didn't confront each other on the issue; we just lived more and more apart. We went through the motions of enjoying each other's company when we were together, bur that's all it was.

It was September 1981 before I received the letter I had half expected. The Band had just done a summer season around the south of France tourist spots and Paula was due to return home in October.

'My darling Liam,

Over recent times, or perhaps longer than that, we have been drifting apart. In all the time I have known you, your support and love have been with me; even after I let you down so badly when I had the drug problem.

I have been a burden to you all this time and I am so deeply sorry for that. It's no good us continuing on the way we are and it is not your fault in any way the way things have gone. My work has always taken first place and you have always understood and put up with it, but it's time I released you from the chains I have held you in.

My time with the group and in particular, Andre, has brought Andre and me closer together as we have drifted apart. We have now developed a loving relationship and I have been unfaithful to you. I know I promised so much, but I have failed you again and you would be better off without me.

I think it would be for the best if you would consider a divorce. I will not contest it and I will agree to any and all obligations that would entail. The least I can do is to make it as easy as possible for you. Please agree. Please let me go and be rid of me. Find someone who you can really love; who will stay by you and look after you in the manner you so richly deserve.

I am so very sorry. I believe I can make a new life here with the new love of my life. We will be together all the time and I think it can work. You will be better off without me, you know it too. You deserve better.

You may not believe this but there will always be a place in my heart for you and if we can remain friends then Andre says you will always be welcome as our guest. He likes you and genuinely hopes we can be friends.

I don't know whether you would like to meet or just write to sort matters out. Whatever you decide will be fine. You can also call me if you wish.

Love, Paula."

The letter was on the hall mat when I got home one evening. I read it and re read it. Then I just sat in my armchair holding it in my hand. My thoughts drifted all over the place, a jumble of nonsense. The letter dropped from my hand. I stood and made my way to the kitchen where I poured myself a very large whiskey and drank it in one go. Then I poured another and drank it more respectfully as I tried to consider what to do. Sitting at the table I placed my head in my hands and cried. Several more glasses passed my lips before I decided to go for a walk. Walking always helped me think things out. All I remember is walking for a long time. My surroundings didn't sink in. I had no plan; I just walked aimlessly until at 1.30am. I found myself at a metal railing looking into the black waters of the river Mersey at the Pier Head, Liverpool. I was now about 12 miles from home and remembered nothing of my journey. I leaned on the rail and my legs felt hot and tired. I had set off on a mild evening but now there was a chill in the breeze.

I looked across the river at the lights of Birkenhead. I took in the panorama of the whole Wirral towards the flame of the Oil terminal up river. My eyes were diverted upwards on hearing the engine of a jet approaching the airport. I followed the flashing wing lights 'till it disappeared behind Garston docks. Now there was quiet except for the lapping of the waves around the landing stage and the stone wall below me. I leaned over and peered at the black smelly water enhanced by the light of the moon. I lit a cigarette taking in deep draws for effect. I wondered what it would be like to drown. How long would it take? Would I feel cold? Would my life flash before my eyes as I drifted into death? I was strangely attracted to the dancing waves. Then, placing one foot on the bottom rail I lifted myself higher. For some ridiculous reason I told myself not to waste the fag and hurried through the last half of it. The resolve had set in. I was ready to end my suffering there and then.

The hand on my shoulder eased me down again. I turned to see the face of a young man. I just focussed on the face at first, but then as questions were directed at me, more of him came into view, together with a second older face. I didn't take in what was being said at first but while I was gathering my thoughts again the Silver Badges and Helmets identified my new friends. Two of Liverpool's finest, enquiring as to my wellbeing. Once I was able to identify myself with proof in the form of wallet documents, I managed to maintain reasoned conversation. I quickly thought up the excuse that my car had broken down and I was awaiting a relative to pick me up. I'm not sure that they were entirely convinced, but an urgent message came through which had them rushing off to something urgent.

This fortuitous meeting brought me back down to earth and I began to make my way back towards the City Centre. Being more aware now I was surprised to see the number of people sleeping rough in doorways and on benches. It was now after 3am. I was very tired and I, too, settled myself down in a side doorway of Blacklers and fell asleep. I awoke at 5.30 to the increasing noise of traffic, street cleaners and a bin waggon. I didn't realise that so much went on at 5.30 in the morning. I found the stop for the number 10 bus soon after 6 and fell asleep again on the journey to Prescot. From there I got another bus to Home where I slept for 14 hours.

CHAPTER 44

I kept the secret of my overnight experiences to myself, never revealing it to anyone. I missed a day at work but passed it off as illness. My work was now just that, work. The soul had gone out of it and I don't know if it was the hospital that had changed or me, but whatever it was I needed to make changes. My life didn't seem to be my own. I was carried along by outside influences all the time. I decided that I must now take charge. Important decisions had to be made if my life was to improve and I was to get over this difficult period.

A year later, now divorced, I found myself being accepted for the post of Officer In Charge of a Residential Home run by Social Services. The home was at Sefton Park in Liverpool. During my final days at Rainhill I frequently walked the grounds, my thoughts of all the wonderful experiences I had over the years; the friends, the loves, the patients, the Hospital itself with its imposing buildings, the beautiful grounds and the comforting feeling of belonging to a large family. It was time to move on, time to file all the memories and start afresh. At the end of the final day, after the big staff party send off. I made my last walk along the drive. At the gate I hesitated, turned and said a quiet goodbye to my old friend Rainhill Hospital. There were mixed emotions but I was looking forward to my new job. The post was residential and I had one month grace to leave the hospital house. I decided to have the month off to recharge my batteries.

Now there would be time to do the rounds of family and friends. Everyone had been so supportive at home and at work. Now that everything was settled with the divorce I had come out of it financially quite well off. Both Paula and Andre had coughed up considerable guilt money. I hadn't so far taken up the invitation to visit them but I hadn't yet ruled it out. Some nights when I stepped out of the shower before bed I would look at and touch the 'Paula scar' and momentarily re live the attack. I could still feel the pain of that event. Occasionally I would have a nightmare about it. Even so I wanted deep down to see Paula again. The mind plays strange tricks on you sometimes.

When I visited JP, Annette, John Paul, now six years old and bounding with energy and Sarah, I was informed that JP was now ready to sell his beloved Harley. I immediately bought it on a whim, at the same time deciding to go on tour with it. I hadn't ridden a motor cycle since the time JP allowed me to ride it when we first met. However, that was not going to put me off. My mind was made up and I asked JP to help me get used to riding again. It was a big machine and some guidance and practice was required. We spent a day together doing a refresher course after which I was ready and eager to get going.

I decided to go where my whims and fancies took me on a tour of Britain. My intention was to go up the west coast to Scotland then cross country and down the East Coast to the South of England, across again to the West Coast and return through Wales to home. That was the plan anyway, but it didn't quite work out that way. I set off heading for the lakes and spent my first night in Grassmere. I stayed in the Youth Hostel which gave me the opportunity to wind down, meet new people and set the tone for a nice relaxing holiday. I loved it so much that I stayed for a second night so my schedule was already destroyed. I thought I would just take it as it comes, relax and enjoy. I loved Grassmere, the quaint little place in the Lake District, with lots of History and some of the best scenery in the world and lovely people. I strolled around the countryside, had lovely meals in many of the cafes, explored the ancient church and sat for ages on the benches on the village green people watching.

The Harley D was a lovely machine on which to relax and enjoy the ride, smooth, comfortable and attractive; just like me. It was my next stop in Glasgow which was to delay my plan even more. I stayed at The Murrayfield Guest House in the City. The Proprietors were Jock and Marie Macferrin. The welcome was great and the food just amazing. The room was very comfortable but without a good view, it was at the rear of the house and backed by other dull stone houses. On the first night I met a few of the guests and our hosts looked after us very well. I immediately got the sense that Marie had more than a passing interest in me. I had a lot of fine whiskey and good food, but the sight of the haggis made me feel sick. I was encouraged to try it, but knowing what it was made me retreat to the toilet to get rid of it. My first evening therefore could have been better. The copious quantity of whiskey sent me off into a long deep sleep and I arose too late for breakfast servings, but Marie made sure I was looked after and made a special exception for me.

I spent the day exploring the wonderful city of Glasgow. I doubt that I saw very much of it as I spent a lot of time talking to lovely people, People everywhere, standing in bus queues, working in shops, bus drivers, Policemen, everybody was so friendly. I met Americans, Chinese, Africans, Indians; lots of foreign visitors. I just loved meeting such a wide variety of people. I got back to the Guesthouse about 6pm. I had a nice tea and then it was back to the bar for general conversation. The conversation centred mainly on Marie. She was about 40 but looked after herself well. I fancied her and she knew it. The feeling was obviously mutual. Marie was about six inches below my own 5' 11" frame. She seemed to prefer one piece dresses in pastel shades which hugged her figure and with a hem line just above the knee. She liked to display her ample breasts which I would agree she could be proud of. Her tummy struggled to be held in and she herself complained about her 'big bum'. The legs were still shapely and firm, perhaps assisted by the high heels. The deep red curly hair completed the true Scottish look. Her Husband was not flavour of the day, or maybe even the year, so as the whiskey flowed so did my chat up lines. My stay was extended.

In the early hours my ability to talk sense was diminishing, even I could tell. As the lights around the bar began to mingle with the labels on the bottles I decided it was time to retire for the night. The lift refused to obey my commands to come. A giggling Marie came to my rescue, pointing out that I was pressing a piece of fancy moulding in the woodwork rather than the call button. She escorted me to my room whilst I talked none sense to her. We held onto each other and just before we left the lift I felt compelled to kiss her. There was no objection. I was told that I was "a naughty boy", a phrase which sounded very sexy in a Scottish accent.

My escort took me right into the room. I knew I was drunk and I knew; with what few brain cells continued to function, that water was needed to offset the effects of the alcohol. I briefly let my escort go while I went to the bathroom. I had a long pee, followed by a long drink of water. Then a quick wash and a check in the mirror helped me to recover a bit from my confused state. Returning to the bedroom I discovered that the bed was already occupied by Marie. She patted the space next to her which I was keen to occupy. Having got under the covers I immediately began to explore my new mate. Gently, she suggested that it might be a good idea if I got undressed. We laughed. I apologised and the error was quickly corrected.

My brain, having now sorted out the priorities, switched to sex mode. The effects of the alcohol took second place and I was all over her. I was aware enough to recognise some differences to previous experiences. Marie was possibly 20 years older, had two children and there was more flesh in some places than I was prepared for. She had spent a long day working and the body odours were different. Not really unpleasant, but more natural than the usual perfumes. The 'natural' aromas' designed by Mother Nature were working well. The foreplay between her legs was a sweaty affair and her breath was not too attractive, but I wasn't going to let that put me off. I probably wasn't that great smelling either after an evening of drinking and no special preparation. It had obviously been a long time since either of us had been in this situation. The first attempt at intercourse didn't go to plan. I couldn't ejaculate. Marie urged me to calm down and play more. It was good advice. After a further period of feeling, moaning and pushing the desired effect was achieved. I wanted her to stay, but she insisted she could not. We kissed farewell and I fell into a long deep sleep.

Remarkably I was able to make it down for breakfast within the specified times. I felt good as I entered the dining room. I wandered what Marie's reaction would be. She was very professional, as if nothing had happened, except for the odd cheeky smile at me when no one would notice. I was slightly aroused watching her walk around serving breakfasts. Her teats bounced slightly as she rushed around. I was given special views of the bust line when she attended to me. Sadly; or perhaps luckily, this was to be my last meeting with Marie. I was off on the next phase of my tour. We both knew this was how it must be. It was just a moment of passion not meant to last. By 10am. I was back on the Harley heading south. It was raining and windy but that didn't dampen my spirit. As I left the City the clouds cleared and wonderful views appeared again.

As I glided through the mountain passes between lakes and sturdy stone settlements, my mind wondered through some of the events of this year; the Wedding of Charles and Dianna. I wondered if they would fare any better than I had. I hoped they would. The troubles in Ireland continued but there seemed to be hope of a resolution. My Irish roots brought about thoughts of the case of Bobby Sands and his hunger strike, ending in his death in May. The thoughts of death had me re visiting the death of Kathy and this coincided with a sudden view of a building which looked just like St. Helens Crematorium. The rain increased and some tears stung my cheeks beneath my visor. The groan of the Harley engine was punctuated with splashes as I gently bounced through puddles. I had to stop. Placing the bike on its stand I stood away from it and stared at the paintwork. It looked dull and sad in the rain. It looked like I felt.

I removed my helmet, wiped my eyes with gloved hands and lifted my face to be bathed by the rain. I hoped the rain drops would wash away my sadness. Then walking a little I found a partly sheltered spot beneath a tree and lit a cigarette. More mixed thoughts wandered around my mind as I calmed down to a better frame of mind. I didn't know it at the time, but this would not be the last time I would be wet today.

Back in the saddle I made my way onward to discover new things, new people and new adventures. The sky cleared and the scenery opened up its treasures once again. Traffic was light and I was enjoying the gentle bends and glorious mountains. Ahead of me in the distance I heard the sounds of several emergency vehicles getting closer. I wondered what poor soul may be having a bad day. A sharp right hand blind bend loomed and I slowed down, keeping well over to my left. The ambulance or police sound was quite close now. Suddenly a Ford Cortina came towards me on my side of the road at high speed. The driver lost some control on the bend. He was closely followed by two police cars. The Cortina wobbled. The driver's eyes glared at me as the car hit me with a glancing blow. I remember smashing through a wooden fence to my left and then I was struggling for my breath under water. It was freezing. My heavy motor cycle kit was weighing me down. I heard millions of bubbles and swallowed water several times. On a few occasions I remember surfacing but being unable to stay afloat. I was panicking, desperate for breath. I felt the muddy bottom and got tangled in plants. Then I got angry and tried to fight my way out. My heart was pounding and my head wanted to explode, then nothing.

Voices and someone pounding my chest brought me spluttering to consciousness on the bank of the river which had nearly claimed me. A burly Police Sergeant had pounded me into existence again. At the time all I could see was the three bright white stripes on his sleeve. I was very cold but a covering of some sort soon made me feel a bit better and my shivering reduced. Then it was lights out again until I found myself listening to more sirens. It was the ambulance I was now inside. Now warmer and with a very painful chest, I was being reassured by an ambulance man. Then the oxygen mask was applied and I was in dream land again. I was lucky. No bones broken. After just two days I was discharged. Annette and JP came to rescue me from Scotland. I had given my statements to the Police; attempted to meet the Sergeant who probably saved my life, but he was unavailable at the time. I noted his details in order to thank him by letter. It seems that the Police were chasing an armed robber in the speeding Ford. He lost control on the bend and struck me but I wasn't the only victim that day. He later crashed into a bus shelter seriously injuring a woman waiting there. I was told it was possible that I may be called as a witness to court at a later date.

On the journey home I kept saying how sorry I was about the demise of the Harley. It had been recovered from the river and was deemed a write off. When I got home I was greeted with the sight of the seriously injured motor bike next to the front door. I was also inundated with calls from concerned relatives and friends. I salvaged what I could from the wreck before arranging for it to be taken away for scrap. JP thought it could be revived, but the insurance company would not have re—insured it. So off it went. After two more days I was off again, this time in the car, to resume what was left of my holiday.

CHAPTER 45

I arranged to spend the rest of my holiday with John Cook on the Isle of White. I thought it best to just relax now and wind down before taking on my new job. I loved it on the Isle of White; the scenery, the quaint villages and small towns. John and Jane were great to be with. I went sailing quite a lot with John. He taught me about the basics of navigation and general sailing techniques including survival advice, safety at sea. The area was very busy with shipping so I had to learn' the rules of the road' so to speak. I loved it. I loved the new challenges and I learned so much in a very short time. A lot of the time spent with the boat was a bit frustrating at first. Checking and re checking equipment, cleaning and polishing and chatting to the other boat owners, often spending hours drinking and socialising after an afternoon sailing. John had a crew to boss about again but I didn't mind at all. I had a wonderful time. One day I found myself being selected to help crew the boat on a trip to Santandare. Jane came along together with two ex Navy buddies who were friends of John. Unfortunately the weather turned against us just two hours out of port and we had to return. There was a commitment to try again but it never happened. We were so badly tossed about on that trip that I was sick for the first time, my sea legs let me down.

Of course there was also the social scene. The Cooke's moved in higher circles than I was used to. At one gathering in their garden I was introduced, as a sort of match making exercise, to Miranda Royce—Carter. That is Lady Miranda Royce-Carter. This was of course Jane's idea. She thought I needed "a friend". I was encouraged to ask her out for dinner, in this case dinner meant in the evening. I couldn't imagine why Lady Miranda would even want to consider going for a date with me, but she did. I suspect it was in my case, simply to please Jane. It wasn't to be a private dinner; it was an evening with Miranda and friends.

Her Ladyship was quite attractive in a Princess Anne sort of way. She reminded me of the Princess. She was also a 'horsey' sort of person and owned two fine grey Stallions.

The house was a grand affair, in its' own grounds with twelve rooms and several stables. This was to be the venue for my date. It was in the form of a party for one of her friends, Helena Rosana, who had reached an important milestone, 21 years old. I was nervous about it. Her ladyship was out of my league. I was picked up from the Cooke's house by Miranda in her bottle green; I think it was a 4 series MG sports car, the one with the bulge on the bonnet. Then taken at break neck speeds to what she described as "The Main House". I already knew that Miranda had recently graduated from Cambridge University with a first class honours degree in Physics. However, she wasn't in a hurry to do anything with it. It was her time to relax and enjoy life for a while.

On the journey to the house we chatted a little between hair raising bends. Miranda's Father was a retired Diplomat who had served mostly in Australia. Her Mother was the "Diplomatic Wife' who looked after everything social and administrative. Miranda had spent much of her childhood in private schools and was looked after by staff on the whole. Her Parents returned permanently to England when she started University. Now, like many of her friends, she was living off 'Daddies Money' until she could be eased gently into some sort of job. She fancied working in aircraft or space technology. I asked a few questions about the car but she knew absolutely nothing about its pedigree, but she had an intimate knowledge of how it all worked.

She pressed a button on the dash and the elaborately decorated twin gates opened up before us to reveal a large Victorian House in beautifully manicured gardens. The car slowed to a reasonable pace at last. The gravel crunched beneath the tyres adding to the effect of the approach. Several guests' cars had already arrived and Miranda associated them to names.

'Oh Julia's here, Harry and Benedict; Oh and Ben! you'll like Ben ah, and there's Jennies little Morgan and Peter's Jensen, gorgeous car. There'll be later. I think we're expecting about thirty guests. Benson made all the arrangements.'

I asked who Benson was. I wasn't surprised to be told he was the butler. Miranda closed the car door and reached for her hand bag from the back seat. I stood for a moment to take in the view of the house and garden. As I stood there near the front of the car I could smell the heat from the over revved engine. I heard the odd crack and clonk as the poor beast cooled down.

Miranda took my hand and led me in like a trophy. First I was introduced to the Stallions, Mr Ed and Silver. Yes, they were named after the T.V. Horses. Then after being bitten by Mr Ed; I was escorted by a giggly Miranda to the front door. Benson greeted us and we entered what was for me a new world. The walk on rich deep pile carpet felt like pure luxury. Paintings; real paintings as per art gallery, decorated the walls. I recognised some items of Chippendale and Hepplewhite furniture. I knew about them from my school studies in woodwork. A Chesterfield suite stood proudly in the lounge, here called a drawing room and a grand piano glistened near the bay windows. Two young men sat playing chess. They were introduced as Harry and Benedict. They lifted their eyes briefly to say 'Hi' then resumed a very serious game. In the garden I was introduced to the remaining early guests and Mum and Dad who seemed very nice people.

The main feature of the garden was the pool; yes a pool and quite a large one at that. Several parasols protected garden furniture sets from the sun, although it wasn't gracing us with its presence at this time. A few small groups stood chatting and I was introduced to some of them. First it was Sam (Samantha), a tall elegant lady in a floral pattern dress and red shoes. She was pretty and shapely with bright red lipstick and tightly curled light brown hair. She smiled and said hello, grasping my hand firmly in greeting. I noticed her painted red nails too and a whiff of expensive perfume filled my nostrils. It was at this moment that I became acutely aware of my 'catalogue clothing range'. I bought all my clothes and shoes from Trafford catalogue for which Annette was an agent. I felt that everyone was now scrutinising me and assessing how poor I was compared with them. Probably not true, but I felt like a peasant.

In company with Sam, who was an interior designer, was John, a Stock Market Trader. John was a bit shorter than me, bald, open neck striped shirt and grey trousers which were held around his plump waist by a pair of brightly coloured bracers. The brown leather shoes were quality items. He had a gold tooth which I couldn't take my eyes off when he spoke.

Then there was Mark; a Captain in the Royal Artillery. Six feet tall with jet black hair. His tanned face was slightly freckled. I suspect that his nose had been broken at some point, I could see the signs. He was smoking a cigar which I got a strong smell of when he said hello. Mark was smartly dressed in a casual sort of way. A light blue shirt and regimental tie and matching cuff links. Black sharply creased trousers and black highly polished shoes. That was probably as casual as he got.

I was greeted politely and they seemed friendly enough, but I still felt out of place. The introductions stopped as I was taken under the wing of Miranda's Parents, Julia and Graham. Julia placed a glass of Champagne in my hand and sat me down on one of the garden chairs to quiz me. Graham went off to talk to other guests. I detected that hidden within the polite and friendly questions was a desire to find out exactly what my status was and how I managed to arrive as a guest of her daughter. I wasn't entirely sure about the friendliness; perhaps just the experienced diplomats wife. Once I passed muster and was no longer considered a threat to the family fortune, I was released back into the party.

All the guests had now arrived with the addition of a violin quartet, four elegant ladies in evening gowns playing a variety of beautiful pieces throughout the evening. I settled with the small group I was first introduced to Stock Market Trader, John He was intrigued by my job. He asked me if I found it very difficult to deal with crazy people all day. I replied that it was no more difficult than dealing with some of the crazy people around us that evening. That made everyone laugh and my work wasn't mentioned again. I must say I enjoyed the evening very much. I saw very little of Miranda and at midnight I was driven back to the Cooke's house by Benson at a more leisurely pace in the Austin Princess Limo. Benson, first name Harry, was a very nice chap. He also asked about my job but with genuine interest. He told me something of himself. He had been a Royal Marine Commando and on his retirement took up the post of Butler, come security officer for the Diplomatic Service. He had been with this family for twelve years and he retired with his boss to remain in his service. He loved his job and was treated like family. On my return I was asked to report on my date. There was disappointment that I hadn't made the grade. Not from me though.

Much to my surprise I found James and Sandra had come for a few days. I was delighted, friends who I could enjoy myself with. I shook James's hand firmly and I had a broad smile to match his. I got a big hug from Sandra. Christine and Lorna had been put to bed. John and Jane insisted we go out together and have some fun. It had passed midnight but Cowes was still alive and well. So off we went. We visited a few night clubs in the last few hours of business. Each of us had reasons to let our hair down. In one place we sang Liverpool songs together to an enthusiastic audience. 'In my Liverpool Home,' 'Liverpool Lou,' 'I Wish I Was Back In Liverpool' and for some reason we included 'The Martians Have Landed In Wigan.' Everyone who could joined in, together with those who couldn't. At 3.30am, we were sat on a bench overlooking a line of moored boats. The cold September breeze rattled flag ropes and mast bells jingled, sleepless pigeons begged for food on the night shift and two young girls assisted each other to have what they thought was a secret pee on a jetty right in front of us. We stayed there until dawn telling each other stories and silly jokes. Sandra lay along the bench with her head on James's lap and her feet across my legs and fell asleep.

That was the best time I had enjoyed for a long time. We were drunk, cold, but very happy. As the sun attempted to rise behind us it was quickly snubbed out by clouds. It began to rain. Sandra was awakened by a pigeon landing briefly on her knee. It had no fear and having stared me in the eye for a moment; it took of steeply to perch on a nearby roof. We made our way, more sober now, back to the house. We had a great few days together. The proud doting Grandparents were happy to spoil the children while we explored the island. All too soon I found myself back at home making my last moves out to the accommodation of my new job.

CHAPTER 46

October 1st 1981. I started my new job at Sefton View Home for the Elderly. I had visited a few times earlier to get a general view of things. I knew there was a lot of work to do in order to reach the goals I had set myself. I had a vision of how I would like it to be but I didn't want to rush in like a 'Bull In A china Shop' and alienate every one. The first few days were a matter of settling in to my spacious flat. The building was Victorian and in keeping with what I had been used to at Rainhill in many ways. My flat had a very spacious living room's kitchen which was as big as my room at Rainhill had been and a large bedroom with en suite bathroom. There was also a store room and an odd little ante room just big enough to accommodate a large arm chair and small table. It had a deep window which allowed a lovely view of the park across the road. This was to be my chill out and thinking room in times to come. Each room has large sash windows with scenic views and the radiators were very efficient, a home, from home. I was delighted with it. Family and friends came to inspect it and on the first Friday evening I held a reception for family and staff. It was big enough.

The first week was a time of 'Getting To Know You' meetings in company with Mary Thompson, my Deputy Officer In Charge. She had worked here for eight years and had applied for my post. I understood that this must be difficult for her but we seemed to get on fine; for now. I was soon to turn her world upside down with my new regime.

I spent time interviewing all the staff to get to know them well; I also told them everything they needed to know about me. I looked at the residents files in detail and spent a lot of time in one to one conversations with them. I had meetings with Doctors and Care Staff from other agencies, Residents family and friends and I managed to get out a good press release about the home. I had meetings with my Senior Managers about budgets and various requirements to improve the general atmosphere of the home. I made a request to change the name to Sefton Grange in order to take away the 'Old People's Home' image. It was a busy time but so fruitful. The name change was approved, much to my surprise and delight. However the wheels of administration grind slowly and it would not happen for months.

Suddenly, Christmas was upon us. In the past it had been a case of putting up decorations, an increase in the food order and a couple of parties. I was in Rainhill mode. This year we decorated the trees outside with lighting donated by a local company. The internal decorations were placed throughout the building, again donated by a City Department Store with a naked man above the door. I asked the local Rotary club to visit with their Fr. Christmas Sleigh and Elves. I also pressed local schools into providing entertainment on most evenings over the festive season. Nobody had ever invited local Clergy to conduct services before so, this was done. The atmosphere was so inviting that staff came in on their own time to take part, even the 'Jobs Worths'. We had 28 residents but at a time like this it seemed like 128. I invited the Staff and Senior Managers in small groups to special receptions in my flat. This helped to break down traditional barriers. The bosses were now less remote and had real personalities.

Although met with some resistance at first, we now had proper lounges arranged for people to associate instead of sitting around the edges of the room. The T.V was removed from the main lounge where it entertained itself most of the time and set into a small dedicated T.V. room. Dining tables were re-set from the regimented rows to a more restaurant like arrangement and covered with table cloths. Less convenient for staff but friendlier for the residents. Residents, who were able to make the choice, went to bed and got up at their leisure. I was able to get funding to decorate the public areas and a Specialist Cleaning Contractor to do a one off deep clean inside the building. I made sure that I was frequently seen to be willing to do exactly the same jobs as every member of staff including night duty. I held weekly Staff Meetings to iron out or prevent any problems from arising. Each month I had a relatives and friends meeting with one member of Senior Management attending. I persuaded 3 residents to produce a newsletter for residents and visitors. A local printer did the copy for nothing. His Mother was one of our residents.

I was so pleased with progress but it wasn't all plain sailing. I battled constantly with an over stretched Social Services Department who tried to place people with us who would be better suited for a Nursing Home or Psychiatric Unit. I argued that the morale of existing residents would be liable to slide if they were to live with people who required specialist care.

It would also undermine my aspirations to provide a peaceful, homely place of retirement. In the event, I was forced to take 8 who were now better described as Patients rather than Residents. This required further training and further stress on my staff. Much of the training I provided myself as the provision made by my bosses fell short of what was required. Now the budget was stretched even more with the requirement of more specialised equipment and increased laundry costs, specialist waste disposal, secure medication cabinets and administration to go with it and an increase in mortality rates. More bodies leaving in what the residents called 'The Meat Wagon'. This made the residents less confident about their future in 'Gods waiting room.'

At meetings I stressed the need for staff to be upbeat about the situation, to continue to provide a happy atmosphere. I lost two good staff who felt they hadn't signed up for Home Care Duties. We managed to carry on with enthusiasm mustered, but it was never going to be the same again. In February '82 the name of the house was formerly changed to Sexton Grange. By now my compliment of Patients had increased to 14. 50% of my residents now needed 24 hour care of one sort or another. I could measure the negative effects this had on the more agile residents who became less interested in leading an active life. Much of the one on one time with staff, which we had worked so hard to achieve, had now gone, the patients now taking up much of our time. However, there was one unexpected positive event which came about in March that year. A new resident who came to us as the result of a death; this was the way it was all too frequently. A smartly dressed Gentleman called John Hughes came to us. He was in general good health for his elderly status except for the fact that he had suffered a stroke a few months earlier, which left him with poor mobility on his left side and he was suffering some memory loss. However, he was very independent with the bearing of a Military Officer; he was also' One for the Ladies.' The great surprise was though that when his first visitor came on the evening of his admission; a Mrs Roberts, I immediately recognised her. Angela. Angela Hughes. My first teacher crushes at school.

One of the policies I had introduced was to meet all first time visitors to introduce them to the house and talk about the Care Programme. It was also an opportunity to get to know friends and relatives which would make consultations easier should there be any concerns in the future. So it was that my first meeting with Angela since school was about to take place. I was nervous. I laughed at myself for feeling like a school boy again. I sat in the office awaiting the arrival of my guest. I released the knot my tie a little and opened a window. My mouth was dry so I sipped water. The knock on the door startled me and I coughed, spitting some water onto my note pad.

'Come in,' I gargled whist patting the wet area with blotting paper and trying to quickly dry the front of my shirt. One of the girls escorted Angela into my office and made the formal introductions.

She didn't recognise me. Why I expected that she should I have no idea. She was still very beautiful and again wore a business suit which brought back all those memories as if it was yesterday. Regaining my composure I reeled off all the introductory talk as I had done so often. She offered no questions. I brought up the subject of school and she seemed quite delighted to be remembered. I didn't realise it at the time but Angela had been a student teacher at the time I first met her. She was on a practical training period from the C.F. Mott Training College. So actually she couldn't have been a lot older than me. She qualified but found teaching was not her calling. She was now a Freelance Journalist, having spent some years with the Liverpool Echo prior to becoming solo. After the brief reunion Angela went to spend a while with her Father. This was a very frustrating period for me. I was itching to know more. My heart was pounding as it did all that time ago. Her effect on me was almost debilitating. I made sure that my duties confined me to an area around the main door so that she couldn't escape my attention on the way out. After what seemed an eternity she appeared once more. We had a brief conversation about how the visit had gone and she talked a little more about her Dad. She became emotional and I held both her hands whilst reassuring her that he would be well looked after and that she was welcome at any time. I wanted so much to hold and kiss her but that was out of the question.

She left, holding my handkerchief which I had offered to dab her tears. At least something of me went with her. She visited frequently and our conversations became longer and more personal. Angela had been married to a fellow journalist from the Echo but it hadn't worked out. Divorce proceedings were under way. I offered my sympathy but it wasn't sincere. I was delighted. There may be a chance of a date, although a remote chance. After only two weeks the date was on. I couldn't believe it. I kept going over and over the same question in my mind. How could this be possible?

The first date was a lunch. She was very busy and we met between assignments at a café opposite the Forum in Lime Street. I worried about what to talk about. I didn't want to talk about her Dad except to say he was fine. I didn't think she'd want to talk about her work; so what? As it happened she babbled on almost constantly about her job. She was so excited and enthusiastic about it and it was all really interesting. I rarely read the press but it seemed that her name was well known in what they called 'The Broad Sheets, the posh papers. Her, not for much longer, Husband was a sub Editor at the Echo so she didn't get any work from them now.

Lately she had worked in Israel on President Sadat's peace initiative up to him being gunned down by Moslem Extremists in October last year. She also reported on his resulting State funeral. She covered the launch of the Columbia Shuttle in April last year. She travelled all over the World in her job leading such an interesting life. The 90 minute lunch date seemed like 30 seconds. After lunch she was dashing off to do an interview with Gypsies in Rochdale who were having a stand-off with the Council over an illegal camp site. I was surprised and pleased to be given a quick but meaningful kiss on our departure from the café.

We had several dates in the coming weeks. Nothing serious, just fun times and a little guarded romance began to bloom. I was not keen to rush things and she had her concerns over the divorce. The Husband was being cited for his affairs so it was not a good idea to get too serious under those circumstances. Then, early in April she didn't turn up for one of our dates. I tried phoning but just got the answerphone. For 2 days there was no contact, then, I got a message originating from the QE11. Angela was on board on her way to the Falkland Islands. Argentina had invaded on April 6th. And now my new girlfriend was on her way to a War Zone. She was not on a luxury cruise but a converted troop ship. That news was an immediate concern. She was on one of the largest ships in the world, on her way to a Conflict Zone. I didn't know at this point what the status of the Argentinian Armed Forces was, but whatever they could muster at sea would find the QE 11 an easy target.

News from Angela would be sparse under the circumstances so I eagerly followed the news. Diplomatic efforts failed to resolve the disagreements so the Task Force duly arrived to take on the Argentinians. It turned out that the Occupying Forces were not about to wave the white flag immediately so the battles commenced. HMS Hermes started the main action with her Harriers with no losses. The Argentinians fought back with Exocet missiles, which sank several British Frigates. Now I was deeply concerned.

I didn't know if the journalists would be kept on board ship or allowed in with the troops. I received a telegram from Angela assuring me that all was fine and they were in no real danger. If Prince Andrew was allowed to be there then the danger would be minimal. Then I heard about Sir Galahad being hit with many casualties. Sir Galahad was a supply ship. The Mirage Jets continued to attack the ships supporting the Invasion Force. Argentina was not going away quickly and putting up a serious fight.

The few telegrams I received were up-beat but I wasn't convinced. Then came the news of the British attack on Goose Green and the fall of Mount Harriet and Twin Sisters. Then 15000 Argentinian soldiers were surrounded and General Menendes surrendered. 254 British and 750 Argentinian soldiers lost their lives. Angela got through it unscathed and managed to get a lot of material out to the media. I expected that when the Fleet returned that Angela and I would meet up again, but it was not to be. Almost immediately after, Angela was off to the Middle East. She had a hunch that things were about to 'Kick Off' there. Her hunch proved to be correct. Early in June the Israeli Ambassador in London was wounded by a Palestinian Gunman. Again Israel and Palestine were embroiled in a full scale conflict and Angela was in the thick of it. We were now pen pals rather than lovers as I had hoped. It didn't stop there. She was off around the globe again with her shoulder bag and camera reporting on The Lebanon and Palestine conflict, the death of Princess Grace of Monaco. She visited N.A.S.S.A, several times, in connection with the Shuttle Programme. Early '84 saw her again in Lebanon. Then President Regan visit to London. She visited India to cover the after effects of the assassination of Indira Ghandi. And so it went on. She kept returning to Lebanon were on one occasion she was held captive for a month after being wounded. She was released after Diplomatic Negotiations

If that wasn't enough she turned up next in Cambodia, 'Out Of The Frying Pan Into The Fire.' Then I heard nothing for a year or so. I thought that was it, one of those relationships that fades away. Then I got a letter at the end of January '86, apologising for the long period without communication. The letter contained another long list of all the Danger Zones she had been in and names of famous people she had met. She had been present at the launch and destruction of Challenger on January 26th. Out of all the things she had seen and done so far, this has affected her emotionally quite a lot. She had spent a lot of time with the seven crew members, before the mission, to do personal stories about them they had become friends. She came back to see her Father who was still quite well and in good spirits. He was rightly very proud of her. She thanked me for looking after him so well. We went out for just one evening before she was due to leave again. I told her I was considering leaving and that the home was under continuing pressure to become a Nursing Home rather than a Residence. I advised her to look at a private care solution. This was agreed and I was appointed agent for doing so. The divorce had now been finalised and I asked what her plans were for the future. I was asked to be patient and understanding. She had a lot of things to do now, ambitions to fulfil. She wasn't for settling down yet. I asked did she think there was any future for us.

She said. 'I'd love to think that there would be. If I was to leave or curtail my career now, I think it would lead to resentment and destroy everything.' I had to agree with the logic, but I was disappointed. Again we parted with a seriously loving kiss. She was due at the airport in just hours for more adventures and risks.

CHAPTER 47

At home my life began to change direction. My first priority was to arrange for Mr Hughes to be set up in a Private Rest Home of quality. I found such a place in Woolton. Angela was so pleased with the arrangements. Angela still travelled extensively in pursuit of her journalistic career. We kept in touch mainly by telephone from wherever she happened to be in the world. This wasn't easy and some assignments meant we would be out of touch for long periods. I also had to make arrangements for my own home when I left Social Services. I had never had to do this before so it was quite a trial. Time passed so quickly and there was a lot of paperwork and searching for a mortgage, which didn't look promising anyway. I settled for a rented flat above Longview shops in Huyton. It was a temporary solution.

I gave my notice to Social Services. The home was being degraded and my vision for it smashed. I took up the long standing offer from James to work for him in 'The Rag Trade.' I trained in the warehouse for a year doing all the jobs from cleaning to management. My Heavy Goods licence was gained at the companies expense and I enjoyed delivering and collecting goods nationwide and to the near Continent. I got to know the country very well. By March '87 I was Assistant Manager, Warehouse and Distribution of 'Styletto Fashions'. It was the hardest job I had done to date. The pressure was on; most of the time, to get orders out on time and make sure everything ran smoothly. There were times when I had to do some of those other jobs I had trained in, Often driving a truck to the far reaches of the land, then catching up with the office work later. The weekends were very welcome. My last driving job before being officially promoted was to take a van abroad to Belgium. I had done one such trip before to France but I didn't have to venture far into the country before reaching my destination.

The Belgian trip was to Bruges and Ostend via the Dover, Zeebrugge Ferry. I left on March 4th. '87. The premises, of the Bruges distributor was found more with luck than skill, on the following day, then, on to Ostend on the return trip. The Ostend pick up was easier to find and I was able to make up time to catch an earlier ferry than anticipated. I enjoyed the trip and found some places I would like to re-visit on a holiday. For now there was no time. I had to get back. On 6th, I arrived at Zeebrugge just in time for the ferry, having been lost a few times. Still I was quite pleased and proud to have made an earlier ferry.

Passport control went smoothly, many wagon and coach drivers complained about delays, but today was fine. I got in quite early in the loading process and was able to get a snack before going up on to the highest observation deck on the starboard side. At six O'clock I leaned against the rail and lit a cigarette. I was in conversation with a Coach Driver from Shearings who had also made and earlier ferry than expected and he was looking forward to a more leisurely journey, than usua,l to his change over place at Cranage, Cheshire. Five past six and the throbbing of the engines eased us away from the quay. The coach driver left to go and check on his passengers. He told me that keeping in touch meant better tipping. With engines 'Slow Ahead' we steamed out of port. It was a bright evening but the breeze was quite cold. I thought that after the fag I would return inside where it would be warmer.

I looked across to the quayside to see more Lorries arriving and cars queuing up. No doubt being disappointed at having to wait for the next ferry. There were fork lifts with flashing lights and official port vehicles busily going about their business. Some people lined the dock area, one or two with fishing rods. 2 little girls waved and I waved back. We passed the two light towers at the Harbour entrance and the engines powered up for sea. I discarded the last bit of cigarette over the side and turned to make my way to one of the doors. There was a sudden lurch to port. I stopped and looked ahead. The leaning righted itself so I turned again towards the door. I gripped the handle and began to slide it open. It was heavy so I was delayed. Then it wouldn't shift at all and as I tugged I realised that I was now being pressed against the bulk head. Looking ahead again I could not believe my eyes. The list was now very bad and within seconds had become a complete turn onto one side. The engines changed tone to a whine. I fell into the gap in the door, managing to grab the outer handle to hold myself in place.

I couldn't move for a while. There were sounds of banging and smashing from within the ship. Everything was shifting or falling. There were chilling cries and screams from terrified people inside. My first thought wasn't as you might expect, perhaps 'this is it,' my first thought was what James would say about the loss of his van, always assuming I was to survive this. I expected to be swimming soon. The water would be icy cold but we had only just left port and I estimated that I could possibly make the half mile or so to the Harbour Wall. I didn't have a life jacket so I hoped to find floating debris as the ship went under. Then all my frantic planning for survival came to an abrupt end as the ship settled and most of the noise stopped for a moment. We must have capsized into shallow water. Then clanging and crashing sounds filled the air as vehicles, equipment and anything not fastened down fell to one side of the vessel. The noise was deafening for a few minutes. This noise was replaced by the sounds of desperate shouts and screams from passengers inside. Hot steam enveloped me for a moment as it escaped through the gap I had made.

I realised that I was now dangling in the door gap. My upper body and arms were above the door and the deck was right in front of my face. My feet were inside the vessel and I couldn't feel anything to support my weight. My ribs and hips were hurting but seemingly no broken bones. I pulled myself out of the gap and crawled a little way along the bulk Head, avoiding windows as I didn't know if they would support my weight. Other people appeared around me, some shouting out names. I tried to gather my thoughts, but passed out for a while. I was awakened by the sound of a helicopter. It was very cold now and the light wasn't as good. I looked at my watch. It was now 6.40pm. The rescue had started and I was helped by a Naval Officer down a rope ladder to a small boat and with others transferred to a Belgian Navy ship which I think was a Frigate. A few hours later I was back in port. Lots of survivors were being looked after by a variety of Port Officials and Navy Personnel. Despite my insistence to be allowed to stay in port, I was taken by ambulance to a local Hospital to be checked. I think it was the Red Cross who contacted home for me. The Casualty Unit was packed. I suspect other hospitals were also used. I estimated there must have been about 500 people on the Ferry. As it didn't sink I hoped everyone would be ok except for injuries.

The T.V. news told a different story. I hadn't noted the name of the ferry before now, but it was the 'Herald of Free Enterprise.' 459 on board and 193 killed. I was so lucky to be here. Had that door not stuck I would have been inside and may not have got out. I was still worried about the loss of the van.

A day later, after filling in statements and forms and answering questions from lots of people, I was met by Mum and Dad and Annette and JP, and taken home. From the moment we sat in the car at the port of Dover until we arrived at Page Moss, I slept.

For the following week I was a celebrity. I did press and radio interviews but kept the bones of my story for Angela to use if she wished. After a week of celebrity status I was keen to get back to work. I was now ready to take on my new management roll but James was still concerned for me and insisted I take it easy for a while. However, that wasn't me. I threw myself full steam into the job. For some time after the Ferry event I did suffer from flash backs and bad dreams. I kept hearing the cries for help and cursed myself for not doing anything for anyone else. Was I a coward? I don't know but there were several commendations for those who were brave and thoughtful enough to do more. Then there was the legal stuff to get through after the event. It was nine months before James got a settlement for the van and goods. After two years my own case for compensation was cleared. For others it was a lot longer as legal cases dragged on.

Angela would get in touch as often as possible from many of the trouble spots in the world. There seemed to be no end to them. There were a number of Royal Occasions around this time but Angela would be more about gauging reactions abroad than in England. Having spent 6 days in an open boat in the South China Sea with Vietnamese Refugees and being attacked by Pirates and losing all her equipment, she decided it might be a good idea to write a book about her journalist years. I thought that was a great idea. Months later, it came to light that she was almost raped during that ordeal but for the intervention of one of the pirate bosses who beat off the potential rapist. They took two Vietnamese girls with them though. Angela thought she would be taken for ransom but for some reason that didn't happen. She said she felt insulted to be thought worthless. I urged her to think about retiring. No chance of that for now. Angela spent the first half of 1988 in Palestine where there was always news. By September she was in Seoul for the Olympic Games. I was in Liverpool thinking about a holiday.

My flat was basic but comfortable. I couldn't get fond of it. I felt it was a transient place. The area wasn't good. There was a lot of vandalism and trouble in the evenings. Youths gathered and created problems. I knew the Police better than I knew the neighbours. I searched newspapers each day for a better pad. When I had the time I'd visit an Estate agent but nothing was jumping out at me which was affordable and in a good location.

A period of family turmoil followed. I lost My Father in June 1989 to a Heart Attack at only 66 years old. Then only three months later my Mother died resulting from Breast Cancer. My Father's death probably helped the process along. She was 63. Annette and I inherited the house at Page Moss and Annette agreed to allow me to buy her out, so the house became mine, when the legal process was completed in November. I moved out of my lonely flat and into a larger lonely house. Angela was able to return to England to attend my Mother's funeral. She stayed for a week at a hotel and we began to finally become more serious about our relationship. During this visit a new business venture was discussed. As a well known journalist she had got to know many prominent people and understood their lifestyle and their needs. She thought there would be a lucrative market in the Private Aircraft Hire Business. She was so enthusiastic about it and thought it would be a good retirement plan to serve two purposes, to end her journalistic career and write the book, plus the opportunity to travel.

I loved the idea but I pointed out that if she intended to host the flights then we would be back to square one in our 'On Hold' relationship. Then the bombshell, It was then suggested that I; yes I, take the training course for the Pilot's Licence. I was stunned. I knew nothing about flying and even after a course I wouldn't be fit to fly Senior Executives or Politicians everywhere. Of course she understood that. She offered to pay for the course and on qualification I would be able to work with a friend of hers who had such a business and was looking to retire. He agreed to continue my training with him until I was fully competent, perhaps up to a year. Well that was something to consider out of the blue. After our romantic week cementing our bond; I was amazed that under the circumstances we had one. Angela was off again. Now though we had chances to be together between assignments and I was to accompany her on a few of them.

CHAPTER 48

In November Angela was in Czechoslovakia where foreign journalists were invited to cover events involving Vaclav Havel who had formed the Civil Forum as an opposition party to the 'Old Guard'. She covered a demonstration in Wenceslaus square on the 19th February, which attracted 250,000 people. On the 21st. she attended a Press Conference where Alexander Dubcek spoke for the first time since the 1968 Reforms. Then she returned home to spend Christmas and New Year with her Father and me. I was so pleased. She still had itchy feet though as World affairs continued without her. Czechoslovakia was still throbbing with tension and the Americans and Russians were concluding the 'Cold War' and Hong Kong was stirring. However, she managed to contain herself for the festive season.

After completing all her work for the year and getting everything off to the various newspapers and magazines, Angela arrived out of the blue a week before Christmas. It was a rainy evening and I answered the door to a wonderful sight. Angela stood before me in a full length cream coat lined with some sort of fluffy material which spilled over the edges including the hood which was up over her head. She lifted her head to receive a welcoming kiss and I eased her into the hallway holding both her hands. I removed her coat and was bathed in the aroma of quality perfume. Her hair was darker than I had seen before, a deep, brunette held in a pony tail by a ring of coloured beads. The jacket and skirt matched the overcoat and she peeled off the jacket, handing it to for me to hang up. She turned to me, placed her arms around my neck and pulled me to her for a long kiss. Briefly her eyes met mine before the lips locked on to each other. I held her to me and felt her beautiful form. It was just wonderful to see her again and I whispered as much into her right ear. We held onto each other for a moment while I wondered what to do next. The thought occurred to me that I didn't have much food in and that it was only bachelor rubbish any way.

I don't remember the transition to the lounge but here we were sitting on the sofa. I held her hand and looked at her as she described her journey from London. I didn't take much of it in. I just looked at her. She was beautiful. Only a little make up had been used but in my opinion she didn't even need that. The blouse reminded me of the first meeting at school when I had those 'cleavage Moments' and I was having them again. I leaned to one side to rest on the arm of the sofa. Angela followed me and we half lay, my arm around her shoulder. We talked about what had happened since our last meeting which seemed like years ago. After a while she fell silent. She was asleep. The long day had taken its toll and I now wondered what was to happen next. Had she come to stay with me? Had she booked a Hotel? I remembered that she didn't have a bag with her when she came in. That didn't give me much of a clue about her intention to stay here or not. Gingerly, I eased my way out from under her and walked to the window to see if there was a car outside. I couldn't see properly because of the hedges so I went to look from the door. It was still raining so I was reluctant to go outside. I could see my own car but again the hedges spoilt my view of other vehicles. I walked to the gate and spotted a white Mercedes which was probably hers. The house door slammed shut. I was still outside without a key. I hurried back and tried it. It was firmly shut. I walked towards the window to find a gap in the curtains so I could check if Angela had woken up. I fell over a plant pot. My failure to unblock a drain a few days earlier was rewarded now when I fell headlong into a pool of muddy water. A cat, sheltering from the rain under the hedge was startled into crying out in terror as this Alien invaded its space and escaped over the top of me digging its claws into my scalp as it did so. I started to pull myself up using the window ledge. I was almost there when I lost my grip and fell again, this time on my back.

I finally managed to get to my feet. I found the gap in the curtains. Angela was beginning to wake up. She looked around the room for me. I tapped on the window, then louder. The rain was heavy now and she probably couldn't hear me. I took a coin from my pocket and tapped on the window. She heard that and came to the window. On opening the curtains she screamed and ran back into the room. I shouted

'Angela, it's me Liam!

From her position of security behind the sofa she emerged once more to check out the familiar voice outside the window.

'Oh my God, what happened to you?'

'Well, if you let me in I'll tell you,'

She laughed her way to the door. 'You frightened me to death, what are you doing?'

I explained. We both laughed about it. I returned to her car to retrieve her luggage. She was staying with me. I went to the bathroom to see what monster had frightened her. I nearly frightened myself. Before me was a filthy hulk with mud and blood stains running down my face. My shirt was in the same state and I looked like a prisoner on the run through one of those American Swamps. I washed my face, turned on the shower above the bath, stripped and stepped in. I poured shower gell all over my body and began to feel the benefit almost at once. My head was stinging where the cat had clawed me. My eyes were also stinging because of the soap. Then I felt a naked Angela slip in behind me. First she held me from behind. I felt her gorgeous breasts pressing against my back. Then she released and used a large sponge to wash my back.

Everything except Angela shut off in my brain. I no longer had any cares. Nothing hurt. Nothing stung; the only action taking place was in my penis. The dates we had never got to this stage. I had never seen Angela naked, never had any more than a sexy cuddle before. Now this was what I had dreamed of but never quite sure it would happen. This was the 'Wet Dream' I had at school, never believing it could possibly happen. This is the woman on whom, at the age of sixteen I would masturbate and imagine having wild sex with. Now she is actually here with me in the shower about to make my dream come true. How strange is that? How exciting and unbelievable is that?

We turned to face each other. A loving smile beamed across her face. I pulled her to me and we kissed passionately. Swishing, sucking and tonguing. We parted slightly while I soaped her front with the big sponge. I was able to create foam patterns over her breasts and suck and kiss her nipples. Pink, firm nipples. Then kneeling I washed her pubic hairs and watched the soapy water hesitate for a moment in the tight black curls, then drip away down her thighs. I felt her buttocks with one hand while I fingered her with the other until she moaned and shuddered with the orgasms. Returning to the standing position and Angela not being very steady now, we exited the bath and made love on the floor. She was so hot inside, so tight. The ribbed effect in her vagina gave me the best thrill ever. It wasn't rushed but fast. We both wanted each other so much at that moment. I felt like I had the guns of HMS Belfast firing from me and Angela fucked me like there was no tomorrow.

Soon, too soon, we were lying side by side recovering. Now we began to feel the hard surface of the floor and sensibly retired to the bed. Not long after, we slept. Now I couldn't think of any reason why I should ease away from her and go for a mud bath in the garden.

I was the first to wake up in the morning. Angela was still fast asleep. I turned to her and gently run my hand over her firm smooth bum. I was aroused but decided to let her sleep. I got up and made breakfast. Nice bacon, overdone eggs, and fried tomatoes, some on the plate, some on my shirt. I tried squashing them in the pan but they didn't want to stay in the pan. I don't blame them. Angela emerged from the hallway dressed only in one of my clean shirts. We greeted each other with a kiss and I invited her to the breakfast table. She looked at my shirt and giggled. We had breakfast and just talked. It was decided to take her Dad out today. It was a bright and nippy winter day. However, John was still fit for his years and I thought he would like a nostalgic tour of the City Centre with a mixture of driving and walking. My Mercedes 500, although a classic was perfect for the job. The limousine body had lots of room in the back with fully adjustable seats. It was after all made for an Ambassador. The bullet proof windows and reinforced floor were probably surplus to requirements for this trip. It did about 18 miles per gallon. Built like a tank but drove, like a Rolls.

We arrived at 'The Mount' retirement home around mid—morning. This was a lovely homely mansion set on the edge of Woolton Park. The well groomed gardens gave it the feel of a Stately Home. It reminded me again of the job I wish I had never left. We were greeted in the reception lounge. Having been shown to comfortable seats in the window bay, we were brought the requested drinks. Angela thanked me again for choosing such a lovely place for her Father. In his letters to her he expressed his love for the place. Soon, the receptionist returned to escort us to John's room. There was a lift but we opted to use the grand staircase. A deep-pile Indian carpet cushioned each step to an upper reading room and onward to the bed rooms. The Victorian building was kept very clean and fresh flowers scented the communal areas. This was my vision for Sefton Grange. Our escort knocked on the oak door at room 10. I remarked that it was like Downing Street with carpets outside. John called us in. We entered a large en suite room with tasteful furniture and fittings. The large bay window looked out over the park and the main road was also in view to add some activity to the scene. John was dressed in a tweed jacket and sports trousers, a check shirt and cravat completed the 'Country Gent' look. John was now ready for his jaunt. As we left the room John took hold of a walking cane. I asked if he would be OK to walk awhile in Town. He said he was fine and that the cane was just a 'Bird Puller.' Angela laughed and gently smacked his shoulder.

CHAPTER 49

John had never been in my car before. He was impressed by its size and comfort, due to the vast area of space in the rear, Angela thought it best to sit with her Dad so he wouldn't feel isolated. The inner screen from the chauffeur days had been removed but rear passengers were still a long way from the driver. I suspect there may have been additional fold down seats in the past.

We set off on our Liverpool Adventure, floating along in our 4.5ltr. stead and feeling good. John even gave a 'royal wave' to staff as we left. The first port of call was Sefton Park, to feed the ducks. Actually I wanted to spy on my old place of employment. I was sad to see the poor state of the building and garden. It was obviously in need of investment but unlikely to get it. We did feed the ducks, not that they needed it, then a stroll part way around the lake. The low winter sun made it a sun glasses day but none of us had any.

Then it was a pub lunch. I found out more about John. He was an ex Royal Navy man which enabled me to bond more with him through my relationship with another John, that being John Cooke. I told him about my adventures on the Catamaran and my sea training around Cowes. John Hughes had been a Petty Officer and had served on a number of ships, mainly Frigates. I had seen a batch of campaign medals in his room but he made no mention of his service at this stage so I didn't press him on the subject. Later I asked Angela about his Naval Service but she said he rarely talked about it so she didn't know much either.

We moved on to the City. I parked in Rodney Street and suggested we explore the immediate area. I knew quite a lot about the History of Liverpool. I tried to make it interesting for my fellow day trippers. Both John and the car looked the part for Rodney Street. It was the place to live for the well healed in days gone by. Now it was mainly high class businesses in the main. In the 19th, Century it would have been cobbled but the character of the Tree Lined Street and Georgian Houses was unspoiled. The area around Mount Pleasant and Canning Street is rich in period houses, in many cases complete with window boxes, now in their dormant winter stage but blooming in the summer. The first American Consul, James Maury lived at 4 Rodney Street. Several properties were birth places of famous Poets and Writers such as Aurthur Clouch, Nicholas Monsarrat and William Gladstone who was Prime Minister four times. He lived at No. 59. We strolled along whilst I gave my potted history talk. We returned to the car for the short drive to the Anglican Cathedral.

Our next stop was St. James Cemetery. John felt inclined to insist that he wasn't quite ready for that yet. Here I pointed out the initials J.C. carved into the rock and the date1876. In another place nearby is a well carved date 1727. This is scarred by marks made by dray horses ropes drawing sandstone from the site. The Catacombs are found here. Many of the occupants were citizens of various American States, plus people who had died at sea. Sarah Biffin is here, whose name was used in Nicholas Nickleby, Captain John Oliver of the Battle of the Nile, the first man to be killed by a train at Rainhill, William Huskisson M.P. I also thought that there was the grave of a victim of the Titanic disaster, but on several visits I was unable to find it. This site is a wealth of historic information. Clambering around rough footpaths and ramps took its toll on poor John who did well to keep up the pace. We got back to the car and left for the City, passing 'Paddies Wigwam' on the way. John expressed a wish to look inside another day. I said I had shares in it having donated money towards it's building at school. My name was supposed to be in a book somewhere inside. I made my way to John Street car park. We found a restaurant nearby and enjoyed a lovely meal.

In the evening we made our way to the Waterfront at the Pier Head. Now it was bitterly cold so we didn't spent very long there. Then I drove to Ottespool and we viewed the river from the raised car park near the pub on the front. At 9pm. we headed back to Woolton Grange and spent another half hour there with John. He thanked us profusely for the wonderful day out and we promised more to come. We left. As I drove away towards Gateacre, Angela became tearful. I held her hand and she told me she felt she had let her Dad down by being away so much. I assured her that he was the proudest Dad on the Planet and that she should regret nothing. We stopped at a set of lights at the top end of Belle Vale. A couple of young men in a Mini Cooper stopped on my offside. The Cooper's engine was revving ready to leave the old Merc. behind in a cloud of dust. The lights changed and the Mini revved hard causing a bit of wheel spin. Sadly for his ego he quickly disappeared in my rear view mirror, a moment of pure joy. It cheered Angela up and I felt like a teenager for just a moment.

We arrived home about 11pm. A bottle of white wine was retrieved from the fridge and we played Strip Poker. I was good at it so Angela was naked within 15 minutes. I had removed my jumper. However the sight of a naked Angela ended up in the only way it could. I sat on an upright dining chair and Angela sat astride me. We kissed and fondled each other. As the passion increased I sucked on her nipples and pulled her onto me. I loved this position as it was easy to get full penetration. I could look at her as we moved in unison. She grabbed my hair and pressed me to her breast. The ultimate moment approached, the excitement reached fever pitch. The chair back broke and we ended up in a heap on the floor. The moment was lost in a fit of laughter and my back reduced to severe pain. After recovering we partly dressed and sat on the sofa to regain our composure. I saw the lights of a bus pass by the window. The curtains were still wide open. I don't know if we had an audience, but if we did they may have been turned on and amused all for the price of one ticket.

The remainder of the time leading up to Christmas was a mixture of visiting relatives and friends and frequent love making; with the curtains closed and more often in bed. We spent Christmas with J.P. and Annette. The House was a lovely modern detached house but I'm not sure I would like to live within the curtilage of a truck depot. Still it was very well appointed inside. The trucks were parked up until the 28th. So there was no noise. On the 23rd. it was the Staff Party. The drivers and admin staff were invited to party at the house together with their families. It was a great night with lots of food and drink plus a D.J. There were plenty of party games for kids and adults and the party went on until 4am. It wasn't a residential area so we could be as manic as we wanted to be. Angela always seemed to have an audience. She could tell lots of exciting stories about her worldwide adventures. However, by 1am, neither she nor her audience knew what on earth she was talking about. Almost all the children had gone by this time. We danced our way in long lines between the trucks, played blindfold skittles; hit the road sign with a football, glamorous Grandma Competition in drag and two of the fork lift drivers did a dance using their vehicles. It would have been good had they not been drunk. The mad games settled by about 3am. Then we just sat around talking rubbish until taxis arrived to carry off the wounded. We slept in the spare room until about 1pm. Christmas Eve.

The afternoon was spent clearing up after the party. We filled a skip with rubbish. A couple emerged from one of the sleeper cab trucks having spent the night and most of the day there. It was one of the drivers and the girl wasn't his wife. Sheepishly they found his car and departed without a word. Later we were visited by all the Cooke Family. We spent two hours playing Monopoly with the children. The day ended with a lovely Christmas Meal prepared by Annette and Angela. We retired at midnight and made Christmas love.

Christmas day was parcel opening day for the Children, John Paul and Sarah, now in their mid teens. It was mainly new clothes, videos and smellies. We adults also exchanged presents. Later we went to the Cookes and did much the same thing. The time between Christmas and New Year was spent going on days out, just for us. We were in love and the world outside us just passed by like a film. We talked a lot about our future. The new business featured a lot in our plans. I was to start my flying lessons in the New Year at Blackpool Airport. I took Angela on a few more historical tours of the City. I loved the architecture in the City. We visited Queen Avenue and explored the arcade in which the Royal Bank, with Greek columns and carved seashells was situated, and the other magnificent bank buildings around Castle Street and Church Street. The Town Hall I always loved with its busy inner square. Victoria Chambers on Castle Street is so beautiful. Angela likened it to a posh wedding cake. The old National and Provincial Bank on Water Street has two lion's heads on the massive bronze doors. In days gone by visiting sailors from distant lands would rub these heads for good luck. We decided to do the same.

We also visited Manchester for shopping. I didn't know much of the History of Manchester but I loved the Midland Hotel, the Town Hall and Library buildings. The shopping was enjoyable with lots of nooks and crannies to explore. The Britania Hotel was wonderful, laid out in the style of a Luxury Liner. We promised each other a night there for posh sex. We visited for a while and sat in the Lounge Bar for a relaxing drink. The central hub of Piccadilly Gardens was a popular gathering place and the Christmas lights display a wonder to behold, but was marred by the presence of beggars and people of suspect appearance. We enjoyed the market very much and contributed a lot to the local economy that day. We had a drive around the city centre admiring the lights and window displays before wending our way down the East Lancs Road and home.

New Year we spent in Scotland. A long held dream for Angela. This was to be a relaxing romantic break, just the two of us. We rented a cottage within reasonable driving distance from Edinburgh. We wanted to take part in the New Year celebrations in the City. The cottage was quite remote and took some finding. However it was well worth the effort. It was an old Farm Labourer's cottage, built in rugged weathered stone with white wooden windows and heavy oak door. It had a well kept garden hedged with privets. The garden was in a bare winter state and the hanging baskets were empty. When we arrived the cottage was bathed in a cold swirling mist which gave it an air of mystery. The lane was very narrow so I parked the car in the entrance to a crumbling barn nearby. As I returned to the cottage Angela was stood at the door with our cases. She was looking around and she was so obviously happy.

'Oh, isn't it lovely?'

I had to agree. I took out the chunky key and turned the stiff lock. I pushed open the heavy door and we were welcomed by a lovely burst of warm air. The owner had thought to light the coal fire. I considered lifting Angela inside but remembered what happened with Lacey Jay and thought better of it. That thought stirred some emotions but I said nothing about it.

We stepped straight into the living room. The floor was slate with rugs here and there. It was like stepping back to a different era. The furniture was probably antique, solid but comfortable with cushions. There was a two seat sofa and a large armchair beautifully upholstered in floral patterns, an upright piano and stool. The piano lid was open and a book of sheet music was set upon the rack. The book was open on the page with the music for 'Have I Told You Lately That I Love you.' The fire must have been alight some time as it was now quite low. I topped it up from the scuttle and emptied the ash in the yard at the back where I also discovered the coal bin which had plenty of stock. Interestingly, the back door, which leads out from the small kitchen, had a latch but no lock. When I pointed this out to Angela she came to have a look. She noticed something obvious which I hadn't. There were two large hooks on the back of the door and a short thick plank leaning against the sink. That was the lock. The plank was place into the hooks across the door. The owner must have forgotten to secure the door when he was getting the place ready earlier. Problem solved. I inspected the kitchen. There was an AGA cooker range which I had no idea how to use. A large stone sink and a ringer. There were some wall cupboards and an ARP cycle. Some ropes for hanging washing I suppose and a tall metal oven contraption for which purpose I had no idea. Angela thought it might be for smoking fish but I couldn't imagine why they would want that inside. The mist had now cleared and we could see mountains in the distance through the small kitchen window.

Back in the lounge or living room we looked around some more. The dresser had a display of old photographs and decorative plates interspaced by ornaments. The cupboard contained everyday use crockery and the drawer stored the cutlery. A white drape covered an old rocking chair. The interior was thickly plastered and the walls decorated with prints of Scottish landscapes. Above the fireplace hung a large framed plaid with mounted crossed swords. The fireplace stonework reached up to the roof to be topped off by a double pot chimney with crown tops. The open plan wooden staircase enticed you to a landing, also plastered and displaying old faded black and white family photographs. For some reason some one thought it was a good idea to fix a scythe to the bedroom door. Not a decorative feature I would have thought of. There were two rooms upstairs, a basic bathroom, that is a bath and sink accompanied by an upright wooden chair. No where to put anything. Oh, there was one ultra modern accessory, a towel ring.

The bedroom was cosy and welcoming. The bulky double bed had a thick comfortable mattress, crisp white sheets and a thick woollen bedspread. Again the room was basic. There was a big wooden dressing table with massive mirror. Some of the silvering around the edges had faded but the bottom edge had engravings of beautiful swans and bull rushes. The wardrobe was in matching style on top of which were two top hat cases. I had forgotten to bring my top hats.

There was a knock at the door. The Landlord had come to welcome us. I got a much needed course in working the AGA and he started it up for us so it would warm the kitchen which was freezing. The heat from the lounge fire convected upstairs so that part of the house was fine. He showed me where to put the ash from the fire which was a hint to move my little mound of ash to the correct place. Electricity was by way of a meter so he made sure he brought us enough change for it. There was no phone so he supplied us with an ex army two way radio. His farm house wasn't far away. It was a bulky hand held unit in army green; that's the radio, not the farmhouse. However it was fit for purpose. Monty, that was the landlord's name, told us about the daily visit by Erick and Maureen with their mobile shop. They could supply all the essentials we needed and I was asked if I required a fishing licence. I declined. I didn't fancy having to kill something myself in order to eat it.

Then, another knock on the door, I thought it was going to be peaceful. It was Erick and Maureen. Monty introduced us and we walked outside to inspect the mobile shop. It was an ex Army Ambulance on a Land Rover chassis. It still had the big Red Cross on the side and the blue light on top. Monty proudly announced that Erick would get to his customers whatever the weather conditions. I quipped, 'and to Hospital as well if needs be?' I got a laugh.

Soon our visitors had gone. We settled together on the sofa and watched the News on the most modern item in the cottage, a T.V. After 15 minutes of news we switched off the set and I suggested we play chess. Angela told me she didn't mind but she would need tuition which I was pleased to provide. After about 20 minutes she seemed happy with the rules so the first serious game commenced. After only 17 moves I was in Check mate. I was stunned until Angela admitted that journalism was made up of 10 minutes action followed by 5 hours of waiting around. Chess was played a lot during those quiet times and she had been rarely beaten. We laughed about my being duped. We were about to go to bed when there was another knock on the door. It was now dark and I wandered who it could be. I opened the door to be slightly startled by the presence of a very large bearded Police Sergeant, .his rough brown hair fighting to get out from beneath his flat cap. Fortunately he was just introducing himself and letting us know he was in the area. He asked if everything was OK and details of who we were and off he went in his ancient Ford Anglia panda car. I thought they had been discontinued ages ago, seemingly not in these parts. At last we were alone to do what lovers do, in that lovely inviting bed. Both we and the field mice had a lovely night.

CHAPTER 50

We quickly got used to living in the style of days gone by with occasional assistance from Monty. We walked a lot amongst the scenic beauty of the place, although summer might have been better. Across the narrow lane in front of the cottage was a large reservoir, at the far end of which there was a small settlement and some sailing boats. On one of the days I hired one and showed off my sailing skills to Angela. It turned out to be more of an endurance test than a pleasant sail. It was very cold and the spray stung my face like razor blades. The wind was brisk and the craft fought me every inch of the way. After two hours we stiffly made our way to the pub to warm up with a couple of Brandies.

Soon the big day was upon us. New Years Eve. We hired a taxi for the trip into Edinburgh. We arrived about 2pm and the City was already alive with activity. We explored the streets and back alleys to seek out interesting events and people. Everyone was in the festive mood and many were on the verge of drunken stupor by tea time. It seemed that the place to be by about 10pm was Princess Street beneath the Castle. That's where all the main activities would take place. Between 5 and 7pm we tried to find a restaurant with space to eat. It was impossible so we ended up at MacDonalds in an hour long queue wading through rubbish to get what we didn't ask for from stressed out staff. Still, any food was welcome by this time.

The night was not disappointing. It was one hell of a party, Thousands of people celebrating with only one aim; to have a great time and bring in 1990 with a bang. We met and drank with so many wonderful people who didn't know and didn't care who you were or where you came from. Everybody was your mate tonight. You loved everybody and everything. I remember seeing only a handful of Police and they were as happy as everyone else. At Midnight there were fireworks, dancing, kissing and no doubt a lot of shagging going on. Our turn would come later, much later.

We neglected to make plans for our return. We started trying for a Taxi at 12.30; and actually got one at 5.30am. We were back at the cottage by 6.10am. The fire had gone out. The AGA was dead as a door nail and soon we were too. Flat out. Angela was the first to awake at 3pm. I followed in a daze half an hour later. It took me ages to get the fire going, soon followed by the AGA. Our first meal of 1990 was at 7.15pm, New Year's Day. However, it wasn't due to our efforts. Monty and his wife visited. They wished us a Happy New Year and presented us with a wonderful cooked meal, freshly caught Salmon from their own fish farm with home grown potatoes and vegetables. A steamed fruit sponge with a brandy source and a bottle of fine Scottish single malt whiskey. We were amazed. Monty made sure we were ok with everything, checking the fire and the AGA and even the fridge. Then the bid us farewell and off they went. What a lovely gesture. We were starving so the meal went down very well. Angela washed up all the plates and kitchenware our benefactors provided.

That evening we discussed our plans for the immediate future. In a few days we would be back at work. Angela had a few more distant assignments but promised to try and curtail her worldwide interests in favour of more UK work. We looked through the prospectus for the Flying School with whom I was soon to start training. I estimated that it would take upwards of a year to gain my Commercial Licence. After that I would be doing further practical training as a Co Pilot and learning about the business before we could take over. Even with the promise of on-going support it was still a daunting prospect. Angela was convinced everything would be fine. She had already researched potential customers and done some of the costing. Her friend in the business, John Moorcroft, agreed to work with us for up to a year after we took over in order to ensure we were properly prepared to be independent. He would remain a Director and Shareholder. That gave me more confidence. All this business talk was tiring. The bed was inviting and so was Angela.

The holiday was over. We said our good byes to Monty and 'Mrs Monty' as I called her. We promised to return. We also stopped off to say good bye to Erick and Maureen and the unique mobile shop. We were sad to leave. It was a wonderful holiday. It wasn't a pleasant journey back. It rained heavily. The scenery was blanked out by road spray and low cloud. The slow traffic and occasional accident scene extended our journey time to six hours. Not until Preston on the M6 could we see more than half a mile ahead and the rain finally stopped. It was good to be home. Annette and J.P. had stocked up the fridge and food cupboard. The heating was on and a card on the dining table welcomed us home. Angela's poor white Merc was filthy having been parked on the main road for two weeks. After unloading our bags my first job was to take her car to the car wash at Old Swan. For the last couple of days before returning to work we spent much of our time entertaining visitors and repeating over and over again our holiday experiences and going through the photographs. Angela said photograph albums would soon be a thing of the past. Technology was moving on fast.

Back at work and James informed me that he was to open a new distribution centre in Kirkby, Liverpool. This was to serve Wales and the South. Warrington was to close and another new depot was to be set up in Carlyle to serve the North and Scotland. I was offered the job of Manager of the Liverpool Depot. After 30 seconds thought, I accepted. James was to be Managing Director and we both set about conducting interviews for the Carlyle Manager. This was a very exciting and demanding period. Between interviews we travelled around selecting equipment and vehicles for the expanded business. James was a tough negotiator and fought hard for the best prices on everything from trucks to toilet paper. The feeling of importance was very satisfying as we had meetings with property agents at prospective premises. I learned a lot about dealing. James would not only get lease payments down and shorter periods offered, but he would get agreements on lots of building work not originally in the agreement. Eventually we settled on a warehouse very close to the East Lancs Road. It needed little in the way of refurbishment so it was just a matter of moving equipment in. The unit would be ready by early February so we had to get a move on to get everything we needed to commence operation. That was now my job. I was also tasked to do a budget for the first year. That alone took me a week. We also went to Commercial Auctions to buy vehicles. I loved the auctions, exciting and nerve racking at the same time. It occurred to me that we would now save money by employing our own vehicle fitters. The cost of farming the work out was considerable. My bright idea back fired on me as that also became my job to cost and sort out.

James and Sandra bought a House in Carlyle. No more living in the depot. It was a stone cottage contained within a small plot of land overlooking the South Lakeland hills I helped with the move and saw the property in its empty state. The garden was well kept. It was difficult getting everything inside. The cottage had not been designed with ease of access for furniture. A house warming was hopefully in the pipeline for two weeks hence.

By April everything was in place and both new Depots were up and running. I was still working on setting up our own maintenance workshop. Liverpool was the larger premises so I decided to set it up there. It wasn't easy getting the right people to work in the garage. There were plenty of fitters around with good qualifications but reliability records were not good on the whole. I never took application forms on face value, digging deeper revealed lots of flaws. I also discovered the astronomical cost of fitting out a workshop for commercial vehicles. This meant more visits to auctions to buy bankrupt stock. I did this in company with my first workshop manager. Keith Meadowcroft. We opened the new vehicle workshop on the 1st. of June. In order to make the workshop pay its way I opened it up for general commercial vehicle repairs and servicing. This proved to be both a blessing and a curse as the yard quickly filled up with Lorries needing repairs. This also led to a new accounts department for the garage side of the business.

All this progression called more and more on my time. Now it was often the case that when Angela was at home I was often called out to solve problems to do with the garage. James advised me to delegate more. I wasn't expected to manage everything 'hands on.' I also found myself juggling my time with the Flying Lessons. The theory was hard going as I was often exhausted when trying to study. The vast quantities of paperwork concerning regulations and the technical aspects of navigation, inspections and maintenance were very difficult to cope with. There were times when I wanted to call it a day, but after discussing it with James and Angela I persevered.

Once I had worked out a reasonable balance between all these tasks, Angela and I managed most weekends together. As we got to know more about each other, it came to light that Angela was keen on country music. I told her about my experiences with Lacey Jay. She knew the basic story but now I was able to go into more detail about life 'On The Road' with the group.

This represented our lifestyle throughout 1990/91. Whilst I was getting to grips with my new responsibilities, Angela was being Angela, rushing all over the place to get the story. The first big job after Christmas was early January when 50000 people demonstrated in London in support of the on-going Ambulance strike. Then in mid January major storms hit England killing 33 people. In February Ayatollah Khomaini hit the headlines with his Fatwa on Salmon Rushdie of 'Satanic Verses' fame. Then there were the floods in Towyn, North Wales which killed 14. That was late in the Month, so far so good. All home based work.

Then Angela was off to South Africa to do a profile on Nelson Mandela who had recently been released from a 27 year prison sentence. She got some personal time with him. She returned home just in time for the Brixton Riots in London. Here she was injured and spent a couple of days in Hospital. I went to bring her home as her prized Mercedes was destroyed by vandals. At the end of March Angela was again in London to report on 20000 protesters marching against the Poll Tax. Then a local story when 19 prisoners at Strangeways in Manchester had a rooftop protest about prison conditions. Then came the local elections in May when Labour came out on top.

In June we went on Holiday to Rhodes. This was a very welcome break for both of us. We arrived at night after a smooth flight from Manchester. Leaving the plane we were greeted with warm welcoming air. I had arranged a hire car for our journey to the Hotel near Lindos. It was a beautiful drive. We passed quaint buildings and small settlements. Taking the Coast Road offered us views of the beaches lit by hotels and lots of palm trees. I seemed to be upsetting the coach drivers rushing holiday makers to their resorts. Still, we made the most of our leisurely drive at 4 in the morning.

We arrived at the magnificent Princess Hotel Lindos. In our country this would be a 5 star hotel but in addition we had several swimming pools, outside bars and eating areas and beautiful décor. We didn't have to queue with lots of coach passengers. The service was swift and pleasant. Our room would have been at home in Buckingham Palace. It was 4.50am. I flopped down on the bed while Angela explored the room and views. Even though she had been all over the globe, this place excited her so much. Later, half awake, I felt myself being undressed, kissed and covered up. I was out for the count.

Our stay was for three weeks. The first week was spent exploring. We sun bathed and shopped in many places. Rhodes City was not quite what I expected. It seemed disorganised and laid back. So much so that in one of the squares packed with people there was a local lady, possibly in her 40s and obviously one of the poorer in the community bathing naked in one of the fountains. Nobody took any notice, except me that is. Angela was quite amused. It was in Pylona that I managed to sneak away for a while to buy a couple of special presents for Angela. On our first Saturday night we walked into the centre of Lindos for the first time. Dodging Mercedes Taxis, we walked down the steep, kerb-less hill to the Taxi Rank. The drivers stood chatting and laughing, some polishing their pristine cars with not only pride but love. We sat on a bench there to people watch for a while. A large ancient tree acted as a roundabout at the turn around point. The bottom of the tree was painted white as a deterrent to hitting it but there was evidence that a few people hadn't seen it. The shopping area seemed to be covered and as it was now dark. The warm lighting invited us to explore the interior. The shops and restaurants were typical of the Island, but the atmosphere and character were quite distinctive. The covering effect was created by large vines living in harmony with the buildings. There was so much infective happiness here. We resisted shopping and found a delightful rooftop restaurant. A waitress escorted us up the narrow winding wooden staircase to the cooler open air. Lanterns enhanced the romantic atmosphere. We both wore wide smiles as we were seated with a view of the street. A musician with a guitar sang to us for a few minutes. I felt embarrassed but Angela was lapping it up. The menu came and the musician left with his tip for another table. We ordered a fruit starter followed by stifado and the ice cream. Everything was beautiful. The food, the service the table flowers and candle.

We talked about lots of things, but a recurring theme was the need to sort our lives out better, to make more time for us rather than our work. The future business also featured in our deliberations and I expressed my concern over the volume of work required to get the licence. I didn't want to let Angela down. She was totally confident that I would easily get through. Her supreme confidence made me a little uneasy but I went along with it. I remembered the two gifts I had secreted away in my shoulder bag. A bottle of local wine was delivered to our table and we began to share it. I passed a black velvet covered box to Angela which I opened to reveal a silver Aires pendant on a chain. Her eyes lit up. I left my seat to help place it around her neck. It complemented her black evening dress beautifully. For that I received a long loving kiss and a 'thank you darling, it s lovely.' Then I handed her the multi coloured gift bag as I returned to my seat. She peeled back the sticky tape and emptied out the small tissue paper parcel. As she pulled at it the parcel burst open and the gold ring with diamond setting spun for a moment like a coin before settling next to her wine glass.

There was a moment of silence. We both looked at the ring. She looked up at me with questioning eyes. I broke the silence.

'If you could possibly find a little time between assignments, do you think you would like to marry me?'

Silence again. My heart pounded and my eyes dried along with my mouth. She looked directly at me, eyes wide and gaping mouth. The Worldly Wise Journalist was stunned. She picked up the ring. I hoped it wasn't to throw at me. Her eyes filled with tears. Shakily she poured two glasses of wine and lifted hers as in a toast. I did the same.

'Yes,' she said. Gulped her whole glass down and said again. 'Yes.'

People nearby witnessed this occasion and announced it to everyone else. Applause rang out into the night air and words of congratulations in several languages. I stood and offered my hand to Angela to stand. I placed the ring on her finger. It was a bit loose. I wasn't able to guess the size exactly so it would have to be adjusted later. We kissed like we had never kissed. The whole restaurant was in uproar. Now three musicians came to the table to serenade us. The Owner or Manager brought out a cake and three waitresses cut it up for distribution. Every customer's glass was topped up for a toast, it was like a wedding. Our evening at the restaurant concluded with almost all the men kissing Angela and some of the women kissing me. From others it was a hug or hand-shake. Angela got the best deal though; she was the best looking.

News travels fast in Lindos. When we returned to the hotel, many of the staff on duty clapped us through Reception and there was a large bunch of flowers and a big bowl of chocolates in the room together with a bottle of Champagne, all on the house. Fantastic, Angela said over and over again how unexpected this was. How excited she was. How emotional it made her feel.

After dipping into the Champagne and chocolates we retired to bed. Tonight was the most important so far for us. Tonight we made love as a firm commitment to each other. Not just for fun, for the total love of each other. It felt different. It had new meaning. It was a union unlike before. Even on such tender and loving occasions our minds can play silly tricks. All I could think of was how I could top this on our wedding night.

CHAPTER 51

The holiday was a wonderful experience. Rest and relaxation evaded us both in our working lives. We fully recharged our batteries and returned home with our tans and gifts for relatives and friends. News of the engagement was greeted with great excitement at home. We had not yet set a date. We were torn between having the wedding soon regardless of our present lifestyles; or wait until Angela could reduce her workload and I get the pilot's licence. Then we could start everything afresh, marriage, business, new home, everything. That decision was put on hold.

Angela returned to her busy schedule and I increased my efforts to gain my pilot's licence, including forgoing a 2 week holiday to study full time and get the flying hours up. I also spent time on almost every weekend going on jobs with our future partner in his aircraft to gain experience in the business. I enjoyed this part of the training very much. I got hands on experience and visited lots of places around Great Britain and the near continent. My views were mostly from the air though. There was little time to go beyond the Airports. Just before I qualified in September 1991 the company acquired a very attractive second hand aircraft. The Cessna was sold off and replaced by a Beechcraft King Air 200. A turbo prop engine executive aircraft, eight-seated and luxuriously fitted out. I loved it. A Beechcraft King Air Helicopter also appeared on the scene which required me to take another course and licence to cover that. However I could take more time over that and I now had the 'Flying Bug.' The business owner, John Moorcroft, delayed his retirement still further to accommodate our needs. Really I don't think he could bring himself to let it all go just yet. The company 'Flights of Fancy' had operated since 1970. The core business was executive hire but pleasure flights were also on the books. It was quite expensive to hire but the costs were high too. However the company made good profits.

By the time my qualification was confirmed Angela had retired from her journalistic career and had been working in the office of 'Flights of

Fancy' getting to know the 'Nittygritty' of the business. Her final decision was aided by having a rough time as a correspondent on contract to 'Time Magazine' during the Gulf War. She described it as a 100 day night mare. Like many of the troops she came home with a non defined illness typified by symptoms such as nausea, shortage of breath and lethargy. Compared with some, her symptoms were mild and after three months she seemed to recover completely. It was a worrying time but she refused to give in and kept working throughout the period of significant discomfort.

Towards the end of 1991 I left Styletto, and began to work full time for 'Flights of Fancy'. The winter months were quiet enough to concentrate on maintenance between cleaning and more cleaning and meetings to plan for the following busy season. Angela and I went to trade shows and exhibitions all over the country to promote our business. I managed to secure a contract for an aerial photography company starting in the spring of '92. I thought that would be interesting. It was a hard negotiation and I didn't get the best price but I thought it may be a job we could do ourselves in the future. Business bookings remained steady except for occasional weather blips but now I was being given more responsibility. Captain Moorcroft became more relaxed and I was given control more frequently as his confidence in me grew. I was still going to lots of places in the UK and in Europe but seeing little of the cities I visited. The longest stay was four days at a Conference for Politicians in Brussels. I enjoyed Brussels. I didn't know the language, but then most people spoke English anyway.

Christmas 1992 and John retired. I became Captain Liam Parry. I put an extra gold stripe on my epaulettes. Angela decided to start her flight training in January. We would fly together and employ an office manager. Our main aircraft required a crew of two. Therefore I had to find a new pilot to help us. That came in the form of a man called Simon Bentham. He was very experienced. Simon had flown Air Ambulances in Australia and Africa. He had flown scientists and equipment to remote locations around the globe. His references indicated that he could land any plane anywhere. Perhaps he may be bored with us but it was a temporary contract any way. In a year he would be off to the Himalayas working with mountaineers and film crews. He was a larger than life character for whom every third word had an "F" in it. He was a rough diamond but loveable, according to Angela.

Christmas 1992. We set the date for the Wedding. April 1993. April was Angela's month of choice. There was now much to do. Fortunately

Angela's Dad was able to take a full part in planning the arrangements. That made them both very happy. My job was to arrange the venues and transportation and all the legal stuff. My future Bride and Father in Law were tasked with the dresses, catering and the general make up of the day.1 was concerned that maybe we didn't have enough time to get everything arranged. The Wedding was to take place in Rhodes in the town of Lindos. Due to the fact that the Wedding was to be in Greece I expected delays and complications. In order to avoid complications I decided to get the assistance of a specialist Solicitor. The word specialist always costs more, however it was ease of mind. My friend James and I flew out to Greece to make 'on the spot' arrangements and ensure all the 'T's were crossed and the 'I's dotted. That wasn't straight forward. In order to get to Rhodes out of season we had to fly to Athens then overland and ferry to Rhodes. We met the Mayor and the Management of 'The Princess Hotel'; sorted out documentation, times and date and made sure we had all the information we needed. I took away all the information about catering for Angela. I couldn't get much sense out of anyone about cars or other forms of transport. The place was almost shut down like our Northern Wakes weeks.

The round trip took us four days. Things moved ever so slowly in Greece. I advised Angela to keep in constant touch with our Greek friends to ensure that everything she wanted was done on time. So 1993 commenced with a hectic schedule. The Wedding arrangements took up much of our time and concentration. I still had business to conduct and Angela started a full time Flying Course, so her qualification time would be far less than my own. Much of my winter work was for Power Companies who had major projects going on throughout the country. Our Chopper was in demand by management teams overseeing the work taking place. Angela now accompanied me on any work done with the Beechcraft King, as part of her training. One of the many things that amazed me about Angela was that she was able to chat away constantly and still concentrate on the flying. When I was taking off or landing I needed to fully concentrate. Angela would be talking about all sorts of things between communications with ground controllers. She would be told off sometimes for trying to chat with controllers who were already busy with other aircraft.

Angela would be qualified for both fixed wing commercial and Helicopters by June. Less than half the time it took me. She told me she wished she had done it years ago as it would have made her journalistic career much easier. In the meantime though there was the matter of the Wedding. We planned to have the main wedding ceremony in Lindos with selected guests and then a further reception for our wider circle of friends and associates when we returned home after the honeymoon. We did consider the idea of flying out to the wedding in our own aircraft but then decided to have a more leisurely trip on a charter flight. It would be nice for somebody else to be the pilot. Partly retired John and 'gung ho' pilot Simon would look after the business while we were away.

Then there was the shopping. The rings, well that was a job for 'H Samuel' in the City Centre. I was going to buy a suit but Angela wanted me to be in uniform. That saved a few bob I thought, but I had to have a new uniform, tailor made, for the occasion. Then we spent nearly 2 hours at Thompsons travel agency who informed us that they had special packages for weddings, so all Angela's catering job was done by them; very crafty. Actually Thompsons were very good. Everything for the Hotel we wanted, the transport, the catering was all arranged by them. I envisaged arranging it ourselves with lots of telephone calls and letters, possible misunderstandings and complications. So now we were ready as much as we could be. Only close family and friends were invited to Lindos. The day came around so quickly. In the week prior to departure I spent anxious hours checking and re checking documents and arrangements. I was often banned from the bedroom while Angela tried on the dress and worried about putting on an ounce. Relatives and friends also kept calling to re-check details. John and Jane Cooke set off two weeks earlier than the wedding date in their new ocean going cabin cruiser 'English Rose'. They would berth at Lindos and I was told we could borrow the craft anytime during the honeymoon. Wow.

The wedding weekend approaches. Nerves are heightened. We check frequently on Angela's Dad. He is fine. Excited and feeling very well. Everybody is prepared and we are at pains to remind everyone to make sure they don't forget anything, especially passports. We leave earlier than anyone else, on the Wednesday. The guests are leaving on the Friday. The Wedding is on Saturday. I ask JP to look after Angela's Dad for the trip. 4am on Wednesday morning. We sit trying to concentrate on breakfast. Once again I sort through everything to make sure we have all we need. The Taxi is ordered for 5am. At ten past it hasn't arrived. I call the office several times but without reply. Angela begins to get nervous. I begin to get angry; then the knock on the door and tremendous relief. We arrive at Manchester airport by 6.15am much lighter in pocket but with a heavy trolley of luggage. The flight is at 7.20am and it seems like a fortnight waiting. Many children become noisy and irritable with waiting. At last we are called to the gate. A mass of people file towards a narrow gap to show Boarding Passes. Some children suddenly remember that they've left clothes, toys or food back in the waiting area and return to retrieve them. Some people fumble for documents at the last minute and hold up the queue. Finally we squeeze into the aircraft and wait for seemingly endless stoppages to enable fat people with loads of hand luggage to sort themselves out. Then your seat appears, wonderful.

Then the push-back of the plane, the safety stuff and then speeding along the runway. I was casting a professional eye over the take off. It was a good flight to Rhodes. This time we settled for the coach ride to the hotel. Now it was swimming and laughing, drinking and eating followed by relaxation and sun. We decided to comply a little with tradition for some reason and stayed in separate rooms prior to the wedding. Anyway, Angela could excite herself with more trying on of the dress in private. John and Jane Cooke, who were already there, invited us onto the boat on Thursday evening. John came to pick us up in the inflatable. The Cruiser was moored a little way out in the bay. It was a beautiful evening. Calm and pleasantly warm after a very hot day and there was a pleasant breeze from the ocean.

Jane waved to us from the boat as we approached the steps to the deck. When aboard, I looked back at the scenery. Lindos was beautiful, covering the hill. It was dusk and the lights started to glitter from the narrow streets. We could see the taxis weaving their way up and down the steep hill, between the top road and the shops. We sat on leather seats around the rear deck and talked a while. John broke out some cigars and he and I sat like millionaire smoking and joking. John offered us the use of the boat for the first few days of the honeymoon suggesting that we could see more of the islands. We thought that would be great. Greek Weddings were usually late afternoon or evening. John thought it might be a good idea for me to sail with him for a few hours on Saturday to get the feel of the cruiser before I took charge of it for a few days. I looked forward to that.

CHAPTER 52

Saturday morning, it was the Wedding Day. I spent the night on John's Boat; although to him a boat is a submarine. This was so I couldn't spy on the bridal party at the hotel. It seemed that everything that was to happen at the Ceremony was none of my business. My job was to turn up. The Marriage was to take place at the Town Hall and conducted by the local Mayor, as was custom and practice in Greece. Jane served up a full English breakfast. The bacon was always poor here, weak and streaky, decent quality wasn't available. It was so lovely sitting on the after deck eating a lovely breakfast, fresh orange juice and toast, or as one café advertised it 'tost'. The sun was glistening on the calm waters of the bay. with voices and engines signalling the start of the day in Lindos. A few fishing boats returning with their catch. John and Jane joined me. Jane asked me how I felt. I was fine. I didn't feel nervous but perhaps a little vacant. A lot had gone on in recent weeks. I was tired and glad the day had finally arrived. It would have upset Angela to know that I was thinking of my Wedding Day with Paula. Seemed like a different century, like it wasn't real. I thought about Kathy and the way I lost her. Then I told myself to look to the future and not to worry John diverted my mind to familiarisation trip in his cruiser. We set off at 10.30, heading out to sea. I had been given the full safety briefing and tour of the craft. Now I was at the helm, pushing forward the throttles and putting the twin diesel engines through their paces. 'English Rose' was no Kitten. She had bags of power, rather more like a Tiger of the seas. After that bit of excitement I eased off the throttles and turned north, keeping the coast in sight. We consulted the charts. These waters were to be respected with strong currents and undulating reefs. We didn't call in at any ports I just concentrated on getting to know the craft and how she handled. At one point we were closely overtaken by a Police boat. They simply waved at us and moved on. John was a little nervous as they approached.

'You haven't got anything dodgy on board have you?' I asked jovially.

As the Police launch pulled away John told me he did have a gun on board which may have been a problem. Some of the waters he planned to visit could be a bit of a problem. It was licenced in England but not internationally. It was locked in a safe to which I had no access. He assured me it would be fine.

At 3pm we eased our way into Lindos harbour and anchored. I was happy with the boat and John was happy with my handling of it. We lowered the inflatable into the water and loaded it with their luggage for the few days ashore. I accompanied John and Jane to their hotel where I could get changed. We arranged taxis to take us to the Town Hall for 4.30pm. The ceremony was at 5pm. James; my best man arrived at 4pm with his report. Apart from tears, panic, broken straps and zips, runny make up and late hairdressers; everything seemed to be going ok at the Princess Hotel. Seemingly Angela was quite calm amidst the mayhem. I asked James had he seen the dress. 'No, she was naked last time I saw her,' he said with a smile.

I retired to the bedroom to change into the tailored uniform. I put on the full kit and looked at myself in the mirror. I couldn't believe how far I had come to get to this point. When I first walked along that drive at Rainhill Hospital I couldn't have imagined in my wildest dreams that I would one day be standing in front of this mirror, a qualified pilot in my own business about to marry a woman of the world like Angela. Then I thought back further to the day I first fell in love with my teacher, and today, all these years later she is about to say yes to being my wife, incredible. It would be hot outside. I presented myself to my guests in full uniform after putting on my cap, tie and jacket in a bag for the journey to the Town Hall. The Taxis arrived. We piled in enthusiastically. The driver talked constantly about Manchester United. His accent made the team sound sexy. Now we were inside the small lavishly ornate Town Hall. For some reason there were two Policemen at the door. I didn't know if that was usual or just in our honour. They hadn't discovered air conditioning inside but it was slightly cooler than the 80 degrees outside. I thought I'd leave the full uniform until last minute.

11 minutes past 5. My Bride arrives. No 'Here comes the Bride' music. A group of Greek Musicians enter the Hall with guitars and traditional songs. They are followed by Angel and her Father. James and I stand, followed by all the guests. James reminds me that I'm only half dressed. Under cover of a column I quickly put on the rest of my uniform. On coming into view

again, the Mayor indicates with a smile that I should remove the cap for now. The Bride and Father are accompanied by Bridesmaids, Christine Porter now in her early 20s, Lorna Cooke, 19 I think. Sarah Porter also about 19 now. John Paul Porter and his parents were in the guest area together with some Greek People who were just enjoying the occasion.

Angela wore a plain ivory full length dress with high lightly frilled collar . . . The train was fixed to a bushel and supported by the Bridesmaids. Her shoes seemed to be silk rather like those of a Ballet Dancer but I didn't get a good view of them. Around her neck and over the collar was a triple string of pearls which were matched be a double string in her hair supporting the veil. The walk down the aisle was slow and purposeful, almost teasing. I could just detect the smile beneath the veil. The musicians, having reached the front, separated and slightly bowed as the Bride passed between them.

Now my heart was pounding. It was very warm and I was scared of fainting. The ceremony was conducted In Greek with an interpreter quietly repeating the Mayor's words. The final words he said in English.

'Do you, Liam Parry take this woman to be your lawfully wedded Wife, to have and to hold, from this day forward, for richer or poorer, in sickness or in health, till death you do part?'

.'I do.'

'Do you, Angela Megan Hughes,' (She had re taken her maiden name) 'take this man, Liam Parry, to be your lawfully wedded Husband, to live from this day forward, for richer, or poorer, in sickness or health until death do you part?'

'I do.'

'I am so pleased on behalf of the Peoples of Greece and of the Whole World to pronounce you Man and Wife. Then; after winging it on the wording so far, he returned to Greek to say, 'You may kiss the Bride.'

Angela turned to me. Lifted her veil and we gently kissed. There were loud cheers and applause. The band 'kicked' off again and led us out of the building. A significant crowd had gathered outside to cheer us on. Rose petals blew everywhere. The Town Hall had a bell which rang out. A photographer marshalled us around for 45 hot minutes. Then we were driven slowly away in a beautiful white, open topped, Mercedes 600 to the Lindos Taxi rank. We had reserved half of the top floor of the restaurant where we had got engaged for our reception.

The Limousine Driver took us on a tour for about an hour to allow guests to get to the reception first. In the back of the car, the breeze was cooling us down. We marvelled at how well everything had gone. From the high Coastal Road the sun glistened on the light blue sea. Cars and coaches passing us blew their horns and we waved back like a Royal Couple. Soon we were at the top of the steep road down to Lindos. I took a last look at the beautiful sea and Angela excitedly pointed out "English Rose" anchored in the small bay. I couldn't quite believe that we would be aboard tonight. At the taxi rank everyone clapped and cheered. The Greek musicians from the church once more greeted us and played ahead of us through the shopping area to the restaurant. We walked slightly self conscious behind the band to the entrance of the restaurant. More petals were strewn across our path. I felt rather like a Roman Centurion returning from a great victory. It was just wonderful.

As we climbed the stairs to the upper floor I removed my jacket and tie. It was still very warm. At the top of the stairs the clapping and cheering erupted again from everybody, not just our guests. The sound settled as we got to our seats. James looked across to me and gave me a 'Thumbs up.' Sarah blew Angela a kiss. Angela's Dad was beaming with pride. The set up was not like it would be in England. The tables were all set for four people. Our table set at one end had only Angela, her Father and me. I noticed a table in one corner loaded with gifts and cards. Staff rushed around delivering food. I was starving. Music and dancing was put on throughout the meal. Occasionally I would look into Angela's loving eyes. She looked stunning. Annette removed Angela's veil before we were encouraged to start the dancing. There were no speeches. As it became dark the candles and strings of bulbs on dodgy wiring added to the atmosphere. There was lots of music, lots of dancing, lots of plates smashed. The wine took its toll and some fell by the wayside. I don't remember who I talked to or what I said but I managed to stay on my feet. Angela had to dance with every man from miles around. Her feel must have been in serious pain but she laughed her way through it all. After the first dance I never got the chance to touch her again until the end of the party at 3am.

CHAPTER 53

We said good bye to our guests. There were lots of kissing and hand-shakes, pats on the back and tears. John and Jane escorted us to the inflatable. John sought assurance from me that I could get to the Cruiser without help. I said I was fine. Angela and I gingerly got into the little craft. I pulled the starter chord, John untied the rope and off we went. The waves and goodbyes faded as we approached 'English Rose'. We neared the stern and I took the rope to secure the inflatable to the steps or so I thought. My timing was out and I over reached myself and plunged straight into the water. Compared with the air temperature it was freezing. The cold shock stunned me for a moment. I banged my head on the hull of the cruiser then came up next to the inflatable. Angela was just screaming "Oh my God, Oh my God!'

'I'm OK !' I gargled as I reached for the bottom step to the boat. Angela was drifting away.

'Throw me the rope!' I shouted. I felt the rope splash beside me. I pulled in the inflatable and secured it. As I struggled to mount the steps Angela grabbed my shirt to help me out of the water. I lost my grip and in seconds we were both in the water.

'Jesus, its freezing!' she screamed.

The tension suddenly disappeared. We both laughed, held each other for a long wet kiss. We were getting used to the temperature, enough to play a little. Splashing and laughing and even ducking each other. Then a bright light stung my eyes. A fisherman had come to check on us. I waved at him and shouted 'We're fine, it's ok!'

. He kept his light on the steps until we were aboard. We both waved and he returned to his duties, no doubt thinking we were mad.

Now quite chilled and soaked we had a shower; separately. It was quite a small shower cubicle. Angela was second as she wanted longer than my one minute. As she showered and beautified, I returned to the after deck to winch the inflatable on board and secure it in the rack. Then I fixed the wind shields to the rails, poured myself a glass of Greek Red Wine and stood looking at the lights ashore. After a while Angela came on deck and from behind put her arms around my waist.

'What a wonderful day my darling,' she whispered.

'Yes, it was wonderful. I didn't want it to end"

She released her grip allowing me to turn to her. We wore warm monogrammed bath robes. 'English Rose'. We kissed gently telling each other of our love. Fresh perfume filled my senses as the kissing got stronger and longer. Soon the robes were on the deck and we eased down onto the soft waterproof deck covering. We lay side by side. I admired her beautiful body which was enhanced by the moonlight. The bright eyes flashing, the soft light of the moon enhanced her curves and the shape of her breasts. I began to kiss her neck; already she began to make sexy sounds of appreciation. The kissing moved to the nipples and navel, the pubic hairs, fanny and thighs and continued to her feet and toes until there was nothing left to kiss in that direction. Except that I continued to kiss the matting getting further and further away. This made her laugh and call me back. The kissing and fondling continued. It was warm enough to stay naked. The sound of a boat engine passed by which made us suspend operations until the sound dwindled away. I turned Angela onto her front and massaged her neck, shoulders and back. She moaned with appreciation. When I reached the curved firm sexy bum I could resist no longer. My arousal was obvious to her. She turned to accept be between her soft thighs. We kissed briefly before I gently entered her, lifting myself up on outstretched arms so I could look into her eyes. They soon closed and with her mouth slightly open we pushed and panted our way to orgasm. I wanted to be in her, part of her body, as one. I roared as if in agony as I made my final thrusts. She dug her nails into me back as we sank into a vice like grip of each other. We were for one wonderful moment, one person.

We parted. Wet with sweat, laying side by side looking up at the fading stars. Dawn was breaking. The air was cooling so I sat up to peer over the wind breaks to see if we could now get to the cabin un-noticed. There was some activity around the bay so we donned our gowns and retired to the cabin. Snuggling up together in the bed we said nothing, just kissed each other to sleep.

I awoke about 10am. It was now hot in the cabin so I opened the portholes and switched on the fans. Angela slept on so I prepared a full English breakfast for myself and a more healthy option for Angela, coffee and a wedge of water melon. It was something she had started the day with before. I woke her with a gentle kiss and announced breakfast, checking at the same time that my choice was ok. It was. Angela headed for the shower followed by a beautifying session in the' heads' (Bathroom to you and me). I had finished my full English before she emerged. By this time I was in the cockpit consulting charts for our first day trip. Angela soon joined me and we decided together where to go today. As I had been drinking quite late last night I thought it best not to go to sea until at least 2pm. The radio crackled into life. It was John checking that everything was alright. I confirmed that we had everything we needed and thanked him profusely for all he had done. They were going to the City today; everyone else he thought was staying local to shop or sunbathe.

Angela returned to the after deck while I erected the canopy. As I began to secure the canopy frame I heard the clicking of a typewriter.

'I thought you'd retired from all that,' I remarked.

'Oh yes I have. I'm not doing a news piece. I'm starting my own book as you suggested. Your book about us is on-going I know, but I thought I would write a companion book to L.A. Love called 'Angela's story'. What do you think darling?'

'Well, well, an Author in our midst eh? I think that's great my love. I don't know even if I can get my own book published yet. But go for it babe!'

The canopy was secured. It was now quite hot but the sea breeze helped to moderate the temperature. I did all the safety checks on the boat and all the equipment as taught by John. He was a stickler for detail so it took me over half an hour. Then I relaxed a while with Angela who was still typing furiously. We had soft drinks and some fruit. I looked around at the view again. I never got tired of it. Lindos was a popular place. The small marina was full which is why we anchored in the bay. Another larger cruiser had joined us overnight. It was almost twice the size of ours and probably belonged to a millionaire or film star. No one was on deck this morning, perhaps they were ashore.

Angela stopped typing. I had been looking at her for some time, never tired of looking at her either. She wore a blue bikini partly covered with a light flowing gown which fluttered in the breeze. I sat next to her to get a view of the book but she hurriedly put it into a folder, refusing to let me see it. The brief struggle ended to make way for kissing and fondling. We decided to leave the rest until later. It was now about 80 degrees so there was a mutual decision to get going on our adventures.

I folded down the canopy and we climbed up to the cockpit. I started the engine and contacted the port and John with details of our intended course to Faliraki. I eased the throttle forward and the boat began to do a tight circle rather than head out to sea. The stern eased around and the bow remained almost where it was. I stopped the engine. I was confused. I stepped down to the lower deck and went over and over the safety checks in my head. What had I missed? I walked around the deck and there it was the cause of the problem. I had not retracted the anchor. It's a good job John didn't see this. The radio cracked into life. He had seen it. He was laughing his head off. My embarrassment was total. At last we were on our way, heading out to sea.

Now free of the anchor and once clear of the port I pushed the throttle to 50%. The swell was heavier than I had anticipated and we splashed our way into the empty sea ahead. The ferry routes were on the other side of the island and emanated mainly from the busy port of Rhodes City. All I could see now was a wisp of smoke from a distant ship over the horizon. Angela asked for confirmation of our destination. I told her New York. She almost believed me. She had the occasional 'Dumb Blonde' moment which is one of the things I loved about her. Then I confirmed Faliraki. I continued West out to sea for 30 minutes then turned North West up the coast. After over two hours without seeing another boat I turned east heading for Faliraki. As you would expect of an ex Navy Officer we had powerful binoculars mounted on stands on the Port and starboard side of the cockpit. I used one of them to get a look at our destination from quite a way out. There was a lot of small craft activity around Faliraki including jet skis and tiny pleasure craft. I asked Angela to keep a sharp look out for swimmers and small boats when we neared the bay area. The sway of the boat eased quite a lot as we approached the island again. Angela felt at ease enough to bring up some drinks from the galley. It had been quite a bumpy ride at sea today.

It was early evening as we approached the sandy beaches in the wide bay area. The water became calmer. I eased the throttle back to 15% and called the Port Police for berthing instructions. I also contacted John to say we arrived safely. Both Angela and I scanned the area for possible problems, Skiers, divers, snorkelers and small pleasure boats. Some people also liked to swim quite a way out from the beaches. As we slowed down the heat increased. I received my berth instructions after a long delay. Typical Greek 'any day will do.' Angela was now scouring the town with the binoculars.

'Wow, it looks great!'

'You're supposed to be looking for hazards,' I reminded her.

'I am' she said. There seems to be a lot of 'Time Share Idiots' about.'

'No change there then,' I added.

The youngsters on all sorts of floating nightmares were oblivious of the dangers of other craft. I had the answer. A very loud twin air horn on top of the cabin shocked them into evasive action which most of the time saved me from avoiding them. Carefully threading our way through all the 'nutters,' we made our way slowly into our berth for the night; or perhaps two. There were a number of boats here which made me feel like a pauper. Magnificent multi million pound Cruisers from all over the world. We tied up and settled in for tea on board. Then we could freshen up and take on whatever Failraki had to throw at us.

As the temperature became more pleasant we secured the boat and made our way into the Town. It was busy, mainly young people walking about between periods of drunken stupor also some families and the odd couple of lost pensioners who may have strayed into the wrong place on a day trip. The Front and Beach area were very pleasant, lots of space and very clean. Here we saw the first Police. We hadn't seen any on patrol in Lindos, just the two at the Town hall. The large car parks were full and the souvenir shops were doing good trade. We walked and talked arms around each other's waist, towards the main shopping and restaurant areas. We stopped off for coffee and ice cream and relaxed in a Tavern kept in the Traditional Style. Old men played board games and smoked cigars, talking loudly, often with friends across the room or even across the street. The place smelled of wine, cheese and tobacco and the walls were white with old thick wooden beams in the walls and ceilings. The small bar was crammed with a wide variety of drinks. An old Coke Fridge stood, as if embarrassed, in a corner. It was working but seemed to be waiting to die. The tables rocked a little on the uneven floor and the barman hadn't shaved for a week and hadn't changed his dull striped shirt for even longer. Oil paintings of Greek scenes hung unevenly around the walls and cobwebs adorned each corner. This was not a tourist place. It was a local 'couldn't care less' place where everyone was your friend if you wanted them to be. The waiter brought over our coffees and a box of draughts. Perhaps the games were compulsory. Obligingly we entered the spirit of the place and set up for a game. It was just as well because the ice cream took ages to arrive. We loved the place.

One of the things we had done to pass the time on the boat trip here was to start learning some basic Greek phrases. Yes—Neh NO—o-chee. Please—parakalo. Thank you—F caristo. OK—en dak zee. Excuse me—me seen cho ree tek. Hello—yea sas. Goodbye—an dee o. Good morning—Kal ee mera. Good afternoon—Kl lee spera. Good night—Kal nee neech ta. The bill please—ton logarismo parakalo. That was it for now but we resolved to learn more. I won the draughts game. Angela won the hearts of all the men. Now it was out into the world again. The evening life was gearing up to give way soon to the night life. The place was slowly coming alive. Lots of young girls on working holidays stood outside restaurants and clubs trying to entice customers with their charms. Offers galore were everywhere, offers on drinks and food and gifts and of course Time Shares. I remembered the name of one of the streets and told the Time Share bods that we lived here already. That seemed to work. My tan was quite good and Angela had her world tour tan, so we pulled it off.

Into the evening, as the light faded, the great unwashed came out to play. Hundreds of young sun and beer soaked British Revellers thronged the streets and bars looking for fun and frolics. Somehow, the atmosphere drove them mad. Many did things they would never dream of doing in the streets at home. We toured the ever open souvenir shops. There were some crazy looking dolls of women with wide open clown like mouths which drew our attention. Lots of tourist crap and a few quality shops. We decided to have a late meal before returning to the boat. Luckily we managed to find a good table at a good restaurant, overlooking the Street Scene. We decided to try a couple of Greek dishes. Angela ordered Psria plaki. A whole fish baked in an open dish with carrots, leeks and potatoes in a tomato, fennel and olive oil sauce. I chose Keftedes. Ground Beef with egg and bread crumbs, flavoured with herbs, mint and cumin and fried in olive oil, served with Saffron Rice, delicious. We also consumed a generous quantity on Greek Wine and Black Forest Gateau which, though nothing to do with Greece, went down very well.

We waved goodbye to the mayhem that was now Faliraki and headed back to the boat, this time without falling into the sea. In nautical terms we were now 'Three Sheets to the Wind' and fell in a heap onto the top of the bed. It was lights out almost immediately for us that night.

CHAPTER 54

Next stop on the cruise was the Port of Rhodes. The Sea Approach was very busy with Ferries and Cruise Ships. This was the major Port for the Island. The Port Authority here was considerably more organised and we arrived at our designated berth safely.

The City of Rhodes was very much a City of two halves. There was the older area with shops and businesses established for many years in most cases, then the more modern area with International Brands and modern buildings. So we explored the expensive older City and the very expensive newer City. I loved walking and talking with Angela. We did some shopping for gifts here. Everything you could possibly want was available. There were lots of gypsy type people selling trinkets and a lot of Africans selling wooden art work from their own regions. The City had a wonderful mix of styles and cultures which gave it a unique character. We spent two days here; there was so much to see. The Street of Knights concerned with the Crusades and the Knights of St. John, The Mosque of Suleiman, the Turkish Baths, the Tower of the virgin, which I pointed out to Angela that she no longer qualified for, the square of the Jewish Martyrs, the Tower of Italy, the Ancient City walls with many named gates and so much more. Having got lost a number of times on both days we found the Marine gate for the last time, boarded our boat and continued our trip. On the East side of the island we visited Fanes, Kamros, Skala, the small islands of Alimia, Tragusa, Malkri and Glyfada where we anchored for a few nights, then the final harbour of Rasonisi, before returning to Lindos. This time we were able to find a free berth so no dingy trip. Then it was a good clean up of the boat before inviting John and Jane to inspect it. Our tans were now just great. On the more remote periods of our voyage we had both practiced nudism and our tans were now full body. The nudism also gave us a very sexy honeymoon trip. If only we could live that life all the time, tiring, but lots of fun.

We handed over the craft to its owners. Bid a fond farewell to 'English Rose' for now and headed for the Villa we had rented to complete our honeymoon dream. The Villa was a few miles from Lindos, just off the coast road. Access was via a rough road through an olive grove. The House sat on a flat topped mound overlooking the beautiful coastline. The walls of the two story building were cream surmounted by a pantiled roof. A rickety telegraph type pole fed the primitive electricity supply to the building. Two large arches adorned the front ground floor with stone steps to the right leading to the first floor balcony with three large windows, the centre one being in the style of French windows. The woodwork was green.

I parked near the left hand arch on the gravel driveway. We got out of the car and looked out to sea. We held each other and kissed awhile before entering the Villa through a large wooden door beneath the left arch. This was obviously converted to be a garage. Then we moved to the louvered doors behind the right hand arch. This room contained tools, a little vintage tractor and a wine press. It became obvious that the accommodation was upstairs. Angela rushed ahead. She couldn't wait to see what it was like. I took the bags from the car, put the car in the newly discovered garage and puffed up the stairs. Walking through the French windows entrance I was not disappointed. Angela stood wowing the beautiful interior. I took off my sandals to allow my feet to feel the cool tiled floor. Angela had opened the shutters and windows to allow a cool breeze in from the ocean. The furniture was in traditional style, wooden, functional and comfortable seating, lots of highly decorated cushions and wall hangings. The rear of the room was a kitchen dining area beyond which was a raised balcony for the sleeping area. None of the wiring would not have 'Passed Muster' in England. Another set of French Windows at the back of the room opened up to a high walled courtyard with roughly built walls seemingly held up by ancient looking grape vines and there was a gnarled olive tree standing like an arthritic pensioner acting as a centre piece with a circular bench around it. An arched gateway in the rear wall opened out to a wonderful view of the valley of olive trees behind. We instantly fell in love with it.

After exploring our temporary home for the rest of the honeymoon with Angela repeatedly saying, 'Oh isn't it lovely,' 'wow, look at that' and 'Oh It's gorgeous.' I unpacked while Angela got to grips with the kitchen and preparing a meal. I just got everything away in time for burgers and chips washed down with local Greek Red Wine. Then we decided to try out the bed. It was king size, allowing us to roll around and play a bit. Then we fell deeply in love all over again. The kissing was overwhelming, searching out our deepest feelings and translating it into wonderful intimate feelings. A lot was expressed without saying a word. Clothing dissolved into nothing. We felt the smooth firm curves of each other's bodies. Soon we were as one, each reaching into the others mind and soul. No other world existed save for our own. My passion pressed deep into her and she responded in kind until as they say, 'The World Moved,' an earth quake which signalled the culmination of our desire for each other. It's surprising what quality burger can do, or more likely quality Greek wine. Whatever caused it that was fine by me.

When passion subsided, I had a nude smoke in the courtyard after which I had my turn in the shower. This was a wonderful time. We relaxed in the lounge, just talking about all sorts of things. How we met again after so long and talked about possible fate. Explored how it could have been had we met years earlier as Adults, how it may have turned out. Angela began to get a little sad with these thoughts. She made herself sadder when she talked of how much time had been wasted and now our age prevented us from starting a family. She complained that her typing of the novel was quite difficult without good light. Perhaps she needed an Eye Test. She didn't like the idea of having to wear glasses. I put my arm around her, kissed her and told her not to worry. Then, taking her by the hand, I led her to the gate at the back of the courtyard. It was now dark and the stars crammed the clear black sky. There was no sound and no nearby lights. Hugging her and pointing to the sky I asked 'What's that up there?'

'The Moon' she replied. I smiled at her.

'Well how far do you want to see?'

THE END.